# *Romantic* Suspense

## Danger. Passion. Drama.

### Deadly Ranch Hideout
Jenna Night

### Ambush In The Mountains
Mary Alford

# MILLS & BOON

DEADLY RANCH HIDEOUT
© 2024 by Virginia Niten
Philippine Copyright 2024
Australian Copyright 2024
New Zealand Copyright 2024

First Published 2024
First Australian Paperback Edition 2024
ISBN 978 1 038 91750 8

AMBUSH IN THE MOUNTAINS
© 2024 by Mary Eason
Philippine Copyright 2024
Australian Copyright 2024
New Zealand Copyright 2024

First Published 2024
First Australian Paperback Edition 2024
ISBN 978 1 038 91750 8

MIX
Paper | Supporting
responsible forestry
FSC
www.fsc.org    FSC® C001695

Published by
Harlequin Mills & Boon
An imprint of Harlequin Enterprises (Australia) Pty Limited
(ABN 47 001 180 918), a subsidiary of HarperCollins
Publishers Australia Pty Limited
(ABN 36 009 913 517)
Level 19, 201 Elizabeth Street
SYDNEY NSW 2000 AUSTRALIA

Cover art used by arrangement with Harlequin Books S.A.. All rights reserved.

Printed and bound in Australia by McPherson's Printing Group

# Deadly Ranch Hideout
Jenna Night

MILLS & BOON

**Jenna Night** comes from a family of Southern-born natural storytellers. Her parents were avid readers and the house was always filled with books. No wonder she grew up wanting to tell her own stories. She's lived on both coasts but currently resides in the Inland Northwest, where she's astonished by the occasional glimpse of a moose, a herd of elk or a soaring eagle.

Visit the Author Profile page
at millsandboon.com.au for more titles.

For where your treasure is,
there will your heart be also.
—*Matthew* 6:21

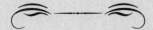

# DEDICATION

To my mum, Esther.
I look forward to seeing you again.

# Chapter One

Monica Larson stared in horror as the black SUV holding her father burst into flames with a bone-rattling *bang*!

The windows blew out, and chunks of safety glass rained down onto the asphalt of the Reno street like a shower of frosty hail. Car alarms blared in both directions along the road.

She stood on the sidewalk across the street with every muscle in her torso knotted up in terror, while at the same time the bones and joints of her legs seemed to melt and her stance became unsteady.

Following the rush of incoming air from the vehicle's broken windows, the flames *whooshed* and flared outside of the SUV, reaching even farther and higher into the sky.

A chunk of metal slammed to the ground by Monica's feet, sending up a spray of debris and snapping her out of her shocked stupor.

*"Dad!"*

She pulled herself together and was finally able to move. As she sprinted across the street toward the smoke and heat, her attention remained laser-focused on rescuing her father. *He could still be alive*, she told herself repeatedly, forcing her legs to pump as fast as possible. *There's still a chance.*

Grief and fear squeezed her throat, making it a fight to breathe. She stumbled over her clumsy feet and fell, barely feeling the pain as she scraped a layer of skin from her chin and the palms of her hands. Crumpled on the ground, she heard a second explosion, and looked up in time to see the SUV lift slightly off the ground before it dropped back to the street as another fireball shot from the vehicle and up into the sky.

*"No!"*

She tried to shove herself back onto her feet, but was derailed by a fit of coughing and gasping as she was nearly overcome by the black, oily smoke roiling toward her.

And then she jerked awake.

After several disoriented seconds ticked by, the impression so strong in her mind that it seemed as if she still smelled the smoke, she began to focus on unfamiliar objects in the darkness of the room where she lay in a sleeping bag atop the lumpy mattress of a bed.

"He's still alive," she whispered to herself, her chest knotted with grief from what she'd seen happen to her dad in the dream. "It wasn't real."

She focused on her breathing, trying to slow it down while sending up a short, brief prayer and reminding herself that right here, right now, she was okay. It was a well-established routine after she'd gotten so much experience grappling with the sudden wallop of panic that often woke her out of a sound sleep. Turned out that witnessing your accountant father being arrested and finding out that he'd been working for an organized crime group for *years* and later seeing him locked up in prison could do some emotional damage to a mobster bookkeeper's daughter.

And then there was the fallout that came *after* her father's imprisonment.

Maybe it was a good thing she couldn't remember some of the more recent events. She rubbed her fingers along the right side of her head, feeling the ridges hidden by her hair where her stitches would completely dissolve eventually. She tried to think back to that missing gap of time after she'd gone to visit her dad in prison and then woken up in the hospital. A car crash, she'd been told, had caused the cuts and bruises and a state of unconsciousness that had apparently lasted for several hours.

She'd been blessed not to suffer major physical injury or significant brain damage, except for the loss of the memory of that short gap of time between going to visit her dad and waking up in the hospital. That was still gone. She might regain it, she'd been told. Then again, she might not. Right now all she had was the impression that the memory was almost in her grasp, like the feeling she typically had just before she recalled a word or fact that was on the tip of her tongue. Her father had been involved in a physical altercation immediately after her visit, and for that reason she was not allowed to call or visit him for the next month.

What she *did* have was the voice memo she'd left for herself on her phone. She'd discovered it shortly after leaving the hospital, and apparently she'd recorded it during that mystery gap of time. It was the reason she'd left her home in Reno, Nevada, and come up here to Cedar Lodge, Montana, to this unfamiliar and rustic cabin outside of town.

*Creak.*

The sound came through the open bedroom door from the direction of the kitchen. She'd arrived around midnight after a long and tiresome drive. She'd unrolled her sleeping bag atop the bed, climbed in while still dressed in jeans and a T-shirt, and immediately fallen into a deep sleep until the nightmare had woken her up.

"Probably just a raccoon," she told herself, wanting desperately to believe that.

But pretending something wasn't happening didn't make it go away. She knew that only too well.

And right now, the smarter part of herself, the part determined to survive, had already shot adrenaline through her system and sent her heart racing.

Should she switch on the bedside light? Would that scare away an intruder if there was one or make her an easier target?

*Creak.*

The sound was definitely coming from the kitchen. Maybe it was a normal noise, like the timber of the old building shifting or the refrigerator cycling on or off. Monica did not want to call the police if she could avoid it. Staying clear of them was included in her plan to keep a low profile while she was here.

She got out of the sleeping bag, dropped her feet to the cold wooden floor and slid them into her shoes.

She was reaching for her phone and key fob when she realized she smelled smoke. *For real.* It wasn't just a lingering impression from her dream.

Her mind raced as she hurried out of the bedroom. She'd been exhausted when she'd arrived after the long drive from Reno. Had she put something on the stove or in the toaster oven and forgotten about it?

Smoke pushed through the gap under the swinging door between the living room and the kitchen. The cabin was old, and Monica could imagine it burning to the ground well before a fire engine could get here.

She grabbed her phone from her pocket, ready to call 9-1-1 if she needed to.

Shoving open the door, she spotted the fire in the dining nook between the refrigerator and the back door. Something was burning beneath the dining table; the table was already engulfed, and flames were crawling up the nearby wall and toward the door.

Pulling the front of her shirt up over her nose to filter some of the smoke, Monica hurried toward the cabinets, hoping to find a pitcher or large bowl that she could fill with water and then douse the flames. Through the fabric she caught a whiff of a familiar yet out-of-place smell.

*Gasoline.*

Her eyes darted toward the rapidly burning table and what must be gasoline-soaked wood or cloth burning beneath it.

Confirmation that this was not some accidental fire caused by forgetfulness on her part or old faulty wiring. This was intentionally set.

*They've found me.* The realization chilled her despite the heat.

In the next instant, someone grabbed her from behind and shoved her toward the fire.

*They want to kill me and make it look like an accident!*

Her father's former criminal bosses must have sent one of their hit men to finish her off as some sort of punishment directed at her dad. Or else the attacker had been hired by Archer Nolan, also employed by the mob, though Monica hadn't been able to prove that fact. Yet. Archer had Monica's mom, Suzanne, convinced that he was a legitimate businessman, and two weeks ago, Suzanne had agreed to marry him in a month. That meant the wedding would happen in two weeks. Monica's mother refused to believe that the man who'd offered her so much comfort after her ex-husband was arrested could also be a criminal when Monica had told her that was the case. Suzanne demanded proof.

Monica was determined to find it. She had to save her mom and protect her family. It was why she'd come to Cedar Lodge.

But right now she was fighting for her life. The heavyset thug who'd grabbed her knocked the phone out of her hand and held her arms pinned to her sides as he continued forcing her toward the flames.

Monica twisted her body as hard as she could, desperate to break free. But it did no good. The masked assailant gripped her tighter, his overwhelming strength enough to propel her forward. She pulled up her feet, hoping the sudden full weight of her body would throw the attacker off balance, but it made no difference.

*Lord, help!*

The flames were growing, and her face was getting hot.

She fought the thug with every bit of strength

she had, but there wasn't much she could do other than twist and stomp her feet back toward him. Unexpectedly, the attacker let go of her arms. But in the next instant he grabbed her neck and began squeezing.

Panic shot through her. She clawed at his hands, but her air supply was already being cut off, and the flaming kitchen began to spin around her. Once she lost consciousness, it would all be over, for good.

Gritting her teeth, she grunted and kicked her heel backward as hard as she could, connecting with his shin. Desperate for a weapon, she dug her hand into her front pocket for the key chain attached to her car fob. It had a couple of metal keys on it, and she slid them between her fingers so they were protruding like a knife point. She clenched to make a fist.

The attacker was so close behind her that she couldn't get much momentum, but she swung back as hard as she could, feeling the tips of the keys jab into the man's stomach. His grip on her neck loosened, and Monica twisted away from him while stomping back toward his ankle. He stumbled, and she took advantage of the moment to yank her neck free from his grip and lurch forward.

Her balance was off and she was dizzy, but she still managed to stagger away and dart through the swinging door to the living room. She grabbed a nearby chair and flung it to the ground behind her. Continuing on, she grabbed at a lamp and threw it down, and then a small end table, desperate to create obstacles for the creep pursuing her so she could get away.

She fumbled with the old-school latch on the front door before flinging it open and feeling a rush of cold, damp air that snapped her senses into focus.

She'd had no idea it was raining, but after the heat of the fire in the kitchen, she happily sprinted into the chilly, steadily falling drops. Her car wasn't far away. It was parked inside the doorless shed. Her phone was back in the cabin, but she still had the fob for her sedan.

Afraid to look back in case the attacker was gaining on her, she focused on getting to the car. She'd start it up, back out as fast as she could, and head down the long driveway through the woods to the main road. She steeled herself to run over the attacker if he tried to stop her. He was determined to kill her. She had no choice.

She was nearly to the shed when a lanky figure appeared out of the shadows in front of her and then began to move toward her. This man didn't have a mask. His knitted cap was pulled down low and his collar flipped up so that most of his face was hidden. But she was able to see the broad, mocking smile on his face.

Her steps staggered as she tried to think which way she should go. A dark feeling of fear and hopelessness edged into her consciousness. Her steps faltered. She was exhausted.

Maybe trying to escape was pointless. Maybe the fatal attack on her was inevitable.

*No. It's not.* She'd made it through so much already. She would not give up now.

The slight nudge of encouragement wasn't a lot, but maybe it was enough to keep her alive.

The only plan she could form was to run into the woods. Were there neighbors nearby who might help? She couldn't remember.

But if she got into the surrounding forest, hunkered down, and stayed absolutely silent, maybe the thugs wouldn't find her. Maybe they would eventually give up and leave.

Or maybe they were excellent trackers who would locate her immediately.

Either way, some part of her had apparently made the decision to give it a try, because she was already running past pine boughs heavy with raindrops at the edge of the long driveway, ignoring the sting as the needles slapped across her face. She tried not to think about the probability that the broken branches would lead the assailants directly to her.

Officer Kris Volker sped down the highway at shortly before four in the morning. While he was not officially on duty, his residence was close to the fire that had been called in by someone living higher up on the mountainside after they'd looked out their window and seen flames at the old Bennett cabin. Kris had gotten the call to respond.

After waking his parents to let them know he was leaving and asking them to make sure his son got to his kindergarten class on time, Kris had hustled out the door to his pickup truck and headed for the two-lane rural highway.

Rain fell at a steady pace, which would hopefully help to contain the flames. Fire and medical emergency crews had been dispatched, but Kris would likely arrive on scene first.

The Bennett cabin had been unoccupied for several months since Ernest, the eldest member of the clan, passed away. Kris wasn't aware of anyone having taken up residence at the old family homestead since then, but maybe they had. Or perhaps a transient had moved in. In any event, if the cabin wasn't fully engulfed in flames, Kris would do his best to search for anyone who might be inside until the firefighters arrived to take over. His thoughts raced as he pictured the layout of the cabin he'd visited countless times as a kid.

He slowed down for the sharp turn onto the winding drive up to the cabin. As he rounded the first curve, his headlights illuminated a flash of something in the woods that didn't belong there. Jeans and a bright blue shirt. A person running. A woman.

Someone who'd set the fire, intentionally or accidentally, and was now running away?

He hit the brakes. His gut instinct was to go after her. Hold her accountable if she'd burned up the cabin.

But what if there was someone still in the old building? Asleep or unconscious. He had to check on that first. He began to move forward again.

At the end of the final straight section of the drive, he saw a faint orange glow shining on the trees at the back of the cabin. It looked like the rain was doing a decent job of controlling the fire. Also, while still some distance away, he spotted an SUV. The hatch was open, the interior was lit, and two men were grabbing long guns. One of the men also shoved a handgun into his waistband. A thick layer of mud had been smeared across the license plate, making it unreadable.

Something was *very* wrong here.

Kris stopped and killed his headlights.

After thinking for a moment, he decided to move forward and then switch on the high beams, temporarily blinding the men and taking advantage of their disorientation to assert control of the situation. But in the moment between making his decision and taking action, he heard one of the men call out to the other, "Go ahead and shoot her if you have to. We can't let her get away." And then they took off jogging into the woods.

Kris glanced at the burning cabin. He didn't know if anyone was in there. He *did* know a woman was running in the forest while these two creeps intended to go after her and kill her.

He knew what he needed to do.

He backed up his rig until he was closer to the spot where he'd seen the woman. Then he grabbed his radio. "Dispatch, Patrol Eighteen.

Advise responders to fire at the old Bennett place that at least two armed gunmen are on scene. I'm checking on female last seen running in the woods. Responders need to use extreme caution on arrival."

"Patrol Eighteen, copy," the dispatcher responded.

Kris turned off the volume on the radio so the bad guys wouldn't hear it.

He got out of the truck, heading in the general direction that he'd seen the woman running, and making adjustments once he spotted snapped branches and twigs and knew he was on her trail.

It appeared she was headed at an angle that would take her to the highway. No doubt when the shadowy men with the rifles picked up her trail—and Kris had little doubt they would, it was that obvious—they would likewise figure out her goal. And they would make sure they were waiting when she got there.

Right now, the potential killers were still behind him and the woman. Kris just needed to find her and help her hide in the darkness without getting tracked and killed himself.

Due to the thick tree canopy overhead, the ground wasn't particularly muddy despite the rain, which helped prevent him from getting bogged down. He spotted pine needles on the ground that formed a low ridge, as if the woman might have begun dragging her feet. Maybe she was injured. Or becoming exhausted.

He sped up and saw her.

For a split second it looked as if she'd seen him. He didn't dare call out since he had no idea how close the gunmen were. He slowed for a second and glanced back but didn't see anyone. When he looked forward again, the woman was gone.

Desperate to catch up with her before she got killed, he pumped his legs harder. As he rounded a thick tree trunk, he felt a branch jut out in his way, causing him to lose his footing. As he fought to right himself, a branch came down hard on the back of his head.

Or maybe it was the barrel of a rifle that had struck him. Somehow the gunmen must have gotten ahead of him.

He thrust his hands forward and managed to catch himself before landing face-first on the forest floor. Then he quickly spun and grabbed at the object that had struck him and yanked it to the side, intending to throw the attacker off balance. It worked.

Somebody stumbled forward and nearly fell on top of him. But it wasn't one of the gunmen. It was the woman.

"It's okay," Kris called out, holding up his arms to fend off blows as she furiously swung the branch at him. "I'm a cop," he called out, trying not to be too loud. The tussle was already making plenty of noise to let the bad guys know where they were, and he didn't want to add to it.

She kept fighting him. He could see the panic in her eyes. He wasn't in his police uniform, and she probably didn't even understand what he was saying.

Obviously the last thing this woman needed at this moment was to be manhandled, but he had no choice. The skin on his back was already itchy as he anticipated a shot coming from one of the attackers any second.

He grabbed both of her hands, and winced when she kicked him in the knee.

"Enough," he said, shaking her hands to try and snap her out of her panic. He knew the visceral feeling of just wanting to stay alive. He'd experienced it himself during a couple of tours overseas in the army. Climbing back down from that height of emotion wasn't an easy thing.

Finally, her gaze focused in a way that told him he had her attention. That she might actually understand him when he spoke.

"I'm a cop with the Cedar Lodge Police Department," he said. "My name's Kris." He quickly explained that he'd gotten the call to respond to the cabin fire and how he'd spotted her running into the woods and then heard the gunmen planning to kill her.

"Great," she said when he finished, breathing heavily, her stance unsteady. She gestured in the direction of the cabin. "Go shoot them."

"I can't."

"Why not?"

*For a lot of reasons.* He shook his head. "I called for backup to deal with the thugs. Other cops will arrive any minute. I don't want to accidentally shoot one of the responders."

"Oh." She looked around and then picked up the branch she'd used to attack him. "So what do we do now?"

"Wait here until the cavalry arrives." Heading back to his vehicle was too much of a risk. Right now he needed to listen for sounds that the assailants had heard his run-in with the woman and located them. Maybe the patter of rainfall had helped muffle the noise they'd made. But it could also mask the footsteps of the assailants approaching them.

He knelt down to make himself less visible if the criminals were nearby and gestured at the woman to do the same.

"Who are those two men?" he asked in a barely audible whisper. "Why do they want to kill you?"

"I don't know."

*Of course you'd say that.* Kris didn't want to be a cynic, but sometimes he was one. In his line of work, he'd come across plenty of "nice" people who weren't so nice. People posing as hapless victims when they were anything but that.

There were many more times, though, when people were targeted and attacked who had done absolutely nothing wrong. Maybe he was being played for a fool, but right now he would give this woman the benefit of the doubt.

*Bang!*

The shot went wild and was followed by several more, some of them smacking the trees and sending splinters of bark and chunks of branch and needles and even pine cones flying.

"They've found us," the woman said in a hoarse whisper. She got to her feet, poised to run. She was still holding the branch to use as a weapon.

Kris shook his head, reached for her free hand and tugged until she squatted back beside him. "If they'd spotted us, they would have snuck up and shot us point-blank. They're trying to panic you and get you to run and show them where you are." He reached for his service weapon, just in case the thugs did pinpoint them. His heart hammered in his chest as he listened for sirens or vehicle engines or any sign of the responders arriving. After a moment, he finally heard something. A high-pitched wail from an approaching patrol car.

With his attention focused in the direction of the siren, he wasn't looking when one of the assailants nearly tripped over them. The thug grabbed the handgun from his own waistband and aimed it at the woman. But then the creep's attention snagged on Kris, and for a moment the shooter hesitated, apparently surprised by seeing an unexpected person.

The woman swung her tree branch and smacked the gunman in the face.

Kris took advantage of the shooter's unsteady steps to grab the woman's arm, shove her behind him, and then back toward the driveway and the arriving cops while pointing his gun in the direction of the attacker.

The gunman and his partner obviously heard the sirens. "You can try to hide but we'll find you!" one of them yelled before firing a couple more shots and then disappearing into the darkness of the forest.

Moments later Kris heard a vehicle start up, and the assailants' SUV tore down the long driveway and turned onto the highway. He keyed his radio and gave the best description he could of the fleeing criminals, their vehicle, and the direction they had gone. "Couldn't get a license plate number," he added.

"Huh," the woman said after his radio communication ended. The two of them continued walking toward the driveway and the flashing red and blue lights visible between the trees.

Not exactly a word, but Kris recognized the feeling of relief she'd expressed.

He thought about the threat voiced by the shooter. For the moment, it made sense for the woman to feel relief. But in the long run, it was apparent that she was still very much in danger. And Kris intended to find out exactly what was going on.

# Chapter Two

Monica forced her leaden legs forward as she trudged alongside Kris toward the arriving cops and emergency medical responders positioned at the lower end of the driveway. The fire trucks had already lumbered past, their engines growling as they headed up the graveled driveway on their way to the cabin to fight the flames.

The rain had stopped, the sky was starting to clear, and there was growing light from the oncoming sunrise.

"What's your name?" Kris asked her as they walked.

"Monica."

"Are you injured?"

She was worn out, scratched up from the race through the woods, and it felt like most of her muscles were on fire. But given all she'd been through, none of that seemed particularly dire. In truth, she was grateful to be alive. "I'm all right."

Moments ago she'd overheard him on his radio requesting the ambulance to stage near the bottom of the driveway with the police cars.

"Are *you* hurt?" She turned to him, realizing that she hadn't given his safety a single thought. He could have been struck by one of the bullets that were flying by while they were under attack.

They cleared the woods and stepped onto the driveway, where she could see him better. He had a sharp jawline, dark brown hair with a hint of rust to it worn in a military-style cut, and icy blue eyes.

"I'm fine," he responded.

He looked like a guy who would typically say that no matter what.

A paramedic hustled toward them. "What's the word?" he asked, giving both Monica and Kris a worried once-over. "Anybody shot? Stabbed? Were you in the burning building and breathed in smoke?"

"Cole, you have an overactive imagination," Kris said.

"Yeah, well, sometimes it saves lives." The medic, a guy with slightly more trendy-looking hair than Kris, turned to Monica. "How are you, ma'am?"

"I'm fine."

"How about we do a quick assessment, just to make sure?"

*"No."* Her response came out more sharply than she'd intended, so she added, "Thank you," to soften it.

"You sure? I'm already here, and it wouldn't take long."

"I'm sure."

The medic gave her a hesitant nod before walking away.

Monica's thoughts were starting to race. How could she get this situation wrapped up with the least amount of fuss so she could maintain her low profile?

She couldn't. Not with shots fired at her *and a cop* and the cabin being set on fire.

Kris threw her a suspicious glance.

She didn't blame him. She was full of suspicions, too. And that included suspicion of the integrity of people in the justice system, like the prison guard who had allowed someone to attack her father while he was in custody so he could be sent to solitary confinement at an especially opportune moment for the crime syndicate. Or the person in the prosecutor's office who repeatedly blocked her dad's attempts to offer expanded information about Boyd Sierra Associates—an innocuous name for a very dangerous organized crime group—in return for a reduction in his prison sentence.

Monica dropped her gaze to the ground and absently reached up to rub the stitches on her head. If only she could remember that meeting with her dad before the car crash, she could just do whatever she needed to do and leave town. Despite what the police reports said, she wasn't convinced it had really been an *accident*.

The night before it happened, Monica had told her mom about her father Hunter's claim that Archer worked for the mob, and Suzanne had dismissed the idea out of hand. Monica hadn't realized that Archer had been eavesdropping beyond an open doorway. When Suzanne stepped out of the room to check on dinner, Archer had extended his threat to Monica in a voice so soft and silken that it had turned her blood ice-cold. "You don't know what you're getting into," he'd said quietly. "We have a long reach. We can get to your dad in prison, to you no matter where you go, and to anybody else in your family if that's what it takes to keep control of the situation. It would be better for you if you just let it all go."

"Why are you doing this?" she'd asked.

"Mainly because I love your mother and I want us to be married."

That moment had been the scariest one of all. Because Monica realized that this seriously messed-up individual really did believe his willingness to do anything to possess her mom truly was the definition of love.

And then there was his use of the word *mainly*. What other reasons did he have? Not honorable ones, Monica was certain of that. It probably also had something to do with making sure that the crime syndicate's secrets were indeed kept secret.

She'd known then that she had to get her mom away from Archer and she had to keep her family from getting sucked in further with his criminal associates.

Whether she would ever be able to completely forgive her dad for all the grief and danger he'd brought down on them, she still didn't know.

For seemingly the thousandth time she tried to remember what he'd told her about Cedar Lodge. The small Montana town where her dad had lived when he was young, and where Monica and her parents had come for ski vacations when she was growing up.

Based on the brief voice memo she'd found on her phone, she only knew that Cedar Lodge was important, and she assumed her dad had left something there. Maybe she was wrong, but it was the only place she knew to start. She didn't know what she was looking for, but she'd planned to begin by speaking with people and visiting places connected to her dad.

She'd suspected Archer and the crime group might figure out a way to track her even though she'd kept her specific plans hidden from her mom and only shared them with the two people she'd needed to help her. One of them being her old friend Shelly, who had provided the cabin. Which was now damaged by fire. Monica shook her head slightly. Somehow she would find a way to compensate her for that. But it might take a while to come up with the money.

"So what's the story here, Monica?" Kris asked, sounding and looking very cop-like. "Who are the two attackers, and why did they come after you?"

Before she could answer, a county sheriff's patrol car pulled onto the drive. A dark-haired deputy quickly got out and strode over to them. "Your shooters got away. A couple of us drove a few miles in each direction on the highway, but your assailants must have turned off onto one of the intersecting roads or old logging trails. Or it could be they've just pulled up somewhere close by and are staying out of sight. We'll keep patrol units in the area and continue looking, but for now we've got nothing."

Kris sighed heavily. "Thanks, Dylan. Keep me posted of any updates."

"You sure there were only the two perps and the one vehicle?" the deputy asked, throwing a glance toward the surrounding forest and the thick pines that were becoming more clearly visible with the brightening sunrise.

*There could be more.* Feeling queasy at the idea, Monica looked around.

"*Could* there be more?" Kris asked Monica with a lifted brow.

She shrugged and wrapped her arms across her midsection. "I don't know. I was asleep. A noise woke me up. I went into the kitchen and it was already on fire. A man attacked me. I got outside, where another man came after me, so I ran into the woods. That's it. That's all I know about any of this."

Kris's radio crackled to life with a report from the captain of the fire crew up at the cabin. "Fire is extinguished. Moderate damage to the kitchen and dining area. Did a search as soon as we arrived on scene. There was no one inside."

"Moderate damage," Kris repeated with a glance at Monica after acknowledging the communication.

"I didn't start the fire," she said. "And now that it's out, I need to go up there and get my belongings." She started walking toward the cabin.

Kris kept pace alongside her. "So, how'd you end up at the old Bennett place?"

Monica wanted to help the police catch the bad guys, but at the same time, it would be like walking a tightrope as she carefully chose what she wanted to say so the authorities wouldn't be alerted to the real reason she was here and then get in her way.

Clearly, in their investigation of what had happened tonight, they would be suspicious of her. She would hope and pray that Kris and his law enforcement friends wouldn't go so far as to surveil her or come along behind her and ask questions of anyone she spoke to. She would also hope and pray that none of the cops or judges in town had connections with the Boyd Sierra criminal group. Like Archer had said in his threat, the association had a long reach.

"My friend Shelly inherited this place from her great-grandpa a few months ago."

"I haven't seen Shelly in ages."

Monica turned to him. "You know her?"

"My family's ranch is just up the road. Our families have been neighbors for generations. How do *you* know Shelly?"

"We met when we were teenagers. Been friends ever since." Monica was aware that this seemingly friendly conversation was actually a subtle interrogation by the cop.

"If you don't know who the attackers were, who do you *think* they might be? What's your best guess on their motive for all of this?"

She shook her head. "I don't know." It wasn't a complete lie. She had no idea who those two creeps were, and she couldn't be certain if this was related to Archer's determination to marry her mom or if some other faction of Boyd Sierra had targeted her, perhaps as a means of scaring her dad into keeping his mouth shut about whatever information he still held regarding their criminal exploits.

They approached the cabin, where a gradually dissipating haze of smoke floated in the air. The kitchen was in the back of the cabin so from the front the building looked mostly okay. She just needed to go inside, grab her stuff, get into the used car she'd bought with the last of her savings after the crash, and go somewhere nearby where she could sit alone and think.

She was scheduled to meet with Esmeralda, an old family friend, at the woman's thrift store in a few hours, and she was determined to keep that appointment. The sooner she got started on what she'd come to Cedar Lodge to do, the better. The last year had taught her that the only way to get out of difficult situations was to go *through* them. Trying to avoid them just made it worse.

"We clear to enter?" Kris asked the fire captain at the front door of the cabin.

"Sure. The power is shut off until an inspector gives the okay to turn it back on. The fire damage messed with some of the wiring."

They walked inside.

Water puddled on the kitchen floor, and droplets fell from the ceiling. The dining table where the fire had started was a pile of soaked, charred wood emitting a strong scorched smell. The window behind it had no glass left in it, and the nearby wall was damaged. In a couple of spots, it had been completely burned through, leaving an irregular hole in its place. Faint sunlight shone into the room.

Monica looked around for her phone. She found it wedged beneath the refrigerator on the side facing away from the fire. It was damp and the screen was cracked, but it had a connection. "It still works," she said in surprise, wiping it with the hem of her shirt.

"We have some extra chargers at the station if you need one."

She turned to him. "I don't want to go to the police station. I have things to take care of today, including calling Shelly and telling her what happened to her cabin." Monica glanced around before retuning her gaze to him. He was handsome. There was no denying that. The brighter light as the sun rose and the clouds rolled away made that quite clear. But what did that have to do with anything? She shook her head slightly, determined to dismiss the observation. "I'd rather just give you my statement here. You already know most of what happened. You were there for it."

He gave her an assessing look that lingered long enough to make her uncomfortable. "Let's talk to the chief together," he finally said in a tone that was light but also left no room for argument. "Maybe having to retell your story from the beginning will help you remember more details."

If she protested too strongly, it would only fuel his curiosity and inflame his suspicion that she was involved in something illegal. The last thing she wanted was a nosy cop keeping an eye on her while she was in town.

"Let me grab my things from the bedroom and put them in my car. I'll follow you to the police station."

"I'll drive you," he said with polite stubbornness. "Afterward, I'll bring you back to get your car. Or drop you off somewhere else if you'd like."

The man's determination was frustrating. But at the same time, she was a little bit grateful despite her annoyance. As she looked around the damaged kitchen, and then walked back to the bedroom to retrieve her belongings, images of the attack flashed in her mind, and fear struck the center of her chest like she'd been punched. She sat on the edge of the bed to steady her breath and regain control of her shaking knees and churning stomach. Since her dad was arrested and her life fell apart, she'd spent a lot of time trying to maintain control of her emotions while dealing with the practical challenges at hand. It never got easy.

It wasn't just the feelings from this attack that were fighting for her attention right now, but also the emotional fallout from the entire last year. Processing all of that was going to take time. Lots more time. Maybe the rest of her life.

She straightened her spine, took a deep breath, wiped her eyes, and got to her feet. Then she grabbed her purse, the backpack stuffed with clothes, and her haphazardly rolled up sleeping bag. At least while riding to the station with Kris she'd feel safe for a while. But she reminded herself not to get used to the feeling of being protected. She still had dangerous work to do.

"So, Monica, what brought you to Cedar Lodge?" Kris asked once they were in his truck and headed down the driveway toward the road.

The young woman beside him kept fiddling with her wavy ash-blond hair, constantly tucking it behind her ears or brushing it from her forehead. When she wasn't doing that, she was adjusting the short necklace she wore or cross-ing and uncrossing her arms.

She was agitated because she was traumatized after nearly being murdered. He understood that. He was fairly unsettled himself. But there was something beyond that bothering her, and he was determined to find out what it was. He wasn't going to badger her, though. He wanted her to *want* to talk to him. That was how he preferred to do things whenever possible.

"So, I noticed Nevada plates on your car," he ventured when she didn't reply after a few moments. "You up here in Montana to check out the scenery?"

"My dad is Hunter Larson." The words burst out of her as if the pressure of holding them back had become too much. That name meant nothing to Kris, but he knew better than to interrupt her before she was finished speaking. "He grew up in Cedar Lodge. We used to come on ski vacations. He's a convicted mob accoun-tant who worked for the Boyd Sierra crime syn-dicate, and this attack probably has something to do with that. I don't know."

The trial and resultant publicity must have been centered down in Nevada, because this wasn't something Kris had heard about. He was,

however, aware of the existence of the dangerous Boyd Sierra syndicate.

"But *I* haven't done anything wrong or broken any laws," she added emphatically.

She was fighting back tears. He could hear
it in her voice.

He felt sorry for her, but at least now they
were getting somewhere. While he wanted to
be compassionate, his ultimate goal was to capture the shooters, and he needed as much information as possible to do that.

But organized crime? That wasn't something
they had in Cedar Lodge. Unless it happened
so efficiently that local law enforcement didn't
know anything about it.

The possibility of that sent a chill through
him. He'd stayed in Cedar Lodge and lived on
the ranch with his parents and son after his wife
died in part because he wanted his boy to grow
up in a safe town. In fact, he wanted everybody he knew and loved here in Cedar Lodge
to live in a safe town. Despite a few inevitable
problems, he'd thought that Cedar Lodge had
mostly remained untouched by large-scale thug
operations like the Boyd Sierra crew. Maybe
he'd been wrong.

*Organized crime.* If the early-morning attackers were professionals, then they might have taken note of his truck as they'd made their getaway. And they weren't likely to give up easily. If they didn't carry through on the directives they'd been given, their employers would be unhappy, and their own lives would be in danger.

For that reason, they likely hadn't fled very far. It's possible they were actually watching Kris and Monica leave the cabin property right now.

Kris repeatedly checked the truck's mirrors—watching for a tail—as they drove into town. At the police department, he took a lingering look around the parking lot and adjacent streets before they climbed out and he escorted her inside to the chief's office.

Chief Gerald Ellis had a pink box full of doughnuts and a coffeepot brewing on a side table in his office. After offering a greeting and then doughnuts and coffee, he sat in his desk chair, and Kris and Monica sat in front of him.

Kris began with the information Monica had just given him about her father. The chief raised his eyebrows slightly at the mention of the criminal group known for everything from extortion to blackmail to drug trafficking in several Western states.

"I've already received reports from the fire department, sheriff's deputies, and other town cops who were on scene. Now, how about you tell me what happened?" His gaze was on Monica.

She took a small bite of doughnut followed by a couple of sips of coffee and then began her story, starting with hearing a noise in the kitchen and ending with the shooters disappearing into the forest. Even for a former solider with combat experience, it was a nightmarish scenario for Kris to imagine as he listened. He admired her courage and ability to keep a cool head through the ordeal.

"How do you think they found you here in Cedar Lodge?" the chief asked. "And why come after you now?"

Monica shrugged. "Maybe they've been keeping an eye on me for a while. And maybe staying alone in a cabin gave them their first good opportunity to come after me."

Kris didn't think she was lying, exactly, but he still sensed she was holding something back. "I could understand a kidnapping attempt to somehow use you as leverage to control your dad. But this wasn't strictly a kidnapping attempt. It was pretty clear they were willing to *kill* you. Why?"

She reached up yet again to tuck her hair behind her ears. "Maybe they wanted to make my dad fear for my mom's life if he talked too much about the syndicate. Make him afraid that they'd kill her like they killed me if he didn't keep his mouth shut. My mom demanded a divorce after my dad was arrested. But he still cares about her. He hasn't made that a secret."

"Why'd you come to Cedar Lodge?" the chief prompted.

"My dad grew up here. He and my grandparents eventually moved away to Reno. That's where I live. But Dad and Mom and I and sometimes family friends or relatives came up here for a ski weekend every year. We usually came in the summer, too, and sometimes just for an easy vacation. It's how I met Shelly Bennett." She offered a half shrug. "A few days ago, I realized I needed to get away and take a break from everything. Cedar Lodge seemed like a good place for that." She made a sound halfway between a laugh and a sob. "Obviously it was a bad idea."

"I imagine you're anxious to get back to

Reno after what's happened." Kris was determined to learn her immediate plans.

She gave a noncommittal shrug.

Sometimes people held back information because they'd done something wrong. But other times it was because they were afraid. Kris thought that might be the situation here. That Monica was afraid to tell them the entire truth.

Chief Ellis leaned back in his chair. "Searching for the thugs will be our top priority. Officer Volker will put together some mug shots for you to look at on the chance the shooters were hired locally. How can we contact you?"

Monica rattled off her phone number, and Ellis typed it into his report form. "Is there anything else you need from me?" Monica asked. "Otherwise, I'd like to get going."

The chief nodded. "That's it for now."

The drive back to the cabin was quiet. Kris gave Monica time to think, hoping she would talk more, but she didn't. Meanwhile, he paid close attention to their surroundings and to other vehicles on the road in case the assailants decided to make another attempt on Monica's life.

When they reached the cabin property, he parked his truck near the shed where Monica had left her car. He exited the vehicle when she did. "I'm happy to take you anywhere you need to go in town," he offered. "Or the county airport if you've changed your mind and want to get out of here in a hurry. Which might be the best idea. You can take care of your car later."

She sighed and ran her fingers through her hair, dislodging a couple of pine needles that had been hidden in there. "I'll be okay."

She glanced toward the cabin, her gaze lingering.

"Whatever is going on, let me help you," Kris said.

She turned to him with a defiant look in her eyes. After a moment it eased into an expression of resolution. "If you want to help, find the shooters who tried to kill the both of us and lock them up."

It was a reasonable response.

"Thank you," she added in a softer tone while standing by the open door of her car. "I sincerely appreciate all you've done. And I'm beyond grateful that you put your life in danger to help me. But I can take care of myself from here."

A crow shot out of the woods, and she startled.

She was obviously still terrified and on edge

after the morning's ordeal. But she'd made it clear she didn't want Kris staying physically beside her, and he needed to respect her wishes.

She started up her vehicle and began down the driveway.

Kris was behind her until they got to the highway and she turned right, toward town. It took some effort to make himself turn left, toward the Double V Ranch, but he did.

He was scheduled to work a patrol shift later today, but first he needed to get back home to make sure his son had gotten to school okay. Then he would saddle up a horse and gather a couple dogs to join him and ride back to the Bennett property as well as the nearby unpaved lanes and fire access roads and homes of the neighbors to see if the bad guys were hiding anywhere around there. The dogs would alert him if there was someone lurking nearby that he didn't see while he conducted his search.

He took one last glance in his rearview mirror before the taillights on Monica's car disappeared from view. An attack like the one this morning in Cedar Lodge was way out of the ordinary. The gunmen had been relentless.

Monica Larson was obviously a smart, tough, and resourceful woman. But Kris still wasn't convinced that she would be all right on her own. He intended to stick very closely to this case because he was certain Monica was still in danger.

# Chapter Three

"I'm not sure helping me is the best decision for you," Monica said to the stoop-shouldered woman in front of her. "You might want to change your mind about letting me work here."

"Change my mind?" Esmeralda Marino asked with the arch of an eyebrow while leaning more heavily on her walking cane. "Now, why would I want to do that?"

They were standing inside Esmeralda's store, Start Again Thrift, near the entrance. It was a few minutes past ten, shortly after the store had opened. A young man stood at the register nearby. Monica gestured toward the other side of the store. "Let's head over there." She wanted to explain today's early-morning attack without anyone listening in.

The two women walked until they were surrounded by neatly arranged racks holding blouses and pullover sweaters and there was no one nearby. "All right," Esmeralda said with a stubborn expression on her face—though compassion still showed in her eyes through the thick lenses of her glasses. "Tell me why I would want to change my mind about helping you."

Monica described the attack.

In the hours since parting ways with Kris, she'd done a lot of praying and thinking while sipping coffee and nibbling at the cheap breakfast sandwich she'd bought at a fast-food restaurant. She'd used the restaurant's restroom to change clothes. The jeans and shirt she'd worn during the attack smelled of smoke and were covered with dirt and mud and bits of forest debris from that terrifying chase. The fresher clothes dug out of her backpack smelled faintly of smoke, too, but they were an improvement.

Monica had originally met Esmeralda through a church activity back when she was a teenager and the older lady was a volunteer and Sunday school teacher. Nominally a Christian, Monica had only gone to the advertised teen event because she'd been in town for a few days and she was bored and hoping to make friends. She did make friends, including Shelly Bennett and Esmeralda. And unbeknownst to Monica, she'd taken the first step toward a faith that would help fill the empty spaces in her heart.

Esmeralda had known Monica's dad since he was a kid who played with some of the children in Esmeralda's own family. She also knew several of his childhood friends. It was Monica's hope that Esmeralda would be aware of places in and around town that were meaningful to Monica's dad. Locations where he may have hidden something. Esmeralda had agreed to do her best to help, but now Monica was fearful of putting her friend in danger.

And while she needed the modest sum Esmeralda had offered to pay her for working at the shop for a few days—the teaching career Monica had prepared for had spiraled out of reach when her dad was arrested and then convicted, and her funds were low—she'd figure out some other way to get by while she was in Cedar Lodge if she had to. Maybe sell her car for whatever small amount she could get out of it.

By the time Monica finished her description of the attack, Esmeralda was firmly shaking her head. "Child, if you think I'll turn you away in your time of need, you don't know me at all."

"Things have changed. It's a potentially deadly situation now."

"And you think helping people escape abuse and addiction through our church outreach programs doesn't throw potential danger my way?" Esmeralda scoffed and tapped her cane a couple of times. "I'm not a foolhardy person. But I'm not going to turn my back on someone who needs my help. Do you really believe I would?"

"No, ma'am. I suppose I don't." Given what Monica had been through, Esmeralda's expression of tough love felt like a hug. The woman's faith and courage and determination to do the right thing made her feel similarly strengthened. And strength was something she would need in abundance.

"Good. Now, I've got a house trailer behind the store that was donated to us. We use the kitchen area of it as an employee break room and the rest of the space for storage when we need to. You can stay there for as long as you'd like."

Monica's eyes welled up with tears. She was filled with gratitude for the reminder that there were still generous and kind people in the world despite the evil that she'd recently witnessed.

Esmeralda led the way outside to the trailer.

On the way, they stopped so Monica could grab her backpack out of her car. She had suitcases in the trunk with more clothes, but she could get those later. As they walked, Monica couldn't resist looking around. It seemed unlikely that the assailants would jump out at her behind the thrift store, but then, so many things that seemed unlikely had happened to her over the last year. She did her best to appear calm and collected even if she didn't exactly feel that way.

"Why don't you stay here and rest for a while?" Esmeralda suggested as she opened the trailer door.

Monica stepped inside and set her backpack on a chair beside a table in the compact dining area. The kitchen appliances and furniture looked dated, but it was tidy and had a faint, clean, lemony scent. Maybe staying in town with stores and people nearby would help keep her safe. A wave of goose bumps rippled across her skin as an image of herself struggling with the thickset attacker in the burning kitchen at the cabin popped into her mind. She did her best to push back the fear. She needed to stay in Cedar Lodge and learn what she could to help protect her family. And she'd have to do it despite being afraid.

"I've already done a lot of sitting around this morning," Monica said after doing a quick walk-through of the trailer. "Right now I'd really like to help out in the store and keep myself busy. Meanwhile, maybe you could suggest a place where Dad might have hidden something, so I can get started looking around and hopefully find something helpful?"

"Have you thought about trying to get permission to search the house and surrounding grounds where your dad grew up?"

"I don't know if that would be worthwhile," Monica said doubtfully. "My dad and grandparents moved out of that house a long time ago."

But after she thought about it for a moment it began to seem like an idea worth checking out. Her dad had become nostalgic after his arrest and spent time talking with her about his childhood and the path his life had taken. Maybe he'd returned there for a visit while he was out on bail and before he started his prison sentence. And perhaps while he was there he'd hidden something on the property.

"Do you remember where that house is?" Monica asked. "Since my grandparents moved out of Cedar Lodge before I was even born, I've only been to the house once, when my dad showed it to me and my mom. I remember the house and the setting, but I don't remember exactly where it's located."

"I used to work at the nearby elementary school, but I haven't been in that part of town in ages," Esmeralda said. She rattled off the names of a couple of cross streets. "I don't recall the house's address, but if you go over to that general area, send me pictures, and I can probably direct you to the right house."

In light of the attack this morning, wandering around where she could be spotted by the thugs who'd tried to kill her earlier in the day wasn't exactly an appealing idea. But in actuality, it was what she'd come to town to do. "Thank you."

Monica had traveled here with the idea of looking around at the resort where she and her parents had stayed when they'd visited Cedar Lodge. Now she had two locations to search for information her dad might have hidden about his mob associates—and his former friend Archer Nolan in particular. Both ideas could be dead ends, but having someplace to start gave her a small spark of hope.

Back inside the store, Esmeralda found a broom and dustpan and handed them to Monica. "Start with this. I find it soothing to sweep sometimes. Maybe you will, too. I've also got some sorting and pricing for you to do whenever you're ready." After sharing a hug with Monica, she turned and walked away, her cane tapping loudly on the shiny linoleum floor.

Monica began to sweep, noticing that her hands were a little shaky as she tried to let the physical work burn off some of her nervous tension. She tried yet again to recall what her dad had told her about the information he had on Archer Nolan when she visited him in prison. Unfortunately, her mind was still a blank when it came to that topic.

She switched her focus to the goal she had already planned for her first day in town, which was a visit to Elk Ridge Resort. Her parents had kept a time-share at the mountainside complex, connected to a ski resort, for several years before her dad's arrest. They'd managed to get the exact same condo each time. Her dad claimed it had the perfect view of the surrounding mountain peaks as well as the town of Cedar Lodge below. The possibility that she'd find what she was looking for at the first location she checked out was a long shot, but maybe he *had* left something there. Maybe he'd tucked away printed documents or photos. Or perhaps he'd set aside a flash drive or external hard drive in a hidden spot for when he needed it.

Monica heard footsteps behind her, and her heart leaped into her throat. The first thing her mind went to was that it was one of the assailants coming back to finish the job. She grabbed the broom handle with both hands, lifting it to use it as a weapon as she spun around.

It took her a moment to recognize the dark blue of a police uniform and the face of the man wearing it.

"Sorry, I didn't mean to startle you." Kris stopped out of range of her broom while wearing a pensive, somewhat suspicious expression. "You didn't tell me you had a job in town."

Monica lowered the broom and then brushed the hair out of her eyes, her heart still racing despite the realization that she was not under attack. "I wasn't sure I would still have one after the fire and the shootings at the cabin." She did her best to take a deep, calming breath. "And it's not long-term. I'm just helping out for a few days while I'm in town."

"Why?" He glanced around and then moved toward her. "What's the connection?"

*Connection?* Did he suspect that she was somehow involved with Boyd Sierra and organized crime? That the attack was related to something illegal that he believed she had been involved in? And that she was in town working some kind of unsavory angle on people?

Insulted, she ignored the question and put forth one of her own. "What are you doing here? Have you been following me?"

"Your car is visible from the street."

Monica gave herself a mental head slap. She should have parked behind the trailer where her vehicle would have been out of view. Not to hide from Kris, but to make it more difficult for the shooters to find her.

"I have some mug shots for you to look at." Kris held out a tablet. "These are local criminals and ex-cons with violent histories. Maybe someone looks familiar. I didn't get a clear look at either of the attackers' faces, so I can't give any input on this."

"I didn't see them clearly, either," Monica said, reaching for the device. "But I'll take a look." She swiped through a couple dozen photos, but none of the images stood out to her. "Sorry," she said, handing the tablet back to Kris. "Nobody looks familiar." Her voice broke on the last word, as it sank in how difficult it might be for the cops to find the assailants. Maybe they wouldn't be able to find the thugs before they attacked her again.

"Try not to be discouraged," Kris said. "This is just a start."

Monica heard the familiar sound of Esmeralda's cane tapping the floor.

"Kris, good to see you," Esmeralda called out, walking up to them.

"Good to see you, too." He smiled at the older lady, and for a moment the expression of cop suspicion on his face was replaced by a sweet, almost boyish, grin. He carried a warm, masculine appeal that would most definitely have attracted Monica's interest if her life circumstances were different. And if he didn't seem so convinced she'd done something wrong.

"So you two know each other," Monica prompted Esmeralda.

"We see each other nearly every Sunday in church." She glanced at Monica with a slight smile on her lips before turning back to Kris. "Were you the officer who responded to the cabin fire and helped her escape those bad men?"

Kris nodded.

"How about that." Esmeralda shook her head.

"Monica first came to our church when she was fifteen years old. I'm surprised you never crossed paths when she was in town and came to services."

An awkward moment passed when it felt like the Sunday school teacher was trying to set them up for a date. Which stirred up a weird mixture of feelings that Monica couldn't even begin to identify. Because she didn't want to. So many things demanded her attention that it didn't really feel like her life was her own anyway. What did it matter if she met an attractive man?

A cashier at the front of the store called out to Esmeralda for assistance.

"You keep this girl safe," Esmeralda said to Kris before walking away.

"I'll be leaving town in a few days," Monica told Kris, trying to send a clear signal that she was not interested in him despite Esmeralda's efforts. She was tired, she was stressed, and she was worried about her parents, both of whom were obviously not so great at making life choices. The last thing she needed to do was stir up any kind of interest she might have in a police officer who apparently thought she was a criminal. At least, his questions made it seem that way.

"I just want to help," Kris said quietly. "Maybe you're being blackmailed. Or it could be you're afraid to speak up about certain information because you fear more attacks. We all make bad decisions sometimes that we regret and that end up causing us trouble. But I'm sure there's a way to make this better."

Was he sincere? Or was he just looking to bust somebody—anybody—to impress his superiors in the police department and help his career? After being told lies by investigators and also witnessing questionable actions in the agencies that were supposed to ensure justice, Monica was determined to be very careful about whom she trusted.

A small voice inside told her Kris might be the real deal. Someone who wanted to do the right thing. Somebody who truly wanted to help her. But right now, she just couldn't take the leap of faith to trust him.

"I'll be fine," she said, turning her attention back to sweeping.

"All right," he said after a moment's hesitation. "But be careful and watch your back."

She listened to him walk away.

After he was gone, she found herself wishing he had stayed. Because he made her feel safe. And she told herself that there was no other reason.

Five hours later, Monica drove up the steep driveway and past the stone signs announcing the Elk Ridge Resort, a complex that included privately owned homes plus time-share condominiums.

She was exhausted but still determined to start her search. The sooner she got going on this—and any other ideas she could think of—the sooner she'd be able to leave town and end any chance of putting Esmeralda in danger by staying on her property.

Maybe she'd seen too many movies, but it did seem possible she could track down the information her father had hidden.

It was upsetting that her mother had dismissed Monica's warnings about Archer and demanded proof before she would even consider the man was not the upstanding citizen he claimed to be. But Suzanne Larson had never been inclined to deal with uncomfortable situations directly. She'd do nearly anything to avoid them. Even a conversation, if it involved something stressful, was dismissed or circumvented. She liked living in her own world of denial as she enjoyed creature comforts and focused on hosting impressive dinner parties.

While Monica had been shocked by the revelation that her dad worked for organized crime, she wondered if her mom had had an inkling that something out of the ordinary was going on. Maybe, since Suzanne hadn't seen any blatant proof of misbehavior, she'd been able to enjoy the generous amount of money pouring into the household without questioning too closely where it came from or how it had been earned.

*Stop it*. Monica told herself she was being uncharitable.

Even if her suspicions were true, that didn't dim Monica's drive to protect her mom and potentially the rest of her family—her aunts and uncles and cousins who could end up endangered by an association with organized crime.

She reached up to touch the scar on her head, wishing she could remember what her dad had said to her before the car crash took away that part of her memories. She huffed in frustration. Quickly, her frustration shifted to fear as her thoughts turned back to this morning's attempt on her life. Nearly being shoved into a fire. Being chased in the woods, anticipating the burn of a bullet smacking into her body. She shuddered and glanced in the rearview mirror to see if anyone was following her. At the moment, there was no one there.

Maybe the two shooters actually had left town.

But if that were the case, the mob would likely send two more.

The long driveway rose in elevation, past forest and toward surrounding jagged peaks and the mountaintop. Late-afternoon sunlight deepened the shadows nearby and higher up the mountainside. Cedar Lodge was located in a river valley that often felt cut off from the rest of the world. The fun, relaxing times Monica had spent here in the past felt like they'd happened a lifetime ago.

Like a lot of people before him, Hunter Larson found faith in prison when he hit rock bottom. Suzanne didn't believe it was real, but Monica did, and her father's faith journey forged a new connection between the two of them, motivating her to put her anger and feelings of betrayal aside and to visit him more often. On one visit, she'd asked him why he'd thrown away a good life to work for organized crime.

"Fool's gold," he'd responded with a sad laugh and a shake of his head. "I don't mean that the money they paid me was fake. It was real enough. But the feeling I was chasing—contentment, I suppose, or a sense that I was making the most of my life and impressing other people—never materialized."

He'd been making decent money as an accountant when he was first introduced to a member of Boyd Sierra Associates by a mutual friend and the organization offered him some very well-paying legitimate accounting work. He'd had no idea that he was working for organized crime at the start. Then, slowly, they'd asked him to change a few numbers here and there and create false financial documentation to replace records that had been "lost."

"Of course I figured out what was going on, but it was great having the extra money in return for very little work," he'd told Monica on one visit, crossing his arms over his chest before blowing out a breath and shaking his head. "But slowly, it started to bug me. I knew it was wrong, and it could cause problems for you and your mom and me farther down the road."

He'd cleared his throat, looking thoughtful at that point.

"I wanted out of the organization, so I started talking to them about moving on to other things. They weren't happy to hear about my intentions, but I began making plans to exit anyway. I put things in place so I'd be ready to get out of the operation and stay out. Then one of the association's front companies that I'd helped launder money through went to the authorities and reported that I'd defrauded them. Now here I am in prison. And ultimately it's nobody's fault but mine. I made the stupid, foolish decisions."

*Put things in place.* Right now those specific words that he'd used swirled around in Monica's head. What *things*? And where was the place?

She pulled up in front of the resort's administrative office and parked.

Inside the office, she spotted a young woman at the reception desk who looked familiar. Hopefully, she'd worked there the last time Monica had come with her family for a visit. If she recognized her, she might be more inclined to help her.

Monica hated to lie, but she didn't want to burden this person with her whole story of dangerous attacks. Especially since it might scare the woman and cause her to turn down Monica's request. So she combined her request to have a look around in their usual condo with a statement that was actually true even if it didn't include the entire story. "I think my dad might have left something behind the last time we were here, and even though it's been a while we only recently realized it. If possible, I'd like to take a quick look around in the condo where we stayed."

"We do thorough cleanings on a regular basis," the receptionist said in a friendly tone. "I think we would have come across it. When that happens, we immediately contact the most recent guest and then ship them the item if they request it."

From her demeanor, Monica got the impression the woman did recognize her from prior trips and either didn't know about Hunter Larson's criminal conviction or didn't hold it against Monica.

"Sometimes things fall into a crack or crevice and they're overlooked," Monica responded with a slight shrug.

The receptionist hesitated for a moment. "Which unit?"

Monica gave her the information.

She'd hoped the woman wouldn't ask specifically what she was looking for—since she didn't know—and was grateful when she didn't.

After a few moments tapping at the screen of the tablet in front of her, the woman looked up. "It's unoccupied right now, so I suppose it wouldn't hurt to take a look."

They headed down one of the narrow lanes in the complex on foot, making their way around a small cement mixer and a truck belonging to a paving company. A man with curly red hair and dirt-covered clothes, carrying a shovel, stepped out from behind the truck and nearly collided with Monica. He muttered an apology and continued on his way.

"We're always doing upkeep," the receptionist said in a chipper tone.

So did that mean if Hunter had left some physical item here, it could have been discovered or disturbed during a routine maintenance project?

They'd walked around the truck when Monica caught the approach of someone from the corner of her eye.

"Hey, look who's back," a man called out.

Monica panicked, thinking he might be another mob gunman putting on a show of friendliness so he could get close enough to kill her. Heart suddenly pounding, she tensed her muscles and got ready to run.

But then she recognized the tall, balding figure of Ryan Fergus. A semiretired former general contractor about twenty years older than Monica's dad, he'd spent time in the Reno area before relocating to Cedar Ridge, where he worked part-time for the resort. He and Monica's dad had hit it off and chatted when her family came to visit.

The knot in her chest shifted from stark fear to dread and apprehension as she waited for the robust older gentleman, who was an affirmed ski bum, to ask about her dad. She really didn't want to talk about all that had happened. For one thing, it still hurt every time she recounted her dad's arrest and imprisonment. And for another, she'd found that, oftentimes, people who inquired about Hunter were hoping for salacious details more than expressing genuine concern.

Beyond that, what if the receptionist overheard their conversation and had second thoughts about letting Monica into the condo?

In the end, Ryan offered a kind smile that reached all the way to his deeply lined eyes and asked, "Monica, how are you?" He reached out for a lingering handshake that gave her the impression he knew about her dad's situation and wanted to be gracious about it.

"I'm well," she replied, anxious to get to the condo and wanting to avoid a full conversation.

"Glad to hear it. My best to your family." He indicated the paving company truck. "I need to get back to supervising some repairs. Hard winters make for good skiing, but they sure do some damage."

He continued on his way, and Monica resumed walking with the receptionist until they reached their destination. The two-story condo had a stylish entrance facing the access road and a modest yard in the back with a patio, a swath of grass, and a white rail fence on the edge of a stony cliff that allowed for a breathtaking view of the entire valley, including the town of Cedar Lodge, down below.

The receptionist settled in the dining area, taking calls for the resort, while indicating to Monica that she was free to look around.

Monica checked hiding places she'd seen on TV cop shows: the undersides of drawers where an object could be taped, the backs of dressers, atop the ceiling tiles near a couple of larger air vents, and the very backs of top shelves in the closets. She even took a close look at the assortment of hardcovers and paperbacks left on a pair of wall shelves in the living room in case something was hidden inside or behind one of them. She tried tapping the stones around the fireplace to see if one of them might be loose. Nothing.

She went outside to look around the backyard. Despite the cool breeze, sweat beaded on her forehead and between her shoulder blades. She imagined someone in the shadows getting a clear view of her on the edge of the cliff and firing a shot. She might be taking a risk standing out here, but this was what she'd come here to do. People's lives were in the balance, including her own, so she did her best to shake off her feeling of unease and power through.

She searched for anything that appeared out of place. Maybe one of those hollowed-out fake rocks where you could hide a key inside. She walked the fence line, looking at the ground there, and then behind the evergreen hedges, but nothing caught her eye.

Swallowing down the disappointment that had her on the verge of tears, she thanked the receptionist, and they walked back to the admin building, where they parted ways.

She headed back down the mountainside to the highway and then into town. The vehicle she drove was nondescript, but Kris mentioned noticing her out-of-state car plates, and she felt like an easy target. Despite gripping the steering wheel, her arms and hands began to feel shaky.

When she thought of the handsome cop, she forced herself to set aside the mental image of him. She didn't want to let her thoughts linger there. Instead, she considered whether it would be wise to hide her car and use rideshare services to get around town. The problem was that the cost would quickly add up, and her credit cards were nearly maxed out.

Figuring her shakiness might be due not only to fear of being found by the bad guys but also to low blood sugar—she hadn't eaten much today—she stopped at a grocery store on her way back to her temporary trailer residence.

After purchasing a couple of bags' worth of food, she walked back out to her car, drove the few blocks to the thrift store, parked in the grass beside the trailer, and walked up the wooden steps that served as a front porch.

She inserted the key Esmeralda had given her, pushed open the door, and heard an odd clicking sound. At the same moment, she noticed a length of wire across the doorframe that hadn't been there earlier.

*Bomb!*

Flinging the bags aside, Monica threw herself off the steps.

# Chapter Four

"I'm all right." Monica clasped her hands together and brought them to her chin. "I just need to rest for a few minutes. And I need some time to think."

Kris stood with one hand on the frame of his patrol car, leaning partway through the open door and peering closely at the mysterious woman seated in front of him. Why was Monica Larson so relentlessly targeted for attack? Just being related to a mob accountant didn't seem like reason enough. And why was she determined to remain in Cedar Lodge after all of this violence?

"Really," she said with a shallow nod and a faint, obviously forced smile. "I'm okay."

Kris's concern must have been evident on his face.

"I don't have any broken bones or sprains or burns," she added. "I flattened myself on the grass after I jumped off the steps, and the force of the blast went over me." She unclasped her hands and looked at them. "Just some scrapes." The nervous smile came back. "And grass stains on my clothes."

Kris had heard the call go out over dispatch after a nearby resident phoned 9-1-1 to report the explosion. Esmeralda had already let him know that Monica was staying on the property. He'd been first on scene, heart dropping to his feet when he'd seen the trailer engulfed in flames, certain the attackers had gotten to Monica and killed her.

It had taken him a moment to spot her silhouette outlined by the fire. She'd been curled up on the grass, clearly terrified and afraid to move. He'd gotten her into his patrol unit just as Fire, EMS, and additional cops arrived. While helping her to his vehicle, he'd kept one hand free, ready to grab his gun if necessary. The attackers might have been lingering nearby, ready to finish her off if she hadn't perished in the fire. But there hadn't been an immediate follow-up attack. Perhaps the thugs had hung around but they hadn't expected a cop to respond so quickly.

There were plenty of police and first responders around now as the fire crew finished dousing the flames that had devoured much of Esmeralda's trailer. It looked like Monica would be safe for the moment. But he had no doubt the assailants would try again.

"Tell me what's really going on," Kris said, doing his best to check his frustration so this didn't sound like an interrogation.

"I already did. The mob's trying to get to my dad by harming me."

"That doesn't tell me why you're determined to stay in town. There must be a reason."

She gave a slight shrug in response.

"Don't you want to go home?" Didn't she have family or friends she could turn to for help?

"I can't go home." She glanced through the windshield of the patrol car at the trailer, where a few small flames lapped at the twisted metal frame of a blown-out window. "If I go back to Reno, I might as well just walk straight toward the thugs who are trying to kill me."

Of course he wouldn't ask her to do that. And she apparently didn't have the financial resources to go far away where she couldn't be found and stay there indefinitely.

How could he help her? He'd called Shelly

Bennett to confirm that Monica had permission to stay in the cabin. Shelly had already known about the initial attack—Monica had called and told her—and Shelly had asked Kris to do whatever he could to help Monica. She'd said that Monica was a good friend and a good person. Esmeralda had likewise vouched for Monica.

So why was Kris so wrapped up with worrying about what might happen to this woman?

Maybe it had something to do with the moment he first spotted her in the woods, running for her life. And the moments later, when he'd been beside her as she'd used the only weapon she could reach—a tree branch—to fight to survive. On her own, and desperate. With only him, a stranger, to help her.

Stationed overseas in the army, he'd seen so many people with their lives torn apart, no home and no one to help them as they grimly tried to hang on and keep living for just one more day. Kris had done his job there the best he could while he was in the military, but he'd seen so many people he couldn't help.

And then there'd been his wife Angie's devastating medical diagnosis eighteen months after Roy had been born. Pancreatic cancer. Spreading quickly. Another sorrowful situation where he couldn't do anything.

But right here, right now, he might be able to assist Monica while at the same time capturing some very bad guys. He hoped to uncover the extent to which organized crime was operating in his town and help crush it. Of course, he also wanted to lock up any local criminals who might be working with these dangerous men.

"I'm going to talk to the chief for a minute." Kris beckoned another officer to stay near the patrol car where Monica was still seated until he came back. The chance of the assailants launching the follow-up attack on Monica that he was worried about might be small, but it was not an impossibility.

Cops had already been dispersed to canvass the nearby residential neighborhood as well as the other businesses on Glacier Street in search of witnesses or helpful video footage. Esmeralda had a couple of outside security cameras that had hopefully recorded some useful images.

Chief Ellis was talking to the fire chief when Kris walked up. As soon as the fire cooled down enough to get a closer look, their intention was to learn as much as possible about the explosive device and see what investigative leads they could develop from there.

Cole was also there with his paramedic crew, waiting for the fire to be completely extinguished and the scene to be officially cleared before he left. Cole had prodded Kris to ask Monica one more time if she was certain she didn't want a quick medical checkup just to confirm that she was all right. Which was what Kris had just done.

"What did she say?" the paramedic asked.

"She said she's okay," Kris reported.

Kris, Cole, and Deputy Dylan Ruiz—along with their friend Henry Walsh, who was away overseas right now—had known each other since they were small and had played football together in high school. After graduation they'd all joined various branches of the military. Kris, Cole, and Dylan had returned to Cedar Lodge and taken jobs protecting the citizens of their town while also working on their family ranches. Henry had gone on to work as a hostage rescue specialist for an international private security company. Nobody was ever quite sure where he was or what he was doing. But he did check in every now and then.

"Okay," Cole said thoughtfully. "Encourage

her to go to the hospital and get checked out if she develops any concerning symptoms."

Kris nodded. Monica obviously didn't think she needed a medical assessment, but she would need a place where she could rest, knowing that she was safe while she thought things through and decided on her next step. He was afraid the thugs would get to her if she stayed in a hotel in town.

Gazing at the smoldering trailer and considering how close she'd come to death twice in one day, he stepped away from Cole and the police chief. He slid his phone out of his pocket and put through a call to his mom, Jill.

"The woman I told you about who was in the fire at the cabin this morning, Monica, has been attacked again," he said after exchanging quick greetings with his mother. "She needs a place to stay. For tonight, at least. I was thinking we could put her up in the bunkhouse. She'll be away from the main house so she won't be around you or Dad or Roy. I'll throw down a sleeping bag outside the bunkhouse door or maybe a small tent so I can keep an eye on things. She's been through a lot, and she could use a break. Would you be okay with that?"

The bunkhouse had actually been remodeled

into a large studio apartment, but they kept the old name. Kris's brother stayed in it whenever he left his job in Alaska to come for a visit.

"Let me talk to your father, and I'll call you right back." Jill disconnected.

Kris's dad, Pete, was a military veteran. His mom had been a competitive barrel racer. Both of them had grown up on ranches on the edge of wilderness, and they'd raised two rambunctious sons who'd gone on to serve in combat zones. Challenges, quickly changing circumstances, and exposure to risk were not unusual or intimidating for Kris's parents.

He was concerned about Roy, though. What if someone came to the ranch looking for Monica? It might be a good night for Roy to sleep over with his cousins. In fact, it might be wise for him to go for a visit even if Monica didn't stay in the bunkhouse. That attack at the cabin was literally close to home, and the possibility existed that the thugs were hiding in the area. There were plenty of vacation homes that weren't occupied by their owners for much of the year. And there were remote campgrounds not too far away.

Kris threw a glance toward Monica inside the patrol car and the cop standing nearby keeping an eye on her. He saw that everything was okay, and then went for a walk around the perimeter of the thrift store and the surrounding property looking for anyone lurking nearby or possibly evidence left behind. Unfortunately, he didn't spot anything helpful.

He was nearly back to his patrol car when his phone rang. It was Jill.

"Listen, I don't want to put you and Dad in a difficult situation," he started out.

"Don't be silly," Jill cut in before he could continue. "Bring Monica here. And we've told Roy that he's going to be staying with his other grandparents tonight. Just to be safe. Hope you're okay with that."

His mom had been one step ahead of him. Of course.

His late wife's parents, Yvonne and Gabriel Durand, were very involved in Roy's life, and the two families had remained close in the aftermath of Angie's passing.

"That sounds like the perfect arrangement," Kris said, mildly annoyed with himself for not having thought of it first.

"Good. Roy's excited that tomorrow morning, they'll be the ones taking him to school for the first time."

"I imagine he is."

"When do you think you'll get here?"

"Within an hour."

"Okay. I'll have dinner ready for the both of you."

"Mom, you don't need to do that. We can pick up something in town and bring it to the house."

"You think you can get better food in town?" she asked with mock sternness.

"No, ma'am."

"Good. See you in a bit. And watch yourself."

Didn't matter that he was a combat veteran and a cop. His mom still couldn't resist reminding him to be careful.

Kris walked back to where the chief and Cole were still standing.

"I'm going to have Campbell take lead on the full investigation of all of this," Ellis said at Kris's approach. "I'll have him start by contacting the feds for any information they're willing to give us on the Boyd Sierra syndicate. We'll also talk to them about any recent bombings using the same kind of device that's present here."

Sam Campbell was one of three detectives in the police department.

"Meanwhile, I want you to keep an eye on Monica. See what you can learn. And keep her alive, obviously."

"Actually, I've already got a plan to run by you regarding that."

"Let's hear it."

"She still refuses to leave town. Going home to Reno is out of the question. I'm afraid if she checks into a hotel, she might not be alive in the morning."

The chief nodded his agreement so far.

"Unless we have some kind of safe house in town that I don't know about, I think the smartest thing to do is have her stay at the Double V Ranch with my family. At least for tonight."

"You sure you want to expose your family to the danger that could potentially come from that?"

Kris explained the planned arrangement.

As he finished, the chief responded to a call over his radio.

"What's this?" Cole asked Kris in a teasing tone while the chief was distracted. "A woman has finally piqued your interest?" He smiled broadly.

"It's not like that," Kris snapped. Yes, Monica

was pretty. But Cedar Lodge was full of pretty women. Well-intentioned friends and family members had tried to set him up with some of them. But between being a cop, working the ranch, and being a dad—the most important job of all—he didn't have time to date. Angie had specifically told him before she passed that she wanted him to find love again—for Roy's benefit as well as for his own sake. But he still felt like *moving on*, as people termed it, would somehow diminish the love he'd had for his late wife. If he'd really loved her, how could he just *move on*?

Right now none of that mattered. He wasn't offering to help Monica because of a romantic interest. He wanted to help because there was so much suffering in the world. Why not do what you could to ease that for someone? To help keep them from getting *murdered*?

Cole dampened down his smile, but not by much. Not even when Kris glared at him.

Ellis completed his radio conversation and turned his attention back to Kris. "Let's go see what Monica thinks about staying at your family's ranch."

At the patrol car, Kris extended his invitation to Monica.

She shook her head in response. "Thanks, but

I've already caused enough trouble. I'll just find a hotel, and I'll lay low for a couple of days."

"I'm not sure you'll last a couple of days," Kris responded.

Her eyes grew wide, and Kris felt a little bad about being so blunt. But not bad enough to backpedal on what he'd said. Because it was the truth.

"You're free to do what you want, of course," the chief said. "But the Double V Ranch would be a good place for you to stay, at least for tonight."

She hesitated for a moment before pressing her lips together and then nodding. "Okay."

"Good," Kris said as he and the chief stepped back from the open door of the patrol car to make room for Monica to get out. He didn't realize until that moment that he'd been holding his breath, waiting for her response. Now he just hoped that the ranch would really be a peaceful place for her to recover from all that had happened to her in one very long day. And that the assailants didn't try to launch another attack tonight.

"I left my groceries flung across the lawn in front of the trailer," Monica said as they neared the edge of town on the way to Kris's ranch.

"Can we stop somewhere so I can grab something to eat?"

Despite nearly being blown to bits, Monica was ravenous. She was tired and had a pounding headache, too. But right now she was focused on food.

"My mom's making us something to eat," Kris said. "But we can stop at the burger place and get you something if you'd rather do that."

"I can wait," she said. A home-cooked meal sounded wonderful.

Kris opened the patrol car's console and pulled out a bottled water and a smashed granola bar. "They've been in here awhile," he said apologetically.

"I don't care." Monica accepted both and ripped off the end of the granola bar wrapper. "Thank you," she managed to add before taking a big bite of oatmeal and chocolate.

"Why are you doing this?" she asked after she finished eating and had drunk all the water. "Why are you sticking your neck out this far and letting me stay at your home?"

She tried to be a charitable person and help others in need, and she understood the drive to do that. But a cop who'd met her less than twenty-four hours ago offering her refuge in his home seemed like a lot. She wasn't sure she could do that for someone, let alone for a complete stranger.

"I want to keep you alive, and I'd also like to get to the bottom of these attacks. The Cedar Lodge PD needs to make sure dangerous thugs don't get the impression that they can run roughshod over this town."

Fair enough. She assumed that he would now press her for more information, but he didn't. And she found herself thinking that maybe she actually was ready to tell him everything. That she was staying in town because she was looking for evidence of Boyd Sierra Associates' criminal activity she believed her father had left here. And that she was desperate to convince her mother to break off her engagement to a mobster before they got married in two weeks.

She took a deep breath, pondering her options.

Full night had fallen, and they rode in the darkness without further conversation. They approached the foot of the drive leading to the Bennett cabin, and Monica felt a shiver pass through her as they drove by.

*Thank You, Lord.*

Her life could have ended this morning. It

was a disquieting thought, to say the least. She glanced over at Kris, his features visible in the dashboard light. Would she have survived if he hadn't been there? There was no way to know. But she was grateful for his help.

They turned off the highway onto a winding tree-lined drive that finally opened to a multiple-acre expanse of meadow and stables and corrals and various outbuildings. A rambling ranch house sat at the edge of a circular unpaved turnaround near the front entrance. The Craftsman-style structure had large windows with light spilling out into the darkness, and there were several vehicles parked nearby.

"You and your parents live here?" Monica asked.

"And my son, Roy."

But not Roy's mother? Were she and Kris separated? Divorced?

*What difference does it make?*

None. It made no difference. Why did she care? She didn't.

Okay, maybe she was a *little* curious about Kris's personal life. Maybe she was a little bit attracted. But it was probably just nerves and fear talking. He'd made her feel safe. That was the appeal. And that was all.

To her surprise, Kris came around and opened the patrol car door for her as she was gathering her backpack and doing what she could to smooth her hair and try to look presentable.

They walked up to the door, and she was feeling oddly nervous. Like she wanted to make a good impression on his family for some silly reason.

Kris opened the door and ushered her ahead of him. As soon as Kris stepped into the house, he was attacked by a small boy dashing across the living room toward him like a runaway colt.

Monica's gaze locked on the boy and his father as Kris picked up the little guy.

Kris had said his son's name was Roy, and Roy had his dad's features but with dark brown eyes instead of blue and dark brown hair instead of Kris's more russet-brown. The child had chubby, rosy cheeks, and he seemed giddy with excitement.

Monica stood by listening as Roy chattered to his dad about his surprise trip to stay at Grammy Yvonne and Grandpa Gabriel's house.

"This is Monica," Kris said to his son.

The exuberant boy had a sudden attack of bashfulness and buried his face in Kris's neck.

Finally, Monica shyly turned to face the

adults. She wasn't certain what kind of reception to expect.

While holding his son in his arms, Kris made the introductions. His mother, Jill, stepped forward first. She was a petite woman with her red hair styled in a pixie cut. A deep tan spoke of time spent working outside. "Welcome," she said to Monica.

His father, Pete, had Kris's muscular build. He, too, offered a friendly "Welcome to our home."

Kris introduced his son's other set of grandparents, and that was when Monica learned that Roy's mother had passed away three years ago.

Kris reported the story in a matter-of-fact tone, but it pierced Monica's heart. This kind man had lost his wife, and this sweet little boy had lost his mother. It was a sorrowful reminder that nearly everyone faced some kind of tragedy in their lifetime.

Maybe it was her own exhaustion combining with compassion for this kind family, or maybe it was a delayed response to the day's terrifying events, but Monica found her eyes were pooling with tears. Embarrassed, she sniffed loudly and turned away to wipe at her eyes with the edge of her sleeve. Then she did her best to pull herself together and politely engage in conversation.

With constant glances at the little boy listening in, and obviously mindful of what they wanted to say in front of him, the grown-ups talked very generally about what had brought Monica here.

After Kris gave his son one last hug and a half dozen more kisses, the little boy excitedly left with his visiting grandparents. Kris stood on the porch, watching until they were out of sight.

"After we eat dinner, I'll get you set up in the bunkhouse," Kris said to Monica. "I'll be sleeping outside the door. And don't worry, it's not as rustic as it sounds. It's pretty nice, really."

"Oh, honey, I already fixed up one of the guest bedrooms for her," Jill said to her son. She turned to Monica. "Shelly Bennett thinks very highly of you." She threw a quick glance at Kris. "You're not the only one who spoke to her today." Her attention reverted back to Monica, and she added, "Shelly asked me to do everything I can to help you. I intend to."

Tears started to well up in Monica's eyes again. So much kindness on the heels of such horror was overwhelming.

Jill offered a sympathetic smile. "I left some

chicken enchiladas and rice in the oven for you two." She walked toward the kitchen, a large space with a breakfast nook. Monica and Kris followed. "There's iced tea in the fridge." She glanced at Kris. "Dad and I already ate."

Pete stood near the kitchen entrance.

"We get up early, we eat dinner early, we go to bed early," Jill explained to Monica with a smile. "That's just what ranch life is like. Now we'll leave you two alone to eat and talk in private about police business. We've got security cameras on the property and spoiled dogs who will bark if anyone comes around."

Monica reached down to pet the large hound of indeterminate breed that had been watching her with interest since she'd arrived. A second, apparently shier dog stayed near Kris's dad.

"That gentle giant you're petting is Betty," Pete said. "The little one is Pepper. The other dogs prefer to stay out in the stables with the horses." Betty followed Jill as she walked toward her husband.

After they were gone, Kris opened the oven to pull out a covered dish and set it on the stove top.

Monica glanced around. "How can I help?"

"Why don't you just sit down and relax. This will be ready in a minute."

A short time later, Monica had a plate of delicious-looking food in front of her, along with utensils and tea.

She was just about to close her eyes and offer a silent prayer of thanks when she saw Kris do the same. She wanted to ask him if he was praying, but she didn't feel like she had the right to. He was a public servant helping her stay alive. They weren't friends.

And yet, she already respected and admired him. He was a gentle man, but he was strong, too. He'd followed through on his determination to help her and work on her case without coercing or pressuring her into doing anything she didn't want to do.

After a few moments she realized she'd been gazing at him for a little too long. Fortunately, he hadn't seemed to notice. A warm bloom of embarrassment spread across her cheeks, and she turned her attention to her food.

The enchiladas were savory and delicious. There wasn't much conversation between the two of them, which gave her time to think. After their meal was completed, Monica knew she wanted to tell Kris everything about why she was here and what she was attempting to do. Even though she suspected he would try to stop her from doing it.

He listened attentively while she went through it all, some of it a repetition of what he'd already heard, but she needed to say it again to give her plans context.

"How's your head?" was the first thing he asked, making her laugh in surprise. She reached up to touch the stitches where her scalp had been split in the crash.

"Everything physical is healing okay. The memories? Not so much. I still have some vague impressions I think might be memories, but they vanish as soon as I try to focus on them."

Kris folded his napkin and set it beside his plate. "I understand what you're attempting to do and why," he said in measured tones. "I also think you realize now why you can't do it alone. Staying with you while you carry out your plan might be one way to investigate the attacks against you and track down the criminals while keeping you safe. Detective Campbell will be doing his research-based investigation. Me shadowing you would give us more boots-on-the-ground-type information. It would broaden the scope of the investigation."

A weight lifted off Monica's chest. The last thing she'd expected was that Kris would offer to help her with what she was doing.

"Let's talk to the chief about this in the morning," he added.

They cleared the table, and then Kris showed her the way to her room. Along the way, he grabbed her backpack from the spot near the front door where she'd set it down.

They passed a den where Jill and Pete were watching a movie. Jill got up and came along to help Monica get situated, showing her where she could find towels in the bathroom connected to her room. Betty and Pepper came with her. This time the little black-and-white terrier mix let Monica pet him.

"We'll let you get some rest," Kris said before leaving Monica alone in her room.

Monica flopped down onto the bed and tried to relax. The Volker family were all very nice people, and they had a beautiful home. But there was no escaping the fact that she was here hiding from people who were trying to kill her. And this was just the end of her second day trying to fight back against the mob to protect her parents and herself. It was going to be a dangerous fight, and there was no guarantee she would win.

## Chapter Five

Sitting beside Monica in Chief Ellis's office while waiting for the chief to return from a brief meeting, Kris looked down at his phone and waved at the video chat image of his son. "Love you, buddy."

"Love you, too, Dad." Roy waved back before shoving the phone into his grandma Yvonne's hand and then scampering away.

Yvonne moved the phone until the camera was at face level. Her expression slightly chagrined, she offered a one-shoulder shrug and said, "He just saw his friends."

Yvonne had taken Roy to school this morning, and while Kris understood his son's need to be social, he still couldn't help feeling a little hurt. Which was silly. Ranch life could be isolating for a kiddo with no siblings, and one of the major benefits of any time Roy spent with

Yvonne and Gabriel was that he'd have several cousins nearby to play with.

Kris reminded himself he should be happy that Roy felt confident enough to be away from his dad for a day or two. That was impressive for the kid's young age.

Still, at times when Monica didn't need him by her side for a short time, he'd pop by to visit his son. He loved every moment spent with that boy. Even the admittedly exhausting and annoying ones.

Kris and Yvonne exchanged goodbyes, and he closed the app.

"I'm sorry to put you through this," Monica said quietly just as Ellis returned to his office carrying a tablet, a stack of file folders, and a coffee cup. "I'll move to a hotel tonight."

"Please don't." Kris had meant it when he'd said he wanted to make helping her his main priority until they solved this case and found her attackers. "If this goes on for very long, we can talk about different arrangements." It wouldn't be fair to ask his son to stay away from home for too long.

"What's this?" Ellis asked, stepping behind his desk and taking a sip of coffee from the oversized mug.

Kris summarized their conversation.

"If I end up having to bring the feds in to work alongside us on this and not just as a source of information, we might be able to get access to some type of safe house somewhere in the state," the chief said. "They must have something somewhere. And speaking of feds, I was just on the phone with both state and federal law enforcement agencies. Use of explosives is always especially concerning, so I gave them the details of what we learned last night about the device connected to the trailer door. The fed confirmed that the fairly simple pressure-triggered assembly made of easily obtainable items is relatively common as far as explosives go, and it doesn't point to any specific criminal or criminal group that he could think of off the top of his head. But they'll add the incident to their own databases along with the possible involvement of the Boyd Sierra syndicate, and he'll let me know if any connection or helpful information pops up."

Ellis tossed the items he'd been carrying onto his desk and sat down. "Detective Campbell has taken up the larger-scale investigation, and right now officers are keeping an eye out for the vehicle described in the initial attack," the chief said to Monica. "Now, I understand from Kris that you have something to tell me?"

Monica recapped what she'd told Kris last night about her plans to find what she needed to help her parents, including her visit to the Elk Ridge Resort as her first stop.

Kris's body tensed as he waited for the chief's response. Ultimately, whether Kris could devote his on-duty time to protecting Monica and helping her with her search was up to Ellis. Whether he'd be allowed to continue offering Monica a place to stay at the ranch was up to his boss, too. Kris was aware that he was skirting a professional and personal line.

Ellis gazed at Monica for what felt like a long time before finally saying, "I can't prevent you from going through with your plans, but I can ask you to stop. For the sake of your own safety. So, will you stop?"

Monica sat up straighter, her posture and her jawline rigid. "No, sir. I will not."

Kris wanted her to be safe, but he also couldn't help admiring her determination and courage.

"I figured as much." Ellis leaned back in his chair. "I'll assign Officer Volker to be your security detail and to assist you for the time being. What's your next step?"

"I know which bank my dad used in town. I want to talk to the manager there. See if they'll confirm if he had a safe-deposit box where he might have left some kind of information on his former bosses."

Ellis frowned. "They won't tell you much without legal authorization from your father."

"I know," Monica said. "But if I can confirm that there's a safe-deposit box, then I'll get started learning how to get access to it."

Ellis nodded. "Okay, that's a good idea. What else have you got planned?"

"Esmeralda Marino is thinking about possible locations where my dad might have hidden something. Places she knows he was connected to when he was growing up here. She suggested I look around his childhood home, so I plan to do that. She said he might have had hiding places on the property as a kid that nobody would know about but him. She's also reaching out to people who knew my dad. Especially old friends. Maybe they have ideas. Maybe he confided in one of them."

*And maybe all of this is a waste of time.* Kris reminded himself that plenty of investigations started with no leads and few clues, but then things grew from there. Maybe some random bit of evidence along the way would bring them to information that was more substantial.

"Esmeralda has helped a lot of people in town, and she's worked with the police department in several situations without asking for anything in return," Ellis said. "There's no telling how many people are waiting for the opportunity to do something good for her, including getting her information that she's seeking. The news about the trailer explosion is all over town. That might make people even more willing to step up. I think you should make talking to her this morning your first priority."

"Okay," Monica said. "And after we talk to her, we can go by the bank."

Kris nodded in agreement.

They left the office and got into Kris's patrol car. Monica had just pulled out her phone when it rang, and she glanced at the screen. "It's Ryan, my dad's friend from the resort."

"Put it on speaker."

She frowned at him.

"If you and I are going to be working together on this, we need to trust each other, and we need to share information. It's better if I hear it directly rather than secondhand as much as possible. If Ryan's making a social call and it's not about the case, then obviously I don't need to hear it."

Her expression softened. "All right." She tapped the screen and shifted the call to the speaker setting. "Ryan, hello."

"Hey, are you okay? I saw the story about the trailer explosion. Of course, rumors are flying around town, but I heard your name connected to the reports. Is it true? Were you there? Was it targeted at you? I can hardly believe it." The words all came out in an anxious rush.

"Yes, I was there, and I'm fine," Monica told him. "Not exactly the kind of thing you'd expect in Cedar Lodge, but I'm going to guess that you already know about my dad's criminal prosecution and the nature of the people he worked for."

"Sadly, I do know," Ryan said, his voice more subdued now.

"Ask him if he has any idea where your dad might have left something for safekeeping," Kris whispered.

She put the question to Ryan, and there was a pause at the other end of the call.

"Only thing that comes to mind is his old locker in the resort gym. But that would have been cleared out when his time-share interest was sold."

"Well, if you think of anything, please let me know."

"Of course."

The call ended, and then Monica tapped the screen to connect to Esmeralda.

Kris listened as the call went to voice mail. "Try again. Maybe she just couldn't get to the phone in time." She still didn't pick up.

"I'll try the thrift shop number," Monica said, tension creeping into her voice.

She'd talked to Esmeralda last night after the explosion. Of course her dear friend had been shocked. Monica had been adamant that she would not return to work despite Esmeralda's protests. She'd exposed her friend to more than enough danger.

Kris had already driven the patrol car to the edge of the driveway. He paused and checked out the side street beside the police facility before pulling out onto the street.

The call to the thrift shop continued to ring until it rolled over to a generic voice mail.

"She didn't mention closing the shop today," Monica said as she disconnected.

"Why don't you try her personal number again?"

Start Again Thrift was closer than her house to their current location. Concerned about Esmeralda's welfare, Kris decided to head there first. Tension tightened his stomach and he prayed that the woman so beloved in the community was okay.

The CLOSED sign hung in the window of Start Again Thrift. The interior lights were off save for one lone fixture always left on near the front door. There were no vehicles parked nearby other than Monica's sedan.

As she gazed at the burnt-out trailer that was to have been her temporary home, fear of what might have happened sent an eerie sensation of goose bumps rippling across her skin. It was followed by the horrifying thought that Esmeralda might have been targeted for attack because she'd helped Monica. Maybe that was why the store was unexpectedly closed and her friend was not answering her phone.

With her phone on speaker, Monica tried to call Esmeralda, but again the call rolled to voice mail. Monica exchanged a worried look with Kris.

He nodded. "We'll head to her house right now."

Moments later, Kris pulled to the curb in front of a sky blue clapboard house with a white picket fence, a front lawn edged in verdant shrubs and bright flowers, and Esmeralda's minivan parked in the driveway. The curtains for the picture window facing the street were tied back. At least one lamp glowed inside. After both Kris and Monica took a lingering look around to make sure it was safe, they got out of the car. Nothing seemed amiss as they walked up the pathway to the front door, with Kris continuing to vigilantly monitor their surroundings.

Nevertheless, Monica's heart beat heavier than usual in her chest under the weight of nervous concern. She didn't want to let the violent events of the last two days turn her into someone who lived her days tormented by fear, but concern for her friend was unavoidable. She offered up a silent prayer for Esmeralda's well-being.

Kris knocked on the white front door, barely waiting for a response before he turned to Monica and said, "Stay behind me." Then he opened the door, which was unlocked as usual, and cautiously stepped inside. "Hello?" he called out. "Esmeralda? Are you home? It's Kris."

There was no human response, but almost immediately, Monica heard the tapping sound of canine toenails hitting the hardwood floor.

A small white fluff ball of a dog with a few bits of grass clippings and dirt in its fur rounded a corner and then stopped short to offer a friendly yap.

Kris leaned down to give the dog a quick pet before continuing in the direction the tiny watchdog had come from. Monica couldn't see much from behind him. But then she saw the cop's broad shoulders visibly relax as he rounded the corner ahead of her. At that point, she could see the open glass slider door and Esmeralda at the edge of the lawn, on her knees, working in a flower bed.

A wave of relief hit Monica so hard she stumbled slightly.

"Hey!" Kris called as he stepped outside, with Monica following. "We've been trying to reach you on the phone."

Esmeralda startled and then turned, tipping her head back to see them from beneath the brim of her floppy sun hat. She offered a contrite smile. "I hope I didn't worry you. I checked in with my kids this morning so they wouldn't be concerned, and then I came out here for a little quiet time with the Lord and my flowers. I intentionally left my phone in the kitchen so I could have a couple of hours of peace."

She reached for her cane to help her stand. A Siamese cat who had been sitting nearby scampered a few feet away and then stopped to turn and watch everything with luminous blue eyes. Kris held out the crook of his arm, and Esmeralda took hold, allowing him to help her to her feet.

"I didn't mean to snap at you," Kris said. "I was just worried when you didn't answer your phone and then we went by the shop and everything was locked up."

"It's all right." She smiled brightly and patted his arm just before she let go of him. "I decided to close the shop and let my employees have a paid day off to come to grips with the explosion and fire last night." By now her smile had faded. "Of course, it happened shortly after we'd closed up the store and left, but they're still upset. Understandably."

"Makes sense," Kris said.

"And it's not me these criminals are coming after." She turned to Monica. "It's you. And you're the person we should be concerned about. How are you? Seriously. You've been through quite a lot."

"Better now that I know you're okay," Monica said.

The fluffy little dog reappeared and offered a couple more friendly barks.

"You're new around here," Kris said, reaching down to scoop up the critter and hold him against his chest.

"That's Rocky," Esmeralda said, smiling fondly at her pooch. "I've had him about two months, and he wants to be everybody's best friend." She began walking toward the house. "Let's go inside."

They settled in the living room after Kris and Monica politely declined Esmeralda's offer of something to drink.

"I know the full story of why Monica is remaining in town, so one of the reasons we were trying to track you down this morning was to find out if you've gotten any new ideas or tips on where we should look for information

Hunter Larson might have documented and hidden regarding his criminal cronies."

Esmeralda leaned back in her floral print chair and clasped her hands in her lap. "I have put the word out, making sure to include my most busybody friends, but I haven't heard anything yet."

"We're going to check out Dad's old house today."

"I've been thinking some more about that, and he might not have left it in the actual house. There's lots of wooded area around that property where he could have put something. Buried it, maybe."

"How would I ever find it?"

"A metal detector?" Esmeralda shrugged. "Based on all the kids' adventure movies I watched as my children were growing up, I'd say search for something that would make a memorable landmark and stand the test of time. A distinctly shaped rock, or pile of rocks, something like that."

"Was your dad released on bail after he was initially arrested?" Kris asked.

Monica nodded.

"So he could have come up to Cedar Lodge and buried something shortly before his trial when he realized he was going to be convicted and locked up. And that would have been, what, about a year ago? We could look for ground that appears as if it's been disturbed relatively recently."

"All of this assuming the owners allow us access to the property," Monica said.

Kris settled his gaze on her. "I think it's worth a try."

He was right.

"Let's go have a look after we stop at the bank to find out if Dad had a safe-deposit box."

With no better ideas, and so much at stake, they had to pursue every potential lead they could think of. And they needed to do it quickly. The longer this was drawn out, the more she and her family and friends—like Esmeralda—would be exposed to danger.

# Chapter Six

"I'm afraid it's against policy for me to give you any information about our clients. Or to even confirm if your father is one of our clients," the bank employee said.

Monica gave a slight nod of understanding as she tried to rein in her frustration. Not with the woman sitting at a desk in front of her in an office cubicle in the bank. But frustration with the situation overall.

She'd tried not to get her hopes up as they'd driven to the bank from Esmeralda's house. It was common knowledge that banks didn't give out depositors' information freely. Still, she had allowed herself a little bit of hope.

"May I offer a suggestion?" the bank employee asked.

"Sure."

"Get a certified power of attorney from your father. With that in hand, most banks will answer your questions and work with you. Us included."

In the blur of activity after her father's arrest and subsequent posting of bail, Monica had accompanied her father on one of his visits with his attorney. She'd signed some things, been shown some documents, and was fairly certain she did have power of attorney. But she hadn't thought about it since then. She didn't think she had an actual copy of it, paper or digitized. And obtaining that would take time.

"What if I have his authorization but I don't have the safe-deposit box key?" Monica asked.

"The lock can be drilled and the box opened. There's a fee for that."

There might be a fee to contact the lawyer for the certified documentation she needed, too. And how certain was she that her dad's attorney was not connected to the Boyd Sierra Associates criminal group?

Not certain at all.

As they stepped out of the bank into bright sunlight, Kris moved in front of Monica to keep her behind him for a few moments until he'd taken a cautious look around. Then they continued to the patrol car and got in.

"Do you think this might be a good time to

contact your mother and see if she has any information or documentation that might help?"

Monica shook her head. "The last thing she wants to do is help me find evidence that her fiancé is a crook. And I can't help thinking she would tell Archer what was going on. If he suspected she might be helping me—even if she wasn't—that could put her in danger."

"Might as well call your dad's attorney's office and see what they can do for you," Kris said while they sat in the parked police car.

Monica had the attorney listed in her directory. She placed a call and spoke with a paralegal, who listened to Monica's request for information and told her she'd get back to her later, despite Monica emphasizing that this was an urgent and time-sensitive request.

"Okay," Monica said after the disappointingly short and unfruitful conversation. "Let's move on to our next step and drive out to my dad's old house."

Kris reached for his phone. "Let me check in with the chief first."

"Put it on speaker so I can hear," Monica said, feeling a slight smile lift the corner of her mouth. "We *are* a team now, right?"

"Yes, we are." He smiled faintly without looking at her.

*He's a good cop and kind person just doing his job*, she told herself after her heart seemed to skip a beat at the sight of his smile. This partnership wasn't going anywhere. Not beyond getting a job done.

Ellis picked up the call. "What have you got to report, Kris?"

"Not much. We can't get information about Hunter Larson at the bank without jumping through some legal hoops. The process has been started but will take time."

"What I expected."

"Esmeralda didn't have any new information or suggestions, but she's still asking around. Right now we're going to head to Hunter Larson's childhood home."

"Good. Campbell and his team are working their confidential informants and also visiting hardware stores to see if anyone remembers selling the items that were used for the explosive device on the trailer. We haven't gotten a hit on the search for the SUV involved in the attack at the Bennett cabin fire, but we're still looking."

After the call ended, Kris pulled away from the curb and drove through downtown. He took a couple of turns that ended with them heading southwest toward a more sparsely populated area. The road quickly became hilly and tree-lined, with jagged snowcapped peaks visible in the distance. Occasionally they crossed a stretch of the winding Meadowlark River.

"My dad always said he loved it here, but there just weren't the financial opportunities he wanted as a young man," Monica said, pondering the amazing beauty of the area. "Financial opportunities were of supreme importance to him until everything started unraveling and he realized he'd gone too far."

"I understand wanting to go see the world," Kris said. "But when I left for the army, I knew I'd come back. And my late wife and I both wanted to raise Roy here."

"Do you hope to expand your family?" *Subtle, Monica.* She cringed a little, but the question had just popped out.

He gave a half shrug. "Between working as a cop and helping at the ranch, my time with Roy is limited enough as it is. I'm not willing to take any more time away from him to date."

Embarrassment heated her cheeks. It sounded as if he was making it clear that he wasn't interested in her. Well, she wasn't interested in him.

Not anymore.

So why had disappointment dropped hard into her stomach like a stale doughnut?

From the corner of her eye, she watched Kris's head move as he shifted his gaze to the rearview mirror and side mirror and then back to the road in front of them.

The feverish, jittery unease that had plagued Monica after the cabin attack yesterday flared up, demanding her attention. She wanted to believe that being in the company of a lawman guaranteed her safety, but Kris's constant vigilance reminded her that simply wasn't true.

"Do you really think someone would have the nerve to tail a patrol car?" she asked while taking a glance at her own side mirror.

"Not usually. But in this case, I'm afraid they might try."

They crested a rise in the road, and Monica was stunned to see an entire development of pricey-looking houses spread across the stretch of flatland and up over the nearby hillside.

"This...is so different from how it looked the last time I was here." She fumbled for words because this used to be a small community of modest homes owned by working-class families dependent on income from the nearby granite quarry. Now, as they drove down the road, she spotted expensive vehicles, trendy stores, and the outpost of a chain coffee shop she would never have expected to see on the fringes of Cedar Lodge, Montana.

"Things change," Kris said. "We have to roll with that fact, like it or not."

She glanced over, intrigued by his tone. It sounded as if he might be thinking about his own personal life and the loss of his wife more than the challenges faced by dramatic changes in a community.

Either way, they needed to stay focused on the task at hand so that she could find the information she needed and head back to Reno, and Kris's young son could move back home to the ranch.

Kris took a turn from the highway, heading deeper into the community toward the intersection of streets that Esmeralda had suggested to Monica as a good starting place. He pulled into the parking lot of an elementary school. "Which way from here?"

"I'm not sure." Monica took a couple of photos of their surroundings and sent them to Esmeralda.

Moments later, Esmeralda called. "Now that I'm looking at the pictures I can remember exactly how to get to your dad's old house from there." She rattled off the directions and ended by encouraging them to be careful and to call her if they needed more help.

Kris pulled out of the parking lot and resumed driving.

After making a series of turns the road changed, becoming wider and smoother. It appeared that the improvements had been made recently.

When they reached the street at the base of the hill where Esmeralda told them they'd find the old house, they were facing a development of new condominiums instead.

"This was it," Monica said dully. "Now that we're here I remember the neighborhood more clearly. This was the spot where my dad lived as a kid."

Kris turned into one of the development parking lots.

Banners tied to poles stuck in the ground and hanging from a couple of second-story balconies advertised the properties for sale.

"The house used to be there." Monica pointed to a spot between a set of dark wood condos. A small body of water was visible a little farther away. "There's the pond that used to be in back of the house."

Driving closer, Kris could see that the pond was now part of a landscaped common area with a wooden walkway around it and a couple of picnic tables on the surrounding grassy area.

"This all looks so new. It must have been done in the last few months," Monica said. "Even if Dad buried something in the ground before he went to prison, it would have been dug up or destroyed when all of this was constructed."

"I think you're right."

She reached up to rub the right side of her head. "This is so frustrating. I wish I could remember what my dad told me." Then she turned to Kris. "What if I've gotten everything wrong? Maybe the notes on my phone showing that I'd researched making a road trip to Cedar Lodge had nothing to do with any of this?" She blew out a puff of air. "I'm sorry for wasting your time."

"It happens. Running up against a dead end sometimes is part of investigative work. And this dead end right here doesn't mean you were wrong to come to Cedar Lodge."

"I suppose." She looked around. "Should we get out and walk around the property on the off chance we actually can find something?" she asked. "Since we're here."

Kris shook his head. "When we talked about doing this, I imagined you looking around inside a house or in a forested area surrounding the house where you'd be hidden from view." He glanced in his mirrors as he'd done the whole trip, and gazed at the nearby parking lot and buildings, as well. "This is too open and exposed. Without a specific reason to think there's been something important buried around here, it's not worth the risk." The Boyd Sierra syndicate had the financial resources to hire excellent help. Despite Kris's vigilance, it was possible they'd been followed from downtown by an expert who'd managed to stay out of view.

"Unless you've got some other thoughts on where to look, I'll take you back to the ranch, and then I'll head back to the police station for the rest of my shift."

She sighed heavily. "Right now I'm all out of ideas."

After they'd driven a couple of miles down the road, Monica said, "If I haven't made any headway with this in the next day or two, I'll move out of your ranch house. I realize you didn't plan on my staying forever."

"Let's just take this one day at a time," Kris responded.

"I know you must miss seeing your son."

"I do. But he loves staying with his other grandparents." And the truth was, Kris had repeatedly promised Yvonne and Gabriel that he would send Roy to their house more often for visits, but he hadn't followed through on that. He was aware that Roy was not simply their beloved grandson but also a living link to the daughter they still mourned. He'd been selfish. And now was a good time to stop that.

But he still planned to stop by and see Roy today if at all possible.

"Can we go by the thrift store?" Monica asked when they were out of the hinterlands and back downtown on Glacier Street. "I'd like to move my car to the ranch. Or at least get my suitcases out of the trunk."

"I'd rather not take the chance of someone seeing you drive your car to the ranch. Then they'll know where you're staying. Maybe just grab your stuff."

He turned into the thrift store parking lot so he could drive completely around the building to see if anyone was lurking nearby. Of course, Monica's car was the only vehicle there since the store was closed. He stopped several feet away.

"Can you open the trunk remotely?" he asked while they were both still in the patrol car.

She pulled a fob out of the cross-body bag she was wearing. "It will pop free of the latch, but it won't open all the way."

"Good enough."

She gave him a questioning look, so he glanced at the burned husk of the trailer and then turned back to her. "If somebody can rig an explosive to the trailer door, they can rig one to your car, too."

Eyes widened, she nodded. She hit the trunk unlock button, and Kris breathed a sigh of relief when nothing exploded. They got out and walked to her car, but before Kris could grab the suitcases from the trunk, Monica walked toward a rear passenger door. "I'm going to grab my laptop from the back, too."

"Wait!"

She froze and turned to face him.

"Stand back and unlock the doors. Then let me have a quick look around before you open any of them."

She pressed the fob, it beeped, and nothing

happened. Still, Kris couldn't release the tightness in his chest. While serving in war zones, he'd seen too many instances where an area seemed safe, only for a bomb to be triggered when a person touched something that appeared completely innocuous.

He took a quick look at the thin coating of dust on the side of the car and the hood, searching for handprints or smudges or any sign that someone had tampered with the vehicle. Nothing. He searched the ground around the car. There were cracks in the asphalt with blades of grass poking up through, and none of them appeared bent or recently trod upon. "Looks good." He pulled open the unlocked door himself. No explosion.

Even then, he couldn't relax. He scanned the surrounding area, something he'd already done at least five times since they'd arrived. "Let's make this quick."

He walked back to the trunk and grabbed her suitcases just before he heard the roar of an engine and the squeal of tires. He stepped aside to look past the raised trunk lid and saw a dark sedan careening into the parking lot and racing full bore toward Monica's car.

Heart pounding in his chest, he yelled to

Monica. Before he could take more than a couple of steps toward her, the speeding vehicle collided with the front of her car. The sound of the impact was a sickening crash of crunching metal and screeching tires. He was forced to leap out of the way as Monica's car spun under the force of the collision.

"Monica!" Kris scrambled to his feet and sprinted toward the side of the car where he'd last seen her, though now it was facing a different direction.

Gears shrieked and the engine growled as the attacking car backed up, preparing to bash Monica's car again.

Kris found Monica hanging halfway out the car door, tangled up in the dangling shoulder harness of a seat belt and a deployed airbag.

"Monica!"

For a moment, she didn't move. Fear twisted into a tight ball in Kris's stomach. Was she unconscious? Was she alive? Had her neck been broken?

"What happened?" she murmured weakly as Kris shoved the shoulder harness and deflating airbag aside and slid his arm under her shoulders. In a perfect situation, he wouldn't move her until he knew the extent of the injuries, but there was no time for being cautious right now.

"You got hit by a car, and he's coming back. We've got to move, *now*!"

Kris heard the grinding of the other car's engine as it roared toward them. Glancing up, he could see it barreling at them through the puzzle-piece pattern of the cracked safety glass in the windshield.

With Monica in his arms, he took several steps backward as quickly as he could before the next impact, this one bashing the front of the car into the back, collapsing the space where Monica would have been if he hadn't gotten her free.

*Thank You, Lord.*

A slight ease of relief moved through him when he realized Monica had gotten her footing and she could at least partially hold her own weight. They had to get moving. They were exposed here, backed up to the thrift shop's exterior brick wall, and they needed to get to cover before the attacking car came after them again.

"Can you make it to the patrol car?" Kris asked, his hands still gripping her in case she didn't have as much strength as he'd thought.

She nodded. "I think so."

The attacker car remained where it had ended up after the last assault, its own front end and right fender damaged. The vehicle made grinding and metallic squealing noises but didn't go anywhere. It sounded like the driver wanted to move but couldn't.

Kris tried to get a look at whoever was behind the wheel, but the tint of the windshield and the sunlight reflecting off it made that difficult. Fearful that the driver would get frustrated and pull out a gun and start shooting, Kris redirected his efforts back to getting Monica and himself back into his police cruiser.

"Let's go!" Kris had a shotgun accessible once they got into his vehicle. He would use it if the attacker tried to crash into the heavier, reinforced patrol car.

They began moving, Monica's balance unsteady and her feet stumbling, when again Kris heard the roar of an engine. Confused, since the original attacker was still stalled in place, he realized the sound was coming from the direction of the entrance on the opposite side of the parking lot.

In an instant, a full-size blue van gunned

toward them, clearly intending to mow them down before they could reach the cop car.

Had the two attackers from the cabin fire each found new vehicles?

Desperate to keep Monica alive, Kris hadn't yet been able to free up his hands long enough to call for assistance. With the van barreling toward them, he couldn't do that now. And with everything happening so fast they didn't have enough time to cover the short distance to his patrol unit.

"The trailer!"

It looked brittle and flimsy after the fire. Clambering inside it probably wouldn't offer much help. But if they could get to the back side of it, where there was a narrow space between the trailer and a cinder-block wall, maybe it would provide refuge long enough for Kris to radio for help and his fellow cops to respond.

They moved as quickly as they could. The lumbering van, which wasn't exactly designed for agile maneuvers, couldn't turn in time and it rocketed past them.

They were just rounding the edge of the trailer to get behind it when Kris heard the crack of a gunshot. Exactly what he'd feared.

Behind the less-than-ideal barrier, Kris freed

his right hand from clasping Monica's arm. He grabbed his radio and called in the attack.

Within seconds, he heard sirens in the distance.

Nearby, more gunshots cracked. Kris hunkered down with Monica, holding her head close to his chest and covering it with his arms.

Finally the shooting stopped. Kris heard the growl of the van's engine fading as it sped away before he could get a clear look at the license plate.

The increasing wails of the sirens indicated that help was almost there.

Daring to release a small sigh of relief, Kris looked down at Monica still clutched in his arms and saw blood on the side of her face.

# Chapter Seven

A robust fire crackled in the fireplace of the family room at the Volker ranch, but Monica still felt chilled to the bone. Several hours had passed since the attack behind the thrift store, but residual anxiety plagued her, making it hard for her to feel anything beyond cold fear.

She was seated on a sofa, feet up and leaning back to rest her stiff neck and shoulder on an oversized pillow. After this attack, Kris's friend Cole had been relentless in badgering Monica to get checked out at the hospital emergency room until she'd finally given in. The doctor had confirmed she had no life-threatening injuries, but she did have sore, strained muscles, a pounding headache, and a few cuts and scratches. Afterward, she and Kris had given their official statements to the police, and Kris was given the remainder of his shift off so that they could both go back to the ranch and get some rest.

It was early evening. The sky had clouded over, and the temperature had dropped. Dinner had been homemade beef barley soup and grilled cheese sandwiches. Monica glanced over at Kris, who was seated in an easy chair, video-chatting with Roy. Jill and Pete were in their home office at the other end of the sprawling ranch house, going over some business issues related to their horse ranch. The Volker family had been so incredibly kind to her. They'd been a blessing she couldn't have even imagined before she hit town.

Sighing heavily, she reminded herself that despite the terrible events, she had a lot to appreciate, even if at the moment she didn't exactly *feel* grateful. What she felt was sore and scared, frustrated and confused, and nearly as angry with her dad as she'd been when he was first arrested and charged with fraud, theft, and participation in a criminal conspiracy.

Realizing she'd probably been looking at Kris a little too long, she shifted her gaze back to the window and the heavy gray clouds outside. Then back to the flickering flames in the fireplace.

*Thank You, Lord, for Your protection. Thank You for the generous and helpful people You have brought into my life. Thank You for the gift of faith to help see me through all of this.*

As had happened to her on so many prior occasions, her prayers of gratitude offered in faith stirred to life the genuine feeling of thankfulness in her heart.

Her phone rang, startling her. Kris looked in her direction, and she grabbed the device to glance at the screen. "It's Esmeralda," she said quietly.

"Dad. *Dad.*" Roy's voice came through the tablet Kris was holding.

"You keep talking to your son," Monica told Kris softly. "I'll let you know what Esmeralda has to say."

After a slight hesitation, Kris nodded and turned back to the screen and his son.

The warm domesticity of the moment hit Monica without warning. A cozy house. A man talking to his little boy—even if it was via technology—by her side. A delicate wisp of a feeling she'd craved in various forms for a long time. First as a child, when she'd wished for siblings and nearby cousins to play with and parents who were more interested in family activities.

And later, when she'd decided to earn a teaching credential so that she could work with children and help them learn and thrive in life.

There wasn't much chance of any of that working out for real now that she had a criminal father and mob assailants trying to kill her. Oh, and one slightly more sophisticated thug doing his best to manipulate her mother into marriage.

She shook her head, trying to discard the feelings, and got a reminder of her sore neck in the process.

"Hey, Esmeralda," she said after tapping the screen of her phone. "How are you?"

"How am *I*? Honey, I waited as long as I could to give you time to rest and then find out how *you* are."

"Sore and shaken up. But it could have been much worse."

Monica gave a brief recap of the attack and mentioned that Kris had asked a friend to tow her car and store it on his property in town. The attacker's wrecked car—which had been stolen—had been impounded by the police while they swept it for evidence.

"The trip to Dad's old house was a bust," Monica said at the end of the update. "The house and trees have been knocked down for condos. The pond is still there. I suppose it's possible Dad hid something in there, but I don't think it's likely."

"I should have anticipated that," Esmeralda said. "I haven't been out that way in ages, but Cedar Lodge has doubled in population in the last few years. Things are bound to be different."

"True enough."

"I'm also calling to offer another suggestion. It's not a location to search for hidden documents, but a person for you to talk to. Your dad's best friend growing up. You ever heard him mention a guy named Brendan Stryker?"

Monica thought for a moment. "Brendan does seem familiar." But a specific instance of her dad mentioning him didn't come to mind. Maybe she was trying to convince herself it sounded familiar because she so desperately wanted to get somewhere with all of this and find the proof of Archer Nolan's criminal nature and activities.

"One of my nephews who's about the same age as your dad said he remembered Hunter and Brendan being buddies from middle school through high school. My nephew's going to try and get contact information for Brendan, and I'll pass that along to you."

"I appreciate it."

They spoke a few more minutes and then disconnected, and Monica related the information to Kris, who had just ended his video call with Roy.

"When I get to the police department tomorrow, I'll see what kind of information I can pull up on Brendan."

"It's worth trying to talk to him." They didn't have any other viable options at this point, so they needed to follow through on even the weakest of leads.

Monica's phone chimed the arrival of a text. "It's Ryan," she said. She tapped to open it and read it aloud: "'Just wrapped up work and saw what happened on the local news app. Man, these people are relentless. The guy who does a lot of the paving work at the resort, Jason Mulhern, has a criminal record and he knew your dad. Maybe check him out? Also, remembered some kind of business group your dad met with when he was here. Will think about it and try to remember details.'"

Kris nodded. "I'll check out Mulhern, and

if he comes up with something on the business group, I'll follow up on that, too."

The implication seemed to be that he would do it alone. Without Monica.

"*We* will follow up on it," she said. Right now it was tempting to hide out someplace safe while the whole horrible situation got resolved. But doing that would not help. It would only slow things down. "You don't know my dad," Monica said. "I have a frame of reference with knowledge that you lack. Timelines in my dad's life. Familiar places. Familiar names. Someone could mention a small detail that would seem insignificant to you, but it would be meaningful to me. I could add it to other information and see a pattern where you couldn't."

"It's your call," he finally said.

It was. It was her decision if she was willing to put herself in danger, despite her fears.

"This doesn't have to be your fight," she said, thinking about Kris's exposure to the attackers today. He hadn't been injured, but he could have been.

"Of course it's my fight." He squared his shoulders. "This isn't just about you and your dad. A criminal syndicate has people launching attacks in my town. There are too many people that I care about in Cedar Lodge to turn away and let the thugs do what they want."

His heated words encouraged a sprout of hope in her heart. The hope that she would get the information she needed to solve her problems.

There was another small hope also alive in her heart that she didn't dare encourage.

She had no chance of a future with Kris and his family, even if she did feel a growing sense of warmth and connection with all of them. Even if she felt like she and Kris understood one another in a way that was more than friendship. Looking at him now, she couldn't stop her heart from beating faster and her stomach from fluttering with a silly burst of delight.

But he might not feel the same way about her.

Beyond that, a cop didn't need the daughter of a convicted criminal in his life. And after everything that had happened, no school in town would ever hire her.

She would continue her effort at uncovering information while doing her best to keep Kris and herself physically safe.

She would keep her heart safe, too.

"Try to get some rest today," Kris said to Monica the next morning as she wandered into the kitchen shortly after sunrise.

He turned to the coffeepot on the counter to refill his thermos mug and add a splash of cream before snapping the lid into place. "I've got to put in a few hours working patrol, and while I'm at the station, I'll check on Brendan Stryker and see what I can find out." He poured a second cup of coffee and offered it to her. She stared back at him with a dull expression before taking a few slurps of coffee, and then she appeared to wake up a little more.

Kris had learned after Monica's first night at the ranch that she wasn't a morning person, but coffee seemed to help brighten her up. This morning it looked like it might take a lot to do the trick.

"If I sit around and rest, I'll be miserable," she finally said. She slumped into a chair at the kitchen table. A few strands of her unruly blond locks had sprung free from her tied-back hair, and there were dark circles under her eyes. "If I'm not busy, my mind races with all the terrible what-ifs I can think of." She took another sip of coffee.

"I'm familiar with that situation." Time spent in combat while in the army was not something Kris had been able to walk away from and quickly forget. "Prayer can help a lot."

"You're right." She nodded sagely and then gave a self-deprecating laugh, shaking her head. "I hand things over to God, but then, before I know it, I've picked them right back up again."

"As soon as you realize you've done that, pray again. That's my best advice. Not that you asked for it."

Jill pulled open the door that led into the kitchen from the mudroom, toed off a pair of work boots, and then walked over to the sink to wash her hands. "The animals are fed and watered, and I think we've earned some breakfast."

Kris smiled at his mom. Of course she'd already been awake and at work for hours. "Give me a few minutes and I'll put together a skillet scramble with some eggs and bacon," Jill said.

"I'm about to leave for the station shortly," Kris replied from his spot leaning against the counter. "Can you clear your schedule to hang out in the house with Monica until early afternoon?"

"I'm sure I'll be fine," Monica interjected. She glanced over at Betty lying on a dog bed. As usual, the old hound interpreted eye contact as a beckon to be petted, and she got up and lumbered over to Monica. Not to be left out, Pepper pushed himself up off the hardwood floor where he'd been splayed and pranced over to Monica so she could pet him, too.

"I don't mind staying in the house," Jill called out as she started grabbing things from the refrigerator. "I've got some bookkeeping to catch up on, and I want to get a batch of whole wheat bread started."

"How do you run this ranch with just the three of you?" Monica asked.

"We're not at full capacity right now." Kris was determined to fight the temptation to linger and chat with Monica.

"We're boarding a few horses and doing some training while saving up and getting ready to expand the operation," Jill added.

Kris was happy that Monica and his mom seemed to be developing a friendship. But at the same time, he hadn't forgotten why Monica was here and that they all needed to remain vigilant.

If he really wanted to help Monica, he needed to get out and do what he could to put an end to the attacks. If he was able to spend a little time at the police station before going out, he might be able to research Brendan Stryker and the paving company guy as well as sit in on Detective Campbell's update to the chief on how his investigation was going.

"All right, I'm leaving." Kris pushed himself away from the counter and grabbed his coffee mug. "Call me if either of you needs anything."

He gave Betty a scratch behind the ears as he walked by her. Pepper was over by Jill, keeping an eagle eye out for any tasty food morsel that Kris's mom might accidentally drop while making breakfast.

He stepped outside and paused on the front porch for a moment to look around. Of course, he'd viewed the security video feed a short time ago, but he wasn't taking any chances. Seeing nothing out of the ordinary near the house, he turned his attention toward the nearest corral. He watched his dad open a gate to the pasture, letting the horses out to run and kick and enjoy the cool grass and space to trot around.

Early-morning sunlight blazed along the tips of the jagged hilltops and ridges that were part of the Volker family property. Kris was blessed to live here. He was blessed to have survived his tours of combat, to have his family, to have his son, and to have had Angela in his life. He felt that painful spark that so often sliced into his heart when he thought of his late wife. And on the heels of that, he felt something else, heavy and unsettling. It took him a moment to realize what it was. Guilt.

He felt guilty because he was seriously attracted to Monica. He didn't just think she was pretty. It was something much more than that.

How could this be possible? Angela had been the love of his life. He'd known it, and he'd told her so more times than he could count. If he could move on to another woman now, did that mean what he'd declared to Angela had been a lie?

He stepped off the porch and walked toward his patrol car. Normally he used his truck to go back and forth to work and only used his police unit when on shift. But these were not normal times. Not for his town. Not for the woman he would help and then see on her way after the job was finished and they both returned to their normal lives.

He heard the front door open and close. He turned to see his mom walking toward him carrying a paper bag. "Here." She shoved the bag at him. "It's a couple of leftover biscuits split with a slice of ham and cheddar cheese in each one."

"Thanks, Mom."

She leaned in to give him a kiss on the cheek. And then she lingered, taking a step back, arms crossed.

If his mom had something to say, Kris knew he would hear it sooner rather than later. "*What*, Mom?"

Cocking her head to one side, she smiled slightly and said, "She's a lovely young woman, isn't she?"

"Monica? Yeah, sure."

"It's nice to see you interested in someone. Even if you met under extreme circumstances."

"*Interested?*" He realized he'd raised his voice and adjusted his volume before adding, "She's not here because I'm interested. She's here because she's got no other options, and if she checked into a hotel, she probably wouldn't live to see another day."

"Son, give me credit for having a few brains in my head. I know what I see right in front of me."

"Now you sound smug."

She shrugged. "Looks to me like she's interested in you, too."

He shook his head. "You're getting your hopes up over nothing." Kris was determined not to do the same. That pointed edge of guilt he'd felt earlier stabbed at him again. "Besides, no one will ever take Angela's place."

"Who said anything about taking someone's place?" This time it was Jill who raised her voice. "More than one thing can be true at once. You realize that, right?" Her voice dropped in volume. "Son, you can love and honor Angela's memory *and* find someone to share your life with for however much time God gives you. Angela *told* you she hoped you would find someone else after she was gone. I heard her say it. More than once."

Kris nodded but didn't speak. His throat closed up with emotion. His mom wasn't wrong. But the present moment wasn't a good time to process all of this. "It still hurts to think about Angela being gone," he finally said, practically forcing out the words. "It doesn't seem fair to a woman to bring her into my life if I still feel that way."

Jill reached for his hands. "You take all the time you need to work through your grief. But since you seem to like Monica, let me give you just a little push."

Kris laughed. *Take your time, but let me give you a little push* pretty much summed up his mom.

"I have Roy, Mom. He's the most important thing in my life. With my job and helping out at the ranch, I don't spend nearly enough time with him. I don't have time to date. And I really don't want to." Awkward dinners with a woman he barely knew, away from his son? Going on *fun* outings where he spent the whole time wondering what his boy was doing? No thanks.

Jill made a scoffing sound. "That boy is your shadow when you're here working the ranch. The right woman will want to get to know Roy. And be patient as she lets him get to know her."

"I don't know, Mom." Kris looked up at the vibrant blue sky before turning back to her. "There's an awful lot going on right now. And I need to get to work." He glanced over at the horses happily munching on grass. His dad was leaning against the outside of the stable, using a garden hose to rinse off the bottoms of his rubber work boots. Kris breathed in and could smell the cedar and aspen and pines growing on the nearby mountainside. He knew enough to enjoy a beautiful moment. Because it could all disappear in an instant.

Images from last night's attack played through his mind. Monica had nearly been killed. And there was no sign the assailants were going to let up on their attacks.

"If you see or hear anything out of the ordinary, let me know." He got into the patrol car and started down the driveway, determined to get his focus back on the job he needed to do. He had to help Monica find her answers while keeping her alive. The emotions tugging at him when he was around her were unimportant.

Doing his job and taking care of Roy. *That* was what mattered.

# Chapter Eight

As he left the late-afternoon meeting at the police station, Kris found himself more worried than ever about Monica's safety.

He'd thought he understood the dangerous reach of the Boyd Sierra crime syndicate. But according to the report he'd just gotten from a federal agent via video call, the syndicate had a large network of sophisticated contract killers they could send to Cedar Lodge. It included young and older female assassins who were proficient at approaching their target without setting off anyone's intuitive safety alarms until it was too late. The clock was ticking to get this case wrapped up before the Boyd Sierra leadership decided to make Monica's death its highest priority.

Shortly before the meeting ended, he'd sent Monica a text letting her know that he'd checked up on Brendan Stryker and learned where he worked. He asked her to be ready to go talk to the man when Kris got back to the ranch. While Detective Campbell and his team continued their standard police investigation, Chief Ellis wanted Kris to continue protecting Monica and working with her to find the evidence she thought her father had hidden somewhere in town, even though no one, not even Monica, had a clue as to what it might tell them.

Traffic was sparse on the highway driving back to the ranch, and Kris was grateful. He hoped to take Monica to talk to Brendan and then return to the ranch before it got completely dark. He glanced out the window at the lowering sun. It would be pushing it. Nighttime driving made it hard to spot anyone tailing them. The only thing visible would be headlights. His former hope that the bad guys might hesitate to tail—or even attack—a patrol car was obviously now gone. Yesterday's nearly deadly demolition derby behind the thrift store made it clear *anything* could happen as the assailants pulled out all the stops to get to Monica.

He turned onto the driveway at the ranch, taking it a little too fast and bumping and jostling along the way. One of the outside dogs,

Alfie, raced across the pasture with what looked like a rawhide bone in his mouth. Lily, smaller than Alfie but younger and more energetic, chased after him. A trio of horses stood together near a corral fence as if having a conversation. Despite the concern nipping at Kris and keeping him worried about Monica, now that he'd returned to the ranch, he was able to let go of some of the tension in his tight neck and shoulder muscles and let his body relax. Everything looked fine.

*Looks can be deceiving.*

That familiar whisper had spoken to him many times in the past when he was a soldier patrolling war-torn regions overseas where it was nearly impossible to anticipate what might happen next. And a few times in equally uncertain situations here in Cedar Lodge, too.

He took a good look around as he got out of his patrol car. Satisfied for the moment that things were quiet and normal, he walked up into the house. The first thing he noticed when he yanked open the front door was the beef and potato scent of shepherd's pie baking in the oven. The second thing he noticed was Monica perched at the edge of a chair in the living room, cross-body bag across her shoulder, clearly anxious to go talk to Brendan.

"What are they saying at the police department?" Monica asked as soon as he'd said hello to her and called out a greeting to his parents in the kitchen.

"Have they got any new information?" Pete asked, walking into the living room, picking up their calico cat, Penny, and then sitting down with her in his lap.

Jill also came around from the kitchen while wiping her hands with a dish towel. She leaned against the doorway to listen.

Kris sat in the chair across from Monica. Like her, he was anxious to get going. But his parents had opened up their home to a complete stranger and taken on the risks associated with that, so they deserved to hear the information he had. He would make it quick.

"Good news on a couple of fronts," Kris started. "The involvement of the Boyd Sierra criminal enterprise has attracted the attention of state and federal agencies, and they're offering help. Right now it's only in the form of whatever supportive investigative work they can do online. They aren't sending agents to Cedar Lodge, but it's something.

"Beyond that, we've learned the car that rammed Monica's sedan yesterday was stolen. No surprise there. Images of the van were picked up on a security camera farther up Glacier Street, and it was stolen, too. Both vehicles were taken from the same part of town, and we've got officers reviewing home security video from that neighborhood. There's a chance the thugs are staying somewhere in that area, so officers will be checking hotels and short-term rentals in the neighborhood, too. Maybe someone will have noticed something helpful."

"That's some good news," Pete said, scratching the cat in his lap behind the ears. "What's the bad news?"

Kris smiled faintly. His dad wasn't a pessimist, but he *was* a realist. Ranch life did that to a person.

Kris turned to Monica. "The feds who have been building a case strong enough to completely take down Boyd Sierra Associates believe the criminals will double down on their efforts to get to you. The fact that your dad decided to leave them and is now willing to turn on them and hand over information to the authorities is a huge blow. No one in that kind of position with the syndicate has ever done that before. If you and your dad are even partially successful in your endeavor, it will make the association look weak to their criminal underground enemies, and they can't have that."

Monica wore a troubled expression. "I guess I wanted to believe that this was happening because Archer Nolan wants to marry my mom and that he had hired a couple of goons to come after me. I didn't want it to be an issue involving the entire syndicate."

Kris got to his feet, and Monica mirrored his move.

"So, where are we going to find Brendan?" Monica asked.

"Fast Engine Car Repair. It's on the south side of town near the river."

They walked out onto the front porch. Kris stepped in front of Monica and took a good look around before escorting her to his patrol car.

Security cameras and alert farm dogs had originally made him assume the Double V Ranch would be a safe haven for her. But now, as he glanced toward the forest on the edge of the pasture and the mountain ridges that rose up behind the house, he couldn't help thinking about the resources at the disposal of the criminal syndicate intent on killing her.

One high-powered rifle in the hands of a skilled shooter could take her out.

The sun was barely lingering above the horizon as Kris pulled up to the curb in front of Fast Engine Car Repair. Monica glanced out her window at the repair bays visible through open roll-up doors, and it looked like most of the employees were gone for the day. The parking lot near the office door was empty.

After a cautious look around, they got out of the patrol car and walked up the sloping drive to one of the open repair bays. A thickset man in blue coveralls walked up to them just before they got inside. "Can I help you?"

Kris quickly stepped between Monica and the man. Monica moved slightly to the side so she could see around him.

For a moment, the man's gaze appeared to settle on the badge pinned to Kris's uniform. Then he slowly nodded, looking none too happy. His eyes flickered between Kris and Monica before focusing on the cop again. "I heard you might be coming out here, and I've got nothing to say to you."

"Good evening," Kris said in an easy tone. "I'm Officer Volker, and this is Monica Larson."

"I've got nothing to do with that mob criminal Hunter Larson." The man's tense stance and tight facial expression matched the borderline hostility of his words. "I'm an honest businessman, and I run an honest shop."

"You must be Brendan Stryker," Kris said calmly as if the outburst hadn't happened. "We're not here to accuse you of anything."

"You'd better not be. If you want to question me, you'll do it in front of my lawyer." He crossed his arms over his chest, still clenching an oily shop rag.

"I heard you and my dad used to be best friends," Monica offered, feeling a slight quiver in the pit of her stomach despite having Kris here to protect her. Brendan and his anger were intimidating.

Brendan stared at her for a minute. "You look like him," he finally said.

Monica tried to relax, hoping a soothing demeanor would get her some answers. "Look, I know my dad broke the law, and he's paying for his actions. Maybe you're disappointed in him because of that. But right now, I'm trying to track down information that could put more of the criminals he worked with behind bars. And yeah, full disclosure, providing that information to the authorities might get my dad a lighter sentence. But that's not the only reason I'm doing this. The entire situation is… *complicated*."

She hadn't meant to give a mini speech, but the words poured out, and she was determined to have her say before Brendan kicked them out of his shop.

His expression relaxed slightly, as did his tone. "I can't help you." He shook his head. "I don't know anything about your dad's criminal activities." Then he glared pointedly at Kris. "And I don't appreciate the cops or anyone else implying otherwise."

The man appeared to be holding back so much rage. And yet Kris kept an easy stance and neutral expression. He didn't look intimidated, nor did he appear compelled to push back equally hard and prove to Brendan how tough he was. Monica found his self-control admirable. It probably made him a good cop, a good soldier back in the day, and a good dad now.

"When's the last time you talked to Hunter Larson?" Kris asked.

Brendan made a scoffing sound. "Years ago. After his family moved down to Reno, he graduated from college, and not long after that he started making big money. He came back for a visit to show off. It was obnoxious and unappreciated." He looked away for a moment and then turned back to Kris. "We were friends in high school. The friendship ended five or six years later."

"Do you have any idea where my dad would have put something if he wanted to hide it here in Cedar Lodge?" Monica felt a little ridiculous for asking at this point, since it was clear her dad and Brendan hadn't been anything like confidants for a long time, but since the opportunity was here, she voiced the question.

"I do not," Brendan said.

She didn't realize she'd actually gotten her hopes up until she felt the weight of disappointment with his answer.

"It's past business hours," Brendan said, finally uncrossing his arms. "I've got work to finish before I close up, and I'd like to get to it."

"Of course," Monica said. "Thank you for your time."

"If you happen to remember anything later that might help us find information Hunter Larson has stashed somewhere in Cedar Lodge, please give me a call." Kris took a business card from the front pocket of his uniform and held it out. Brendan glared at him for a moment before finally taking it.

Monica wondered if the mechanic had something against cops.

"Another dead end," she muttered after they'd gotten back into the patrol car. "He obviously doesn't know anything about my dad and his criminal issues."

"He might not," Kris said, starting up the car's engine. "It could also be that he knows something about your dad's shady past—even where he might have hidden important information—but he's afraid to talk about it. Boyd Sierra Associates are a dangerous bunch. I can understand him not wanting to cross them. Or him wanting to make certain there's no reason for them to think that he's crossed them. It's a small town, and word gets around."

Kris pulled out onto the road. "Tomorrow I should have time to do a deeper background check on him at the station. I spent most of the day today on patrol and got back barely in time for the meeting. Maybe he's had prior run-ins with the police. I've never interacted with him, but that doesn't mean some other cop hasn't."

"He reminded me of the man who attacked me inside the cabin," Monica said.

Kris gave her a sharp look. "Really?"

"I don't think it's him, though. His voice sounded different."

"The police department has been operating under the assumption that Boyd Sierra might have hired local thugs to do their dirty work." He nodded to himself. "I'll definitely take a closer look at Brendan."

Monica considered what he'd said. Was she mistaken? Could Brendan have been one of the assailants at the cabin? Or even involved in the other assaults? She hadn't gotten a clear look at the attackers at the cabin or when they were coming after her with the car behind the thrift shop. Kris had already told her he hadn't been able to see the faces of the thugs driving the car or van behind the store, either.

The drive back to the ranch was quiet, but Monica felt anxious and jittery the whole way. She rubbed the side of her head, frustrated as she tried again to take her mind back to that prison visit with her dad.

"If only I could remember what Dad told me," she muttered as Kris made the turn onto the ranch driveway. "The more I think about it, the more it seems like I remember the two of us talking about *people* rather than *objects* as we sat together in the prison visiting room." Could he have been telling her about a person rather than hidden documentation? "Perhaps I've been searching for the wrong thing all along."

As had happened so many times before, when she tried to focus on the conversation, the memory or thought or imagining or whatever it was seemed to just fade away. It was so frustrating that her dad was still not allowed to receive visits or phone calls because of the fight he'd gotten into.

Ahead, warm light spilled from several windows of the rambling Volker ranch house, giving it a welcoming appeal.

"If you're starting to recall that you and your dad were talking about people rather than physical items, that's making headway. After you get some food in you and a little rest, maybe your memory will become clearer." Kris parked near the front door of the house. He climbed out of the vehicle and strode around to stand close to Monica as she got out, and they walked the short distance to the porch.

"I saw you driving up on the security camera," Pete said from the foyer once they'd stepped inside. A sleepy-looking Betty sat beside him, thumping her tail lightly on the floor. "Everything go okay?"

"For the most part," Kris answered.

"Well, your mom left you two some dinner in the oven. It's getting late for us, so we're about ready to turn in for the night. Holler if you need anything."

Pete ambled down the long hallway, Betty at his heels, and Kris and Monica moved toward the kitchen.

"You sit down," Kris said, pulling out a chair at the dining table for Monica. "I'll have this ready in a minute."

He grabbed a set of pot holders, took the shepherd's pie out of the oven, and set it on the stove top, then reached for plates in the cupboard.

Monica went to see if there was the usual iced tea or lemonade in the refrigerator. Sitting at the table and being waited on by Kris after all he'd done for her didn't seem right. Three days ago, they hadn't even known each other. She shook her head. It was hard to believe it had only been three days.

She'd filled a couple of glasses with ice cubes and was pouring in the tea when she heard a strange buzzing sound. She looked up, focusing on the noise, trying to figure out what it was. It kind of sounded like a car engine now, but it wasn't coming from the direction of the driveway.

She turned to Kris, and by his unmoving stance and the expression of concentration on his face, she knew he heard it, too. "What could that be?" she asked. "Somebody on an ATV cutting across the pasture, maybe?" Though the sound didn't seem to be coming from that direction, either.

Kris darted to the wall and hit the switch to kill the kitchen lights, hiding them in darkness. Then he hurried to the kitchen window, pushed the blinds aside and looked outside.

*Boom!*

It was both a roar and a hideous crushing sound, combined with an impact that shook the house to its foundation.

Kris launched himself atop Monica, taking them both to the floor as a hot cloud of wood and concrete debris shot through the still-shuddering house.

## Chapter Nine

The dust slowly began to settle, and after a moment the air Monica drew into her lungs felt cleaner.

Kris remained propped over her, his arms forming a protective cage around her head.

"Are you okay?" she asked, ending her question with a slight cough.

"Yeah." He adjusted his position so he could look directly at her. "How about you?"

"I'm okay, too." She nodded, grateful to be alive and thankful that she had lived through another potentially deadly attack. Because she was reasonably sure whatever just happened—whatever it turned out to be—was somehow one more attempt on her life.

After a moment, she realized she was grasping Kris's muscular biceps, and she didn't want to let go. Not just yet. Despite the uncertainty of what had just happened, she wanted to rest for a few seconds in the feeling of being safe despite the obvious danger all around. In the feeling of having someone care enough to make her feel like she was someone important.

Was she truly important to him personally? Or was she important in the sense that he was sworn to protect all the citizens of his town? She wanted to believe she already knew. That she'd seen the signs he was interested in her. But she'd misinterpreted situations before. She'd certainly been fooled by her own father when he presented himself as a regular mild-mannered accountant.

She was being ridiculous. Debris still settled around them. There were things going on that were more important than the ridiculous stirrings of romantic hope in her heart.

And then Kris leaned down and tenderly brushed his lips across her forehead.

Her breath caught in her throat. And in the next moment, her entire body relaxed.

Such a small gesture, but a fortifying one. The fear and temptation of falling into hopelessness that had dogged her since the initial attack at the cabin felt as if they had been chased away. At least for the span of a few steady heartbeats, as she turned her attention toward focusing her thoughts.

After a lingering hesitation where they shared a locked gaze, Kris pushed himself up to his feet and then held out his hand, helping Monica get up, too.

"Kris! Monica!" Pete, flashlight in hand, made his way down the hall with Betty and Pepper beside him.

Jill followed, carrying her phone, and already talking to a 9-1-1 operator.

"We're all right," Kris called out. "How about you?"

His dad nodded as he stepped into the kitchen. "We're good."

Kris grabbed his gun from the police utility belt he'd set aside when they'd arrived at the house, and then took Monica's hand as they walked out to the darkened living room. Lights were on in the southern end of the building, but the power was out in the half of the house closer to the point of the explosion.

A light haze of dusty debris still snaked through the air, smelling of concrete and dirt. And something else.

"I smell gasoline," Monica said as she walked cautiously with Kris toward the site of the odd explosion, which was still out of sight. It seemed to be near the family room.

"You feel that draft?" Pete asked. "Windows are broken at the very least."

Monica spotted an orange flicker of light at the end of the hallway. "Something's burning."

Pete shoved his flashlight at Monica and then quickly stepped through the bathroom door beside them, grabbing a small garbage can. He emptied it onto the floor and then started filling it with water.

Meanwhile, after a glance upward to make sure the ceiling was stable, Kris and Monica continued cautiously forward. The floor became more thickly strewn with chunks of wood and drywall. They stepped over part of a lamp and a cushion from one of the family room easy chairs. Still feeling jarred but also curious, Monica stayed beside Kris. The sound of the explosion hadn't been at all like the explosion at the trailer. And the smell in the aftermath of the event was different.

Pete caught up with them just as they entered the family room.

Moderate-sized flames snaked along the wall with the most structural damage, casting shifting light around the otherwise darkened room.

There were holes in the wall and snapped beams at the juncture of the wall and the ceiling. Dirt and debris, tree branches and rocks, were strewn across the room.

Pete doused the fire and then hurried back for more water.

"I'm no expert on explosives," Monica said quietly. "But something about this just seems... *off.*" Goose bumps rippled across the surface of her skin at the sight of the creepy scene in front of her.

Jill aimed her phone flashlight above the smoking fire until it settled on an object punched into the wall halfway between the floor and the ceiling. It was black and circular.

"A tire?" Monica said. And then, just above it, she spotted something curved and metallic. Her brain struggled to put the pieces together into an idea that made sense. Because it couldn't be what she thought it was. "Is that part of a *car*?" That wasn't possible. She shook her head. "It's too far off the ground for someone to have rammed it into the house."

A voice crackled through Jill's phone. She turned off the flashlight function and put the phone up to her ear. "Emergency response is about eight minutes out," she said.

"I'm going to go take a look outside," Kris said.

Monica reached for his arm. "Shouldn't we stay here?"

"It could be that whoever did this plans to bust in, assuming we're injured or addled, and try to finish us off. I'd rather get in the way of that if I can."

Such a hard lesson Monica had learned over the last few days: sometimes there was no safe option.

"Your mom and I will grab a couple of rifles out of the gun safe and go out with you," Pete said.

They all started back toward the other end of the house, with Kris heading to the kitchen door leading to the side yard rather than the main front entrance.

"Might be better if you stay inside," he said to Monica. "You're the one they're after."

She thought back to her desperate fight with the thug at the Bennett cabin. There was no way she wanted to find herself in that kind of situation again. "I'm staying with you."

He glanced at her, and she was relieved when he didn't argue.

"Stay back." Kris grabbed his police radio and then opened the door, initially remaining behind it and using it as a barricade before moving aside to have a better look around. He cocked his head slightly as if listening. Monica, too, listened closely. For footsteps, or voices, or the sound of someone firing a gun.

Jill and Pete appeared, weapons in hand, and the two of them plus Kris made a quick plan for them to look for bad guys, circling the house as efficiently as possible.

Kris was out the door first, head on a swivel as he continually surveyed his surroundings, staying close to the building as he moved toward the right.

His parents stepped outside. Using equal caution, they headed left.

Monica went with Kris, and as they rounded the end of the house, she finally saw for certain that the *explosion* wasn't an explosion so much as an impact.

The bizarre image of a car actually jammed partway through the house, rear wheels on the ground holding it in place at an odd angle, created the unreal image that someone had actually tried to drive up the exterior wall.

"What am I seeing?" Monica whispered. "How could this have happened?" She was stunned and terrified at the same time.

Kris glanced up at the mountain ridge looming above the house and then at the surrounding snapped tree branches and torn-up grass. "I think someone drove off the fire road on the ridge. This thing didn't just tumble over the edge like it possibly could have in an accident. It had to be going fast and would have shot through the air like a bullet."

"You think someone was actually intending to drive off the ridge and crash onto the house?" Monica could barely believe she was saying those words. It was an unfathomable situation.

"Yes." Kris gestured toward the car embedded in the side of the house. "I'm going to see if the driver survived."

Monica heard approaching sirens.

Stepping cautiously around the precariously balanced vehicle, Kris moved to a spot where he could see part of the cracked windshield. He pulled out his phone and flicked on the flashlight app. "I don't see anyone in there," he called out to Monica after a moment. He continued to peer into the other windows. "I don't see blood. I don't see any sign of anyone."

He keyed his radio and informed dispatch of the situation.

Still overwhelmed, Monica shook her head. "Did the criminals think the car would actually land on me and kill me?"

"Maybe." Kris shrugged. "Or it could be they hoped to get us all running outside, disoriented and unarmed, and then they could pick you off from a distance with a rifle. Or it could be they just hope to get you out of the house permanently and back on the run so it's easier for them to get to you."

His parents approached from the other side of the house. "All clear," his mom reported.

"Nobody in the car. I'm going to guess that whoever did this put a weight on the gas pedal, popped it into gear, and let it go over the edge. There's probably a more sophisticated way to make it happen if you know what you're doing."

"Well, I obviously *do* have to leave now," Monica said, feeling horrible about what she'd put this family through by staying here.

*Bam!*

The crack of a rifle shot echoed from the ridgetop, followed by several more shots.

Kris grabbed Monica and pulled her around to the side of the house not facing the ridge. His parents were right behind them.

He keyed his radio. "Shots fired on us at the Volker ranch from Fire Road Thirty-Two!"

"Copy. I'm almost to the ranch." The immediate response, with the sound of a siren in the background, sounded like Kris's friend Dylan rather than an emergency dispatcher. "Dispatch, show Deputy Ruiz responding to shots fired. I'm heading for the ridge."

A second deputy confirmed that she'd respond to the ridge location, as well.

There were no subsequent shots fired, and as the minutes ticked by, Monica hoped they'd finally caught a break in the case and the shooter had been captured.

But when Ruiz finally checked in again, it was to report that he and the other deputy had not come across anyone, so the shooter was still at large.

The following morning, Kris paused from hammering a sheet of plywood into place to take a lingering look around the ranch property and the friends and neighbors who had shown up to help with repairs to the house. *Thank You, Lord.* Last night's horrible event could have been so much worse. He was especially grateful that he'd sent Roy to stay with Angie's parents when Monica first moved in.

He glanced over at Monica, on the porch near the doorway and hopefully out of range of any potential shooter. Penny the calico cat sat beside her, licking her paw and then wiping her face.

The car that had been partially embedded in the house was now at the police impound yard, where it would be swept for evidence. The cable from a winch on a heavy-duty wildlands fire truck had been attached to the sedan and then tightened until it pulled the vehicle to the ground. Kris had quickly confirmed that no one was inside the vehicle. Of course, like the other vehicles used by the attackers, it had been reported stolen.

Kris and Monica had gone with Chief Ellis to take a look at the spot on the fire road where the car had gone over. Tire tracks and footprints were visible in the dirt where the attackers had taken advantage of a small gap between the trees to turn the vehicle into an aimed projectile. If that naturally formed gap had been just a little bit farther to the south, the falling car could have landed in the middle of the house or at the end near the bedrooms, and the outcome could have been much, much worse.

The county roadworks department had already moved a boulder into place so the same insane tactic couldn't be tried twice. The county sheriff had committed to having his deputies patrol that stretch of fire road on a regular basis for at least the next few days. Still, Kris was aware that this didn't necessarily make Monica completely safe. These attackers had proven they would do anything to get to her. Including things Kris could never imagine.

Kris's mom walked by him carrying a couple of wooden planks, and she offered him a tired smile. The chief had left a cop stationed outside the ranch house last night while Monica and the Volkers tried to sleep, but it was fairly evident that none of them had gotten much rest.

Kris glanced at Monica again. It seemed like she had been avoiding him all morning. Was she understandably scared after last night's attack? Or was it something else?

Could she be unhappy about him kissing her on her forehead? In the moment, he'd been so glad she was alive. But had it made things weird between them? Had he overstepped his bounds?

He put down his hammer and walked over

to her. He would apologize if he needed to. Maybe he should offer her a half truth and explain how he'd simply given in to an impulse of the moment. He didn't need to admit he'd been compelled by something more and that a feeling of concern for her had combined with attraction leading to a gesture he now realized was completely out of line.

"I need to get out of here," she said as he approached her on the porch.

She'd mentioned something about leaving last night, and Kris had hoped she'd forgotten about it. He pushed aside a sinking sensation, determined to come across as calm and reasonable despite the fear that she would leave.

"Let's just give it some time before you decide what to do next. I know you're shaken up. We all are." Kris had been through some rough situations in the military and as a cop. As a civilian and the direct target of so much violence, he could only imagine how Monica felt.

She shook her head, and the light breeze blew tendrils of wavy blond hair in front of her face. "How can I stay? Look what happened to your parents' house. Look at how I've put people in danger."

"You aren't to blame for any of this. And you deserve to be protected."

Kris reached out to brush the strands of hair aside and tuck them behind her ear.

She didn't seem to mind the gesture, as unshed tears shimmered in her eyes. The soft feel of her skin made him feel even more protective, and he let his fingertips linger on her cheek for a moment before finally dropping his hand. He couldn't help noticing the flush of color in her cheeks and wondered if his cheeks had been reddened by a rush of emotion, too.

She held his gaze for a moment, then shifted it away. But she didn't step back. And Kris didn't move away from her, either.

There truly was something between them. He knew it now. It wasn't just him. Where he wanted it to go, he still wasn't sure.

Monica's phone chimed, and she slid it out of her pocket to look at the screen. "It's Ryan Fergus. Video call."

She tapped the screen, and Kris stepped beside her. He found himself looking at a fit, older gentleman wearing a dark blue polo shirt with the Elk Ridge Resort logo stitched onto it.

"You're all right," Ryan said. "I wanted to see for myself."

"I'm okay," Monica said before offering a nervous laugh. "They keep trying to kill me, and I keep surviving."

"I've been off my phone most of the morning, and I just now saw on the local news site what happened. Is there anything I can do to help? Do you need me to find a safe place for you to stay here at the resort?"

Kris watched Ryan's glance shift toward him a couple of times.

"I don't need that right now, but I might eventually," Monica said.

"I'm still doing what I can to think of people your dad mentioned who might know something useful and be able to help you out. Or who might have had a grudge against him, for that matter."

"Where were you last night about eight o'clock?" Kris asked. That was roughly the time of the attack.

Ryan drew his head back, rapidly blinking in apparent surprise while Monica looked at Kris from the corner of her eye.

"Ryan is helping me," she said to Kris in a patient, teacher-like tone. "If he wanted to hurt me, he would have had the chance when I walked right up to him at the resort."

Maybe so. But Kris was not taking any chances. And anyone who followed true crime stories, let alone who actually fought crime, had heard of *helpful* people who were actually in on the crime.

"This is Officer Kris Volker," Monica said to Ryan.

"I went out for a late dinner with a couple of friends last night," Ryan finally said, sounding as if he were insulted. "After we ate, we moved to the restaurant lounge to have an after-dinner drink and chat for a while. We met there at seven thirty and stayed a couple of hours."

After Kris got the name of the restaurant, he pulled out his phone and texted a message to Chief Ellis with the specifics, asking if he would have someone check out Ryan's alibi. By the time he hit Send, Monica had ended her conversation with Ryan, and she turned to him. "I hope he doesn't take offense and stop offering assistance. I need all the help I can get."

"If he really was where he said he was, he shouldn't have a problem with the question. Your life is in danger. If he's annoyed, then he obviously isn't much of a friend."

"I don't know that I'd exactly describe him as a friend," Monica said thoughtfully.

The sound of a truck rumbling up the driveway caught Kris's attention. He stepped to where he had a better view and spotted a well-worn green pickup truck with a camper shell on the back moving toward the house. A smile crossed his lips.

"Who is it?" Monica asked, turning to get a clearer look.

"It's Cole. You've met him."

"Oh, the paramedic?"

Kris nodded.

They walked toward the truck as Cole parked it and got out. "Wouldn't want you to work too hard, so I came to help," the medic called out teasingly as a greeting while walking up to Kris and Monica.

"You're just here because you have no social life," Kris shot back with a grin.

"Just not one I tell you about." Cole offered Monica a smile before his expression turned serious. "I am so sorry these terrible things keep happening to you. I was on the other side of the county working a traffic accident when the call about the attack last night came through, so I couldn't respond." He glanced over at Kris's parents, who were standing together by the side of the house, talking. "I'm glad everybody's okay."

"Could have been worse."

"Yeah, and with that in mind…" He gestured toward his truck. "I plan to be out here whenever I'm not working as long as Monica is staying here. I'll sleep in the camper."

Touched by the offer and more than willing to accept his help, Kris scoffed. "Don't be ridiculous. You can sleep in the stable with the horses."

"What?" Monica demanded.

"No, seriously, stay in the bunkhouse. You know how nice it is."

"Dylan's going to stay in there. When he's off shift with the sheriff's department, he'll be here, too."

Kris felt a lump of emotion in his throat. He was blessed to have such good friends.

Knowing that an effusive offer of thanks would only make Cole uncomfortable, Kris cleared his throat and said, "Just don't eat us out of house and home while you're here."

Cole hitched the corner of his mouth up in a half smile. "I'm not making any promises."

The two men exchanged manly thumps on the upper arm, which earned them an eye roll from Monica. After that, Cole turned and walked toward a work crew who were tearing out sections of the damaged wall to prep it for repair.

"Good friends are worth so much," Monica said quietly. "After my dad got arrested, I learned I didn't have as many as I'd thought I did. But the ones who were willing to stand by me in the worst of it have added a lot to my life." She sighed heavily. "Shelly Bennett offered me the use of her family cabin because she wanted to help, and it got set on fire. And now, look at the damage to your house. I don't want my friends to suffer because someone is coming after me."

Kris opened his mouth to say something that would make her agree to stay, though he had no idea what it should be. But he was interrupted when Monica's phone chimed again.

"It's a text from Esmeralda. She says someone told her that my dad liked to hang out at the Wind Ridge golf course when he was in town." She looked up at Kris. "I'd forgotten about that. He did like to play golf in the spring and summer when the weather was good."

She turned back to the screen. "Some friend of Esmeralda's told her they saw Dad hanging out in the clubhouse there a lot. Sometimes with my mom and sometimes alone. He appeared to have the same regular group of friends."

"I don't suppose you'll let me go ask around there and see if I can learn anything while you stay here?"

Monica gave him a direct look. "I want to be safe, obviously. But hiding won't solve anything, and it will likely slow down my efforts. As I've mentioned before, there are details that might not be meaningful to you, but if I heard them, they'd be meaningful to me. Even if your department catches the thugs, I still have to find evidence to prove to my mom that Archer is a criminal before she marries him. And that same information might help take down the entire Boyd Sierra Associates crime syndicate or at least do some serious damage. They're into extortion, drug dealing, all kinds of things. Imagine the potential for misery that could be stopped if they were destroyed. Or at least weakened."

"True. All right, we'll go to the golf course. Maybe there's a bartender or a restaurant manager we can talk to who remembers something about your dad." They walked into the house.

"You ever thought of a future career as a detective?" Kris asked.

Monica shrugged. "Right now, when it comes to looking toward the future, I don't have any specific plans. I would be grateful to just stay alive."

## Chapter Ten

The golf course on the western end of town offered a gorgeous view of the Meadowlark River.

Monica was getting a good look at the scenery because, like Kris, she was glancing around constantly to see if they were being followed. Vigilance had become second nature to her since the cabin attack, and she wondered if it would be a habit that continued through the rest of her life. The possibility that she might need to watch her back forever was chilling.

They were riding in one of the ranch trucks. Kris was concerned that the attackers might be looking for a patrol vehicle to find Monica, so they were traveling discreetly in the old pickup. He was also dressed in regular clothes instead of his uniform because he wanted to keep a lower profile. For all they knew, the bad guys had been watching them from the moment they left ranch property, but they could still do their best to be as safe as possible.

Kris's handheld police radio lay on the bench seat between them, crackling with various transmissions between officers and the town's emergency dispatch center. Everything sounded routine and relatively quiet.

"I came out here a few times as a kid," Monica said as they drew closer to the sprawling golf course. A light breeze sent a spray of water from a fountain in the middle of a water hazard across the bright green grass.

Kris turned into the parking lot and found a space near the portico. After the obligatory few moments looking around to see if they'd been followed, they got out and walked through the smoked-glass doors into the foyer and then veered off toward the restaurant with its adjoining lounge.

The serving table for the breakfast buffet was being disassembled, and it was too early for the lunch crowd. The facility with its large windows, dark wood paneling, and plush maroon carpeting was nearly empty except for a couple of patrons sipping from coffee mugs at a table near the door to the back patio.

A man behind the bar with a clipboard appeared to be taking inventory of the bottles stored on the shelves.

"Looks like he's a manager of some sort," Monica commented. "Maybe he's been employed here long enough to know the regulars, and he's noticed something."

"Worth a shot," Kris said, and they headed toward him.

"Good morning," Kris called out as they approached the man.

Monica reminded herself to smile. Tension had worn her nerves thin, and she was certain her feeling of anxious desperation showed on her face. She couldn't help wondering if she'd already interacted with someone who had useful information, but they were afraid to speak up. If she wanted people to help, she needed to seem somewhat friendly and approachable. She was asking people to stick their necks out, possibly putting themselves in danger if they gave her information in any way related to Boyd Sierra Associates. It was a lot to ask. Being pleasant while she asked for help was the least she could do.

The lounge employee, dressed in black slacks and a dress shirt, turned to offer them a polite, professional smile. "Good morning." A small brass-colored name tag declared him Daniel, and beneath it was written Food and Beverage Services Manager. "May I get you something to drink?"

"Actually, we'd just like to talk to you for a minute," Monica said.

Daniel nodded cautiously. "Sure."

"Have you worked here for a while?" she asked.

"Oh, yeah, I started bussing tables on weekends when I was still in high school." He offered a small smile. "And as you can see, that was a few years ago."

Monica figured he was about forty years old, give or take.

"Good." She nodded, still striving to appear upbeat. "I was hoping to ask you some questions about a customer who's been a seasonal visitor in the past. It's my dad, actually." She pulled out her phone, tapped on a photo and held it up.

Daniel leaned across the bar to have a look. As his gaze went to the picture, Monica said, "His name is Hunter Larson."

Daniel's smile faltered.

"You know who he is," Monica said. It was a statement, not a question.

"Yeah, sure," Daniel said hesitantly. He appeared uncomfortable and then glanced briskly around the lounge and toward the dining room as if looking for an excuse to walk away.

"You know about his criminal conviction," Monica said, figuring there was no point in beating around the bush.

"A couple of our guests were talking about it once and I couldn't help overhearing some of their conversation."

"I understand he liked to hang out with the same group of friends when he came out to play a few rounds, and they'd relax together here afterward. Could you tell me who those friends were?"

Daniel grabbed a bar towel and began rubbing it on a glass that already looked dry. "Why are you asking?"

"I'm trying to track down some information," she said, quickly thinking of how she could state her case as succinctly as possible. "People's lives are at stake. I believe one or more of my dad's associates know things that could help me and that possibly should be shared with the authorities. I just want to talk to them. It seems likely that they're still members here."

He shook his head. "Sorry, but I can't help you."

"Can't or won't?" Kris asked.

Daniel glanced at him. "You're a police of-ficer. I've seen you before."

Kris nodded. "I am. And if you pay attention to the news, you know there are some danger-ous people active in town right now. Any infor-mation you could give us would be a big help."

"I mind my own business," Daniel said with a tone of finality. "There's no way I'm crossing organized crime. Not even with something as simple as telling you who your dad hung out with when he was here. I have no idea who is connected to what, and I don't want to get in-volved. Now, I'm happy to get you something to eat or drink, but that's it."

Monica was frustrated, but she couldn't force the man to give them an answer.

Kris took out a business card and set it on the counter. "In case you change your mind or think of something."

Back outside, Monica looked up at the vi-brant blue sky overhead. Such a beautiful day, such a gorgeous setting. People going about their normal lives all around her. And yet here she was, the target of murderers and getting nowhere in her efforts to set things to rights in her life and get very bad guys sent to jail.

"How do you do it?" She turned to Kris,

who was focused on their surroundings as they walked to the truck.

"I pray a lot. I do the best I can. I accept that ultimately I am not in control," he answered without hesitation. He hadn't needed her to explain what she meant, and it seemed like a confirmation of her feeling that they'd come to understand each other in a ridiculously short amount of time. The basis of that seemed to be that they had faith in common. But there was something more specific to each of them, too. Something that just felt *right*—at least to Monica—when they were together.

She felt comfortable with him. His calmness and strength were reassuring. Having a dad who turned out to be secretly committing white-collar crimes had undermined her trust in people in general. But seeing Kris with his family and friends and coworkers showed her that he truly was the kind of man he presented himself to be. Some people, like him, were trustworthy.

He didn't deserve to have his world turned sideways by a woman whose future was uncertain and who brought danger wherever she went.

Kris had this meaningful life where he was of service to his community. He had an adorable son and a lovely family. Even if things were to move forward between the two of them, how could Monica possibly fit into his life without creating a rift? He was a lawman, and she was the daughter of a dishonest mob accountant. Her dad had come to faith, and she was grateful for that. But he remained accountable for his actions. And her name was associated with his. How could she tarnish the name of Officer Kris Volker?

What were the chances of her getting a teaching job in a town where people might know about her dad? There were undoubtedly more of them who were aware of his exploits since the attacks on Monica had made it into the local news. And what if all her efforts failed and nothing substantial happened to the Boyd Sierra syndicate? What if they carried a grudge against Monica and anyone close to her for the rest of her life?

Kris was kind and brave, and his family was supportive and generous. How could she bring trouble to them? What kind of thank-you was that?

It would be selfish and self-centered. It was something she wouldn't do. Painful as it was, sad as it was, she needed to rein in her emotions and be more controlled in her responses to Kris's attention.

"I want to stop by the police station before we go back to the ranch," Kris said while they were still in the parking lot. A moment later his phone chimed, and he checked it. "Here's some good news for you. Your friend Ryan's alibi checks out. He was at the restaurant when he said he was. Witnesses confirm it, and there's security video footage of him."

"I'm glad to hear it." It was good news. But given the weight of the thoughts on her mind, she didn't exactly feel happy.

"Ryan seems pretty concerned about the guy who was working at the resort when you went up there."

"Jason Mulhern." In her mind, Monica pictured the paving company truck she'd seen and the man she'd almost bumped into. She assumed that had been Jason.

"Talking to him should be our next step." He tapped some information into his cell phone. "Looks like Mulhern's shop isn't far from downtown. Let's stop by and see what he has to say on our way back to the ranch from the police station." He put aside the phone and drove out of the parking lot.

"Brendan was pretty hostile when we went to talk to him last night," Monica said as they rode down the road. "It seemed like he felt as if Dad had betrayed their friendship, but maybe it was something more. Or maybe he's just an angry person all the time." She shrugged. "It's hard to imagine him getting angry and sending a car off a ridge onto your house. That seems far-fetched. But I do wonder if he's somehow connected to the attacks on me. He was the right size for the attacker inside the cabin, but since his voice was different I just don't think he was that guy." She shook her head. "But maybe I'm wrong. Maybe I'm misremember-ing, and he is one of the attackers. He seemed over-the-top defensive. What do you think?"

"Given all that's happened, I think we should stay suspicious of everyone. You coming back to town and going around with a cop asking questions is bound to stir up a few secrets and fears. I'm hoping it will awaken somebody's guilty conscience and prod them to do the right thing. That does happen, but unfortunately it takes time. Maybe we'll start to get some re-sults for our efforts soon."

"I hope so. I don't have time to waste." Not

to mention that she was exhausted by the constant fear weighing her down.

They approached a railroad crossing as the gates dropped down in front of them. Kris stopped and shifted the truck into Park. He glanced in the rearview mirror, did a double take, and then yelled, "Get down!" He lunged across the bench seat, pressing Monica's head down and protecting it with his own body as bullets slammed into the cab's rear window and pounded into the back of the truck.

"We can't move. We're boxed in!" Monica cried out as the shots kept coming. "The train is in front of us, and the shooter is behind us."

"We *have* to move." Kris sat back up behind the steering wheel while keeping his head ducked as much as possible.

They were pinned in by a concrete traffic barrier on one side that made it impossible to do a U-turn and the brick exterior of an industrial building on the other.

"How can we get away? Which direction can we go?" Monica raised her head slightly to peer into her side mirror, where she saw a heavy SUV behind them. She could see the open passenger door, with a gunman crouched behind it, firing through the gap. He paused and looked as though he was getting ready to move forward. Possibly to shoot Monica point-blank through the side window. And then shoot Kris, too.

She knew Kris had a gun, but she could see that the interior of the besieged truck was not a good place to set up some kind of defensive position. Surrounded by glass, and with Monica unarmed, they were too vulnerable.

"Hang on!" Kris slammed the truck into gear and made a right turn so sharp the truck initially struggled to move forward. The vehicle rocked and swayed as he drove off the pavement, around the crossing gates, and onto the dusty right-of-way alongside the rail line.

They raced beside the train. Loud clanks and squeals on the railroad cars launched a frightening assault on Monica's ears. It was accompanied by a deep rumbling vibration that she not only heard but also felt in her gut.

"Call it in on my radio!"

The truck stirred up dust that swirled around them as the truck rattled across the rutted hard-packed dirt.

*Bang! Bang!*

The assailants had followed them!

More shots slammed into the back of the truck's cab. Monica took a quick look in the side mirror and saw the SUV was now frighteningly close on their tail.

She reached for the radio, but it wasn't there. Feeling a flare of panic that sent a grip of fear through her whole body, she looked around and then slid down to the floorboard, where she finally discovered it had slipped under her side of the seat.

"Key it and say *shots fired*," Kris called to her as he fought with the jerking steering wheel on the rough stretch of dirt that wasn't even really a road. "Tell them you're with Officer Volker."

She followed his directions.

"Copy shots fired," a voice on the radio responded. "All units clear the channel. What is your location?"

What *was* their location? What should she say? That they were gunning it alongside a train near the golf course? She had no idea of the nearby street names.

"East of Lampson Street on the southern side of the railroad right-of-way, heading east toward Sunrise Avenue," Kris said in a tone so calm and controlled that Monica actually found it eerie.

Squeezing her eyes shut to help her concentrate, she repeated the words, hearing the shakiness in her voice, which vibrated with every dip and bump along the ground not meant for high-speed driving.

At Kris's prompting, she added a description of the vehicle pursuing them and mentioned there were two shooters.

After that, Monica could hear the dispatcher speaking with police units checking in their estimated response time, but she was more focused on keeping her balance as Kris made another sharp right turn, this time onto the first actual paved street they came to.

"Tell them we're southbound on Sunrise Avenue now."

She wanted to do what he said, but fear had a grip on her so tight she could barely think, let alone move. Her breath felt locked in her chest, and all she could do was stare straight ahead with her hands braced against the dashboard so she'd be ready if he took another sharp turn.

"We'll shake them," Kris said with only a slight hint of concern in his voice. "Just hang on for a little while longer."

This whole race to stay ahead of the shooters felt like deadly, random chaos to Monica. But Kris obviously knew how to deal with it, and his even-tempered focus helped settle her emotions once again. She took a breath and said, "Southbound on Sunrise," into the radio.

They were in an industrial part of town, with brick warehouses and repair garages and light manufacturing businesses.

Kris made a sudden turn into a narrow alley between two warehouses, his truck barely fitting between the oversized blue trash cans pressed against the outer walls of the buildings. Almost immediately after that, he took a turn into another narrow alley before coming to a stop, eyes glued on his rearview mirror.

Without the roar of the train beside them or the whine of the pickup's engine, Monica was finally able to hear emergency sirens.

"What should I tell them now?" she asked, radio near her face, her voice not much more than a whisper. "How do I describe where we are?"

He shook his head. "We don't. We hope and pray the shooters didn't see us make the first turn, or the turn after that. They might have a scanner and be listening to police traffic, so we don't want to say specifically where we are. We had to use the radio to coordinate a response with the other cops, but now we can use a phone so we don't inadvertently tell the thugs how to find us."

*Bang! Bang!*

Just as he finished speaking, they heard shots fired, followed by the sound of brakes squealing and then a car crash. It came from the direction of where they would have been if Kris hadn't turned.

The sound of sirens grew increasingly loud, and it sounded like the cops sped past the alley entrance Kris had turned into as they raced by in pursuit of the assailants.

The sirens wailed in place for a few moments, and then they were silenced.

Radio traffic commenced with an officer reporting the vehicle they'd been pursuing had crashed, two suspects had bailed on foot, and the officers were in pursuit.

The dispatcher responded that the sheriff's department K-9 team was on the way.

Kris drove through the alley until they reached the street and could see the intersection where the SUV had crashed against a light pole. The front doors were hanging open.

Two patrol units were parked on scene, and an officer was on the sidewalk talking to a citizen who gestured as if they were describing everything they'd witnessed.

"Should we stay and help?" Monica asked.

Kris shook his head. "What we need to do is get you out of here. The criminals could double back on foot and come after you if they know you're nearby. They may not be far away. They might even be watching to see if we show up on the scene."

He grabbed his cell and placed a call to dispatch to let them know that he and Monica would be heading to the police station to give their official statements about what had happened. After he was finished, he pulled out onto the street. The cracked spiderweb of safety glass at the back of the cab allowed air to flow through the small spaces that had actually been blown out by bullets. Bullets that could have killed either one of them.

"You have to wonder how many more times we can survive attacks like this," Monica said wearily.

Kris ran a hand through his bristly, military-cut hair as he exhaled a deep sigh. "As many times as we have to."

"So the only thing we've got on Brendan Stryker, at least on record, is that he's a hothead and has faced a few assault charges," Kris said, gaze fixed on his computer screen at the police station. "It could be he's committed other crimes and never got caught, but it could also be true that his temper and inability to resist using his fists to solve conflicts are his only problems." He glanced at Monica, who was seated in a chair across from him, and winced inwardly at the sorrowful expression on her face. She was a good person who'd been through so much, and he was compelled to do everything he could to help her. It was probably a good thing that they were still at the police station after giving their reports on the shooting attack. If they were back at the ranch, he might not have been able to avoid the temptation to take her in his arms and try to offer whatever comfort he could.

"Have you found out anything about Mulhern, the guy with the paving company, that shows him criminally active?" Detective Campbell had returned to the police station after hearing about the criminals' attempt to ambush Monica and Kris while they were stopped at the railroad crossing. "None of my informants know anything about the guy."

Kris shook his head. "He does have a criminal record. He broke into a couple of unoccupied homes and stole a few things when he was young. He did his time, and he's no longer under probation, so I can't force him to come in and talk to me. I was going to stop by his paving business this afternoon and ask him a few questions, but given what's just happened, I think it would be best to get Monica back to the ranch."

He glanced at Monica, and braced for an argument that she had no time to waste and would want to talk to Mulhern as soon as possible. But in this instance, she looked at him, exhaustion written on her face and in her slightly slumped posture, and nodded.

The chief strode out of his office, phone to his ear and a tablet in his hand, finishing a conversation and then disconnecting. "The county K-9 team tracked the suspects from the point where they bailed out of their vehicle to a grocery store parking lot four blocks over, where the scent trail stopped."

"What does that mean?" Monica asked. "That they have accomplices in town who picked them up?"

The chief shook his head. "Actually, it looks like they just stole themselves another car. The manager of the grocery store gave the officers access to security video, and they could see perps who generally looked like the assailants breaking into a car and getting away."

"Maybe we should run a check on all known car thieves in town," Kris said. "These guys seem to be very good at that."

"Not a bad idea," Campbell mused. "Does the video footage show us their faces so we can ID them?"

Ellis tapped the screen a couple of times and then set the tablet on Kris's desk so they could have a look. "You can see their builds and get a sense of their heights," he said as the video played. "But they've got sunglasses on and their jacket collars flipped up. There's not enough for facial recognition."

Kris leaned over to watch as the lackluster-quality video played out. "I'd say these are probably the same men who attacked Monica at the Bennett cabin. Which indicates it's likely been the same attackers all along and the Boyd Sierra syndicate hasn't sent multiple killers to Cedar Lodge. That's been my biggest fear."

He turned to Monica, and she nodded. "I agree. I think the slightly shorter and wider guy is the one who grappled with me at the cabin and tried to force me into the fire. The taller guy is the one who was waiting outside."

"We're going to catch them," Chief Ellis said to Monica. "I know you're in a tough situation and that you're likely getting discouraged, but I want you to know this police department supports you. We're not going to give up until we find these criminals. *I* am not going to give up until I've done all I can to support your efforts to uncover the information you believe your dad left for you. Finding it could benefit the whole town. We want these thugs convinced that it's no longer safe for them to engage in any kind of illegal activities in Cedar Lodge, Montana."

Kris reached out to take Monica's hand and gave it a light squeeze.

The look in her eyes when she turned to him, a glassy-eyed expression of acknowledgment and trust, nearly took his breath away. In his heart, he made a promise to her that he would continue doing all he could to keep her safe and help her protect her family.

She blinked, looked away, and then withdrew her hand from his.

"Going forward, I'm assigning an officer, in addition to Kris, to go with you anytime you leave the Volker family ranch," Ellis said to Monica. "Give me an hour's advance notice, and I'll redirect a cop on patrol to escort you wherever you're going. We're a relatively small department. Given the circumstances, I can justify having Kris assigned to work your case and protect you. I'm afraid I can't justify the cost of a second round-the-clock bodyguard. But I'll do what I can."

"Thank you," Monica said.

"An officer will follow you two back to the Volker ranch as soon as you're ready to go."

Kris's truck would need some windows replaced and holes patched, but he figured on taking care of that later. It was in good enough shape to get them back home.

"Do you have any new leads to follow on this investigation?" Ellis asked. "Beyond talking to Jason Mulhern after you've had time to recover from today's events?"

"No, sir," Kris said. "But we'll find something."

Detective Campbell got to his feet. "My team is still looking for leads, too. I've got another call scheduled tomorrow morning to check in with my federal law enforcement colleagues."

"All right," Chief Ellis said. "Everybody stay alert." He glanced at Kris and said, "Ask whoever is available to follow you home when you're ready to leave." Then he headed back to his office.

Kris turned to Monica. "I'm ready to go now. How about you?"

She nodded.

After finding an officer to escort them, Kris and Monica headed out the door toward the parking lot. They needed to make forward progress on this case soon. Normally quiet Cedar Lodge was starting to feel as dangerous as any combat zone.

# Chapter Eleven

Monica had a robust appetite just hours after she and Kris had nearly been shot to death. She wondered what that said about her. Maybe it meant she was getting used to living on the edge of danger. It was hard to believe her life had turned out like this.

Jill set a casserole dish packed with baked spaghetti on the dining table close to Monica. Her stomach rumbled.

After their return to the ranch, Monica and Kris had given his parents a full report regarding what had happened. Of course everyone was concerned, but at the moment, what more could they do beyond try to stay safe while Monica and Kris tracked down the information Monica was seeking? After the debrief, everyone returned to their routine activities. Jill and Pete had started dinner and declined any offer of help, insisting that Monica and Kris rest.

Shortly before mealtime, they'd been joined by Cole and Dylan, who had both just finished their work shifts.

"This feels like old times with you kids here," Jill said.

*"Kids?"* Kris glanced at Cole and Dylan before dropping his chin and giving his mom a deadpan stare. And then he broke into a wide smile.

He was a man who took dire situations seriously, could talk things out and admit to being worried or afraid. But at some point, he would collect himself and radiate a faith-filled confidence that made Monica feel confident, too. Well, *somewhat* confident.

"You boys will always be kids to your mom," Pete said as he gestured to Monica to help herself to the savory spaghetti in front of her.

She dished up her food, and while waiting for the others, she glanced around the room, her gaze lingering on the rifles propped against the nearby walls. She knew Kris and Dylan were wearing their sidearms. For all she knew, everybody at the table but her was armed. They were enjoying a lighthearted family meal, and yet at the same time, everyone acknowledged that another attack could happen at any moment. Apparently, for the Volker family, huddling together somewhere, overwhelmed with fear, was not an option.

The curtains and blinds around the dining area were closed as a precaution so that no ill-intentioned lurker could see inside the house. Repairs to the damaged section of the home had been partially completed thanks to the help offered by so many people. The Volkers were still awaiting customized items like precisely sized windows and window frames, but eventually the house would look good as new.

"The boys played football together in high school." Jill continued her earlier conversational topic about Kris and his friends as everyone started digging in. "They did junior rodeo. They went hiking and camping and fishing, all that stuff. And man, did they eat us out of house and home when all four of them were here." She turned to Monica. "The fourth musketeer, Henry, works all over the world, and we don't see him much anymore."

Her comment sounded a little wistful to Monica.

Cole, the tall paramedic who Monica had learned was a navy veteran, said, "Henry will come back to town one of these days, and when he does, he'll probably come by here asking for something to eat." He looked down at the huge spoonful of food he'd just scooped up and then glanced up with a guilty expression followed by a grin.

"Don't worry," Jill said, grinning back at him. "I made two casseroles in case we need more. I know who I'm dealing with here."

Dark-haired Dylan turned to his friend and shook his head. "You act like you haven't eaten in days."

Cole shrugged. "I love Mrs. Volker's spaghetti casserole," Cole said. "I always have."

Betty gave a low *woof* from the living room followed by a growl.

Kris, Cole, and Dylan were on their feet in an instant. The others stood, as well.

So much for the appearance of a calm family dinner.

Monica felt the couple of bites of casserole she'd eaten turn to lead in her stomach. Dread settled around her shoulders, giving her a chill. Which direction would the attack come from this time? She followed Betty as the hound moved toward the foyer, seemingly focused on the front door.

"I'll check the security feed." Pete slid his phone out of his pocket and tapped the screen.

Kris was at the dining room window, moving the blind slightly aside to peer out. Cole moved toward the front door, near where Monica was standing, while Dylan took up a position by a living room window.

Betty let out another low bark. Little Pepper stood beside her.

"Looks like it's your police escort," Pete said with his gaze focused on his phone.

It was a cop?

That was strange. They'd had an officer follow them home from the station, but there'd been no plans for him to stay on the property. And there were no other police escorts scheduled to show up at the ranch. Chief Ellis's directions had been that Monica and Kris should call for an officer when they planned to leave the ranch.

What was going on?

Monica walked back to the dining room, where Kris opened the blind a little wider. Monica moved closer to him while staying out of sight. A patrol car rolled slowly up the driveway and then headed past the front entrance and toward the section of the house where the car from the ridge had been partially embedded in the wall.

"Looks like the patrolman is taking a look behind the house," Pete said moments later.

Monica was suddenly aware that fear had tightened her lungs so badly she could barely breathe.

The patrol car came back around.

"I'm going to go talk to the officer," Kris said. He glanced at Cole, and his friend strode out the front door with him.

Monica stood by the partially open door, muscles taut, peeking and listening. Cole stood on the bottom step, continually scanning their surroundings.

The officer stopped and rolled down his window.

"What's up?" Kris called out, approaching the car.

"We've got officers up on the ridge responding to a vehicle fire. I'm just taking a look around and making sure there's nobody on your property that you didn't invite here."

Goose bumps rippled across the surface of Monica's skin as she imagined Boyd Sierra killers creeping down the mountainside and waiting until the home's occupants were asleep before launching another attack.

"None of the dogs barked until you drove up," Kris said.

"Good sign. At least for the moment."

*At least for the moment.* That wasn't very comforting.

A voice came across the patrolman's radio. "I found an SUV up here. No plates. Looks like someone tried to set the interior on fire but it fizzled out. I'll check for a vehicle identification number."

"I wonder if that's the SUV the attackers were driving the night of the fire," Monica said loudly enough for Kris to hear.

He glanced at her, pulled his phone out of his pocket, and placed a call. It sounded like he was talking to the officer up on the ridge and asking for a photo of the car. Moments after he ended the call, his phone pinged. He tapped the screen, looked at the picture, and then stepped toward the door to show it to Monica.

The sight still made Monica's skin crawl. "That's their SUV."

Kris nodded. "I think so, too."

"Why would they do this?" Monica asked, still remaining partially hidden by the door at the house's entrance. "Why ditch it and try to set it on fire on that ridge? And why do it now?"

Kris shrugged. "Maybe they planned to send a flaming car rolling down the hill in another attempt to get us all to run outside so they could shoot you. Or maybe they just wanted a fire on the hill to draw attention. To show that they know where you are. To scare you."

If they wanted to scare her, it was working.

And paired with that fear was dread. How many more attacks would be launched at or around this house? How many times would Kris or his family or friends be put into danger because they were close to her?

Things couldn't keep going the way they were. Something had to change. It wasn't enough for her to try to emotionally distance herself from Kris. It was time to put some physical distance between them, too.

Kris exchanged a few more words with the officer, letting him know that he and Monica had recognized the burned vehicle. Then the patrolman drove off.

"Cole and I are going to have a look around," Kris said before he and his friend set off toward the stables and barn.

"If anybody's hiding out in one of the out-buildings, they'll find them." Dylan stepped up to stand beside Monica.

They kept an eye on the men checking the property until they returned. By the time the two longtime friends came back inside, both were wearing serious expressions. They walked into the center of the house where Kris's parents were waiting.

"We didn't see anything notable, but I still think we should make sure someone is awake and keeping an eye on the security cameras throughout the night," Kris said. "We could split it up into short shifts so we can all still function and do our jobs tomorrow."

Everyone nodded in agreement.

They sat back down to finish eating dinner, but by now, Monica's appetite had drastically diminished. The hard knot in her stomach made it difficult to swallow food, but she did the best she could. With danger all around them, she needed to remain strong and alert.

After dinner, Monica walked up to Kris in the living room, where he'd cast the ranch security feed onto a smart TV on the wall. Jill and Pete were still in the kitchen, talking, while Cole and Dylan had gone to grab the sleeping bags each of them had brought. They'd changed their original plans and were both going to camp out in the ranch house living room instead of Cole staying in his camper and Dylan in the bunkhouse.

"I need to talk to you," Monica said.

Kris turned from the screen. "Sure."

Monica took a deep breath. "Listen, I appreciate everything you have done for me. But I've decided it's time for me to go." She'd pondered it aloud before, but she really meant it now.

Kris stared at her, his face unreadable. So she continued, the words spilling out as she nervously rubbed the stitches on her scalp. "I think I was wrong," she blurted out, tears forming in her eyes because she was scared and sad and frustrated that the pivotal memories of that prison conversation just wouldn't come back. "We haven't gotten anywhere. We haven't found any object or note or key or receipt or anything that could lead us to some clue I thought my dad might have left here. Nobody has come forward with information he entrusted to them."

She brushed away the tears at the corners of her eyes, and then hugged herself, determined to keep going and say what she needed to say.

She wouldn't mention how sorry she was to have brought such danger to him and his family, because he was a generous and honorable man who would tell her that her concern wasn't reason enough for her to leave.

When she looked at Kris's face, she was reminded of the sweet image of his little boy. It was unfair to keep father and son apart any longer. It didn't matter that all reports were that Roy was having a wonderful time with his other set of grandparents and the cousins who lived nearby.

She shook her head slightly, doing her best to dismiss feelings she admittedly had for this man and her appreciation of his family. In the scheme of things, what did her feelings matter?

She'd brought danger to Kris's family home. She couldn't possibly risk bringing danger to his son, and Roy needed to come home eventually.

"I want you to stay," Kris said simply.

She straightened her spine and lifted her chin. "I have a reasonable plan. If I can get to the airport without the Boyd Sierra thugs seeing me, I'd have a good head start. I don't have siblings, but I do have cousins in Nevada, and also in California. It might be wiser if I stayed with them. I wouldn't stand out in a densely populated area the way I do in Cedar Lodge." She paused for a moment before continuing. "We haven't gotten anywhere with our investigation, and I'm running out of time to convince my mom that Archer Nolan is part of the mob before she marries him. But maybe, once the prison officials allow my dad to have visitors again, I'll be able to find the proof that will ultimately make her realize Archer's been lying to her. In the meantime, if you hear back from anyone in town who has some information to share, you can let me know."

"I want you to stay," Kris repeated. Only this time, he took a step closer. The expression on his face shifted. It was hard to believe she'd once thought he looked like a typical skeptical cop. His eyes softened with concern. He reached up to rest his fingertips on her cheek. "I want to help you through this. And then I want to see what happens between us afterward."

There wouldn't be any afterward. That was the thing. Boyd Sierra Associates was a strong criminal organization, and if they stayed angry with her, anyone around her would always be in danger. That included Roy.

Kris was a sensible man. He was probably caught up in the high emotion of the situation they were in, just like she was. Right now she needed to be the calm and logical person. He'd offered that to her when she needed it; now she could offer it to him. Even if he didn't realize it was what was best for him.

His warm hand still rested on her cheek. Her heart fluttered despite her best intentions to keep it settled. A self-interested part of her wanted so badly to tell him that she hadn't chosen to leave Cedar Lodge because she *wanted* to. She felt emotionally torn in half. But she had to do the right thing. Her dad hadn't done the right thing, and look how much damage it had caused for so many people.

*Dear Lord, please give me strength to make the best decision and follow through on it.*

She reached up to rest her hand atop his. "I think Cedar Lodge is a dead end for me," she said. It wasn't a complete lie. It wasn't the complete truth, either. But dragging things out and hinting that they might have some kind of future together would be wrong.

She removed her hand and took a step back, letting his hand fall away from her cheek, not wanting to focus too much on the flicker of confusion in his eyes. Maybe he thought he knew how she felt. Maybe he was right. But if she didn't confirm it, it would be easier for him to let go of any closeness he felt for her and move on.

"I understand your worry for your family and concern for all of us," Kris said, his voice steady. "Maybe it's time to try to connect with your mom and tell her more about what's been going on. Find out if she's okay, too. Maybe that will help you decide to stay a little longer and keep trying."

So far, Monica had responded to her mom's texts with simple reassurances that she was okay. Monica had been worried her mom would relay her whereabouts to Nolan, either deliberately or unintentionally. But at this point, what did it matter? The bad guys obviously knew where Monica had been staying, and it was past time for her mom to face up to how dangerous the whole situation was. She'd indulged in denial long enough. Maybe relating the details of the attacks was the only proof Monica would ever have to show her mom that her fiancé was a terrible and dangerous man.

Monica took out her phone and sent her mom a brief text intended to start a conversation.

While waiting for a reply, she tapped the email icon on her phone to take a quick look at messages waiting in her inbox. The most recent item made her snap her head back in surprise.

"Something wrong?" Kris asked.

"It's from the office of my dad's lawyer. It's about the certified power of attorney I asked for. I thought they were going to call me and tell me if they'd be able to send it." Preparing herself for disappointment, she tapped the screen to open it. As she read, her breath caught in her throat. "It's here," she said. "They sent the power of attorney form."

Kris smiled. "I'll let Chief Ellis know we'll need a patrol car here in the morning so we can be at the bank as soon as they open."

Monica gave in to the impulse to reach out for a celebratory hug. Kris folded his muscled arms around her in response, and she pressed the side of her face against his chest. She could feel and hear the steady beat of his heart. Her own heart gave her away as it raced in her chest under the influence of his touch.

Kris didn't seem to be in any hurry to let go of her. And she wasn't anxious to leave his embrace, either. So she gave herself a few moments to enjoy it. This would be the last time they shared a moment like this one.

There was no guarantee there would even be

a safe-deposit box at the bank belonging to her dad. Or that there would be anything helpful in it. And even if there was something that would keep her mom from marrying Archer and get her dad a reduction in his prison sentence, that wouldn't change things between Monica and Kris. She would still be the criminal's daughter whose family reputation would cast a shadow over Kris's career at the police department. She wouldn't be able to start her teaching career in Cedar Lodge, where the school board would discover her shady family connections. And most important of all, the Boyd Sierra syndicate would still hold a grudge against her, making it risky for anyone to be around her.

Slowly and regretfully, she let go of Kris. And she steeled her heart to the fact that no matter what happened at the bank tomorrow, she would be leaving Cedar Lodge, and she would not look back.

Monica stared down at the open safe-deposit box in front of her. She'd already picked up her grandfather's old pocket watch, her great-grandmother's engraved wedding ring, and a few other pieces of jewelry that had sentimental value for her dad. These must have been the final few belongings of monetary value her father owned that he would not sell to help pay for his legal defense after he'd been arrested.

Everything else had been cashed out to pay the lawyers.

A familiar shaking feeling started in the center of her chest. A sad sensation of loss and sorrow and disappointment for all she and her parents had been through and for the feeling that so much of her happiness as a child must have been built on a lie. She didn't really know her dad at all, never had. Her mother—not always the easiest relationship in her life—had become a stranger. And their shared history as a family seemed to have been reduced to these few objects.

Instead of sending a text reply last night, Suzanne had called her daughter. Torn by indecision, Monica had ultimately not answered the call. She was afraid that once she heard her mother's voice, she would say too much, potentially putting her mom or herself in danger. So she'd sent a text saying that she'd talk to her later.

Suzanne had left an angry voice message after that, but Monica had understood that it was fueled by fear. Whether it was fear for Monica or fear for herself, it was hard to say.

Here, now, inside a private area within the bank vault, Monica stared down at all that space where she'd hoped there would be data storage devices or photographs or documents or *something* that would tell her what she needed to know.

She tried to hold back the trembling sensation that came over her and blink away the tears. She shouldn't have gotten her hopes up. From the moment she left Reno for Cedar Lodge, she shouldn't have thought finding a resolution to all her family problems would be straightforward.

She left the items in the box and beckoned a bank employee to help her get the box secured again.

Disappointment hung heavy on her shoulders. She had no solid plans for what to do next. She and Kris had one more person they'd planned to talk to, Jason Mulhern, who owned the paving company that did work at the Elk Ridge Resort among other places. She was at a loss over what to do after that. It really did make sense for her to just leave town.

She spotted Kris in the lobby before he saw

her. He was standing, his head moving slowly from side to side as he looked around the lobby and presumably out the windows at the surrounding streets of Cedar Lodge, keeping an eye out for potential attackers.

He turned to her just before she reached him, and the shift in his eyes to a sympathetic rather than vigilant expression made her realize that her own emotions must be clearly written on her face.

"What did you find?" he asked cautiously.

"Nothing helpful. A few pieces of jewelry." She shook her head. "There's no secret message attached to any of them or etched into the metal." She'd taken a close look at each item to make sure even though she'd felt foolish doing it.

"I'm sorry. I know this isn't what you'd hoped for. But we aren't at a point for you to give up hope or leave town just yet."

He gave her an encouraging smile, and despite her best intentions, she smiled back. She'd become too aware of the *moments* like this one that they'd shared. When their exchanges were beyond the objective sharing of information between a cop and a citizen in desperate need of help.

When had that even started? When had it all become so personal, this interaction between them? She'd been thinking about it since last night, and she still didn't know. Perhaps it had been that way from the beginning. But she couldn't let it continue.

She schooled her features, letting the smile fade away and keeping her voice impersonal and matter-of-fact as she said, "Hiding out and thinking only of myself isn't something I can live with. And if I'm not making headway here in Cedar Lodge, there's no reason to stay."

His gaze fixed on her, the warmth in his eyes fading. Within seconds he was wearing the cynical *cop face* expression.

She'd made her point. She'd pushed him away. He got the message.

He held up his phone and spoke in a professional tone. "I heard from Detective Campbell while you were in the vault. He's arranged a video meeting with a couple of parole officers who may have some insights into the thugs who've been attacking you."

Monica nodded uncertainly, not sure what kind of information he was talking about.

"Parolees sometimes pass on information to the officers managing their cases," Kris con-

tinued. "Since the parolees are out and about
in the world, some of them pick up useful information. They're supposed to stay away from
other criminals, but they don't always do that.
And sometimes they share information with
their parole officers. Chief Ellis wants me at
the station to listen in. It's a secure meeting, so
I can't have you attend. But I can tell you what
I learn afterward. And we need to get going,
because it's starting soon."

They walked outside. The bank was part of
a commercial complex with shops and stores
that spanned several connected buildings. They
stepped out from a short passageway to the
street, where a cop escort was waiting in a patrol car behind the Volker ranch SUV Kris had
driven to the bank.

"Monica!"

Kris stepped closer to Monica, grasped her
upper arm, and pulled her close to him.

Ryan Fergus walked up to them on the sidewalk. "Sorry, I probably shouldn't have yelled
out your name like that," he said apologetically.
"I'm just glad to see you in person and know
you're all right."

"I'm okay."

"Good. Well, I'm actually here following up on some information that might help you."

"What's that?" Monica asked.

Ryan gestured toward a restaurant kitty-corner from where they stood. "I told you that I'd heard about a local business group with monthly luncheons that your dad sometimes met with. I think the Cedar Lodge Entrepreneur's Club might be that group. There's a meeting today at George's Farmhouse Restaurant over there, and I figured I'd check it out and see if it's the same one. I didn't want to mention anything until I knew for sure."

Despite herself, Monica got her hopes up. She was desperate for leads, and this was a plausible one. "I'll go with you," she said to Ryan. "Maybe I'll see someone I recognize or hear a familiar name."

"We need to get to the police station," Kris said, still holding her arm.

Ryan stepped back. "You don't need to go with me," he said to Monica. "Let me find out if your dad ever attended one of their meetings, and we'll proceed from there. If anybody has anything useful to say, I'll let you know immediately."

"You go to the police station," Monica said,

gently disengaging her arm from Kris's grasp. "And I'll check out this entrepreneur's club."

Kris frowned at her.

She gestured at the officer in the patrol car. "Officer Anderson can keep an eye on me. And the police department is only three blocks away."

When Kris looked like he was not going to move, she started toward the cop car, and he followed. She gave the patrol officer a quick rundown of their plans. Then she turned to Kris. "*Please*, go so you don't miss the start of the meeting. After it's over we'll talk to Mulhern at his paving company shop. And if I learn anything at this meeting at the restaurant, we can follow up on that, too."

She felt energized by the prospect of getting somewhere.

"I don't like it," Kris said, crossing his arms. "Going in different directions."

"At this point, I'm potentially in danger anywhere I go. Even at your house. We might as well take advantage of every opportunity we get and try to follow up on leads as quickly as possible. My mom could marry Archer Nolan in a week, and I don't want that to happen. Ryan will be with me, and Officer Anderson will be keeping an eye on things. He can take me to the police station or back to the ranch."

Appearing hesitant, Kris apparently realized she wasn't going to give up, and he finally agreed. After leaning into the patrol car to say something to Anderson, he walked behind it to the SUV and got in. After a lingering look at Monica, he pulled away from the curb.

Monica glanced around the street, wondering if she'd ever again reach a point in her life when she didn't have to worry about her safety.

"Oh, I left my wallet in my car," Ryan said, patting his pockets. "I was planning to get something to eat while I was at the restaurant. They make fantastic omelets." He gestured toward the passageway behind them that led into the business complex. "If I cut through there, I can get to the side street where I parked my car a little quicker." He looked doubtful. "I don't know if you want to walk with me or wait in the patrol car?"

She didn't especially want to wait in the patrol car. And the side street he indicated was in the direction of the restaurant.

Ryan had already started through the passageway, saying something about Hunter Larson, but Monica couldn't hear it clearly.

She called out to the officer, who'd been watching the whole time, "I'm going with him. We'll be right back."

She turned and hurried into the passageway to catch up with Ryan, who was still talking. She was walking beside him, trying to piece together exactly what he was saying about her dad, when she heard him make a strange sound.

And then everything went dark.

# Chapter Twelve

Kris strode out of the police station conference room, where the video meeting was still on-going. The parole officers had reported none of their parolees knew anything about the attackers who'd targeted Monica, giving strong support to the idea that the assailants were professionals from out of town.

A couple of federal agents had joined the call, working with Detective Campbell on his attempts to track the thugs and tie the case to Boyd Sierra Associates. Kris was more interested in facts and leads that would specifically help to gather information that could help Monica's family. And at the moment, he was particularly concerned about Monica herself.

He'd regretted his decision to give in to Monica's request that they go their different ways the moment he'd driven away. Impatient to get back to her as quickly as possible, he'd interjected himself into the meeting and pushed the questions he and Monica needed answered. After learning that they had no specific leads, he decided it was time for him to go. He could catch up on any pertinent information later.

As he walked across the lobby, Jason Mulhern was at the forefront of his mind. He wanted to see for himself that Monica was okay, but she had a cop watching out for her, and Kris knew if he really wanted to help her, he would do everything he could to move the investigation forward.

The meeting had reminded him that Mulhern was the one specific person of interest he'd wanted to talk to but hadn't. The guy did have a criminal past, and it didn't necessarily follow that he was out of the game simply because there was nothing recent on his record. Maybe he just hadn't gotten caught. And Ryan had mentioned more than once that Mulhern seemed shady.

Rather than call ahead and give Mulhern time to fabricate lies or even slip out the back door, Kris decided to just drive to Mulhern Paving. He'd already looked at the location on his phone, and it wasn't far away.

He couldn't resist the temptation to call

Monica on the way there. Of course, Anderson would have let him know if there was a problem. And dispatch would have alerted him in the meeting if something significant had happened. Still, he called.

She didn't answer. Pushing aside the shot of anxiety that threatened to overtake rational thought, he took a breath and sent a text: Everything okay? Maybe she'd found someone at the restaurant meeting who was offering her helpful information. Though at this point he wasn't clear on what that could possibly be. Computer files? Photos? Voice recordings? Or maybe it would be something completely different.

Monica had talked about her dad having found faith and changed for the better. And while Kris knew that was possible, his cop cynicism wouldn't go away. Maybe the furtive life of a mob accountant wasn't the only secret Hunter Larson had been hiding. Maybe that was why the criminals were so intent on getting to Monica.

He pulled up to a small metal prefab building with a sign reading Mulhern Paving attached to the side. It didn't appear to be a large business. He was about to reach for his police radio to check in with Anderson when an office door opened. A woman walked out and then locked the door behind her.

Kris saw only one vehicle in the parking lot. It appeared that if this woman left, there would be no one for him to talk to. He set aside the radio and got out to walk toward her. She gave him a friendly smile that faltered when he identified himself as a police officer.

"Can I help you?" she asked politely.

"I'd like to speak with Jason Mulhern."

"He not here. I'm Nancy Mulhern, his wife. What did you want to talk to him about?"

Kris glanced at the office window. Could Jason be listening and watching from behind the closed curtain? Had he and his wife seen Kris as he arrived? Perhaps Jason had seen Kris somewhere when Kris was in uniform. It would make sense for a criminal to remember the faces of most cops in town.

Kris didn't hear anything or see any movement around the window, so he turned his attention back to Mrs. Mulhern. "I need to ask your husband a few questions. I won't take much of his time."

"Have you got a specific crime you think my husband committed?" While not rude, she did sound defensive and somewhat annoyed.

"No, I'm not looking for him regarding a particular crime." He would need to see Mulhern and talk to him before he could begin to figure out where he might fit into all the criminal attacks.

Mrs. Mulhern made a scoffing sound. She shook her head and looked down before lifting her gaze again, holding her head slightly tilted. "Jason made some bad decisions fifteen *years* ago. He was twenty years old and desperate, and he paid for his mistakes. And he hasn't broken the law since. Yet whenever one of you cops gets stuck investigating a case involving a burglary or commercial theft and you can't find any solid leads, you come looking for my husband, hoping to pin it on him." She crossed her arms over her chest. "We've had enough of it."

Since Mulhern had served his sentence and completed parole long ago, Kris had no leverage to pressure the man to talk to him.

"There's a woman in town who's been the target of some vicious attacks," Kris began. "If you follow the local news, you've probably seen something about it."

The woman lifted her shoulders. "My husband would never be involved in anything like that."

*Maybe, maybe not.*

"I understand your husband has done a lot of work up at the Elk Ridge Resort. The woman who's been attacked has a connection to that location. Maybe your husband has seen something that would help with the investigation. Maybe he saw something and didn't realize its significance."

*Or maybe he did more than just see something. Maybe he participated.*

Kris especially wanted to find out if Mulhern was a general physical match for the assailants. Neither he nor Monica could make a specific match based on a photo of Mulhern because they hadn't gotten a good look at the assailants' faces.

"Please," Kris added. "It's important. Another attack could happen at any time."

His mind returned to worrying about Monica's safety since she hadn't responded to his call or text, giving him a coiling sensation in the pit of his stomach.

The woman sighed. "Jason got a call for an appraisal this morning. I don't know if he's still there or if he's finished that and gone on to check other projects." She pulled her phone out of her purse and tapped the screen. Kris could hear the call go through and start ringing on the other end. It went to voice mail. The woman left a brief message and disconnected. "He's obviously busy. I've texted him a couple of times this morning, and he hasn't responded yet."

"Where was the appraisal supposed to be done?"

"That old roadhouse east of town. People have said they were going to buy it and renovate it for years, but it looks as if Ryan Fergus is actually going to do it."

*Ryan Fergus?* The same Ryan who had repeatedly said he didn't trust Jason Mulhern and had pointed to him as a likely criminal? And also the same Ryan who was with Monica *right now*?

Monica hadn't responded to Kris's call or text. Jason Mulhern hadn't responded to his wife's attempts to contact him.

Something was *very* wrong.

"Thank you," Kris called out as he turned and jogged toward the SUV, trying again to call Monica. When he got no response, he called Officer Anderson.

"Anderson," the officer responded when he answered.

"You have a visual on Monica right now, correct?"

"No. She and that friend you guys were with

headed back toward the bank. They haven't come out yet."

"You didn't go with them?" Kris practically barked out the words.

"She didn't ask me to go with them. Just like she didn't ask me to go along the first time she went into the bank with you. I figured she had some private financial issue to take care of and after that they'd head over to the restaurant they were talking about."

Through the phone, Kris could hear the sound of a car door opening.

"I'm going inside the bank right now," Anderson said. He disconnected.

With Anderson headed into the bank to look for Monica, Kris made the snap decision to head for the county highway that would take him out to the roadhouse to see if Mulhern was still there. He started off in that direction.

Anderson called moments later. "Monica's not here. I'll head to the restaurant in case they ended up driving there in her friend's car and I didn't realize it."

"Make it fast," Kris snapped, furious that Anderson hadn't insisted on accompanying Monica wherever she went. It didn't matter that Anderson was technically right and he couldn't force his help on Monica. Kris gave him a quick summary of his plan to go to the roadhouse before disconnecting.

*Monica, what were you thinking?* Why hadn't she stayed with Anderson?

Kris did his best to corral his emotions. Monica wasn't a cop. She wasn't used to daily exposure to lies and deceit. She wasn't cynical. She'd known Ryan Fergus for a few years, and he must have seemed completely safe to her. Maybe he was a decent guy and the two of them had been taken by Mulhern. Or Brendan Stryker. Or the two hit men that had been dogging her all along.

Anderson called again. "Monica's not in the restaurant."

"Call Chief Ellis. Tell him what's happening and that we need to track Monica by her phone location." He knew the chief would automatically have dispatch issue a be-on-the-lookout for her. "I'll check in as soon as I get to the roadhouse."

Kris hit the gas pedal harder, already on the eastern edge of town where the highway opened up. He hoped and prayed that he would find Monica before it was too late.

Monica opened her eyes, her gaze fixed on the dusty concrete in front of her while she tried to figure out where she was and what had happened.

She was in a fairly large room that was shadowy and cool. She was lying on her side with her head resting on the concrete. She had a throbbing headache.

*Ryan.* The last thing she remembered was walking with Ryan. Was he here? Had he been kidnapped, too? It was obvious someone had knocked her out and brought her here.

She tried to push herself up into a sitting position, but found that her hands were tied behind her back. Her knees were bent, her ankles secured together with rope like her hands.

She must be in shock, because she felt concerned but not terrified. There wasn't the heart-pounding fear she'd experienced while being shot at or wrestling with an assailant trying to shove her into a fire. It was a strangely detached feeling. Maybe she'd just had all she could take and she was finally letting go.

*No. Do not let go. Do not quit.*

Where had those thoughts come from?

She knew the answer in an instant. From the part of her that had prayed and fought against despair after she'd been taken so low following her dad's arrest.

*Dear Lord, please help me. I'm overwhelmed and tired. Of everything. But I know with You all things are possible. You can and will give me strength.*

The prayer felt like it brought her back to her senses. Literally. Her wrists and ankles hurt. The concrete floor was colder. She felt *more* frightened.

She also felt more *alive*. And strengthened to do everything she could to stay that way.

She couldn't tell if there was anyone else in the room, watching her. What she could see from her awkward position was cabinets and metal doors and a pair of sinks on the other side of the room with a wide window above them, forest visible outside. There was also a set of ovens. So it must be a restaurant kitchen.

But the restaurant she'd intended to go to so she could question the entrepreneur's club about her dad would be busy and full of people right now. Not dusty and lit only by sunlight coming through the windows. Where was she?

Following an awkward series of movements, she was finally able to get herself seated upright with her legs stretched out in front of her but her hands still behind her back. Her hair was in front of her eyes now, so she couldn't see much. She came to rest leaning against a cabinet that had a broken handle. Maybe she could use that to get her hands untied. Tilting her head, she blew out a puff of air to clear the hair from her eyes. She startled when she saw Jason Mulhern seated in a chair several feet away, staring in her direction.

Where was Ryan? Was he tied up somewhere in this building, too?

"You," she said to Jason. Her mouth was dry, and her throat was scratchy. "You're behind all of this? *You've* been trying to kill me?" She looked around, expecting to see an accomplice lurking in the shadows because it had been two men attacking her since she arrived in town.

He moved his head slightly and then said, "No, I haven't been trying to kill you." His words sounded awkward and distorted. She focused her attention more intently on him, and it became clear that he was slumped in the chair. That he was tied to it, actually. His lips were split, and there was blood at the corner of his mouth.

"What?" Her breath caught in her chest as the compulsion to *get out of here now* overtook her, and she was unable to force out any more words. She thought of the broken cabinet handle and pressed against it, hoping to use it to cut through the rope binding her hands.

"You're Monica Larson," he said with a scratchy voice. "I think I saw you at the resort, but I didn't recognize you at the time. It's been so long. I thought you looked a little familiar, but it took me a while to figure out why."

What was he talking about? It was hard to focus on him while trying to cut through the rope bindings on her wrists at the same time. She hardly knew what to say. But at such an extreme point, where her life might nearly be over, there was no reason not to talk blunt truth with him.

"I don't know you," she said. "I've heard you're a criminal. Maybe you've committed crimes with my dad." She shook her head. Acknowledging all that she'd learned about her father over the last year or so was still hard. "I came to Cedar Lodge hoping to find some information I think he wanted me to know. The criminal gang he used to work with is trying to kill me because they're afraid of what I might learn." She gave him a lingering look. "Does that mean you work for Boyd Sierra Associates, too? Are they now trying to kill you, as well?"

And if that was the case, why were they still both alive? Why hadn't the kidnappers already killed them?

"I have the information you're looking for," he said.

Was he lying to her? Was this some kind of trick?

In the quiet, while she tried to figure out what to do next, she heard cars driving by. Not heavy traffic, as if she were in the middle of town. But maybe enough that if she could just get outside, she could flag down help.

So far she hadn't accomplished anything using the broken handle behind her back. She couldn't get the metal edge lined up at the necessary angle to cut through the ropes. Frustrated, she looked around for some other way to get herself free as Jason started talking again.

"Your dad hid information in a folder inside an email account," Jason said. "He told me about it shortly before he went to prison. He told me how to access it and said he might someday send you to look for it."

"Okay, how do I access it?"

*If* she got out of here alive, maybe she would finally get what she'd been looking for. She still had so many questions. Why had her dad not told *her* how to access the information back when he was first arrested and before he was sent to prison? Why had he told Jason?

"First, we need to get out of here. Then I'll tell you everything," Jason said. "You can get up and move. I can't. I'm tied to this chair. Come this way and see if you can somehow untie these ropes."

She didn't trust him. What was his game? But then again, what other choice did she have?

She heard a male voice somewhere else in the building. There was no time to waste. She pulled hard on the broken handle, and it came off. Then she scooted across the cold concrete toward Jason. "I'm holding a broken handle I yanked off the cabinet door," she said. "Maybe it can cut through your ropes or pry them loose or something."

"I can move my hands a little," Jason said. "Give it to me, back up over here, and I'll try to cut your hands loose first."

Maybe he would do what he said. Or maybe he'd use the sharp edge of the broken handle to cut or stab her. In light of all that had happened, she wasn't inclined to trust him. But again, what other choice did she have?

"I'll have so many questions for you once we get out of here," she said.

"I'll tell you everything I know."

She gave him the handle, feeling him take a firm grasp of it with his fingertips. He quickly managed to slide it partially under the ropes that tied her. He began a sawing movement with it, using the sharp edge to cut the fibers.

At the same time, Monica tugged on the ropes as hard as she could. A wave of hope and relief passed through her when the rope finally loosened. Continuing to pull, she felt one hand slip free and then the other.

"Got it." She shook off the ropes.

Again she heard a male voice from somewhere else in the commercial kitchen. It was getting louder. The man was getting closer. Her stomach lurched when she finally recognized the voice and could make out the words. "Yes, you will pay me for her. And I've got a guy here we can kill and then stage the scene so it looks like he's the killer. I'll convince the cops that he grabbed Monica and forced me to come along since I was with her. I'll tell the police he was working with the two assailants they already know about. And I'll give them completely misleading descriptions."

Jason dropped the handle. "Help me get free."

Monica quickly pulled the rope off her ankles and then worked to get Jason's hands loose. They both hurried to get his feet untied and cast off the rope that had bound him to the chair.

As soon as he was free, he jumped up, knocking over the chair. The sound was loud in the nearly empty kitchen.

A door swung open, and Ryan hurried through holding a gun. He fired at Jason.

Jason dove behind the center island.

Terrified, Monica backed into a corner with nowhere to go. She heard a vehicle engine roar up to the building from the direction of the street.

"That would be the two gentlemen who have desperately been trying to eliminate you as a problem for their bosses," Ryan said in an even tone as if they were having a normal conversation. Even his facial expression was calm, almost as if he was simply taking a tour of the building.

He stepped farther into the kitchen, shifting his gaze back and forth between Monica and the area on the other side of the room where Jason had disappeared.

Heart pounding in her chest, Monica could

barely hear the killers entering the building and striding toward them.

"It's nothing personal," Ryan said to Monica with a slight smile. "It's just business."

With that faint smile lingering on his thin lips, he turned at the sound of footsteps.

Kris appeared in the doorway with his gun drawn.

With a look of surprise and the smile finally wiped from his lips, Ryan immediately fired at Kris. The cop crouched and ducked back behind the doorway so that he was out of sight.

Ryan went after him, and Monica sprang forward from the corner of the kitchen. She grabbed the chair Jason had been tied to and swung it at Ryan, connecting with his head and causing him to lurch forward. He regained his balance and spun around while firing a wild shot at Monica. She dropped to the floor, and the bullet missed her.

Kris rushed through the door, and Monica jumped to her feet.

Ryan, now standing directly in front of Monica, faced off with Kris. If Kris fired, the bullet could hit Monica. Ryan could take advantage of that.

Monica was summoning her courage to jump on Ryan's back when Kris shifted his gun to his free hand and threw out a roundhouse punch that connected with Ryan's jaw. The older man spun, but righted himself and pointed his gun at Kris again.

"Drop it!" Kris yelled at the same time he threw out another punch, this time knocking Ryan out cold. Kris immediately grabbed the older man's dropped weapon.

Monica stepped up to wrap her arms around Kris. "We're okay," she said, her voice shaky. There were moments when she was sure she was not going to be okay. That she was going to die. And she'd had moments of the same worry about Kris.

He wrapped an arm around her and squeezed her shoulders while keeping the other hand free so he could cautiously continue to point his gun at Ryan. Still, he managed to brush the top of her head with a kiss. "I wasn't going to stop until I found you."

Her knees nearly buckled with relief.

"Monica, are you okay?" Jason called out as he got to his feet on the other side of the kitchen island.

"Who are you?" Kris demanded, pointing his gun at the man who looked familiar.

"That's Jason Mulhern," Monica said. "Ryan kidnapped him, too."

*Bang! Bang!*

Before Monica could give any further explanation, shots blasted through the windows over the sink. Kris threw himself atop Monica, shielding her with his body. When the shots ended, Kris slowly got to his feet.

A second round of shots blasted through the window, and Kris hit the ground again. Monica closed her eyes tightly and covered her ears with her hands.

When this round of gunfire finally ended, Monica opened her eyes. A heavyset man had snuck through the doorway leading into the kitchen. He was the attacker who had tried to force her into the flames in the cabin fire. She knew it by the look of him and the way he moved.

The man snatched her wrist and yanked her to her feet before she could react.

In the instant it took for Kris to spin around and aim his gun at the assailant, the thug already had the barrel of his gun pressed against Monica's temple.

"Drop your gun," the criminal barked at Kris.

The cop shook his head. "Let her go."

"Drop your gun," the man repeated, grinding out the words. "Or I'll kill her right here in front of you. You know I'll do it."

Kris dropped his gun.

With his weapon still pressed against Monica's head, the attacker dragged Monica through the door of what she now recognized was the old roadhouse outside of town.

There was a van with its engine running in the gravel parking lot. The taller, skinny criminal Monica recognized from the cabin fire ran around from the back of the roadhouse. He must have been the person shooting through the window to draw away everyone's attention while the thickset guy snuck inside to grab Monica.

Kris stepped up to the doorway as the bad guy continued to drag her to the van while keeping his gun aimed at her head.

Why he or the other thug hadn't killed her on the spot, she didn't know. Maybe they were only keeping her alive so they could use her as leverage to escape from Kris.

No doubt once they got her into the van and drove away, her life would be over.

# Chapter Thirteen

Kris heard footsteps coming up behind him and he turned his gun on the red-haired man who immediately held his hands up in a sign of surrender. "I'm not one of the bad guys. Ryan Fergus grabbed me and tied me up here before he kidnapped Monica."

Kris realized he'd seen a photo of the guy as well as his face on the Mulhern Paving company's website. "Jason Mulhern."

Jason gave a curt nod and cautiously put his hands down.

Kris had no idea what the former criminal was doing here or if he could even trust him, but grilling the man for information wasn't his highest priority at the moment. What he really cared about was the woman being taken away at gunpoint.

"I'll go out the back of the roadhouse and then come around the side and make a lot of noise," Jason said. "Maybe it will distract the guy holding Monica enough that he'll loosen his grip and you can get a clear shot at him."

It wasn't a terrible idea. Firing his gun anywhere near Monica wasn't a *good* idea, but Kris couldn't risk them getting away and killing her before he could stop them. He held on to Ryan's gun, still not trusting Jason enough to give it to him.

"Go!"

Kris heard Jason run back inside the roadhouse so he could go through and out the back. At the same time, he took aim at the criminal who clutched Monica's head in the crook of his arm while waving his gun and screaming threats at Kris. They were almost to the side door of the van.

The skinny assailant slid into the driver's seat. The second Monica was in the van, he would hit the gas pedal and they'd be gone. They might even kill her as soon as they were far enough away that Kris and his gun no longer posed a threat to them.

Kris stepped through the doorway onto the covered porch that ran the length of the roadhouse. The thug holding Monica yelled to his accomplice, and the skinny guy moved to open the door from inside the van.

Kris couldn't wait for Jason to create his distraction. For all he knew, the former thief had taken the opportunity to run away. So he locked gazes with Monica, who was staring at him, wide-eyed. There was a moment when he felt they understood one another. Maybe it was wishful thinking on his part. Maybe it was the continuing intensity of two people working so closely together in dangerous situations over the last few days. But the perception felt real. He was certain she understood he was about to do something drastic because they were beyond the point where they had any other choice.

The slider door began to open. Kris held Monica's gaze and gave a slight nod of his head. She mirrored the gesture. He took a breath and aimed his gun, ready to open fire.

*"Hey! Let her go!"* Jason popped his head around the corner of the building, waving his arms and yelling toward the attackers at the van before darting out of range.

In that moment, Monica lunged back from the criminal holding her, twisting away from the gun pointed at her head and ducking down.

Clearly aware that Kris was the greater danger to him, the attacker immediately fired at him.

Kris shot back.

Monica broke free from the kidnapper's grip. She began a stumbling run toward the side of the building and away from the line of fire as Kris and the kidnapper traded shots. From behind one of the porch's wooden posts, he glanced over to make certain she was okay.

*Dear Lord, please protect her.*

Meanwhile, the driver had slipped out of the van and started shooting at Kris, too.

As soon as Monica neared the corner of the roadhouse and the relative protection of the building, she turned to Kris as if checking to see that he was okay.

*Run!* he thought just before she disappeared from sight. He ducked behind the splintered porch railing and finally had a second to key his radio and call for help. He turned his focus back on the assailants, watching as both men clambered into the van and put it in Reverse.

Maybe they were admitting defeat.

But after backing a short distance, the driver shifted gears and barreled toward the side of the building where Monica had just been. The attackers weren't giving up. They were going after her until the bitter end.

*Please let her have run into the woods.*

There was a grassy area all around the old building where it had once been cleared for extra parking. But close to that, the ground became uneven and tilted downward into a wash. And there were trees everywhere. The van's engine was already making a grinding noise and sounded like it was no longer moving.

Were the bad guys already out of the van? Would they be waiting for him to chase after them?

He ran back into the roadhouse, through the dining and dance area and into the kitchen, where Ryan lay slumped on the floor, moaning. He continued out the back door, where he sprinted across a cracked concrete patio with a couple of broken-down picnic tables and beyond a swath of wild grass into the cover of the woods.

He looked through the dappled light, desperate to see a flash of color that matched Monica's clothes. Or even Jason's clothes. Anything to let him know where the two of them had gone. Because right now, he assumed the two of them were together.

Moving fast downhill through the shadowy forest, he quickly found the lowest part of the wash where it had a relatively even bottom and he could move at a fast pace. Years of search and rescue training had taught him that when people in the wilderness had no other plan, they typically moved downhill and took the path of least resistance.

He raced along, all the while scanning his surroundings, looking for broken tree branches or trampled plants or anything that might indicate which way he should go. He turned the volume down on his radio so the thugs wouldn't hear any of the transmissions. He'd given dispatch all the information they needed. At this point he was intent on rescuing Monica.

The assailants weren't visible, but he could hear them to his right and a little behind him. They were noisy in the forest and either not realizing or not caring that their voices carried as they spoke to one another, talking about which way Monica might have gone.

If these were the two men who'd attacked Monica at the cabin, they'd already demonstrated that they could track her in the woods. He sped up, feeling a rush of relief when he saw a small pine sapling with a recently snapped branch.

He stepped out of the wash into the cover of thicker trees and knelt to make himself less visible.

There, ahead of him behind a large deadfall tree, he saw leaves flutter where nothing else was moving. Maybe Monica was hiding back there.

The attackers had gone silent. There'd been no sound of a vehicle engine starting up, so Kris knew they hadn't driven away. Maybe they, too, had seen the wash and were following it right behind him.

Drawing closer to the downed tree lying on the ground, he caught a glimpse of Monica's booted foot. "It's Kris," he said as he approached, barely louder than a whisper. "Stay down," he cautioned. "I think they're nearby."

He rounded the fallen old tree, relieved to see Monica. He dropped down to the ground beside her. She was holding a tree branch, looking understandably wild-eyed. Beside her, Jason clutched a multipurpose tool with the blade extended.

"Are you okay?" Kris whispered.

Monica nodded. "I was worried you'd been shot."

"I'm fine." Kris could see a dark red mark on

the side of her face. It looked like she'd been struck, and he pressed his lips together and felt a knot in his gut. Drawing in a steadying breath, he turned toward Jason.

"Have you got a plan?" Jason asked.

"Stay hidden until help arrives. Cops are on the way." What else could they do? Training and instinct combined with combat experience prodded him to take the offensive and go after the bad guys, but that could put Monica in greater danger. So they would wait.

As he lay there on the ground, Kris's senses were heightened. Not only was he looking and listening for the approaching criminals, but he was almost overwhelmingly aware of his determination to protect Monica. Keeping her safe was more important than his own safety. He glanced at her, admiring the determined set of her features. She'd been through so much, and she'd done everything she could to help her parents. She didn't deserve to be lying here in the dirt, fearful of losing her life.

The sound of snapping twigs behind them sent Kris spinning to face that way while still staying as low as possible. He pointed his gun in the direction of the sound.

Monica had also turned around, gripping her

tree branch with both hands. Jason positioned himself with one foot and one knee on the ground, as if ready to sprint forward if needed.

The snapping noises sounded again, but they weren't very loud. Were they getting closer? It was hard for Kris to tell. Maybe if they were quiet, the thugs would continue on their way. He listened closely, and then he heard the much louder sounds of crashing branches coming from the direction of the roadhouse, the direction they'd originally been facing.

Kris spun back around in time to see the heavyset assailant moving forward, gun drawn. The criminal began shooting as he moved closer to them.

"Get down!" Kris called out. As the only one of them with a gun, he was the only one who stood a chance of stopping the shooter's deadly charge.

Kris fired a shot, and the thug ducked behind a tree, disappearing into the shadows only to suddenly reappear to Kris's right. The attacker was nearly to Monica, reaching out as if to grab her as she lifted the tree branch to defend herself. Kris had no choice but to shoot the man, his bullet striking him in the lower arm.

The creep grunted in pain and dropped his

gun. When he reached down to retrieve it, Jason sprinted forward to grab it. As they grappled over the weapon the second thug dashed out of the woods from a different direction.

Kris looked up to see the skinny criminal pointing a gun at him.

Before the assailant could fire, Monica swung her tree branch and hit him in the face. Kris jumped the guy, quickly pinning him to the ground with his knee in the center of the man's back. He glanced over to confirm that Jason had the injured attacker's gun so that both men were subdued.

Sirens sounded in the distance.

"Grab my radio," Kris said to Monica. "It's attached to my belt. You'll need to turn on the volume."

For a moment, she just stared at him. He wouldn't blame her if she was in shock.

"It's going to be okay," he said calmly. "But I don't want to let go of this jerk and risk him getting away. We need to let the officers know where we are."

Monica reached for the radio, her hand trembling from the fear and adrenaline still overwhelming her mind and body. She keyed it, identified herself, stated that she was with Officer Volker, and then began describing what had happened and where they were located. In the distance it sounded like the initial responders were pulling into the roadhouse parking lot. Seconds later, she heard the cops reporting their arrival to dispatch.

Shifting her gaze between Kris and Jason as they kept control of the criminals, Monica offered up a silent prayer. *Thank You, Lord.* The long list of specifics she was thankful for would probably be in her mind for the rest of her life. For now, she was mostly grateful that she and Kris and Jason were alive.

She heard the sound of breaking branches and snapping twigs coming downhill in their direction. When she saw a flash of dark blue police uniform between the trees, she called out, "We're over here."

It seemed as if the three Cedar Lodge police officers, and Kris's deputy friend Dylan, appeared in an instant, guns drawn, looking grim.

"Kris, are you and Monica all right?" Cole was behind them carrying his paramedic gear, with an EMT in tow.

"Yeah, we're okay," Kris said. "I shot one of the perps in the arm, so you'll need to assess that. There's also an assailant inside the road-house who was knocked out. The last I saw of him, he was unconscious."

*Ryan Fergus.* The shock of discovering he'd betrayed Monica hadn't yet worn off. Beyond being a surprise, it made no sense. He'd had so many opportunities to kill her. Why hadn't he completed the job?

The EMT and one of the cops headed back up toward the roadhouse to see after Ryan.

Watching them go, Monica felt her initial sense of relief dissipate. There were still so many unanswered questions about everything, not only Ryan's role in the attacks. Did Jason Mul-hern actually have information entrusted to him by her father? Would it be significant enough to make any difference, and would it be enough to stop the Boyd Sierra syndicate from hounding her? And why would her father hide whatever it was with Jason and not with his own daughter? In the end, capturing these two goons—and Ryan—solved the most pressing issues of the at-tacks against her, but it didn't solve everything.

She turned to Kris, who had just handed over the assailant he was restraining to one of the officers. He locked gazes with Monica, and for a moment they just stared at each other. And then he smiled.

Heartbreak radiated from Monica's head to her toes. Kris Volker was such a good man. A kind and loving man. A *family* man. And yes, a handsome man. Everything she'd ever wanted.

But wrapping up this particular battle didn't put a complete end to the danger that had been stalking her. There were still potential threats looming on the horizon and unanswered questions. And that meant if she pursued a relationship with Kris, she would put not only him in danger, but potentially his son and his parents, as well.

Kris stepped forward through the tall grass and wrapped his arms around her.

Despite her earlier determination to hide her feelings, she clung to him in return, giving herself this moment to feel the reassurance of his muscular arms wrapped around her and the comfort of hearing his heart beat steadily in his chest.

She looked up at him and he leaned down for a kiss, the tender press of his lips against hers making her heart skip several beats as a warm blush raced over her skin.

They'd survived this together. The creeps

who'd tried to kill her the night she'd first arrived in Cedar Lodge and several times after were in custody. That was something to celebrate. She would relish the accomplishment and let herself enjoy the feeling of being held in Kris's arms for the moment.

But she couldn't deny reality forever. That would be too dangerous.

"We did it," Kris said.

"Yes, we did."

"I was afraid I was going to lose you."

She looked away, knowing exactly what that declaration meant. The words were right there on the tip of her tongue, ready to be said back to him. She cared about Kris. *A lot.*

"I was afraid for you, too," she finally said, regretfully pulling away from him. "That was some kind of Wild West shooting, cowboy. Both when we were up there in front of the roadhouse and then afterward when we got ambushed here, too."

She forced a wide smile on her lips and offered a challenging lift of her chin. She would shift the tone from a romantic connection to something more like friends.

"Thanks." Kris's expression seemed to sadden before her eyes. She'd hurt him by not responding the way he'd wanted her to. An ache formed in her chest that she quickly identified as sorrow for having seemingly rejected him. She reminded herself that he would look and feel infinitely more hurt if a new set of criminals came after her and Roy got caught in the crossfire.

She really did love Kris. It was impossible not to. And because she loved him, she wanted to protect him and his son.

The injury to the kidnapper Kris had shot was not life-threatening. Cole and an officer helped the man up the incline toward the flat ground at the roadhouse where the criminal could be put into an ambulance. The other bad guy had already been handcuffed and walked up to one of the patrol cars.

"Well, this kind of thing has happened enough times that I already know I'll have to give an official statement, and you'll need to write a report."

Kris nodded. "You are correct."

As Monica started to walk beside him back toward the roadhouse, she moved unsteadily. "My knees are wobbly. I'm not sure why."

"Residual adrenaline," Kris said.

He offered his hand, and Monica clasped it.

Didn't matter what her brain told her about shuttering any romantic feelings she had for him. Her stubborn heart did a little dance in response to his touch anyway.

She tightened her hold on him, knowing that it wouldn't last for long. Her time in Cedar Lodge was just about wrapped up.

## Chapter Fourteen

Kris pulled his SUV into the police station parking lot the following morning with Monica seated beside him.

They'd been here yesterday afternoon, giving statements about the kidnapping and shooting at the roadhouse. But after a couple of hours during which all three perps were uncooperative and information was not forthcoming, Chief Ellis had told them to go back to the ranch with the assurance that he'd fill them in on the pertinent details when he finally had them.

Early this morning, Kris had gotten a text from Ellis asking Kris and Monica to show up for a meeting with Detective Campbell and Jason Mulhern at ten o'clock. Kris and Monica had not spoken with Mulhern after the arrests at the roadhouse when he'd been taken aside to give his own account of what had happened.

"I don't know why, but I feel nervous about

this," Monica said as Kris parked and killed the engine. "I guess because the last twenty-four hours has been so overwhelming. It's hard to process all that's happened."

"If you want me to take you back to the ranch, I will," Kris offered. It would probably scare her if he told her he would do pretty much whatever she wanted if it made her happy. Even let her cut him out of her life and head back to Reno.

Monica had been quiet and emotionally distant when the two of them were at the police station yesterday. Even more so after they'd gone back to the ranch. She'd avoided him beyond making polite conversation when the family sat down for dinner.

Kris knew something of the struggle to process difficult emotions, and it was plain that Monica still had a lot to work out about her dad and her relationship with her mom.

In some ways, Kris would always be emotionally processing the sad passing of his late wife. He didn't want to forget about her. And he was determined to talk about her around Roy so that his son could have some feeling that he *knew* her. The boy's actual memories of his mother were sparse and mostly impressions rather than specific events or even what she looked like.

Could Monica accept that? He didn't know. But he would like to. And if he were going to be selfish, he wanted her to stay in Cedar Lodge. For his own sake as well as his son's.

After nearly losing Monica—more than once—he finally understood to the core of his being that the best thing he could do for his late wife's memory was to continue on with a full life for their son as well as himself.

And he wanted to explore what a full life with Monica might be like. He'd never met another woman like her. He'd been afraid that if he got seriously involved with someone, he would compare her with his late wife. And he had made the comparison, a little bit, at first. But the more he knew Monica, the more she was completely her own woman in his mind. And surprisingly, he didn't feel guilty about his growing feelings for her.

He hopped out of the truck and walked around to open Monica's door for her. Habit had him glancing around, just to make sure it was safe.

Inside the police department, they headed for the largest conference room. Chief Ellis and

Detective Campbell were there, along with Jason Mulhern.

"We've already interviewed Mr. Mulhern," Chief Ellis said to Monica. "He told us there were some things he had to say, and he wanted to make sure you heard them."

"I'm curious to know what information you have about my dad," Monica said to Jason as everyone was seated. "But I'm a little bit afraid to find out what it is, too." She turned to Kris with a faint smile and rubbed the side of her head. "I *still* don't remember what my dad said to me during that prison visit before the car crash. I guess I never will."

Jason turned to Monica. "I want you to know that I wasn't intentionally trying to hide anything from you." He glanced at Ellis for a moment as if wanting to confirm that the chief acknowledged what he was saying. "I own my business," he continued, addressing Monica. "I've got a family. Four children. My wife says I'm a workaholic, and maybe I am. I don't keep a close eye on the news, so I didn't know you were attacked here in town. When I saw you at the resort, I didn't realize you were Hunter Larson's daughter. You were a kid the last time I saw you." He offered her a slight smile. "Ryan

Fergus contacted me and asked if I'd meet him at the roadhouse and give him an estimate on what it would cost to pave the parking area and the patio in back, so I did. One minute we were talking in the kitchen. The next I was waking up after he'd apparently knocked me out and tied me up. Later, he carried you in and set you on the floor. Between overhearing him on his phone mentioning Monica Larson and looking at you lying there, I realized who you were."

"Who are you to my dad?" Monica asked. "Why would he hide information with you instead of me? What did Ryan have to do with this?"

"When I was younger, I was desperate for money, and I did some stupid things," Jason said with a shake of his head. "After I got out of lockup, the only job I could get was cleaning up the gym at the resort. I met your dad, and we'd chat a little once in a while. That's when I saw you and your mom sometimes. It's not like we were best buddies, but when I told him my story, your dad said encouraging things to me. Stuff that gave me hope that I could turn my life around."

Kris glanced at Monica and saw her smiling softly. At least she would get to hear one good thing about her dad today. It sounded like he was basically a kind man.

"Anyway, Mr. Larson and I met a few times for lunch over the years when he was in town." This time Jason turned his gaze to Kris and Detective Campbell and then to Chief Ellis. "I was shocked when he contacted me a little over a year ago and told me I was the only person he could trust with some information. That he was going to prison. Maybe for a long time."

"He didn't trust me?" Monica said sadly.

"He didn't want to put you in a position where you'd have to lie or hide anything for him," Jason said. "He told me I could opt out of holding on to the information for him, but I felt I owed him, and I wanted to help. It was simple enough. He'd set up an email account with several dummy folders with random stuff in them, and one significant folder had all kinds of important information in it. He gave me the email address and the login and password. He told me that you or your mom might come to me one day and ask for it, and I should help you."

"Of course you took a peek at it," Kris said.

Jason shook his head. "I was tempted to at first. But when my wife told me about Mr. Larson being in the news down in Reno—we kept track of him over the years since he'd been so kind—I realized he was connected to organized crime and I decided to stay out of it."

"So, what was in there?" Monica asked.

Jason gestured toward Detective Campbell. "That's what I'd like to know. I told the police last night how to access the information your dad had hidden."

"There's a lot in there about Boyd Sierra Associates," Campbell said with a broad smile. "Banking information. Summaries of many of their illegal operations. Names of members and descriptions of crimes they committed. Government employees and justice system employees on their payroll. Photos and voice recordings. I've shared it with my colleagues in federal law enforcement who have been working with me since the initial attack on you in Cedar Lodge. Specifically because of the suspected organized crime connection. They'll be combing through everything and getting ready to take down the top-level bad guys."

"What about Archer Nolan, my dad's *friend* who swooped in and swept my mom off her feet?" Monica's tone was steeped in sarcasm. "Is there anything about him in there?"

Campbell nodded. "He's in the notes. There are photos of him with known thugs. Voice recordings of him giving directions for crimes. A warrant is being issued for his arrest."

"Should be enough to convince your mom," Kris said. He knew how important that had been to her.

She sighed heavily. "I hope so." Then she turned to Chief Ellis. "So, what's next? Do you think the Boyd Sierra people will keep coming after me? Especially after some of them start getting arrested. They'll know you got the information because of me, and they'll be furious."

"The ones who are most furious will be the ones who are locked up," Campbell interjected. "And the ones who aren't locked up will be busy lawyering up and covering their tracks."

"What these kind of people do isn't some impulse crime spurred by emotion," Ellis added. "They're coldhearted businesspeople. Chasing you down or hiring someone to do that would be a waste of resources and make them vulnerable to further charges. I think they'll be busy for a while. There won't be anything for them to gain by coming after you at this point. Their goal in attacking you was to prevent all of this criminal information from getting to the authorities. Obviously, it's too late for that now. As a practical matter, I think they'll cut their losses and leave you alone."

Kris watched Monica's face for a reaction, hoping she'd turn to look at him. If this case was closed, at least for her, did that mean she would consider staying?

He thought he'd already indicated clearly enough how he felt about her. But maybe he needed to do more. *Say* more. They'd been through so much together under such stressful circumstances that they hadn't been able to focus on each other personally.

"What about Ryan Fergus and the two thugs who have been after me since I arrived in town?" Monica asked the police chief.

"Ryan quickly got a lawyer, and they immediately negotiated a plea deal. So he's already talking. He claims he was never employed by the Boyd Sierra people, but he'd met a few of them while working on buildings owned by them when he still lived in Reno. Part of the reason he and your dad chatted was that, professionally, they traveled in some of the same circles. When you showed up in town and the attacks started, he had a feeling they might be connected to your dad being on the outs with the Boyd Sierra syndicate.

"It took him a few days to connect with someone in Reno because he wasn't part of their organization. He didn't try to contact their hit men in town, but not because he was afraid of them. Actually, he was in competition with them. He wanted to grab you first and get paid for delivering you to them. They were willing to pay him if he got to you before their thugs did. So he formed his plan, which included making it look like Mr. Mulhern had kidnapped you and then been murdered by unidentified assailants. Ryan intended to have it appear to the authorities that he'd been kidnapped and physically assaulted, too.

"In the end, the thugs in town had been contacted to meet up with Ryan at the roadhouse and take custody of you."

"And kill me."

Ellis nodded. "Most likely. I think the only reason they didn't kill you at the roadhouse was that they were afraid of getting shot by Kris."

"Are either of the two assailants talking?" Kris asked.

"Not yet," Ellis said. "I'm sure they're more afraid of their employers than they are of going to prison." He got to his feet. "Now, Campbell and I have got a lot of work to do." He turned to Kris. "You'll be back to work your regular shift tomorrow, right?"

"Yes, sir." Now that he thought the family ranch would be a safe haven again, he was anxious to get his son and bring him home. He glanced at Monica as everyone stood and began exiting the conference room. It would feel more like a home—for him and his son—if Monica were there, too.

He had to know if she would give him and Roy a chance. If she would linger in town long enough to find out if the connection they felt was real.

"I'll book an airline ticket back to Reno and then get a rideshare out to the airport," Monica said as Kris made the turn onto the drive up to the house at the Double V Ranch.

When they'd gone past the nearby road up to the Bennett cabin a few moments ago, she'd expected to feel that familiar twist of anxiety in her gut and the reminder of all the danger she'd been subjected to. But she hadn't. Instead, surprisingly, she'd felt a sense of completion. At least when it came to the dangerous Boyd Sierra Associates.

There were still so many things in her personal life that remained disordered and chaotic. She *had* to go back and take care of them. Even though what she most wanted in her life was right here beside her. Kris Volker was a man with deep roots in Cedar Lodge, Montana. He wasn't going anywhere.

She held her breath for a moment, hoping that Kris would ask her to stay. But he didn't. Trying to focus on gratitude for all he'd done rather than disappointment that he didn't want to pursue a relationship with her, she pasted a quivering smile on her lips and said, "Thank you for all your help." She kept it short so there was less chance of her bursting into tears.

"What do you need to do back in Reno?" he finally asked.

They were parked now and getting out of the truck.

"There's a lot of stuff I've got to work out with both my parents." Maybe by now her dad was allowed to have visitors again. And the conversation she'd have with her mom when she arrived back in town would be complicated, to say the least. "I don't know how grateful my mother will be for all of our efforts after Archer is arrested. I'm confident in time she'll appreciate having her criminal fiancé unmasked, but at first, not so much."

"And what happens after that? After you get your *stuff* worked out?"

He held his hand out to her. It was a small gesture physically, but it was big in meaning since it appeared to express a desire for a romantic relationship now that their working partnership was over.

Monica felt a cautious flutter in her heart as she took his hand. She was afraid to hope, but she couldn't help it.

To her surprise, rather than walking to the house, Kris led the way to the stables and the nearby corral where several horses languidly nibbled grass. She hadn't seen much of the stables—or the ranch at all, really—because people had been trying to kill her. It had seemed sensible to stay inside the house when she wasn't out with Kris trying to get her awful family predicament sorted out.

"What happens after I talk at length with my mom and dad?" she responded. "I don't know. I figure out how I'm going to restart my life, I guess."

He laughed softly. Confused, she turned to look at him.

"Restarting your life sounds like a good thing. It's something I've needed to do for a while, too. In some ways, my life stopped when Angela passed away. And it didn't start again until I met you."

Her heart pounded almost painfully in her chest. When she'd thought her investigation was putting his family at risk and that it might have reached a dead end anyway, she'd told him it was time for her to go. He'd asked her to stay, and she'd rebuffed him. She'd known it had hurt him, but it had felt like the right thing.

After the dust had settled at the roadhouse yesterday and the three perps were arrested, she'd had second thoughts about leaving. Fact was, she realized she wanted to continue to have Officer Kris Volker by her side. All the time. But she figured she'd ruined her chance. And that weighed heavy on her heart.

She felt at home on this ranch. Kris's parents had been so kind to her, and his friends Cole and Dylan had joked with her a little and treated her like a buddy even though she'd known them such a short time.

What she wanted for the rest of her life, what

she'd always dreamed of, was right here. Most especially in the form of the man standing beside her at the corral railing while they watched the horses.

She looked at her hand, still clasped by his. She understood what he was indirectly asking her, just like she'd understood so much about him almost from the beginning. It seemed only fair that she take her turn and admit her true feelings. She gathered her courage. Her life had been on the line, and now she had to willingly put her heart out there.

"I need to leave for a while," she said, giving his hand a squeeze. "But I'd like to have a reason to come back."

He turned to her, lifting an eyebrow. "Would you, now?"

She'd made herself vulnerable and he was going to tease her? *Really?*

But then he let go of her hand and wrapped his arms around her instead, holding her loosely and gazing down at her face. "I want you to have a reason to come back here, too." He lifted a hand to her cheek, trailing a finger along the line of her jaw.

Monica sighed deeply, the fluttering sensation in the center of her chest combining wonderfully with a feeling of safety and certainty she hadn't felt in a long time.

Kris leaned down to gently press his forehead to hers. She pulled him closer, and he moved in for a lingering kiss that was warm and tender. Monica held on to him for several moments after the kiss ended, enjoying the sheltering feeling of his arms wrapped around her and the solid certainty of him holding her tight.

"Being associated with the daughter of a mob accountant could harm your career," she said hesitantly. "Are you sure you're okay with that?"

He replied with a half smile. "People can always find a reason to be critical if they want to. Beyond that, anybody who cares about me or works with me knows what kind of man I am. And when they see us together, they'll figure out what kind of woman you are, too."

"And Roy?" She knew his little boy was his number one priority, as he should be.

Kris's smile broadened at the sound of his son's name. "Roy has a big heart. He looks for reasons to like everybody. He'll be back here at the ranch later today." He shook his head. "My kid sounds like he doesn't want to leave his grandparents' house, and I'm a little sore about that." It was clear by his tone that he was joking.

His smile faded slowly, and his tone became more serious. "For his sake, we'll need to take things slow. Which might be a nice change since things have moved so fast from the moment I first saw you."

That might seem like it lacked excitement to someone else, but not to her. After so many betrayals—from her father turning out to be a criminal to Ryan Fergus attempting to exchange her for payment from the killers—a slow and steady building of trust sounded like just what her heart needed to heal.

"Slow can be good," she said after a moment.

"I agree." He leaned in for a slow and toe-curling kiss.

Monica had no doubt that as soon as she got things wrapped up in Reno, she'd get back to Cedar Lodge and the Double V Ranch as fast as she could.

# Epilogue

*One Year Later*

"I love you," Kris said, his dark blue eyes filled with emotion.

"I love you, too." Monica closed her eyes as Kris leaned in for a kiss, enjoying the moment. She'd spent the day savoring moments. It began with putting on her wedding dress and was followed by walking down the aisle and then seeing Kris in his tuxedo waiting for her with Roy in a matching tuxedo beside him. After that she'd felt humbled by the solemnity of the moment when she and Kris exchanged rings and the pastor had pronounced them husband and wife.

After the kiss ended, Kris moved until he was beside her, his arm across her waist. They were standing at the end of a pier at Bear Lake. The wedding reception was being held at a lakeside venue across the street from the church where they'd exchanged their vows. Esmeralda had provided the flowers from her own gardens. And now everyone was relaxing, enjoying themselves.

Roy in particular seemed to be having an especially good time. He let out a squeal, and Monica glanced over to watch him and his cousins and young friends race around and play in the lakeside grass. The sounds of mellow instrumental music could be heard. It was dusk, and stars were visible in the purple-blue sky. Fairy lights twinkled from the venue's outside dance floor as well as the railings on the pier. Cole and Dylan were both dancing with their dates for the evening.

For the first few weeks after the attacks on her a year ago, Monica had experienced brief flashbacks of the most harrowing moments. But the occurrences had slowed, and the accompanying anxiety had eased until it finally vanished. Spending lots of time with Kris and his friends and family had helped with that.

So had getting a chance to talk with her dad and tell him about the events. She still hadn't recovered her memory of that pivotal meeting with him at the prison, but he did confirm that he'd told her to contact Jason Mulhern in Cedar Lodge, Montana. She missed having her father at her wedding, but she was determined to focus on the future. And right now it looked especially good.

Monica's mom had been present when Archer Nolan was arrested. Once she got past the shock, she'd been appreciative of all Monica had done. Their relationship had gotten closer over the last year, and her mom was here now. While some of the relationships in Monica's life had been wildly irregular, she'd come to realize that all strong relationships came with problems and challenges and the need for forgiveness on both sides.

A small Christian school in town had been willing to hire Monica on Kris's and Esmeralda's recommendations. That had allowed Monica to rent a small apartment in Cedar Lodge while she and Kris—and Roy—all began to get to know each other better.

Monica and Kris had fallen in love quickly, but they'd given it time. Mostly for Roy's sake.

Monica now had the kind of life she'd dreamed of. It had needed time to take shape, but it was here now. She finally had the love and the family and the sense of belonging that she'd always longed for.

She and Kris remained standing, side by side, until it almost felt as if they'd melted together into one person, both helping to keep the other strong and upright. After a few moments, Monica realized she heard a commotion behind them. She and Kris turned around. The wedding guests on the outside dance floor were waving at them and yelling their names.

"Hey, come on back and dance!" Cole called out to them with his hands cupped around his mouth.

"Kris has two left feet, but you're stuck with him now!" Dylan added.

*The dance!* Between greeting guests and keeping track of Roy and then eating some dinner and cutting the cake, they hadn't had their first dance yet.

Beside her, Kris was laughing. "You realize you're stuck with all of us now, right?"

She leaned in for a quick kiss. "I wouldn't have it any other way."

Hand in hand, they strode from the end of the pier toward the lake's grassy shore. When they got there, Roy raced over to tackle his dad.

Kris picked him up and set him on his shoulders. Then he reached for Monica's hand.

Monica smiled, feeling the warmth of the moment settle in her heart. Here was *another* moment to savor. And she had no doubt there would be many, many more such moments to come.

★ ★ ★ ★ ★

# Ambush In The Mountains

Mary Alford

MILLS & BOON

**Mary Alford** is a *USA TODAY* bestselling author who loves giving her readers the unexpected, combining unforgettable characters with unpredictable plots that result in stories the reader can't put down. Her titles have been finalists for several awards, including the Daphne du Maurier, the Beverly, the Maggie and the Selah. She and her husband live in the heart of Texas in the middle of seventy acres with two cats and one dog. Learn more about Mary at www.maryalford.net.

Visit the Author Profile page
at millsandboon.com.au for more titles.

He healeth the broken in heart,
and bindeth up their wounds.
—*Psalm* 147:3

## DEDICATION

To those who are free and to those who are captive
still. We pray. Continually and always. Until all are
free from the bounds of human trafficking and
those responsible are brought to justice.
Because no life is for sale!

*Ambush in the Mountains* deals with topics that some readers
may find difficult, including human trafficking.

# Chapter One

Something soft and wet touched her face. It was so cold. Snow. Happy memories made her smile. Just for a second, she was back on the farm with her *mamm* and *daed*. Younger *bruders*, Peter and Eli. Winters were always such fun in her Amish community. After chores were finished, she'd take Peter and Eli to go ice skating on the pond near their farm. *Mamm* would make them hot chocolate.

But this wasn't Ohio, and those memories weren't real any longer. At times Summer wondered if they'd ever been. Maybe her brain had created happy memories in order to deal with the nightmare.

This was real. *He* was real. His angry face replaced the sweetness in her mind. With a gasp, Summer's eyes flew open. Darkness surrounded her. Waking so quickly left her disoriented. Her breath fogged the air in front of her. So cold. It had been snowing for a while—the white flakes covered her clothes and hair.

She hadn't meant to fall asleep. Just rest her aching body for a little while. The hours of tramping through the woods, stumbling and sometimes falling, had taken their toll. She'd only wanted to take a break for a second and had ended up wasting valuable time.

"No, no, no." Summer struggled to a sitting position, difficult with the added weight of the baby. Being eight months pregnant made it difficult to do most things.

How much time had passed? *Please let it be only a few minutes*. The sky above revealed nothing but pretty white flakes, yet her sweatshirt was covered in snow.

Summer shivered from the cold and listened over the panic beat of her heart. Were those voices or the noises of the woods?

It had barely been daylight when she'd slipped out of the house while Ray and the others slept. Many hours had past, and a storm had moved.

*I'll find you and when I do, I'll kill you.*

He'd warned what he'd do to her if she escaped. Ray had bragged about the ones who tried. He'd told her he'd buried them where no one would ever find them.

She had to go. Had to keep moving. With the help of the tree she'd rested beneath, Summer slowly rose, her swollen feet shooting pins and needles up her legs. The mere effort of standing exhausted her. How could she possibly go any farther?

The temptation to give up and accept her fate was great. After all, she deserved it.

"No!" She wouldn't feel sorry for herself. She'd escaped. Summer touched her burgeoning midsection. She'd saved her baby's life by running. Now was not the time to give up, because it wasn't just her—she had to think about the baby.

According to Ray, Summer had aged out long ago and was all used up. She wasn't the type of girl his clients would request anymore. They only wanted young women between the ages of thirteen and twenty. Instead of letting her go like he promised, he'd forced her to "handle the other girls' needs" as he'd put it. That meant keeping them calm and cooperating. Ray believed that if the other girls saw her still working for him at twenty-six, they'd think the same was possible for them eventually.

But that wasn't the case at all. Summer wasn't

working for Ray because she had any other choice. It was out of sheer survival.

She'd memorized as many of the girls' names and faces as possible to help find them in the future. Ray had gotten so used to having her around that he'd become careless with keeping his secrets. She knew things and she'd managed to download a lot of Ray's files onto a thumb drive, including one folder labeled simply "Barn," which she hadn't been able to open.

She'd promised herself that when the opportunity came, she'd escape and tell the police everything. But that was before Ray told her he had cops on his payroll. Her world had collapsed that day. There was no one to turn to for help except herself.

When Ray found out he was going to be a father, he wanted to get rid of the baby...until he'd figured out he could get money for the child.

There was no way she'd let Ray sell her baby.

He'd thought he broke her will to escape long ago, but he had no idea what she'd do to save her baby.

Drawing in a handful of breaths, Summer started walking again as fast as the exhaustion in her limbs would allow. By now, he would know she'd run. He'd send men to look for her because he couldn't afford to let her live. She'd been part of their operation for a long time. She knew things. Terrible things.

Summer. The name he'd given her didn't fit, but she'd been Summer for so long she barely remembered the woman she was before. Elizabeth Wyse was an innocent eighteen-year-old Amish girl who met up with the wrong person while on *rumspringa*, and her life had changed forever. She'd lost her family and everything she held precious, and had been plunged into a seedy world of human trafficking for more than eight years.

Tears she hadn't allowed herself to release for so long scalded her cheeks, and she swiped them away with an angry hand.

Before escaping, Summer had hidden the thumb drive in one of the walls of the living room. It was at the house where Ray and the other members of the ring stayed along with the girls. It would be bad for her if Ray found out she'd copied his files.

More noises behind her confirmed that what she'd heard earlier wasn't simply sounds of the woods. She jerked in that direction. Someone was coming. She'd wasted too much time rest-

ing and now they were close. There was no
time for self-pity. She imagined Ray's angry
face and it spurred her on. If he caught her,
he'd hurt her badly.

*Gott, I need Your strength.*

Her body felt lighter as she broke into a run.
Up ahead the woods thinned out. Lights appeared. Different from a flashlight. They were
much bigger. Car headlights. She'd reached a
road. A vehicle was coming. *Please let it be help
and not him.*

Stumbling, she kept her focus on the headlights. If she could reach the car before they
found her...

She half slid, half tripped out onto the road,
her breathing coming in ragged gasps. Summer
turned toward the vehicle. It approached much
faster than she imagined.

As she stared at the growing headlights, she
wondered if the driver would see her in time.
She held on to her baby as the truck continued
to barrel down on her.

Her legs gave out and she dropped to her
knees, unable to find the strength to stay standing. Would she and her child die here? For years,
she'd prayed for death, but now she wanted to

live. Wanted to be the mother her baby deserved. She didn't want Ray to write her ending.

Axel Sterling stomped on the brake pedal and jerked the steering wheel hard to the left—away from the woman in the middle of the road. The headlights captured her frightened expression. Why wasn't she moving?

"Don't let me hit her." The woman's swollen belly had him begging God for help. He'd killed enough in his lifetime. Most had been enemy soldiers. She wasn't.

"Hang on, Camo." The Belgian Malinois that had been his constant companion was tossed against the door as the car skidded across the pavement. The dog whimpered. "Sorry, buddy." Axel grabbed for him and scooted him closer. He'd do his best to protect his friend.

The brakes caught and locked. He could smell burning rubber. Axel let the dog go and grabbed the wheel with both hands, worried the truck would flip.

"Come on!" he yelled and fought to keep from barreling off the side of the mountain and to certain death. He white-knuckled the steering wheel for several more yards before it came to a shuddering stop.

Axel blew out a big shaky breath and held up his trembling hands. He looked over his shoulder. The woman had managed to stand. She'd turned toward his vehicle.

What was she doing out here in the first place with one of the worst storms of the season moving in? He had no business being out here himself. Axel's only excuse was, he'd thought he had time to reach the store, grab his needed supplies and get home before the brunt of it hit, which wasn't supposed to be until dark. He'd been wrong. The storm had turned the late afternoon to night before he made it home and the skies had dumped snow at an alarming rate.

Axel opened the cab door. Camo's full attention was on the woman. He barked aggressively, as if realizing there was more to the situation than simply saving a frightened young woman.

Camo had been a scout and patrol dog for the military until he retired and Axel had taken him in. The canine soldier had experienced a lot of danger in his lifetime. The hackles raised on his back confirmed that whatever was happening here was going to be bad.

The woman's frightened eyes went to the dog. She seemed to shrink away from the threat she perceived Camo represented.

"Stay," Axel told the dog and because he'd seen combat himself and knew sometimes the most innocent of things were not, he tucked his handgun beneath his coat and hurried over to help the woman who was noticeably pregnant.

"Are you hurt?" he asked when he reached her side. She instinctively put space between them. The reaction made him wonder if it was because of Camo's barking or him? What was she doing out here alone in weather such as this? She wore only a sweatshirt and jeans and no coat despite the cold. Her feet were clad in flip-flops. Not exactly appropriate attire for this weather. Was she running from someone who had hurt her?

Axel slipped out of his heavy down jacket and started to place it around her shoulders, but she backed farther away, her dark eyes filled with terror.

"I'm not going to hurt you," he said gently. "I want to help. Are you lost?" She certainly didn't appear to be a hiker in those clothes. Her blond hair was soaked from the falling snow. Her cheeks sunken. Eyes hollow and filled with a dread that went much deeper than being lost in the woods.

He took a step back. "My name is Axel."

Past her shoulder, he spotted four flashlights weaving through the woods.

She jerked around. "Oh, no. Please, you can't let him take me."

Axel tugged the coat tighter around her. "Then come with me." She hesitated only a second before following him to the truck, still keeping her distance.

Two feet from the back, a sound he hoped to never hear again had him grabbing the woman and pushing her toward the cover of the truck. Gunfire. The people with the flashlights were shooting at them!

"Get down low," Axel warned and steadied her when she stumbled. He whipped his handgun out and returned fire, forcing the shooters to take cover.

"Hurry." Axel grabbed her arm, ignoring the way she tried to pull free. He ushered her inside the cab before jumping in beside her. Camo, who had ducked at the sound of the gunshots, growled low immediately on alert by this new person.

"It's okay, Camo. She's a friend." He scooted the dog over and glanced at the woman who he wasn't anywhere close to being convinced was a friend. Who knew what she'd gotten herself involved in that had intruded in his peaceful existence? Yet the soldier in him wouldn't let him leave her to those wolves.

He fired the truck engine up and shoved it into Drive before speeding away. Several shots came far too close. Axel swerved around a curve and was grateful that the roads weren't slick enough to send them flying down the side of the mountain. He glanced in his rearview mirror, thinking they'd escaped the shooters on foot. But multiple sets of headlights assured him they had vehicles waiting near the road.

Staying alive was his only priority right now. He'd question the woman later once they were safe.

"Put your seat belt on." The words came out a little too sharply. "There's a small road up ahead. If I can make it without being spotted, we stand a chance at losing them."

He glanced at Camo. The dog watched the stranger with open distrust. "Camo, get on the floorboard."

The canine grumbled but hopped down at her feet while keeping a close eye on her.

Once she'd secured the seat belt, Axel killed the lights including the interior ones. She screamed as the world around them went pitch-black.

"It's okay," he said. "I don't want them to see where we're going." He needed to put space between them and those headlights so their attackers couldn't pick up the change in direction.

He rounded another curve in the road and squinted through the windshield at nothing but darkness. "The road is on the right-hand side and it's hard to see."

She leaned against the door as if to put as much distance between them as possible.

Axel realized he didn't know what to call her and asked her name. When she didn't respond, he looked her way again. She wasn't giving away any answers, and her huge brown eyes were glued to him as if she expected him to attack her at any minute.

It was going to be difficult to get her to open up to him when she didn't trust him. He let the questions go for now. "Can you help me watch for the road? It should be coming up soon."

Another look confirmed she still clung to the door, but she leaned forward, searching the darkness past the windshield. Strands of her wet hair fell across her face. She tucked it behind her ear. It was then that he noticed a scar across her hand. Someone had hurt her. The men coming after her? What was going on?

"There." She pointed to what could barely be considered an opening.

"I see it." Axel slowed enough to make the turn. The truck slid sideways, and the woman screamed again.

Camo looked up at him without concern. They knew each other and trust had been well established.

Once he had the vehicle straightened and under control, Axel watched the rearview mirror. "So far, I don't see anyone." He slowed enough to traverse the pitted road without causing damage to the truck. After they'd traveled a while he said, "We should be safe enough to use the lights again." Axel flipped them on and the countryside around them illuminated.

His mind mentally calculated what route he'd have to take to reach his place. This road intersected with one of the main county roads. If he took it, he could eventually backtrack to his home.

While Axel tried to untangle what he could possibly be dealing with that would bring armed men after this woman, a far more disturbing thought had him wondering if they had the ability to track the vehicle through his license plate. If so, his mountain sanctuary would be compromised.

Axel wasn't one to do anything without a plan. To formulate one, he needed answers from her now.

"Who are those men back there?" He waited for her to speak but she just stared at him with those huge dark eyes.

"Look, I'm trying to help you, but I don't understand what's happening."

If possible, she shrank even farther away from him.

"At least tell me your name," he said, unable to keep his frustration out of his tone.

Camo, as if sensing her distress, seemed to accept her into his space. He licked her hand. The gesture had her staring at the dog for the longest time before a smile spread across her face.

Nice going, boy.

Camo might have been a soldier in his previous career, but he'd adjusted okay to civilian life, and he enjoyed attention on his terms. The dog had a way of sensing when Axel's darkness came upon him, and he'd usually do something as simple as lie down at his feet or lick his hand like he had hers.

"My name is Summer." Tears glistened in her eyes as she spoke in a shaky voice.

A small victory in Axel's opinion. "Nice to meet you, Summer. You're safe now."

She scrubbed her hands across her face. "I'm not. He's coming after me."

"Who are you talking about?"

She set her chin and refused to answer.

Axel tried another tactic. "I only want to help." That she didn't believe him was clear. "Where are you from? I can help you get back home." He wondered if he could reach out to her family to let them know she was safe before going to the sheriff to report the crime.

She shook her head. "No. That's not possible."

"Why not?" He looked her way when she didn't respond.

"Because... I—I can't go back there. Not like this." She touched her swollen belly.

Axel sensed she wasn't going to tell him anything more about her past.

"How far along are you?"

Summer hesitated for the longest time. She didn't trust him. He believed there were few people she did trust.

"Eight months, I think," she said in barely a

whisper. "When he found out I was pregnant, at first he wanted to get rid of the child, but then he figured out a way to sell the baby. I couldn't let that happen."

Disgust rose in Axel's throat. His hands tightened on the wheel. "Who is this man?"

She wiped at her face once more. "I don't know."

Was it true or was she somehow protecting this monster?

Axel let go of his misgivings. "We'll figure it out. Right now, we need to put as much space as possible between us and those shooters."

She turned away and stared out the side window. Her story was going to be horrendous when it came but she wasn't ready to share it yet.

Axel's attention returned to the bumpy road ahead. He of all people understood how hard it was to return to the life you left behind. He'd been struggling to find his place since he'd returned from the war. He'd gone home and wanted to fit back into his old life in Colorado but nothing about it felt right anymore. And so, he'd traveled around the country looking for someplace to feel like he belonged. Then Brayden told him about Elk Ridge, Montana.

When he'd ended up in almost total isolation on a cabin atop a mountain in the Tobacco Root Mountains, Axel realized this was where he felt the most normal. He'd bought the place right away.

The army had given him a purpose. He'd excelled at becoming a sniper. Life was going well. He'd realized he'd found someone to love for the first time in his life...

Axel shut down that way of thinking before the darkness could set in. Summer needed his help. He had a purpose. A mission. That he understood.

The blackness in his rearview mirror made him grateful. At least for the moment, those dangerous men hadn't caught the diversion.

Camo settled on the floorboards with a har-umph and closed his eyes, content with the peace of the moment. In war, a soldier learned to take advantage of the downtimes because you never knew when they would disappear.

The woman seated beside Axel was far from being at peace. Her eyes were glued to the side mirror with good reason. Those men wouldn't be coming after her with such force if she didn't pose a threat.

A pit formed in his stomach. It warned him

this was far from over. They weren't going to simply let her get away and give up.

"Are you hungry?" he asked and remembered he'd purchased some snacks for the ride home. "There's some chips and bottled water in the bag there. Oh, and a couple of candy bars." His guilty pleasure was the occasional binge on junk food. "I realize it's probably not the healthiest of snacks," he said when she hesitated. "Especially for the baby." But it was all he had.

She opened the grocery bag and dug out the chips. "I'm starving." She tore the bag open and munched several chips before holding the bag out to Axel.

"No thanks. You enjoy." He'd make a more nutritious meal once they reached the house.

Now that his pulse had finally returned to normal, he began working out the details of getting to his cabin without taking any of the main county roads. Unfortunately, he couldn't avoid the one coming up.

Once they reached the cabin, he'd call the sheriff on his satellite phone. Everything would be okay. So, why didn't it feel that way? Why couldn't he relax?

Because of the fear written all over her face, and the truth he knew in his gut.

# Chapter Two

She wiped her cheese-dust-covered fingers on her jeans. With the gnawing hunger abated, Summer drank deeply from a water bottle.

When she'd managed to escape while Ray and the rest of his people were sleeping, Summer had one thought and that was saving her child.

Ray had given her more freedom since she'd begun working for the ring. She wasn't locked away at night like the other girls. Ray believed she'd do whatever he told her to…even give up her baby.

Unfamiliar tears stung her eyes once more. They sickened her because they represented weakness. The things she'd been forced to do had made her numb on the inside. Yet as much as she tried to admonish the tears away, they wouldn't stop coming. It seemed as if all those pent-up emotions had been set free and she couldn't will them away.

"Are you okay?" The man who said his name was Axel asked as if he really did care. There was concern in his blue eyes.

"I'm fine," she said in a tone that sounded harsh. She owed him hers and her baby's lives, but that didn't mean she trusted him. Summer had learned men hurt you. "I— I'm sorry I haven't thanked you for saving me."

"It's okay and you're welcome. I'm glad I came along when I did. Where were you coming from?" He waited for an answer she wouldn't give before asking again, "Who are those men, Summer?"

She flinched at the sincerity on Axel's face. Ray had pretended to care about her and had her believing he loved her. He'd convinced her to leave her home and everyone she trusted and then he'd hurt her badly. Forced her to do things she didn't understand and had seemed unimaginable. The love he'd confessed evaporated, and the real monster remained in all his cruelty.

She was just one of many young women Ray had misled into trusting him. Like her, the other girls had been every bit as convinced he meant those words of love until he'd gotten them away from their families and anyone who could help them.

"Your family must be worried about you." Axel glanced over. "If you tell me where they live, I can help get you home." She almost believed him. Summer stared down at the dog, who had opened his eyes at their brief exchange. Camo seemed to realize she needed a friend and licked her hand again while she petted his head.

Eight years. Had it really been more than eight years since she'd turned eighteen and made that fateful mistake to talk to Ray even though every instinct in her body warned her not to.

But it was at the end of her *rumspringa*, and she wanted to try new things. Be daring.

"My place is on the other side of the mountain. You can warm up while I call the sheriff. He can reach out to your parents and let them know you're safe."

"No—you can't. No police." Ray's bragging came to mind. He'd told her that he had people in places to protect his operation, and then he'd looked at her and she believed he'd meant he had people in law enforcement working for him.

"Why not?" he said gently and touched her arm. Summer immediately jerked free and put as much space as she could between them. She hated this reaction, but after the things she'd been forced to endure because of Ray, she'd developed an aversion to being touched.

"Sorry." Axel quickly removed his hand, those sharp blue eyes held hers, waiting for an explanation she had no plan to give.

Axel apparently gave up on getting answers and focused on the road while Summer returned to that dark place once more. In the beginning, Summer believed Ray loved her. She couldn't imagine her luck at finding someone as nice to love her back. When he'd suggested leaving the Amish way of life for good, it had seemed impossible to consider, but the more time she spent with him, the more she wanted a life with Ray no matter what it cost her. She'd find a way to stay in touch with her family.

Summer had snuck out late one night after her parents and *bruders* had fallen asleep and met Ray on the road near their house.

She'd giggled when he swept her into his arms. Summer never imagined being so happy. And then…

Everything changed. He'd taken her to a

run-down farmhouse and told her what was expected of her. When she'd cried, he made her believe everything was her fault. He'd demoralized her to the point of thinking her parents wouldn't want her back. He was all she had.

Summer clenched her hands into fists until her jagged nails dug into her palms. Keeping a clear head was all that had helped her escape Ray.

As the time grew closer to when she'd deliver the baby, Summer knew she had to make her move. She'd been so terrified. When she'd reached the front hall without being spotted, Summer had swung the door open. The creaking sound it made almost had her giving up. But then she thought about her baby, and she'd run.

She'd snatched a steak knife from the kitchen the day before because it was all she could find to use as a weapon. Having it made her feel somewhat protected.

"Camo likes you."

She didn't need to look at Axel to realize he was watching her, probably trying to draw her out of her shell.

"And Camo doesn't like just anyone," Axel was saying.

As if to bring the point home, Camo laid his

head in Summer's lap. She couldn't not smile. The dog reminded her of her family dog, Pepper. She'd loved that dog. Was he still alive after so long?

Tears struggled to be set free and she bit down hard on her bottom lip until she tasted blood. A coping mechanism she'd used to get through all those horrific experiences. If she ever truly let go of her guard, she'd be crying for days.

Summer patted the dog's head and felt inside her jeans pocket where the cold metal of the knife gave her some sense of being in control.

Axel slowed the truck to a stop, forcing her attention to him.

"What are you doing?" She searched his face, waiting for him to reveal his true self.

"There's an intersection coming up. I'm worried."

She understood. Ray and his evil people weren't likely to give up so easily. "What should we do?" She forced the words out.

Summer so wanted to trust this man who had rescued her, but after everything she'd gone through, it was hard to make that leap.

He looked behind them. "We can't take the chance of returning the way we came. Eventually, those men will circle back. If they have any knowledge of the countryside, they'll know about the upcoming intersection. Wait here. I'll take a look." He got out and started walking down the road in front of them, the headlights picking up his sure steps. Snow covered his dark blond hair and plaid shirt. Summer glanced down and realized she still wore his jacket. It must be freezing out and yet he hadn't asked for the garment back. A simple act of kindness like this surely was genuine.

When he rounded the bend in the road and disappeared from sight, fear pressed in on all sides. Summer stroked the dog's fur with one hand and held on to the knife with the other. She counted the seconds, another way of coping when a situation became too much for her to get through on her own. She'd count.

One minute passed. She kept counting. At five minutes he reappeared, and she breathed out a relieved sigh. Camo barked his happiness when Axel got back in.

"I don't see anything. The road that intersects is one of the main county roads. Thankfully, we don't have to be on it too long."

He looked at her—waiting for a response she couldn't give—before he put the truck in gear and started slowly down the road. As he neared the intersection, Axel shut off the lights once more. The darkness was terrifying.

"So far so good," Axel said almost to himself. He rolled to a stop at the sign and looked both ways before turning left.

Summer watched the side mirror. It couldn't be this easy. She knew better. Ray had taken great pleasure in telling her about what he'd done to the girls who thought they could escape him, and it had been brutal.

If he found her, Ray would make her pay for leaving and he'd kill Axel for helping her.

Axel braked hard. Summer grabbed the door handle to keep from being thrown forward despite the seat belt.

"What is it?" She looked his way, but Axel was staring straight ahead. Her attention flew to the windshield and the darkness beyond. Lights glowed almost as if suspended in midair. A heartbeat later, Summer realized it was interior car lights. Soon, the rest of the vehicle became clear as her eyes adjusted. The driver had pulled the car sideways onto the road to block any oncoming traffic.

"It's him. It's Ray." The words flew out before she could stop them.

"Hold on." Axel shoved the truck into Reverse and flew backward until they'd reached the turnoff road. Once he was even with it, he hit Drive and sped down the road.

Summer looked behind them. "They're coming after us." More than one set of lights now followed.

Axel handled the vehicle skillfully. "We've got to get off the road. I noticed a place a little farther up."

She wasn't sure what he meant but she didn't see a viable way to leave the road that didn't sound frightening.

"From what I could tell, the vehicles behind us are all cars," Axel said. "They won't be able to make it through the rough terrain. At best, it will take a four-wheel-drive vehicle like this."

At best.

He slowed enough to put the truck in four-wheel drive before edging into the woods on Summer's side.

"Help me watch for obstacles," he told her. "We can't afford to use the lights and have them pick up our location."

Tree branches slapped the sides of the truck as Axel did his best to maneuver through them.

Summer leaned forward trying to see in near

impossible conditions. "Wait, there's a large tree coming up on my side."

Axel squinted through the windshield. "I see it." He inched the truck past it while barely keeping from clipping another on his side.

Camo whined as the vehicle rocked back and forth and climbed precariously over downed limbs and tree stumps. The dog jumped up onto the seat and fixed his attention on Axel.

"It's okay, buddy." Axel patted his friend's head.

But was it?

Summer spotted lights in the side mirror and jerked around. "They've reached the place where we went off-road."

Axel glanced quickly at the rearview mirror. "They're trying to follow." The move clearly caught him by surprise. "They won't make it far, but still…"

The lead car's headlights entered the woods.

Summer covered her stomach with her hands. Her baby. She hadn't realized what it was like to love someone she didn't know until she'd felt the baby kick. That was when Summer had known—she wasn't going to let Ray sell her baby. She couldn't let him capture her again.

She'd fight with everything she had to keep that from happening.

"We need help, Summer, but unfortunately my sat phone is at my place." Axel explained that a sat phone connected the phone to networks by radio link through satellites orbiting the Earth instead of cell towers. Apparently it proved to be more reliable. "Without it, we have no way to call anyone." He looked her way. "In other words, we're on our own."

A shiver chased down her back. If they reached his cabin safely, he'd want to call and report the attack. She couldn't let that happen. Couldn't risk Ray's mole within the police force alerting him to where she was.

The lead car's headlights caught up with the back of the truck.

"They're gaining!" Summer couldn't control the panic in her voice.

"Hold on to something." Axel punched the gas. With one hand she grabbed the door and with the other she tugged Camo closer.

Behind them, a rapid succession of loud pops had her turning.

"Gunshots." Axel eyed her. "They're shooting at us again. Get down."

Summer did her best to get out of sight, but it was hard with the baby.

The bullets reached them and bounced off the truck bed.

"How are they getting past all that debris?" Axel said in amazement.

One bullet hit the back window and it shattered on contact. Cold air and snow whipped in. Axel automatically ducked then rose enough to see over the dash.

"What's happening?" Summer yelled over the noise of gunfire.

"There's more than one car in the woods now." From his low stance, Axel glanced behind them as the truck climbed over downed trees and kept moving at a steady pace.

A sharp pain shot through Summer's midsection, and she let the dog go to grab hold of her baby, closing her eyes.

Axel saw her expression. "Are you okay?"

"It's just a cramp. I need to sit up." She did and prayed the pain would pass. After a few deep breaths it abated. "I'm okay."

Axel blew out a breath and nodded. Another round of shots had her jumping.

"They're too far to reach us now," he said.

"It looks as if the lead car is stuck. We have the advantage. Let's keep going."

Summer kept her attention behind them for the longest time. Had they really escaped?

Axel's hands relaxed a little on the steering wheel. "I haven't seen an attack like this since I left Afghanistan."

He was a soldier. That explained the way he'd protected her. Summer shifted a little to study his profile. His strong jaw was covered in slightly darker stubble. A small bump on the bridge of his nose had her wondering if it were natural or if his nose had been broken at one time. He wore such a serious look on his face.

Axel turned in time to see her watching. "Are you feeling better?"

Summer nodded and faced forward. The darkness beyond the windshield was filled with unknowns just like her life. "Where does this lead?" she asked in an unsteady voice.

Axel cranked the wheel hard to miss a fallen tree that had come up almost too quick to dodge. "That was close. I'm going to have to turn on the headlights. The woods are getting thicker."

He flipped them on and the world in front of them came out of the darkness. Summer got her first real look at what Axel had been fighting. The floor of the woods was littered with trees in various stages of decay.

"There's a small road coming up once we top this ridge and head down the other side." He pointed to the incline they were heading for. "It will connect to another that leads to my place up on the top of the mountain."

A shiver of fear returned along with her distrust. Axel had saved her life and he seemed to be genuinely trying to help her, but Ray had appeared believable as well. She'd thought he'd cared about her until the real Ray showed up and the truth became clear. He'd kidnapped her and forced her into prostitution.

"Is one of those men the father?" Axel asked quietly. "Is that why they're coming after you with so much manpower?"

Saying the words aloud made what she'd become real. How could she tell him the things she'd been forced to do to survive? The men who hadn't bothered to wonder how old she or the other girls were. Or if they were being treated badly. After she'd aged out, Ray had kept her for himself. She'd hated those times. He had asked to hear stories about growing up

Amish in Ohio and then he'd make fun of her simple ways.

She'd thought when she became pregnant, things would be different. Ray might actually look forward to having the baby, but nothing could be further from the truth.

She hung her head without answering.

Axel's deep blue eyes bored into hers. "What's really going on, Summer."

If she told, he'd look at her the way the other men had, as if she were worthless. Once more tears of frustration blurred everything in sight. Would there ever be a time when she didn't feel like nothing?

"Hey, it's okay," he said gently. "No matter what you've gone through, everything is going to be okay. I'm not going to let any of those men hurt you again."

Wouldn't it be nice to believe him? Summer scrubbed her hand over her eyes and glanced at Camo, who appeared to be watching her. The dog laid his head in her lap again and she lost a little of her heart to him. She choked out a laugh, the sound of it foreign. She hadn't laughed in a long time. It gave her hope. Maybe it was possible to survive Ray and find her place in the world again.

★ ★ ★

Though she didn't say it, Axel believed Summer had escaped from a human trafficking ring. He couldn't imagine the things she'd endured, probably from a young age. She couldn't be more than in her mid-twenties.

Every time he made a move, she shrank away, putting as much distance between them as the truck's cab would allow. He'd tried to assure her she could trust him and finally resorted to showing her.

At least one car was disabled. He'd counted three sets of headlights before. Axel tried to remember how many had chased them after he'd saved Summer.

"It looks as if it's stuck." Summer had seen the same thing he had.

Axel grunted an answer. He didn't want to tell her as much, but he was worried. She'd mentioned one name. Ray. If he was calling the shots like Summer's reactions seemed to confirm, then for whatever reason, they weren't going to give up so easily. Those men had come after her with guns blazing. Summer was important enough for them to kill to get her back. Axel had his handgun and the shotgun he carried with him but that was it.

"Can you shoot?" he asked, the question clearly surprising her.

"I've never fired a weapon, but I can learn."

Would he be making a mistake arming a frightened amateur who clearly didn't trust him? He'd hate for her to turn the weapon on him out of some misguided attempt to protect herself because of what'd she'd survived.

"Why do you ask?" she pressed when Axel's thoughts ran a mile a minute.

He decided they both needed to trust each other and that meant him telling her what he suspected would happen when they reached the road.

"I'm afraid there may be men waiting for us." He watched the horrified expression that had only just begun to evaporate return in full force.

"There must be another way out. I can't go back with him."

"There isn't," he told her. The alarm on her face was clearly justified. Behind them, several men had flashlights and were coming after them on foot. He had to act fast. Sitting still would allow the pursuers time to catch up.

Axel killed the lights and jerked the wheel to the right. "We can't use the lights if we stand a chance at escaping. I'm not sure if this is the best way to go since it will basically take us back to the road where they were waiting for us before."

Summer looked behind them. "Do you think they'll figure out which way we're going?"

He'd made a promise to himself to tell her the truth no matter how bad. "Eventually. I'm just hoping not before we have the chance to get away."

Summer returned to petting Camo as if it gave her comfort. Camo didn't mind. He'd developed a softness for her. Axel was glad for the distraction his pooch provided. He needed time to think of what to do.

What was happening went way beyond anything Axel felt equipped to deal with despite his training. He'd been living in almost total isolation in his mountaintop haven trying to heal.

He'd lost so much to the war. With only two months before being discharged, Axel realized he'd fallen in love with his childhood friend and fellow soldier. He'd planned to tell Erin about his feelings when her unit was attacked and she was killed. He never got to tell her how he felt about her. Instead, he was left with a broken heart that wouldn't heal. He'd become the shell of the person he was today, seeking out his own company because he wasn't fit to be with anyone else. Except Camo.

Axel's only neighbors were the Amish couple who lived down below him. They ran a rescue mission for animals as well as a farm. Abram took in all sorts of animals including retired dogs of service. That's where Axel had met Camo. They'd clicked from the start. Both had seen things in battle they wished they could forget.

Axel carefully weaved his way along through the massive amount of trees that were dead due to beetles. He kept his attention on what little he could see beyond the hood and tried to stay ahead of wrecking the truck. They couldn't afford to lose their only means of transportation. The snow was the first of the fall, but it was dark, and the temperatures were below freezing.

Not to mention armed men were hunting them down.

He hit the brakes, startling Summer and Camo. He'd barely missed a massive tree trunk by inches. Axel pulled in a shaky breath and let it go. "Sorry. That was close." He backed up. "I can't see a way around it from here. Sit tight. I'll have a look." The men with the flashlights were still some distance.

"No, wait." The fear in her voice stopped him.

"It's okay," he said gently. "I'll be right back. I'm just going to see if I can find a way past the tree." He waited for a long moment. She'd been through unimaginable things. A little patience was necessary.

"Okay," she said softly.

"You're safe, I promise." With that assurance, he got out and carefully closed the door so as to not alert anyone below.

Bitter cold nailed him the second he left the protection of the truck. This storm had hit quickly. According to all weather reports, it would arrive late in the evening. He'd managed to grab the necessary groceries for himself and Camo, plus feed for the two mares and handful of cows at his place. Axel had been a couple miles outside the nearest town, Elk Ridge, when the gray foreboding clouds had let loose, and snow mixed with ice had Axel worried if he'd make it home without incident. He'd thought the weather would be his only problem.

The downed spruce was much bigger than he could move by himself. He had a winch on the back of the truck, but the time it would take to move the limb, not to mention the sound, proved too risky.

He walked a little way to the right, searching for a better spot to take the truck through. The choices weren't great, but Axel found one place that might work.

He returned to the truck. The fear on Summer's face hadn't eased any.

"Can you move it?" she asked.

He shook his head. "No, but I found another way around."

He put the truck in Reverse and backed up. "It's going to be tight."

The brake and backup lights were probably giving away their location. A quick look behind confirmed the men had discovered their change of direction. "They know where we are." He shoved the truck into Drive and headed toward a narrow opening between trees. Sparks flew from both sides as the tree trunks scraped across the vehicle.

Camo barked aggressively at the noise. As soon as the truck cleared, Axel pushed it as fast as he dared while once more Summer clutched the door.

"The road shouldn't be much farther, but I'm worried," he admitted. "They know the direction we're going by now. There might be cars there to cut us off."

He kept the speed up until the road came into view. No matter what he found waiting for them, he couldn't slow down. Because Axel was convinced the terror he'd seen in Summer was real and he didn't want to find out what those men would do if they caught her again.

# Chapter Three

"There's a fence!" Summer screamed. "We can't make it through."

"We don't have a choice. We're going through it."

Summer grasped Camo and couldn't look at the barbed wire fence coming up too quickly. She kept her attention on Axel. He didn't appear afraid. Why didn't he appear afraid?

The front of the truck struck the gate hard. The resistance it gave to the speeding vehicle was only temporary but enough to throw Summer forward and then back when each strand of the wire snapped free.

Axel's attention was on the stretch of ditch that would prove as difficult as anything they'd survived so far.

"No. Axel!" she shrieked when the truck hit the ditch and vaulted into midair. Before Axel had time to warn her to hold on, it slammed onto the road hard. A loud pop had her attention jerking behind them expecting another shootout but there was nothing.

Summer closed her eyes and prayed hard.

*Help us. Please, help us.*

Axel brought the truck to a shuddering stop. "I think we may have blown a tire. Let me check." She wanted to warn him it was too dangerous. What if Ray had men waiting in the woods? What if those who had been following them caught up?

"We're safe for now," he said, reading her thoughts. "I don't see any sign of them. I'll only be a second." He hopped out and checked. It didn't take long before he returned and put the truck in Drive. "The front right tire is blown. But we'll have to keep going."

"Won't it destroy the wheel?"

"Probably." He tossed the word her way before putting the truck in gear. It sounded as if it were riding on a wooden block as Axel wrangled the injured wheel down the road.

Summer couldn't believe the things that had happened in just a short amount of time. Ray was determined to find her. He knew the things she'd seen. Enough to put him and his crew away for a long time. She had no doubt of the outcome if it came to keeping her alive to get the money for the baby or silencing her before she could reveal what she knew.

"Uh-oh."

Axel's words had her wrenching his way. His focus was behind them.

A set of headlights appeared. An innocent traveler or…?

"I can't afford to drive too fast on this bad tire." He ran a hand through his hair. "I think there's a smaller road coming up on the right. Unfortunately, it's going to take us farther away from my place." He kept his attention on the lights. "I just hope we make it before they catch us."

*Thunk, thunk, thunk.* Every turn of the blown wheel thumped along her stretched-thin nerves. She stared out the side window to keep track of the lights. They'd never make it. The vehicle was closing in on them at a rapid rate.

Soon, inches off their bumper, the driver struck the truck hard, sending them all forward in their seats.

Summer couldn't hold back the scream.

Another ram had Axel fighting for control as the truck careened toward the ditch.

"They're trying to run us off the road. I'm going to try something."

Summer anticipated his warning to hold on and grabbed for the door again.

He sped up enough to put space between them before he jerked the wheel hard to the left and the truck swung sideways then faced the approaching car. Axel turned the lights on bright.

When it became apparent what he had planned, Summer prayed all the harder.

Axel slammed the heavier truck into the oncoming car. The impact sent them spinning on the slick road. Axel hit the brakes and managed to stop despite the disabled tire.

The car driver's panicked expression flashed before them before he slammed into the ditch hard, lodging the vehicle nose first.

"They're getting out." Four men climbed from the vehicle and opened fire. Summer automatically ducked low as the bullets bounced off the cab and Axel spun his truck around and drove away as fast as possible.

"At least we won't have to worry about them coming after us on wheels." He gave her a lopsided grin before telling her it was safe to sit up.

Summer rose and noticed the men were standing in the middle of the road. One appeared to be talking on a phone. "Axel, they're calling for help."

His attention shifted from the space in front of them to the men.

Once more, he shut off the lights. "We need to get out of sight fast." He drove for some distance before they reached a small opening on the right side of the road. "There's our turn. I don't think they'll notice."

The blown tire clearly made it difficult to steer the vehicle.

"We should be out of sight enough to use the headlights again." He flipped them on. As soon as Summer glimpsed the road in front of them, her unease returned. It was barely big enough for the truck to fit down and it didn't appear to have been used in a long time. The recently fallen snow covered the road undisturbed.

All the trust she'd built for Axel evaporated as memories of that night returned. Ray had taken her down a road like this one leading to that farmhouse and the beginning of her eight-year-long nightmare.

"Are you sure this is the way?" she asked uneasily.

Axel checked they weren't being followed before answering. "This is the road. I realize it doesn't look like much, but my Amish friends use it often. They took me down it once. Very few people know about it. Even if the men behind us are familiar with the area, they may not know about this road. As you can see, if you weren't looking for it specifically, you would never know it was there." His gaze softened as he held hers.

He had friends who were Amish. Summer clenched her hands to keep from showing any reaction. She'd lived eighteen years in the Plain world of Ohio in the Holmes Community.

Until her *rumspringa*, Summer hadn't known there was life beyond her family and the community. When she and Hannah, her friend, had gone through their "running around time," they started hanging out at some of the *Englischer* businesses around town.

She still remembered the first time she'd seen Ray. He'd looked so handsome and trustworthy. Ray had spotted them and come over. He'd flirted with her and Hannah before singling her out.

Summer told herself it was because he found her attractive. Now she knew the truth. Of the two of them, she was the most gullible.

"I don't know what you've gone through,

Summer, but you can trust me. I would never hurt you." Axel's sincere voice broke through the memories of that time.

Trusting Axel still didn't sit well with her, but it was her only option right now. He pulled the wheel hard to the left to avoid a pit in the road. "We'll have to circle back to my place. Unfortunately, there aren't any houses around with phones. There's an Amish settlement nearby but they don't allow phones." He said it as if she didn't know. The words fell like knives to her heart. What she wouldn't give to be back at her family home helping her *mamm* with the evening meal. Doing chores along with *Daed* and her little brothers, Peter and Eli.

Through the years, she wondered if they thought about her. Summer hadn't told anyone she was running away with an *Englischer*. She'd simply run away in the middle of the night. Did her family try to find her through the years? Did they miss her as much as she missed them?

"Here's our road," Axel was saying. Summer pushed those memories aside. She wasn't that girl anymore.

"How are you holding up?" Axel asked with another captivating smile. "The road was rougher than I remembered."

"I'm...fine." She'd almost said *oke*. Just for a second, the past had bled into her reality. The language of her youth still came easy enough. Ray made her speak it so he could laugh at her and call her simple.

"You live amongst the Amish?" she asked because she needed something to take her mind off everything she'd given up.

"I've lived near the small Amish settlement since..." He stopped. She wondered what secrets he had hidden. "My place is the last house up the mountain and some distance from the settlement, but there's one Amish couple who live close by." He looked her way briefly. "That's where I found Camo. He served in the military like me."

The dog watched him with wisdom that seemed to hint he understood exactly what Axel said.

She never realized dogs could be part of the military and told Axel as much.

"Oh, yes." Axel nodded. "They're used in all sorts of capacities from search and rescue, scout and patrol, guard and sentry as well as narcotics and weapons detection." He glanced down at the dog. "Camo, here, was a scout and patrol dog. According to Abram and Lainey, he was trained to work in silence in order to detect possible ambushes, snipers or other types of enemy attacks."

Summer was surprised. "What an amazing creature you are, Camo."

Axel smiled at her description, and she wished this moment of quiet reprieve could last forever. "According to what I've read about the scouts," he said, "they're a bit of an elite group among the military working dogs. Only dogs with both superior intelligence and a quiet disposition can be selected for this specialty. Scout and patrol dogs are generally sent out with their handlers to walk point during combat patrols, well ahead of the infantry patrol." He stopped. "Sorry, I'm probably boring you with so many details. Needless to say, I'm proud of Camo's service."

"Not at all." Summer was impressed. Though she loved their family dog, she wished she'd had one like Camo. Perhaps he would have helped her see the truth about Ray before she'd made the worst mistake of her life.

The familiar road to his cabin rose beneath the injured truck. It could barely be called a road actually. More like a path filled with gravel. He wondered how well the four-wheel-drive feature would work with the tire gone and on its rim. Under normal conditions, Axel was happy his place was two miles up the mountain and virtually inaccessible during the winter months except with his Jeep, which had snow chains on it.

"You live up here by yourself?" she asked.

Her distrust had returned, and he couldn't blame her. She didn't really know him, and they'd been thrown together in a difficult situation. He wanted to ask her the questions racing through his head but first he'd have to gain her trust. He just hoped there'd be time before the next attack because Axel had no doubt they hadn't seen the last of the assailants, and he needed to understand what they were up against.

His arms ached from forcing the truck to do as he wished. Once he got home, he'd get the tire changed and hope there wouldn't be any lasting damage to the vehicle.

As they drew closer to the top of the mountain, the path narrowed. On Summer's side there was a sheer drop-off that would mean certain death if one false move sent them over the side.

She grew increasingly uneasy watching the treacherous slope. Axel edged away from it for both their benefits.

"How do you get around in the winter?" she asked.

He told her about his Jeep. "It works well for traversing the snow."

The snow continued to fall heavier at this higher altitude, peppering the headlights. The storm appeared to be growing in strength. It was hard to see far ahead. He clutched the wheel tight. Beside him, Camo sat watching the familiar path.

"Almost home, boy," he said as he had through all the trips up the mountain he'd made with Camo.

The dog cast those soulful eyes his way. Every time Axel looked into them, he saw the battles Camo had fought for his country.

Axel edged around the last curve in the road. His place sat dark against the stormy backdrop.

He hadn't bothered with leaving lights on because he'd been certain he'd be back before the weather moved in.

He shook his head. He'd grown up in Colorado and was used to the weather in higher elevations. He knew storms could pop up quickly and it was best to be prepared.

The headlights spanned the cabin. Nothing foreboding appeared.

He parked as close as he could. "Hang on, I'll get the place unlocked and the lights on." Her huge eyes found him. She didn't want to be alone. "Why don't you and Camo come with me?"

He got out and went around to her side, opening the door. Axel held out his hand for her. Summer hesitated for a long moment before she clasped it and stepped from the truck. Once more her pregnancy reminded him that they'd be at a disadvantage if they had to escape on foot.

He quickly unlocked the door and ushered her inside, flipping on the lights.

The dying fire in the woodstove had burned down to embers. "Come in and get comfortable." He tossed some firewood on the embers and added crumpled paper until the fire caught.

"I need to check on the Jeep to make sure it's ready in case we need to leave quickly," he said once she'd slipped into the rocker near the fire. Axel brought her some socks and a blanket to warm her up. She understood what he hadn't said. In case the men coming after them found Axel's house.

"But first, I need to try and reach the sheriff."

"No, please, you can't," she said a little too quickly.

"Why not?" He had to know why she refused to go to the police for help.

"He told me he has people in law enforcement." Her huge eyes found his.

Axel had met the sheriff and several of his people. His good friend Brayden was on the force. He didn't believe any of them were on the take.

Her gaze pleaded with him. "Please, Axel. You can't."

By not reaching out for help, it would be just them, and he wasn't sure he could protect her against so many.

"All right. For now, I won't call them, but if it comes to it, we may not have a choice."

She dropped her hand. "Thank you."

"I'll carry in the groceries and then change the tire." He hesitated. "And then I really need you to tell me what's going on."

Her expression grew suspicious immediately.

"Summer, I want to protect you. To do so, I must know what we're up against."

She held his gaze for the longest time before she nodded. "Okay, we'll talk."

He smiled. At least he'd won a small battle.

Axel headed outside and brought in the couple of bags in the back seat. He reentered the house, saying, "As soon as I return, I'll make us something to eat."

Summer didn't answer and he stepped outside into the storm once more. The howling wind made it hard to hear anything at all. He returned to the driver's seat and pulled the truck into the barn he used to house the cows and horses in bad weather.

After he'd made sure the Jeep was ready for travel, Axel moved it around behind the house, then fed and watered the animals. While in the barn, he changed the destroyed tire on the truck.

For reasons he couldn't explain, his gut warned him to keep the truck inside the barn, which wasn't its normal spot. Though it was a tight fit, the cows had room to move about. He checked on the horses again before stepping out into weather that was getting worse by the minute.

Axel started for the house when a sound that

seemed out of place caught his attention. He listened but didn't hear it again. The wind?

After what happened, he couldn't accept it was anything as simple. He didn't believe the attackers' cars would make it up his mountain road but still, they were determined and would find a way if they realized this was where he'd taken Summer.

He couldn't go back inside without checking things out. Axel grabbed the old coat he kept in the barn and put it on. Treading carefully, he headed down the mountain while slipping and sliding at times.

As he walked, he heard the noise again. An engine! Fear quickly weaved through him. Just someone innocently driving down the road that intersected with his drive? Before tonight, he wouldn't have given it much thought.

He eased farther down until he could see the county road. Headlights crawled along it. Despite the storm, the passenger window was down, and someone flashed a light around. They were searching. Axel ducked behind a tree to keep from being spotted. The car hesitated at his driveway opening and Axel prayed the weather had covered up their earlier tracks.

He held his breath. Inside the car, snatches

of conversation came his way. One name had him frozen in place. His name. Whoever these people were, they had the capability of running his plates and had found out his name… like someone in law enforcement might do. Was Summer right about not trusting the cops? If that was true, who could they go to for help… No one. They were on their own.

# Chapter Four

Summer kept watch on the door as the minutes ticked by. So far, she'd counted off fifteen of them and still no sign of Axel. All sorts of dreadful scenarios flew through her head. Had Ray's people found him? Or worse yet, what if Axel wasn't the nice man he appeared to be? What if he worked for Ray.

She clutched the knife she'd brought with her in one hand and the armrest with the other, ready to spring into action at the slightest sign something was off. No matter what, she wouldn't let Ray take her again. He'd make an example out of her for all those other girls. And the evidence she believed she had on him would remain hidden in the walls of that old house. She wouldn't let Ray win. He'd taken enough. Summer thought about the other girls. She was so worried about them. Were they safe?

Somehow, she had to survive in order to save them and future victims.

She touched her midsection. "I love you, baby." Summer had no idea if she was having a girl or a boy. Yet, she'd gotten into the habit of referring to the baby as a girl. Seeing a doctor had been forbidden. They ask too many questions according to Ray.

An unfamiliar noise outside captured her attention. She sucked in a breath and shot from her seat. Camo, who had been lying at her feet peacefully, did the same. His attention pivoted from her startled face to the door. A second later, he lay back down in front of the fire. Surely the dog would be more worried if there were trouble coming.

She went over to the window but hesitated. If she opened the curtains, looked out and saw Ray, she'd fall apart. But she had to be brave for the baby. Easier said than done.

Killing the lights, Summer inched the curtains apart. Snow mixed with sleet peppered the window. Nothing beyond the weather could be seen. Summer blew out a breath. The storm was getting worse. So far, Axel had offered only kindness. Should she go look for him?

The dog whimpered. She swung toward

him quickly. Camo watched her with those keen eyes. Axel told her he'd once been part of the military. She couldn't imagine the things Camo had seen during his time there. But he wasn't concerned about his master. Perhaps she shouldn't be either.

"Okay. I trust you, boy." She flipped on the lights and returned to her seat, still clutching the knife. The dog licked her hand as if to say thank you.

"You're a good dog," Summer said with a little laugh. She rocked back and forth, the chair making a faint squeaking sound that seemed to be in sync with her heartbeat.

The wind outside howled like a wild animal trying to break into the house...or something far worse.

"He's not out there. You're free," she whispered to herself. "You're free." And she was. At least for the moment.

She glanced around the simple room that gave little away about its owner. Only the barest of furniture in the living room. A sofa and two rockers. The woodstove. And a chest in the corner of the room. It reminded her of the one in the living room of her home in Ohio.

*Mamm* had a chest just like it where she kept their handmade quilts.

Looking over her shoulder, she saw that a small dining room led into the dark kitchen. She couldn't make out much about it. She leaned forward and peered down the hall where a couple of doors led to other rooms.

Axel Sterling had chosen to live a simple life isolated from most human contact for a reason. What was that reason? His only companion appeared to be Camo. She sensed he was trying to escape his own kind of nightmares. If that were true, they had something in common.

A breath escaped her, drawing Camo's attention. Despite her worries, the dog made her happy. "It's okay, Camo. I'm just curious about your friend."

The dog grumbled before settling back into his position.

The baby kicked and she grabbed her belly. Her child was active. When she wasn't waking her up in the middle of the night with movement she was stomping on her bladder. Like now.

"There, there, little one. Everything's going to be okay."

Eventually the baby settled down. Summer

closed her eyes. She'd just rest for a moment until Axel returned. The wind continued to do its damage outside but soon became background sounds to memories of the farm and a simpler life.

At times, especially at night, she'd go there in her memories when things became too fearful. She could almost see her *daed's* face. *Mamm* and her *bruders* smiling around the table as they shared a meal together. *Daed* praying silently over their food. Both *bruders* roughhousing and sometimes kicking each other under the table. Summer trying to shush them...

The door flew open. Summer shot up from her chair, the knife poised as a weapon, eyes wild.

Axel stood in the open space, watching her wield the knife.

She sank back down, relieved, a heavy breath shooting through her body.

"Sorry, I didn't mean to startle you," Axel said. "The wind blew the door from my grasp."

She willed her heartbeat to return to normal. "No, it's okay. You didn't..." But he had and the tremor in her voice mocked her words.

"Are you warm enough?" he asked, ignoring the knife. The concern written on his face seemed genuine. He removed his coat and crossed to the trunk. Axel pulled out a quilt that reminded her of the many she'd helped her *mamm* complete. He placed it gently around her shoulders.

"Thank you." She did her best not to flinch when his fingers brushed her shoulder.

Axel slipped into the rocker beside her and petted Camo absently.

The frown on his face had her worried. "Something happened," she said.

He sat back and turned his face toward her. "Yes. I went down to the county road."

Summer's grip tightened on the arms of the rocker while she waited and prayed their location hadn't been exposed.

"There was a car out there," Axel continued. He told her about the window being down and the light searching. "They mentioned my name, Summer. They obviously ran my plates and know that I live somewhere down this way. But with the weather and the fact that I don't have a mailbox at the edge of my property, well, I don't think they'll be able to find us."

But she could tell he wasn't sure. He couldn't give her the guarantees she craved. Could they take that chance? "What if they do. Maybe we should leave."

His intense blue eyes skimmed over her face. "The storm's intensifying. A car like that won't be able to make it up the drive. They left and I waited to make sure they didn't come back. Chances are, they'll wait out the storm somewhere safe. It may not break until morning. We should be safe until then. It will give us time to figure out what to do next."

She wished she could believe his assurances. "What happens if we need to make a run for it? How will we get away?" She inadvertently clutched her swollen middle. The baby. She had to think about her child above everything else. If Axel's answer wasn't good enough, she'd find another way herself. The cost of going back to Ray was too great.

He slowly smiled. "I have a four-wheel-drive Jeep with snow chains parked out back. It can get us through anything." Axel hesitated and she believed she knew what he would say. "My good friend is a deputy. I know the sheriff and many of his people and I have to tell you, they're all good as they get. They aren't corrupt, Summer."

She twisted her hands together. "I can't take

that chance. Ray told me he had cops on his payroll. Cops as in plural. I'm sorry, I can't."

He slowly nodded. "All right, but to help you, I need to know what I'm up against."

Telling her story aloud would mean disclosing the whole ugly truth about how she was the one who had fallen for Ray's lies.

"Summer, whatever it is, none of it is your fault."

She clenched her hands into fists until she felt her nails biting into her palms. "But it is." She glanced his way and knew she had his full attention.

"Please tell me what happened to you," he said quietly.

She pulled in a breath and told him about how she had met Ray and how he'd made her believe she was special. "He asked me to run away with him." Summer couldn't believe she'd acted so recklessly. "I thought I loved him, and I believed he loved me, too."

"But he didn't."

Her mouth twisted. "No, he didn't. As soon as he got me away from everyone I knew, it became clear what was expected of me, and it had nothing to do with love."

The terrible things she'd been forced to do made her feel unclean.

Axel's expression was intense. "He's a human trafficker."

Summer hated those words. "Yes. He took me and several other girls to a house and forced us to do things for money. He told us if we ever left, he'd kill us." Thinking about that time and the innocent young woman she'd been back then had her fighting back tears once more. It was difficult sharing her story for the first time with anyone. It made her feel vulnerable. Would he judge her? See her as less-than?

The look on Axel's face held nothing but compassion.

Summer gathered the courage to tell him about the girls who had disappeared. "He used to brag about how he'd buried them where no one would ever find them."

A look of disgust crossed Axel's face. "What happened when he realized you were pregnant?"

Ray had allowed her a certain amount of freedom in her roll of working for his organization. She took care of the girls. Eventually, she even handled the books for him.

She shared Ray's plans to sell their child.

"I had to fight for my baby." Summer looked down at her belly and told Axel how she'd waited until just the right moment when Ray was sleeping. Ray was a night owl and stayed up until early in the morning. When he'd finally fallen asleep it was right around dawn. She'd slipped out of the house with plans to get as far away as possible before he noticed "I was so afraid he'd catch me before I got away," she said once she'd finished.

"You're very brave, Summer," he told her with what sounded like admiration. "I can't imagine what you've been forced to go through. I want you to know, you're not alone anymore. And I promise I'll do whatever I can to protect you from this Ray and his people. I hope that you'll trust me to know when we need to reach out to the sheriff."

She looked into his eyes and realized every single one of his words were true. "I do trust you." Her faith in him was a surprise. She'd long ago stopped trusting anyone. But he'd listened to her story—one she'd never told anyone—and hadn't found her lacking. He wanted to help. And she found she wanted to let him.

He slowly smiled. "Good. I'll check down the road again soon. In the meantime, you need something good to eat." He rose and started for the dark kitchen. For reasons she couldn't explain, she didn't want to be alone. Summer followed him into the kitchen while Camo padded after them.

He didn't question why she'd come. Just pointed to the table. "Make yourself comfortable. How about eggs, bacon and biscuits?"

She couldn't remember the last time she'd had anything substantial to eat. Before she ran away, the food supply at the house was almost nonexistent. Ray hadn't sent anyone to do the shopping in days. Her final meal there had consisted of a sandwich, some chips and water.

"That sounds nice. I can help."

He barely let her finish before he shook his head. "I've got this. You stay off your feet. You've done enough running around lately."

Summer settled into a chair. She wasn't used to kindness. It naturally made her a little suspicious.

"I'm not much of a chef," Axel said. "Usually, it's something simple like breakfast or the occasional steak or burger."

Real food sounded wonderful. She closed her eyes. A pan clanged, causing her to startle. Would there ever be a time where she could be at peace? As long as she was running from Ray, it would be impossible.

Soon, the aromas reminded her of the hours that had passed since she'd eaten that last handful of chips.

She'd been walking for hours when she'd finally stopped to rest and had fallen asleep under that tree only to awaken to the storm. She'd waisted hours of daylight by sleeping.

When Axel had picked her up it was late afternoon, yet the storm made it appear like night. She and Axel had spent hours trying to escape Ray's people before arriving at his home. It had to be close to ten by now.

Fresh-brewed coffee teased her senses. Ray hated coffee and wouldn't allow it in the house where they stayed. Most meals were prepared by Summer. After she'd aged out, she'd been allowed to eat meals with Ray and his men.

She tried to recall the last time she'd had coffee. Probably before she left the farm.

"Food's ready. I know it's not morning, but I hope you like breakfast. It's kind of what I'm good at fixing." The sound of Axel's voice, so unexpected, had her jerking toward it. "Sorry, I didn't mean to startle you."

She hated being so jumpy. "No, It's okay."

Summer stopped and drew in a breath. Once more, she struggled to free herself of Ray's influence. He was always there in her head, reminding her of the violence he could do.

At this moment, she was safe. Summer held on to that. She rose clumsily to her feet. At this late stage in her pregnancy, doing anything was hard.

"I'd like to wash my hands."

He pointed to the sink where there was soap and paper towels nearby. Though Summer had never been to a doctor, she calculated this to be late in her eighth month of pregnancy. More than anything she wished she had her *mamm* close to guide her through what was coming.

Axel stepped back to let her pass by as she returned to the table that looked handmade and well-worn.

"Do you want coffee…sorry, I'm not sure if you can drink coffee."

She hadn't been around too many women who were pregnant in the past. Summer had still been a child herself when her *bruders* came along one year after the other. She'd done her best to avoid caffeine during her pregnancy but occasionally slipped up when Ray brought home sodas.

"How about water instead." Axel went over to a cabinet and brought out a glass filling it from the sink.

"Thank you." She accepted the glass from him and pulled out the closest chair.

Axel poured himself some coffee and then brought over two plates before sitting across from her.

"Do you mind if we pray?" he asked with a little uncertainty.

She nodded without words. Prayers at her family home consisted of the silent prayer at meals. *Daed* ending it with an amen. Summer would pray for wisdom for the future while lying in her bed at night. Her father always ended their Bible studies with a prayer.

Axel bowed his head and closed his eyes. "Father, thank You. For allowing me to help Summer. For bringing us safely to my home. Protect us. Don't let those men find us again. Help Summer know she can trust me and help her to heal from what she's suffered. And, Father, protect her baby. Amen."

She quickly ducked her head when he opened his eyes. The prayer was a simple one and yet it brought tears to her eyes. Someone had prayed over her. She couldn't remember that ever happening before.

"Dig in. Oh, there's biscuits." Axel scraped back his chair and went over to the stove. He returned carrying a pan of warm biscuits. "Butter?"

She cleared her throat. "Yes, please." It felt strange having someone wait on her.

She buttered a biscuit and bit into it. The warmth and melted butter tasted delicious. It reminded her of *Mamm's* homemade buttermilk biscuits. She and her *bruders* would always sneak a couple while *Mamm* wasn't looking.

Soon Summer had polished off the biscuit and started on another.

The rumble of Axel's laughter drew her attention to his face. It was a handsome face. He had caring eyes. Dark blond hair that touched the collar of his sweater. He swept it back from his face often, almost as an unconscious gesture or perhaps a nervous habit. She certainly had her own ticks.

He smiled. It embodied kindness—a trait she'd almost forgotten existed. "I'll take a second serving as a compliment to my biscuit making skills."

She swallowed. "They're very good." Summer wiped her hands and then tucked into the eggs and bacon.

Camo nudged at her leg making his presence known. He looked up at her with a hopeful expression and she smiled.

"He loves bacon," Axel said. "Don't worry, boy. I have a few pieces for you." He set a bacon strip on the floor near the dog, who wolfed it down. "Pace yourself, my friend."

"He's a good dog."

Axel's attention returned to Summer. Those startling blue eyes left her feeling a little unbalanced. "He *is* a good dog. He and I have kind of helped each other through a lot."

There were layers upon layers of unspoken emotions behind those words.

"How long have you lived here?" She and Axel had been through so much already, yet there was a lot about him she didn't know.

"A few years—since I left the service." His hands tightened into fists on the table, then slowly relaxed. There was a story behind that reaction. Axel had seen darkness, like her. "I bought it from the Amish family who lived here before. They got tired of the cold and moved to a warmer climate." He skimmed the room.

"Personally, I love the cold and the isolation. It's peaceful."

Summer nodded then finished off her food without answering.

"Did you get enough to eat?"

She realized she'd been ravenous. Ray kept her fed but certainly not without hunger. "Yes, thank you."

Axel pushed back his plate and sipped his coffee.

She dropped her eyes to her empty plate. Axel had saved her life. Had protected her through several attacks that could have ended badly without Axel's skills. He had proven himself a good man. Still that little voice in the back of her head couldn't let her give her confidence completely. She'd made a life-altering mistake in trusting Ray. He'd said all the right words and made her feel as if she was the most important person in the world to him. And look how that had turned out.

His protective instincts increased every time he was eyewitness to the terror that seemed to have become part of who Summer was.

Axel's hands tightened around his coffee cup. When he thought about what she'd undoubtedly been through at the hands of the man she called Ray, all the anger he thought he'd buried with the man he'd once been resurfaced. He wanted to do bad things to this person who'd caused Summer so much pain.

But that was the old Axel. Now he prayed and trusted God to fight his battles.

Since he'd moved to Montana, a lot had changed about him. He'd found God. Gave Him all the anger and bitterness that had infested his heart after losing the woman he loved, because Axel didn't know how to deal with it himself.

Erin's unit had been attacked by enemy combatants outside of Kabul. Erin and her entire unit had died. Then Axel's world had collapsed. At that time, he thought he had everything figured out when he realized he'd fallen in love with his childhood friend. He believed Erin felt the same way about him. They'd have a wonderful future together with a house full of kids.

"I'm so embarrassed…" The softest of whispered words came from across the table. The past and the anger went fleeing. Summer needed him.

"Why? This isn't your fault. None of it."

She glanced his way for half a second. "It is. *I* left with him."

He waited for her to continue. She'd said she'd been a young naive Amish woman who thought Ray loved her. He'd gotten her away from her family and those who could protect her...then the true monster came out.

Summer didn't look at him once. When she told him about how Ray and the rest of his goons had used violence and threats against her family to get Summer—and probably many other young women—to submit to their will, he understood why she feared Axel. It was how she'd react to any man.

Axel's jaw tightened. "I'm glad you managed to escape."

She lifted her head. "I couldn't have done it without you. They would have caught me and..."

The horror she'd gone through broke the ice away from his heart. Axel knew then this was only the beginning of what he'd do to keep her safe. No matter what, he'd fight for her because so many others had let her down.

"What about your family?" he asked. "I know you don't want to reach out to the sher-

iff, but I could take you home if you'd like...
They love you and want you back, Summer."

She shook her head. "I can't."

He let the matter go for the moment. "Why
don't you stretch out on the bed and get some
rest. I'll finish up the dishes and then I'd like
to take another look around outside."

Right away the distrust returned.

"There's a guest bedroom down the hall.
You'll be safe there. If you'd like, you can get
cleaned up."

She searched his face for the longest time.
Probably looking for some hint that he wasn't
going to turn into Ray.

"I would never hurt you, Summer. I might
have an extra set of sweats you can use. They'll
probably be too big for you, but at least they'll
keep you warm."

She slowly let go of a breath and said tentatively, "That would be nice."

Axel was grateful for the small amount of
trust he'd earned. It felt as if he'd overcome a
huge hurdle.

"Great. I'll get them." He rose and went to
his room to retrieve the sweats. Outside the
window, the wind screamed its anger. The
storm appeared to be picking up still. It would

be impossible to hear anything coming up on the house. The thought made him uneasy. He would have no way of knowing if Ray and his people were close until they were right on top of the cabin.

Axel gathered himself. He didn't want to alarm Summer.

He returned to the kitchen and handed her the clothing and a second pair of his socks. "I'll just check around outside."

"Wait." The panic in her voice stopped him dead.

"What is it?" His attention went to her stomach. He had no knowledge of how to deliver a baby. If it were her time, he'd have to try and get her to the hospital, and in the current weather conditions it wouldn't be easy.

"Do you mind waiting to leave until I'm finished cleaning up?"

Relieved, he assured her he would. "I'll be in the living room. Come on, Camo."

The dog followed. Axel added more wood to the fire against the chill that seemed to be permeating the house despite the blaze. He returned to the kitchen and cleared away the dishes.

Once the cleanup was finished, he slipped

into his favorite rocker in front of the fire. His thoughts went over what Summer had told him about Ray.

His good friend Lainey was a victim of a human trafficking ring operating in the area a few years back. The county's own district attorney had been indicted along with a police officer Axel didn't know.

Summer believed Ray had police officers working for him now. Someone had run his plates and found out the general vicinity where he lived. If he did reach out to the sheriff's people, would he be leading Ray straight to them?

A short time later, Summer emerged wearing his old military sweats, her blond hair a darker shade from being wet.

"Thank you. I feel much better." She slipped into the rocker beside him.

"You're welcome. But you really should get some rest." He didn't want to tell her they might have to leave at a moment's notice.

"Is it okay if I stretch out on your sofa?"

She didn't completely trust him yet. "Sure. I'll leave Camo here to keep you company and I'll be back soon."

He rose and started for the door. Camo didn't argue when he told the dog to stay.

"I'm going to lock the door behind me," he told her. "I have a key I can use to get back inside in case you're sleeping." Axel put on his heavy coat and gloves, then slipped into his boots. He grabbed his flashlight and stepped out into the nightmare storm.

Blowing snow swirled all around him, chilling any exposed skin. Up on top of the mountain, the snow accumulation was much deeper, muffling sound further. He listened but it was impossible to hear anything, much less see more than his hand in front of his face.

The light didn't pick up anything that resembled footsteps but with the amount of snow and driving wind, any tracks would be quickly covered. Axel killed the light and went by his instincts alone. He trudged through the deep snow that had already accumulated.

Once he reached the bottom of his drive, which intersected with the road, Axel stepped out into it and clicked on the light. A set of tire tracks had him quickly switching off the flashlight. There was no way those were from earlier. Someone had been here recently.

Axel's heart thundered in his chest when he caught something over the screaming wind. An engine. A vehicle was moving this way. They were likely trying to pinpoint the location of his place. He prayed they hadn't yet.

He hurried back to the trees covering his property and ducked out of sight. The noise grew closer, yet there were no lights. The driver wasn't using any headlights. How were they staying on the road in this weather?

The hairs on the back of Axel's neck stood up. The car's occupants didn't want anyone to know they were coming. Worst-case scenarios played through his head.

The vehicle was now even with where Axel was hiding. He eased a little away from the spot, but with the storm it was impossible to make out anything about the car as it eased past.

On the right side of his property was the Bureau of Land Management, or BLM land. It was undeveloped and unused.

He started walking toward the fence line that separated his property from the BLM land to make sure the car had kept going. Axel climbed the fence onto the government land and headed toward the road again. Before he reached it, car doors slammed shut. Axel froze in place. Low murmurs whipped his way. Enough for him to realize the occupants of the car had been sent to find him and Summer.

His first thought was her safety. He had to get to her now.

Before he had the chance to slip back to his place, a flashlight beam homed in on him.

"There's someone out here!" a man yelled. A heartbeat later, gunshots lit up the space where the shooters were. Axel dropped to the ground and crawled to the closest tree coverage.

"Get him!" the same man shouted. "Don't let him get away."

Like it or not, he would probably be shot in the back if he ran, and if he did manage to escape, he'd lead them straight to Summer.

Axel whipped out his handgun and fired in the direction of the shots. Someone screamed. He'd hit his mark. How many others were still out there?

"I'm shot. Help me!" the wounded man called to his partners.

"David, get Jim back to the car. We'll deal with this guy."

There were at least four men.

Axel eased forward to try and see what was coming. Another round of shots from at least two shooters had him ducking once more.

When he'd left Afghanistan, he thought he'd seen the last of battle but like it or not, he was going to have to take down these men—all of them—in order to protect Summer. Her story had been heartbreaking. The things that had been done to her…he couldn't let that happen again. Not matter what—no matter the cost— he'd protect her because she deserved someone who would fight for her.

More shots fired had him getting as close to the tree as he could. They were using the gun-fire to keep him pinned down. He waited for the last of the shots to ring out and then fired toward one of the shooters. Another scream. Another perp had been hit.

Footsteps running away seemed to confirm the last shooter was retreating. What about the man he'd hit? Had Axel's shot been a kill shot? Why else would they leave a man behind?

He slipped from his coverage and rushed after the fleeing man. If they got away, they'd know where Summer was and send backup.

Through the storm he caught movement and fired. A yelp told him the man was hit. He didn't go down but returned fire forcing Axel to take cover. Once the shots ended, he left his coverage, but couldn't pick up the man's move-ments again in the storm.

A car door slammed shut. Seconds later, taillights penetrated the weather. Axel ran out into the road and aimed at the lights. Bullets tinged off the back. The car didn't slow down. They'd gotten away, which meant he and Summer wouldn't have long before Ray's people converged on his mountain.

Axel started back toward his cabin at a fast pace. Once he reached the spot where the shooting had taken place, he found the dead man. He'd been shot in the head. Axel searched the man's pockets, not surprised that he didn't have a cell phone on him. He pulled out the man's wallet. Barry Harper was the name on the driver's license. It didn't ring a bell. Axel knew all the deputy's names and a few of the local police. There was no badge on the man. The weapon was a Glock. Some law enforcement agencies used them.

With nothing else giving any answers, Axel stuck the man's wallet in his pocket and headed back to the fence. Perhaps Summer would know him. Right now, they were in trouble. With her not wanting to involve the police, it limited Axel to where he could turn for help.

As bad as he hated bringing this deadly situation to his friends, at this point, Axel didn't see any other option. If they could reach Abram and Lainey's place before their pursuers found them, they stood a chance of escaping.

Unfortunately, the trip down the mountain wouldn't be easy in the Jeep. A rough ride under normal circumstances, the weather would make it much more difficult. With Summer being pregnant, the trip would be filled with dangers. Still, he had no doubt those men would have called for more backup by now. He'd engaged them and they knew he and Summer were close by.

He climbed over the fence and started toward the house while every stray sound had him jerking toward it. How big was this organization that Summer had inadvertently gotten herself involved in? How was it connected to what had happened before?

Questions flew through his head without any valid answers.

He neared the house—the lights inside had always been a welcome sight in the past. Even though it was only him and Camo, they reminded him that this was his home. His little sanctuary up on the mountain.

He removed his glove and fished out the house key. The wisest thing was to get the sheriff on the sat phone and tell him everything.

That wasn't an option.

Axel slipped the key into the lock and opened the door. He hoped Summer had managed to get some sleep. As bad as he hated to wake her, there wasn't a choice. This location was compromised.

He stepped through the entrance. Camo made a sound and looked up from where he lay on the floor near where Summer was stretched out on the sofa. She appeared to be resting.

Axel closed the door and hurried over to her. As he neared, she became aware of him and sat up quickly. She had the steak knife in her hand again.

He stopped. "Hey, it's me."

Her panic slowly eased and she lowered the knife. "What's wrong?"

Axel told her about what he'd gone through. "We can't stay here. There's one man dead down there. Although I injured two of the three remaining, they got away. They know I'm the one who helped you. They'll come back with others."

Summer stumbled to her feet. "What do we do?"

He hated risking taking a pregnant woman through some of the most rugged mountainous country to reach a cabin on the other side, but there wasn't a choice.

"There's a place we can go." He reminded her about his Amish friends. "They have a small place on the other side of the mountain, and it will be some rough riding."

She clutched her belly. "I'll be okay."

He had serious doubts. Unfortunately, they were all out of choices. "We'll take the Jeep." Axel glanced around the living room. "I have an extra set of boots." The flip-flops wouldn't work. Axel retrieved the lined boots and gave them to her.

"I'll gather some supplies for the trip in case…" He didn't finish, but there was a good chance they might not make it if the weather continued this way.

He ran his hand through his hair, a habit he had when he was trying to work things out in his head. They'd need blankets for warmth and food just in case. "Stay close to the fire. I'll be right back."

He grabbed the sat phone from the drawer in the kitchen and stuck it in his pocket. If things got worse, he wouldn't have a choice. Whether Summer liked it or not, he was calling the sheriff.

He retrieved extra blankets from the closet and carried them out.

Summer turned as he entered the room. "Let me do something."

He hesitated—torn between wanting her to rest after her ordeal and needing her help.

"You can help me carry some food." He went to the kitchen with her and grabbed a couple of bags then loaded as much food as he could into them. Taking up the heavier ones, he handed Summer a couple of lighter ones.

"Here, use this coat." With his free hand, he gave her the warmest one and slipped on the second one he kept near the door before grabbing the blankets. "The Jeep is behind the house." He looked into her eyes. "Stay close to me. Come, Camo."

Axel opened the back door and stepped out into a storm that was far worse than before.

Camo realized where they were going and trotted out in front of them as Axel locked up. Though only a short distance from the house, it felt as if it took forever to reach the Jeep. Axel opened the door and ushered Summer inside and out of the weather. He quickly loaded the supplies in the back of the Jeep and let Camo hop in.

He didn't waste time getting behind the wheel. Axel started the Jeep and quickly reversed while hoping the driving snow would soon cover up their tracks.

Like it or not, he wouldn't have a choice but to use the headlights. The terrain summiting the mountain was going to be difficult enough to maneuver.

Soon the rocks that littered the place became more intense.

Summer grabbed the door handle. "Where are we going?" She shot him a suspicious look.

"I told you. To my friends' place. We can stay with them until we figure out our next move. They're good people."

"This is the couple who gave you Camo."

He nodded, glad she appeared less worried. Axel understood what she'd gone through made it hard to trust. He'd just have to find ways to show her that she could trust him.

"What if they come after us there?" she asked.

"Then we'll figure it out."

His attention returned to the nightmare in front of them as the Jeep climbed over rocks that were almost as big as it.

"The snow should cover our tracks," he assured her. "It's really blowing. If they come to the house, and I believe they will, there should be no way they'd know about the small Amish community down below." Axel prayed those words would prove true, but Summer had been kept in the area. It stood to reason that Ray was staying somewhere close by. How well did he know the part of the state in which he was hiding?

The lights of the house disappeared in the swirling snow. He'd done his best to make sure his place looked as if the owners had simply left for a visit or a trip to town.

Summer's attention was fixed on the obstacles in front of them while Axel did his best to avoid damaging the Jeep. If they got stuck up here, they could die long before Ray's people reached them.

Though he'd gone down this way to visit his friends many times in the past, it had never been in these conditions. Axel was worried. He couldn't keep from checking the rearview and side mirrors expecting danger to appear at any moment. He could just see hisdriveway off to his right. So far, no sign of the traffickers. They had a moment of reprieve that he didn't believe would last.

He prayed they'd summit and be heading

down the mountain before those men discovered the way up to his house.

His hands tightened on the wheel. He needed something to take his mind off the danger they faced. Then Axel remembered the identity of the man he'd shot.

"Do you know a man by the name of Barry Harper?" he asked and swung toward Summer. The look on her face was one of sheer terror. It was brutally clear she knew the man he'd killed. And she was afraid of him.

# Chapter Five

Barry Harper. Hearing the name made her almost physically ill. Barry's cruel face would be imprinted in her brain forever. Just seeing him enter a room used to fill her with fear.

"You know him," Axel apparently deduced from her expression.

She swallowed several times before she found her voice. "Yes, I know him."

"He's dead. I shot him."

Her head jerked his way. He'd been forced to kill a man for her. "I'm sorry you had to do that." Yet her emotions were torn between knowing what he had to do was wrong and happy that the man who'd been capable of such cruelty was no longer able to hurt anyone else.

His expression softened. "I had to kill him to protect you, Summer. And from the look on your face, I can see he was a bad man."

She ducked her head, her blond hair covering her face. Barry was that and more. Ray had nicknamed Barry The Enforcer. When one of the girls tried to run away for the first time, Barry would hurt them, and Ray would force all the women to watch the cruelty to scare them into obedience.

"He works for Ray. And you're right, he's a very bad man." After she'd tried to escape the first time, Ray had taken pleasure in calling in Barry. The Enforcer had beat her so badly that she thought she would die. She'd been left with her wounds untreated for days until she'd finally gotten the strength to get up. Eat. The other girls did their best to protect her from Ray whenever he'd demand to know why Summer wasn't working. He'd raged at them and told them that every day she was feeling sorry for herself was a day that cost him money. Everything was about money with Ray.

As much as she'd wanted to try and escape again, the thought of what Barry had put her through kept her from doing it...until now.

Axel glanced her way. "How many others were part of Ray's organization?"

Summer had lost track of the ones who'd come in and out of Ray's life. "Many. More than a dozen at least that I know of."

His attention shot past her to something over her right shoulder.

Summer turned toward it. Two sets of headlights crawled around the mountainside heading up Axel's drive. Ray's people were homing in on their location.

Axel killed the lights immediately, plunging them into darkness.

"Let's hope they didn't see our headlights, otherwise they'll follow." He leaned forward. "I can't see anything." A tremor of apprehension entered his voice.

Summer kept her attention on the driveway. The headlights appeared to stop. "They're struggling to get up the mountainside." At least it was something. She watched as the two cars appeared to turn around. "Are they heading back down? Maybe they're giving up?" She looked with hope to Axel. He was anything but hopeful.

"I don't think so." Axel kept the Jeep's speed at a crawl. "We've reached the summit that's close to my place," he said with relief.

The Jeep started down at a steep incline. Though she wore a seat belt, she was forced forward at the direction the Jeep was going. "I can't see the lights anymore."

Axel braked sharply, jostling the occupants of the vehicle. Camo straightened himself and then barked his complaint.

"Sorry, buddy." Axel put the Jeep into Park. "I'm going to slip over to the driveway and see what they're up to." The mountain's summit was less than a quarter mile from his place. He shifted toward her. "I'll be right back."

It took everything inside her not to beg him to stay. Axel was doing his best to keep them alive.

He waited a second longer for her to say something. When she couldn't, he quietly opened the door and closed it gently. Camo groaned as if sensing his master was in danger.

"It's okay. He'll be okay." She petted the dog's head while looking in the direction Axel had left. She couldn't see anything through the blizzard.

Once more she counted off the seconds, the routine giving only a small amount of comfort. Camo placed his paws over the back of the seat and waited while Summer continued to mark off the seconds under her breath.

One, two, three...

The wind rocked the Jeep back and forth, further straining her taut nerves.

Ten, eleven, twelve…

Beyond the darkness and the embattled Jeep, she saw flashlights down the drive. Ray's cronies had abandoned their vehicles and were coming after them on foot.

"Hurry, Axel."

Every second they were standing still gave Ray a chance to find them.

Someone materialized near her side of the Jeep. Summer bit back a scream when she realized it was Axel.

He slipped into the Jeep and closed the door. "There's at least six men down there. Having to come in on foot will slow them down, but if they find the pickup, they might use it to pursue."

He put the Jeep into Drive and started downhill. "I'm hoping we're far enough down that they won't see the headlights because I'm driving blind here. I can't see anything."

Pulling in a breath, Axel flipped on the lights. The path in front of them was immediately illuminated. It was far worse than Summer imagined. Huge rocks littered the way.

Axel did his best to avoid most. The rest he ended up crawling the Jeep over.

"How far is your friends' place?" she asked

while gripping the hand rest and the seat. The jarring of the vehicle made her nauseous.

"Maybe four miles. Are you holding up okay?" Axel's concern for her was clear.

She pulled in several breaths. The nausea subsided somewhat. "Yes, I think so." Four miles in these conditions? It could take hours to reach his friends.

She looked over her shoulder. The flashlights were no longer visible. "I don't see anyone coming after us."

"That's a good thing." He offered a half smile. "With the wind squalling, I don't think they'll hear the Jeep's engine." Axel leaned forward to scan the path in front of them. He continued dodging rocks until they began to thin away to be replaced by trees.

"I'd forgotten how hairy the trip down can be under normal conditions and in the daylight. Everything okay?" Axel looked her way.

She managed a nod. Truth be told she was terrified. Of the weather—one false move could result in death. Of the people hunting them who appeared relentless in their pursuit. If they kept coming like this...

"What do you think will happen when they don't find us at your house?" she asked. "They'll know we've been there because of the wood-stove." Even though Axel had done his best to extinguish the fire, it still smoldered.

"After what happened on BLM land, I'm hoping they think we fled the area using my driveway. It would make sense to me but..."

What about their tracks near the shed? Would the relentless snowstorm cover it up in time? As much as she wanted to believe Ray's people wouldn't search the property too closely, she knew Ray. Those who worked for him were as frightened of Ray as Summer was. They'd turn over every rock looking for her and Axel because having to tell Ray they'd escaped was not a solution. Ray required complete loyalty and he'd do whatever was necessary to protect his investment from the threat Summer posed. She knew so much about his organization. He'd thought her weak and easy to intimidate but he'd been wrong. She'd listened when he hadn't realized it and she had a good memory. Plus, there was enough on that thumb drive to put Ray and everyone in his organization in jail.

One of their conversations played through her mind. It happened when the other girls were out, and it was just the two of them. Ray got bored easily. On this particular occasion, he'd been pacing around the house with too much pent-up energy. He'd told her something that terrified her.

Ray had bragged about how much he enjoyed killing people. She'd been horrified and yet he'd laughed at her shock. Ray had let something slip probably because he was certain she was too afraid of him to tell anyone. He'd said he'd killed lots of people when he was young. He got this creepy faraway look on his face as if he were reliving the kills. He'd told her how exciting it was to watch life slip from someone's body as you choked them. He'd been inches away from her, no doubt seeing the same fear in her as he had in his previous victims.

She thought she would die that day. And then he'd snapped out of it and been his normal self. For a long time after that, she was terrified she'd be his next victim.

"Looks like we've reached the bottom of the mountain." Axel sighed in relief. Through the headlights, tall trees appeared to grow thicker. They were entering a wooded area.

"Does your friend live in the woods?" Summer asked, the doubt returning to her tone. "I'm sorry… Eight years has made me jaded. I want to fix that before my child comes." She didn't want to pass on fear to the baby.

"It's okay. They live just past the trees actually. There's another mountain range beyond here. They live right before the foothills. There's a small Amish settlement with a handful of farms."

"We're close to Amish country." A glance her way confirmed she was struggling to hold onto her emotions. "Once Ray told me what was expected of me in the future, he moved me and a handful of other girls out west." A tiny smile touched her lips. "We passed many Amish buggies along the way. I couldn't take my eyes off them. I tried to memorize every detail of the life I'd been so willing to give up." She shrugged. "Through these nightmare years, I can't tell you how often I've longed to return to the girl I'd been back then."

Her story broke his heart and he vowed he'd help her get back to her family someday. Maybe then, he'd be able to let go of the regret he still held onto because of Erin. Axel had hesitated to tell Erin how he felt about her. Would knowing about his love have made those final moments easier? He'd never know.

Once they reached the trees the storm seemed slightly more subdued.

Summer turned around in her seat. "No sign we've been followed."

Axel nodded. "I figure by now, even with this weather, they're almost at the house. I'd like to be through the woods when that happens." He couldn't keep the worried edge out of his voice.

"Will your friends be okay with us bringing our troubles to their doorstep? I don't want to bring shame to their family."

"Hey, no one's judging you, Summer. You didn't choose this way of life. It was forced on you."

She slowly nodded.

"Last year, something like this happened. Both Abram and his wife, Lainey, got sucked into the nightmare." He told her about how Lainey had been kidnapped by a man named Harley Owens who had proceeded to take a deputy hostage. "They almost died. Then Abram and his brother-in-law rescued them."

"That's awful."

"It was. Owens and Phillip Hollis, the county's district attorney, were involved along with a local cop." He glanced her way. "According to my friend, Brayden, who joined the sheriff's department after the incident, a thorough investigation confirmed there were never any other officers indicted." He said that to put her mind at ease.

"I recognize two of the names you mentioned. Ray met up with Harley Owens once, along with another man who tried to keep his identity a secret. A short time after the meeting, Harley and the other man—Phillip Hollis— were arrested along with part of Ray's crew. He was furious." She told him how Ray had been enraged for weeks afterward and had taken out his anger on everyone around him. He berated those who had landed in custody and had become paranoid that the police were closing in on him. He'd been forced to suspend his enterprise and move it to another location until the heat settled from the county.

"Ray said he had to take different precautions to prevent that from ever happening again. He tightened security. He didn't trust anyone he came in contact with."

Axel's hands tightened on the wheel. "That must have been horrible. What an evil human being."

"You don't know the half of it."

"I have no doubt." His mouth thinned. Ray deserved to be in jail.

"Most of the girls were so young," Summer said in a strangled voice. "I hated what they had to go through. They'd cry after their first initiation into the business, and I tried to quiet them. Ray hated tears. He said it showed weakness and he wasn't one to allow weakness. I'd do my best to keep them calm and assure them everything would be okay even though I knew it wouldn't." She told him many of the girls eventually gave in and accepted their fate. Others fought. For those it was the hardest. A few tried to run. They never returned.

Ray was a true monster preying on the innocent. How many lives had he ruined because of greed?

"Have you lived here in Montana all your life?" Summer asked, the question intruding into his dark thoughts.

"For several years now." Camo made a sound as he settled into his seat, and Axel glanced his way briefly. "I grew up in Colorado. It was just me and my parents, but it always felt like I was protected from everything. Joining the military really opened my eyes to the real world."

"I'd give anything to be able to go back to another time," Summer said earnestly.

He wished he could wipe away every bad thing Ray had done to her.

Lights appeared up ahead. "Those are from Abram's home." Summer focused on where he pointed. A tiny pin light was all that was visible through the storm.

She wrung her hands. "I really hate that we have to involve them."

"Trust me, Abram and Lainey are good people. They'll want to help." He told her about how Lainey had joined the Amish faith after what happened with the previous trafficking ring a few years back. She and Abram had wed and made a life together farming and helping animals in need.

"They sound nice."

"They don't judge," he said, sensing her concerns.

The woods had been cleared away as they drew closer to the house. As bad as what they'd gone through so far was, the thought of the unknowns that lay in front of them had Axel's stomach doing a somersault.

The barn appeared off to the right, then the house.

Summer swallowed as Axel stopped the Jeep in front.

He barely had time to park the vehicle before

Abram stepped from the porch with a lantern held high. Worry on his face. He recognized the Jeep and smiled.

Axel waved and shifted to her. "Let me explain things to them. Stay here with Camo where it's warm." She appeared grateful at his offer.

Axel shoved the door open against the wind and got out. It slammed shut before he could close it. He noticed Summer jump nervously.

He hurried up the steps and shook Abram's hand.

"What brings you out on a night like this, my friend?" Abram's joy at seeing Axel soon turned to concern. He glanced through the snow-covered window at Summer. The Amish man's brow creased. "Something has happened." When Axel struggled to find the words, he added, "Is it bad?"

"It's bad." Axel did his best to explain what Summer had gone through and what they'd battled so far. "We need a place to hide out and warm up. I'm sorry to have to bring this to you, Abram, but I didn't know where else to go."

Abram shook his head. "Nonsense. You did the right thing. Please, come inside."

"Thank you, my friend." Axel came around

to Summer's side. He helped her out and held on to her arm when the wind would have blown her around. "Let's get you inside." As they headed for the porch, Axel scanned the snowy world around them and wondered how long they would have before they were found and forced into another battle Axel wasn't sure they could win.

# Chapter Six

Summer searched Axel's handsome face and wished she could erase the things that were forever imprinted in her heart, keeping her from experiencing anything close to a human emotion again. But she couldn't. She was damaged beyond repair.

He cleared his throat. "Are you okay?" The huskiness in his voice made her wonder what he was thinking.

She nodded because saying words seemed impossible.

"Come, Camo." The dog trotted up the porch steps.

Abram had opened the door and was standing in the threshold with a woman who appeared to be in her early twenties.

Camo ran past them into the house and the young woman laughed. "Please come inside and make yourself at home like Camo." She bunched her apron in her hands. "I'm Lainey and this is my husband, Abram."

"Summer." She hated the name because of all it represented.

"It's nice to meet you, Summer. Please, come in and sit by the fire." Lainey pointed to the warmth permeating from the woodstove.

"Thank you." Summer slipped into one of the chairs, her attention glued on Axel. Despite her hesitation to trust anyone, he made her feel safe.

"I should get the Jeep out of sight," Axel told her and immediately what little bit of progress she'd made at letting go of her fears evaporated.

He came over to where she sat and knelt beside her. "I'll be right back, I promise. In the meantime, you're safe here. Is it okay if I use the barn?" he asked Abram.

"*Jah*," Abram confirmed. "I'll come with you to get the doors."

"Thanks, Abram." Axel turned to her with eyes that held encouragement. "I won't be long."

When the two men stepped outside, Lainey brought over a quilt and placed it on Summer's lap. She slipped into the vacant chair.

"I'm glad you both made it safely. Abram

told me Axel mentioned you were attacked?" Lainey's expression was kind. She was looking for answers Summer wasn't sure she could give.

"Yes. There are some bad men coming after me. Axel saved me." She swallowed. If only it was that simple. "They followed us to his house." Camo once more stuck his head in Summer's lap as if realizing she was struggling.

Lainey laughed at the dog's behavior. "He really likes you. Except for Axel, Camo doesn't normally warm up to others easily."

"He's been a *gut* watchdog." Summer smiled down at the dog and stroked his head.

"Are you Amish?" Lainey asked in surprise. Summer realized she'd slipped up.

"Not anymore." She looked at the other woman and saw sympathy there.

"I'm a new Amish believer myself. I'm still adjusting to the language difference. My *mann* and I met when something bad happened here a few years back. Through all the bad, *Gott* brought us together." She smiled warmly. "When is your baby due?"

"In another month I think." If Lainey considered it strange that Summer didn't know the exact time of her birth she didn't comment.

She held Summer's gaze. "It could have been

me. What happened to you could have been me." The words were said so softly that she almost didn't catch them. But she understood. Lainey could have suffered the same fate as Summer.

She cleared her throat, but the tears refused to stay back. She covered her face with her hands.

"I'm so sorry that happened to you," Lainey said gently, "but you're safe here."

Summer scrubbed her face. "I'm not sure for how long. Ray's people are searching for us now." She sniffed several times. "How long before they come here."

"Those terrible men," Lainey muttered, her lips thinning. "I can't believe such awful things are still happening here in our county."

Summer blew out a shuddering sigh. "I'm sorry for bringing this to you and Abram."

Lainey shook her head. "*Nay.* You have nothing to apologize for. These men must be stopped. Did Axel call the sheriff?"

Immediately Summer's guard was up. "No, and we can't call them ever." She told Lainey about what Ray had said.

"I know in the past there was a police officer involved, but not the sheriff's men. I trust them. I have a *gut* friend who works for them, and I know Axel's friend Brayden does as well. You can trust them."

Before Summer could respond, Axel returned with Abram. He zeroed in on her face, no doubt seeing the turmoil there. "Everything good here?"

She did her best to reassure him it was, and he didn't press.

"The vehicle is secured for now." He pulled up another chair near her. "We need to try to reach the sheriff. It's time, Summer. We're safe for now, but I don't believe those men will give up. It's only a matter of time before they widen their search."

She shivered. Trusting Axel and Lainey, when they both assured her she could rely on the sheriff, was hard. Yet something in Lainey's story got to her. She had a friend who was on the force, too. Summer slowly nodded. "Okay."

He smiled and rose, pulling out the sat phone he'd brought with him. He dialed a number and waited. "Nothing but a fast busy signal." His gaze locked with Abram's. "Either the weather's preventing the call from going through or there are too many people trying to use the service."

An uneasy feeling coiled down into the pit of her stomach. They had no way of calling for help and there were armed men after them who wouldn't hesitate to take all of their lives.

Axel had never felt more helpless. He'd convinced Summer to call for help and now he couldn't get the call to go through.

"Maybe once the storm lets up," Abram said and clamped Axel's shoulder for encouragement.

Waiting didn't ease Axel's anxiety one little bit. Would they have that long?

"I could saddle the horse and ride over to Elk Ridge," Abram suggested. "They aren't looking for me."

Axel turned toward his friend while his tired brain worked out the details. "That might work, but I think it would be best if both you and Lainey went together in case…" He didn't finish. If the threat showed up here, he didn't want his friends to get caught in the cross fire of a gunfight.

"I understand." He looked to his wife, who was listening to the conversation. "I will get the buggy ready."

"Let me help." Axel started for the door, but Abram stopped him.

"No, my friend. You're exhausted. Stay and

rest. That will do you better than assisting me. I'll be back in no time."

Lainey stood. "Would you like something to eat while we wait? I made Yumasetti casserole and bread for yesterday's meal. There's plenty."

"That's very kind of you, but not necessary. We ate at my place earlier," Axel told her.

"Well, if you get hungry later please help yourselves." She beamed at Axel. "*Komm* and sit for a while, Axel. Perhaps the phone service will return soon and none of this will be necessary."

The clock on the wall of the living room chimed the time. Just past midnight. Hours before daylight.

Despite his worries, Axel smiled at Lainey's use of the simple Pennsylvania Dutch word. She'd told him how difficult it was to learn it in order to become Amish.

"Nicely done," he told her as she disappeared into the kitchen.

Axel slipped into Lainey's vacated seat and tried not to show Summer his concern. "Are you warm enough?"

She nodded. "Your friends are nice. I like them."

He smiled. "I do, too. They've been good to me." He didn't elaborate on how he'd found comfort in the simple ways of the Amish. He'd helped Abram and Lainey with their growing family of animals. Life for them appeared simple even though he knew it wasn't. Abram had shared about the time when he and Lainey were taken hostage. It had left Lainey with nightmares for a long time. She'd found solace in helping him care for the animals.

He leaned his head against the back of the chair, his fingers drumming a staccato beat on the armrest. The desire to be doing something to prevent what he believed to be coming their way had been ingrained in him since his military days. Waiting wasn't something Axel was accustomed to.

He tried the phone again. When it didn't go through, he returned it to his pocket.

"Do you think they'll check this far down the mountain?" Summer kept her attention on his face. She'd see it if he lied.

"I'd say there's a strong likelihood."

The door opened suddenly, drawing both his and Summer's attention to the gust of wind and snow entering the house.

Abram forced the door closed against the storm. "We're all set."

Lainey came out of the kitchen wiping her

hands on her apron. She reached for her cloak from the peg by the door and slipped it on.

Axel rose and helped Summer to her feet. "Please be careful, you two. These men are dangerous."

"Don't worry about us. We will be *oke*. Remember, they aren't looking for an Amish couple." Abram opened the door, and he and Lainey stepped out onto the porch. Axel and Summer followed them outside.

The storm hadn't eased one bit.

Abram held his wife's arm as they made their way to the enclosed buggy. He opened the door and assisted Lainey inside before turning back to them. "Stay safe and keep your eyes open."

Axel nodded. "We will try our best. If enemies show up, we won't have a choice. We'll have to leave."

"We will be praying for you." Abram climbed up into the buggy. A short time later, he guided it away.

Axel glanced around at the darkness. More than the cold had him shivering. "Let's go back inside." As soon as they entered, he locked the door, a gesture that didn't go unnoticed by Summer.

"How long will it take them to reach the

sheriff's office?" Summer asked, rubbing her hands down her arms.

"Not long. Maybe an hour in these conditions."

"What's wrong?" She'd picked up on the anxiety he couldn't hide.

"Nothing. I'm just wondering if we should leave now instead of waiting for Abram and Lainey to reach the sheriff." He hesitated. "I have a friend who is former military and part of the sheriff's department. His place isn't far from here. If we can reach it…"

Axel tried to relax enough to come up with a clear plan, but it was hard.

"You don't think we should wait for Abram and Lainey to return?"

"Maybe—I'm not sure." He hated sounding so uncertain. "We'll see what happens. I don't want to be taken by surprise. If we're on the move, we stand a better chance at staying ahead of them."

Both returned to their places by the fire.

"We should pray." Axel felt the need to talk to God. He bowed his head. "We need Your help, Lord. We're running out of options. We need Your deliverance. Please give us the strength to get through what's coming and help me protect Summer and keep Abram and Lainey safe. Amen."

Axel lifted his eyes and found Summer watching him. Had she prayed, too? Did she hold to the faith of her people still? He could certainly understand if she had doubts after going through the horrible things she had.

"Yumasetti casserole was my *daed*'s favorite meal," Summer said softly, capturing his attention. "*Mamm* used to make it for him all the time."

Axel couldn't take his eyes off her. "How old are your brothers?"

"Peter would be eighteen now. Eli fifteen— fifteen. I can't believe my baby *bruder* is fifteen."

He was silent for a minute. "I have two younger sisters myself. Kim and Bridgette. They're all grown up now with families of their own. Yet most times, I still see them as those little girls who followed me around." He hesitated before saying, "After this is over, you need to see your family, Summer. They must be worried about you."

She didn't look at him. "I don't think I can. I hurt them badly. I ran away in the middle of the night and never even left them a note. They must have been so worried. I wonder if they ever tried to find me."

"I'm sure they did."

"I can't believe I chose Ray over my family, or that I ever believed he loved me and would take care of me."

Axel's jaw tightened. "He's good at manipulating young women into believing he cares about them."

"I wish I could go back in time and warn the younger me of what would come." She swiped at her eyes and his heart broke for her. How many times had he wished the same. Even if he couldn't have changed the outcome of what happened to Erin, he might have let her know how much he loved her.

Every noise outside set his nerves on edge. It felt like danger was breathing down their necks, and staying in one place for long was too risky.

"I'm going to take a look around and see if I can find a place where the phone will pick up service."

"Can I come with you?" Summer asked, surprising him.

He was worried something would happen to her that would cause harm to the baby. His first thought was to ask her to stay inside where it was safe and warm, but he remembered how strong she was. She'd gone through things some people could never understand and she was still fighting.

"I don't want to be alone…and I feel safe with you."

"Sure. We'll take Camo as well."

Axel walked with her to the door where their coats hung. He helped Summer into his over-size coat careful not to touch her. He'd sensed she didn't like to be touched and he could certainly understand.

He pushed his arms through his coat and zipped it up. "Take my cap. It will help keep your ears warm."

He handed her the camo-colored knit cap and watched her place it down low over her ears before pushing up the hood of the coat. He had an extra set of gloves in his coat and let her use them.

Once they were ready, Axel opened the door. Camo ran past him as he stepped out into the storm that wasn't showing any sign of letting up.

"Stay close to me," Axel said near her ear so she could hear. She nodded and they started toward the barn. It was impossible to hear anything. Ray's men could be right on top of them before he'd know.

Camo trotted off ahead. At the back of the barn, he tried to call out again. The call rang once and then dropped and he gripped it tight. Of all times for the sat phone not to be able to pick up service.

"It's not going to work, is it?"

He turned slightly to see her clearly. She didn't seem fearful like before but almost resigned.

"What if Ray's guys find us before the sheriff can help?"

Axel squashed his own doubts. "I'm not going to let that happen. We have options." He started walking again and she fell into step beside him. Still, Axel didn't like sitting still. They'd talked in the kitchen for a while, and enough time had passed for Abram and Lainey to have reached the sheriff's department by now. Would he be risking both their lives by waiting for help? The soldier in him screamed they needed to keep moving.

"But you're worried," Summer said, correctly reading his mood.

They reached the edge of the woods they'd gone through, and Camo kept in the lead. "I am. I think we need to leave, Summer. If we can reach Brayden's place, he has a police radio." Yet there was a lot of rugged countryside between them and Brayden's, which was only accessible by snowmobile in bad weather.

Brayden had lived in the Tobacco Root Mountains growing up and had told Axel all about them. He'd invited Axel to stay with him at this small cabin. A few days of peace and quiet in the mountains and Axel had been convinced this was the place for him. He'd used all his savings to buy the house and stake his claim to a piece of the Roots, as the locals called them.

Brayden's place was even more isolated than Axel's. He'd built his cabin on the property that had once belonged to his people. The old family homestead was just down the mountain from Brayden's newer place.

Though the house was accessible through a county road, it took almost twice as long to reach that road. Brayden had carved a four-wheel path down the side of the mountain and had a shed at the base of it. Sometimes, he kept his snowcat, which he used to keep the path clear, down there. Did Axel dare risk taking Summer up the mountain even in the snowcat?

A few more tries of the phone confirmed it would be useless trying to reach anyone who could assist.

As much as he wished Abram and Lainey had an extra buggy to keep them disguised, the couple only possessed the one they'd left in. Should he and Summer have to leave soon, they'd be forced to use the Jeep, which might bring them unwelcome attention by Ray's crew.

"I don't see anyone," Axel said. "But then again, with this weather it would be impossible. Let's head back inside."

He and Summer turned and started back toward the house. Camo had been investigating something near the barn. The dog was focused on the trees near the back. When Axel spotted the hackles on the back of Camo's coat standing at attention, he stopped abruptly.

Axel placed his finger over his lips and pointed to the animal. "Stay here," he whispered before slowly approaching the dog's location. As he neared, Camo growled, his teeth bared. Axel immediately retrieved his weapon from the pocket where he'd placed it in. He looked back to Summer and motioned her to go back to the house.

She hesitated, but eventually started toward

it. He turned back toward Camo. The dog growled again and lunged for something.

Axel raced to assist his friend, thinking it might be a wild animal that had Camo so disturbed—until someone screamed as the dog chomped down on his leg.

It was a man dressed in a heavy dark jacket, his face obscured by a knit balaclava.

Before he had the chance to advance on the man, movement out of the corner of his eye had Axel whirling. Another person charged. Relying on his quick instincts, Axel whirled around, his weapon pointed at the assailant. The man stopped dead in his tracks.

"Take it easy, buddy," the stranger said. "We don't want any trouble. We just got turned around in the storm." He carried an assault rifle assuring Axel this man wasn't here because he was lost.

"Drop the weapon." Axel kept his weapon pointed at the intruder.

The man didn't make a move to comply. "Look, all we want is the woman. Summer."

Axel tried not to react. There was no doubt: these were members of the ring. "I said, drop the weapon."

The man slowly smiled. "I'm afraid I can't do that. Call your dog off before I shoot him."

Camo had the first man pinned to the ground and wasn't easing on his hold.

"Not going to happen," Axel said.

The man shifted slightly, his weapon now trained on Camo.

Axel wasn't about to let him hurt his dog. He covered the space between himself and the man before he had the chance to react and slammed the butt of the gun against the man's head hard enough to knock him unconscious immediately.

The assailant on the ground used his free leg to kick Camo off him. He grabbed his weapon, which had gotten lost in the attack, and aimed it straight at Axel.

Axel fired one shot striking the man's chest. He dropped without making a sound, but the noise of the gunshot echoed all around. If there were others close by, they'd hear it and come to investigate. Axel noticed someone running his way and he whipped the weapon out only to realize it was Summer.

"What happened?" she panted.

Axel lowered his gun and blew out a relieved breath before explaining. "I had to shoot one. The other's unconscious. There'll be others coming." He glanced down at the unconscious man. "I'll need to get him in the barn and tied up."

He reached for the man when a noise captured his attention. Hooves pounding the earth. Axel dropped the man and hurried to the front of the barn. The buggy Abram and Lainey had driven came to a quick stop.

Abram jumped out and helped his wife down. "There are armed men canvassing the road," his friend said. "They stopped us and asked questions. I believe they suspected something because they tried to pull me from the buggy. I managed to get away, but they fired on us as if they wanted to kill us. Still, I think we lost them. As we neared the property, we heard shots."

Axel explained what happened. "Summer and I are putting your lives in danger. We need to leave. Can you help me get him to the barn first?" He gestured to the unconscious man.

"*Jah*, I can."

Axel faced Summer. "Why don't you and Lainey go to the house where it's warm."

Lainey put her arm around Summer and ushered her inside, closing the door to keep the cold out.

Once the women were safe, Abram slung the shotgun he used for hunting over his shoulder. As an Amish man, Abram was a pacifist, but he'd also seen what bad men were capable of and he wouldn't hesitate to offer assistance to Axel.

Together, they got the unconscious man inside the barn as he came to and started yelling at the top of his lungs.

"Keep quiet," Axel warned but it didn't silence him any.

While Axel guarded him at gunpoint, Abram grabbed rope and secured his arms and legs to one of the stalls while the man kept a close watch on the dog. Axel suppressed a smile. Camo could be intimidating when needed.

"We'll have to gag him otherwise he'll keep alerting his people," Axel said.

"Use this." Abram handed him a handkerchief.

Once the man was silenced, they brought in the other man. Axel double-checked for a pulse that wasn't there. Killing had been part of his job in the past, but he'd tried to put that behind him. Unfortunately, bad guys didn't live by the same code of conduct.

"I need to get Summer and leave." He didn't

want to think what might happen if Ray's people found them again and he wasn't able to fight them off.

# Chapter Seven

Summer huddled next to Lainey as they listened. Nothing but the storm. Were Axel and Abram okay?

"I'm going to look for them." Summer started for the door when the baby kicked several times as if she, too, sensed the danger they were facing. She grabbed her stomach.

Lainey hurried to her side. "What's happening?"

"The baby is kicking. I'm fine."

"Still, you mustn't go out there. It could be dangerous for you and the child. Come and sit."

"No, I have to help him." Summer reached for the door handle. It twisted in her hand, and she jumped back.

Axel's attention landed on her. He stepped inside with Camo. The taut set of his face assured her more bad had happened.

"We need to leave. Now." He looked past

her to Lainey. "Abram is bringing the buggy up to the front of the house. He's going to try a different route to reach Elk Ridge. You must go with him."

Lainey nodded. "What about supplies for you?"

Axel shook his head. "We brought some in case we couldn't reach the house." His attention returned to Summer once more. "The Jeep's just outside." He held out his hand to her.

Summer hugged Lainey tight before she stepped out with Axel.

They headed toward the Jeep with Camo staying close. Axel opened the passenger door for her, and she struggled inside. The added weight of the baby had her moving much slower these days.

Once she was safely inside, he shut the door and opened the back for Camo. The dog had gotten proficient in maneuvering in and out of vehicles as if accustomed to riding everywhere with Axel.

Axel climbed behind the wheel and turned to her. "This isn't going to be an easy trip." Fear shot through her body as he held her gaze. It was barely a new day and still hours before dawn. The trip so far had been dreadful. What else was in store for them?

Summer secured her seat belt and waited while he did the same before putting the Jeep into Drive. They started away from the farm. In the side mirror, Summer watched the lanterns from the house disappear.

"I can hardly see a thing," Axel muttered and leaned forward, his face close to the windshield. "The weather is deteriorating into all-out blizzard conditions."

She noticed the tension in his profile, the way he gripped the steering wheel and his knuckles turned white.

Her anxiety doubled. If someone accustomed to this type of weather was uneasy, then she should be as well.

They reached the edge of the property that had been cleared and bordered more woods.

"How many more of Ray's men do you think are out here in this weather?" She couldn't help but wonder why just two would have wandered so far from the rest.

Axel frowned. "I don't know. It seems kind of strange that those two would be alone. How'd they get to the farm on foot?" He slowed as they traversed the dark woods.

Summer thought about what he'd said. It didn't seem likely they were part of the team searching Axel's house. And even if they were, they couldn't have walked all the way to the farm especially in the middle of a blizzard.

Axel stomped the brakes suddenly, throwing her forward against the seat belt. "Sorry," he apologized.

She saw what had caused the move. A huge tree had fallen over.

Axel backed up and nudged the vehicle around the obstacle.

"There's a road not far from Abram's place. It leads past the Amish community and then eventually to a county road…" He hesitated, his thoughts likely running along the same line as hers. "They couldn't have walked in from there. It's too far."

"Then where's their vehicle?"

His gaze locked with hers. "There could be more men waiting in the parked vehicle. We have to go back. Abram and Lainey are in danger."

He stopped the Jeep and reversed enough to where he could turn around in the narrow space afforded by the trees.

Summer held on while Axel picked up speed as best he could under the circumstances.

As they neared the Amish home, a rapid release of gunfire assured Summer they were too late.

Axel floored the gas pedal as they cleared the final trees. He flipped the lights on bright. "Get down low," he warned.

She caught a glimpse of several men advancing on the house. They were shooting at Abram. The Amish man quickly raced inside and slammed the door closed.

As the men heard the vehicle approaching, they whirled toward the Jeep and opened fire narrowly missing it.

Axel whipped the vehicle around the back of the house. He bailed out and ran up the steps. "Open up, Abram, it's me."

The door swung open. Abram's worry was clear on his face.

"You and Lainey come with us," Axel told him.

Abram nodded rapidly and turned toward his wife. Before they had the chance to leave the house, another round of gunfire took out the front windows of the house.

"Hurry, it's our only chance!" Axel grabbed

Lainey's arm and ushered her into the Jeep while Abram followed. He carried his shotgun, further reinforcing the gravity of the situation. Abram would protect his family and friends from death no matter his beliefs.

As soon as the couple was inside, Axel raced the Jeep toward the woods at the back of the property. Behind them, armed men rushed around the corner.

"Get down!" Axel yelled. The occupants of the Jeep got out of sight while he managed to avoid a stray bullet. He killed the lights and plunged the vehicle into the woods while shots kept coming their way. "At least the engine hasn't been hit. We can't go to the county road. They'll have men there waiting. Brayden's place is the only option."

Camo growled as if ready to defend them no matter the personal cost.

"It's okay, buddy," Axel told the dog. "We should be far enough away so you can get up now."

Summer sat up in her seat and glanced back to where Lainey's terrified expression showed how difficult this was. "Our poor house," Lainey murmured.

Abram placed his arm around her shoulder.

"It can be repaired. I worry about Martha, our mare, though. She's out in this storm."

"I'm so sorry." Summer felt terrible. "This is all my fault."

"It isn't," Axel assured her. "None of this is on you."

Both Lainey and Abram nodded.

"You can't blame yourself for what criminals choose to do." Abram looked behind them. "I see flashlights and something else...perhaps car headlights."

"That must be the vehicle they used to get here." Axel watched the rearview mirror. "If that's the same one that came after Summer and me, then they're all cars. They won't be able to follow us far." He smiled over at her. "That's one thing we can be grateful for. They didn't plan on the storm when they came after you."

She tried to hold on to the hope that at least her captors couldn't follow.

"My *daed* will have heard the shots and come to investigate." In the rearview, Abram appeared concerned about his father's safety.

"Your father is a wise man," Axel assured him. "He will know that that many shots mean trouble and will stay put."

Summer couldn't bear it if someone innocent died.

She glanced in the side mirror. "I don't see the headlights anymore."

Axel checked behind them. "I'm guessing they realized their car wouldn't make it up this way. Unfortunately, they'll look for another route."

Summer's frown deepened. "Is there one?"

He looked her way. "There are dozens of small roads around these mountains. If they're familiar with the area, they could find a way to cut us off."

Summer sat back in her seat with an uneasy feeling settling around her. What started out as a flee to save her and her baby's lives had ended up involving three other people. People now in jeopardy simply because they'd tried to help. Now they were about to involve someone else. If Ray's men figured out where they were going, Brayden's life could be in danger… just like theirs.

Axel was grateful he had the wheel to hold on to because his hands shook. What had happened back there at Abram's place could have turned out much worse.

He stopped the Jeep, immediately garnering Summer's attention.

"I'm going to slip back to Abram's place and see what they're up to," he decided. "I'll be right back."

She shook her head. "No, we need to keep going. If they catch us…"

He did his best to reassure her. "I won't be long."

"Let me go with you." Abram leaned forward with a serious expression. "In case there's trouble."

As much as Axel didn't want to put his friend in further danger, the man was an excellent shot.

"Thank you, Abram."

He carefully opened the door and blocked Camo from going with them. "Stay, boy. Take care of Summer and Lainey." Camo whined his displeasure at being left behind before settling down next to Summer.

With Abram close, the two headed at a diagonal angle. After walking at a brisk pace for ten minutes, they covered the quarter of a mile to Abram's farm. As much as Axel was hoping their attackers had left the property and were searching for another way to head them off, it soon became clear they hadn't.

Armed men were everywhere around the property. The car that had attempted to follow was parked out back.

"What are they doing?" Abram whispered.

"I don't know." Axel watched the activity. They weren't showing any sign of leaving.

Axel struggled to make the right decision. He doubted Brayden would have heard the commotion from his place, especially with the storm.

He shifted to Abram. "I don't want to put you and Lainey in further danger. I'm going to circle close to the Amish community and drop you both off. From there, it's a straight shot to Brayden's if we head east."

Abram searched his face. "It's too dangerous for you and Summer to go it alone."

"We'll be okay." Axel couldn't put his friends in jeopardy any longer. "Maybe you can warn the community about the danger coming."

Abram reluctantly agreed. "I'll saddle one of my *daed*'s horses and take the backroads to Elk Ridge. Be careful, my friend. There are an awful lot of armed men roaming the countryside."

"I will. I just hope the gunmen don't happen upon the community." Had they gotten a good look at Abram earlier? If not, even if they managed to come across Abram's parents' place, there would be no way for them to know Abram was the one they'd fired upon.

As much as he wanted to protect Summer by having her stay with Abram's parents, Henry and Esther, if their pursuers searched the place and found her, everyone would be in danger and Summer would be dead.

"We should head back," Axel said and led the way to the Jeep. As soon as they were inside, he told Summer and Lainey the plan.

"Oh, Axel, I'm worried about you and Summer," Lainey exclaimed, her concern evident in her voice.

"We'll be careful," Axel assured her with more confidence than he felt. He put the Jeep into gear and kept going the way they were pointing for a while. It took all his driving skills to keep the vehicle from striking a tree.

Abram leaned close to his window. "You should be safe to turn toward the settlement now."

Axel guided the Jeep carefully around several trees before shifting their direction. His thoughts went a mile a minute as he maneuvered his way through the woods.

One thought kept popping into his head concerning the previous arrests for human trafficking. Close to a dozen had been taken into custody years back. Many had been sentenced already. The sheriff's department had believed they'd broken the back of the trafficking rings in Montana. They'd clearly underestimated the magnitude of this criminal enterprise. At this point, Sheriff McCallister and his people weren't looking for traffickers. Axel needed to figure out what details they had to understand exactly how this type of organization worked. Summer would have insight into the way Ray operated.

He glanced at her. "Summer, what else can you tell us about Ray's operation. Is he working with someone else?"

"Ray oversaw the entire operation in Montana. Harley Owens and Phillip Hollis worked for him, though it wasn't always that way. Ray started out recruiting girls, but over the past eight years since I've been with him, he's moved up. He doesn't get his hands dirty recruiting the girls anymore."

Lainey sucked in a breath. "Oh, I recognize both those names you mentioned." She reached for Abram's hand. "I will never forget those terrible men."

Axel couldn't imagine the things Lainey had suffered at the traffickers' hands. He frowned. "What do you know about Ray personally?" She didn't seem to understand what he meant, and he added, "I'm just wondering how someone like Ray got to be in charge of such an enormous operation."

She considered the question. "He told me he once lived in Montana with his family. He said he moved away after he graduated from college and went to work for an international organization."

This had Axel's attention right away. "What type of organization?" Was it possible Ray worked for a much larger trafficking ring?

"I don't know. All he said was he'd worked his way up quickly to be in a position of power. He was so proud of what he'd accomplished." Her lips twisted in apparent disgust. "Ray drove an expensive car and wore nice clothes. A watch that he told me cost thousands of dollars."

Ray's organization was likely part of a much bigger one. He doubted Ray controlled the entire operation himself. What if Summer had seen the real person in charge without realizing it. "Did you ever see anyone visit Ray that wasn't one of his employees?" If they could figure out who this person was, hopefully Sheriff McCallister could make an arrest.

She started to shake her head but then hesitated. "There were four men and a woman who came to the house we stayed in once right after the arrests." She stopped as if recalling the moment. "They had accents, and they all gave me the creeps."

Axel sat up straighter. A woman? "Do you know what type of accents?"

She thought about it for a moment. "I'm not certain—maybe Russian? They were all armed and the woman with them was in charge."

His blood ran cold. Was the trafficking ring in Montana associated with the Russian mafia? Who was this woman in charge?

"They were all very suspicious," Summer continued. "They shut the door to Ray's office, but not before I heard Ray mention the woman's name. Vitaliy. I'd never seen him look so worried before."

The name wasn't familiar, but Ray's reaction seemed to confirm Axel's suspicions. Vitaliy, the Russian boss, must be running the entire operation. It would make sense that the Russian mafia would be concerned following the arrests. Those who were picked up might talk to shave time off their sentences—especially Harley and Phillip. "If the mafia is involved in what's happening, then this is bad on so many levels. Ray's life is in danger if he lets you get away knowing the things you do about the organization. I'd say chances are they'll probably kill Ray once you're located."

Summer's fear was etched on her face and Axel's concern ratcheted up to a whole new level. What if he couldn't protect her? Letting Ray capture her again was unthinkable.

It felt as if it took forever to cover the distance to the Amish community. When the first lights could be seen, the relief he felt was physical.

Abram's father, Henry, lived not far from where they were now. His place was a little away from the other farms. For this, he was grateful.

The farm butted up against the woods, which would allow for plenty of coverage. Axel parked the Jeep in the trees and turned toward the back seat. "Can you go to your father and tell him what's happening? You and Lainey. We will wait here."

Abram agreed. He assisted his wife from the vehicle.

Axel rolled down his window.

"There's a good chance those men may come here."

Abram nodded. "Don't worry about us. Watch your backs. These are dangerous people."

Axel swallowed uneasily, feeling the weight of what lay ahead. Could he keep Summer safe against so many? "We will."

Abram shook his hand and nodded to Summer. "I hope you will come visit us when the baby comes."

Her eyes shone with emotion. "I'd like that."

Abram stepped back and closed the door quietly. Axel backed out of the woods and headed toward the mountain where Brayden lived.

"Will they be safe?" Summer asked, her attention on the side mirror as she watched Abram return to the house.

"I hope so." But he wasn't sure. He was worried for his friends. He'd met Henry and Esther many times. They were good people who'd gone out of their way to make Axel feel welcome.

His thoughts flew in a dozen different directions. The time on the Jeep's dash said it was almost three in the morning.

"You should try and get some sleep," Axel urged. Brayden might still be awake when they arrived. His friend had told him many times about how difficult it was to sleep through the night even after being out of the military for a long time. Axel could relate. He struggled with the same issue. Too many bad things waited for him in his dreams.

Brayden had lost a lot to the war. His marriage to his college sweetheart had ended after he returned stateside. For anyone who hadn't gone through war, it was hard to understand.

"I'm too keyed up," she told him. "You said your friend's a police officer?" The reluctance in Summer's tone was clear.

"He's a deputy for the sheriff's department. Brayden and I served together in the military. I'd trust him with my life. You can, too."

A soft breath escaped her as doubts warred on her face. "I'm sorry. I wasn't always like this."

His heart went out to her. "Don't be. You've been through things that would break most people."

She swallowed and fought emotions that seemed close to the surface. "Thank you. For being there to save me. For understanding. I don't want to be this way for the rest of my life." Summer brushed her hand across her eyes. At that moment, he'd do everything within his power to make sure she survived Ray's reign of terror and had the chance at living a normal life.

He knew Summer saw herself as damaged goods. In his mind she was anything but. She was strong and courageous and beautiful on the inside and out.

"You won't," he said in a voice rough with things he hadn't felt in a while. Realizing he'd fallen in love with Erin had snuck up on him little by little. A lifetime of being there for each other. Sharing things he hadn't shared with anyone else had made him love her. But he'd lost her and for a time he'd thought he'd lost himself as well.

"In time, once this is all over and you no longer live in fear, you'll come back to yourself. And you have the baby to help you." The real Summer was in there somewhere. He wanted to know her.

Still, it would no doubt be difficult for her to move forward as a single parent. His mouth thinned. He thought about his own parents. He'd been ten when his dad had taken off and he'd never seen him again. For months afterward, he'd cried himself to sleep at night. The scariest time was when he'd stopped crying. He'd stuffed his feelings down deep and tried to pretend he didn't care that his father had not only left their mother but also Axel and his two sisters, Kim and Bridgette.

Erin had been there with him through it all. They'd joined the service together. Been sent to Afghanistan. As long as he had her to keep him level, he was okay.

Summer touched her belly. "I've been fighting so hard to escape Ray and live that I haven't really allowed myself to think about the future." She glanced lovingly down at the place where the child rested. "I don't have a home, a job—how am I going to take care of my baby? I can't go back to my family—not like this. I don't have anyone."

"You have me." He didn't hesitate to add, "You'll always have a place to stay and someone to lean on, Summer. Always."

The look of awe on her face made him feel as if he'd done the right thing. Made him always want to do the right thing for her.

Camo made a sound from the back seat almost as if to remind them he was there.

Axel chuckled. "Sorry, buddy, are we not giving you the attention you deserve?"

The dog grumbled again, and Axel petted his head.

For a while, it had been just him and Camo. They'd gotten good at reading each other. Camo had played a huge part in pulling Axel from the darkness he'd sunk into following Erin's death.

"I'm going to flip on the headlights," he said. "We'll be facing some precarious countryside up ahead."

Summer's attention returned to the windshield while Axel prayed this was the right decision. So far, it felt as if he'd made a lot of bad ones that had ended in close calls and putting innocent people in danger.

She blew out a breath. "Abram and Lainey have been through so much. I hate that their house has been damaged. It's just one more thing to be sorry for."

Axel wasn't about to let her blame that on herself. "No, Summer. That's not on you. Don't let him win."

She ducked her head. "It's hard. He told me I was worthless for so long—that no one else would ever want me."

"He lied," Axel said softly. "Ray lied."

While she continued to study his profile as if wondering what he meant, it took all of Axel's attention to focus on the path ahead.

The mountain where Brayden lived was over seven thousand feet high. The deep snow accumulation prevented Axel from being able to see the dangers that lay beneath.

Summer told him about her family's farm in Ohio. "Where we lived there weren't any mountains. The winters were hard, but we were always able to get to town for supplies." She turned toward him. "How do you do it?"

He'd talked to many people who asked him the same question. His sister Kim was among them whenever she brought his mom and her family for a visit. Axel couldn't explain but it was the very isolation of the place that made him feel at home.

He shrugged. "I guess I find it comforting. Just me and Camo taking care of each other." He looked her way and noticed a far-off look on her face.

"Actually, that sounds nice. I'd be okay with not having to run into anyone again…or at least not anyone I didn't want to." Her expression turned hard.

"I felt that way when I came here after leaving the service," he said gently. "I didn't want to be around anyone, and I blamed everyone for what happened to…"

Very few people knew about Erin's death. Brayden of course and his family.

"You lost someone you loved," she concluded.

He nodded. "Her name was Erin. We grew up together. I was going to ask her to marry me when she died."

"Oh, Axel, I'm so sorry."

He swallowed back the bitterness that always made an appearance whenever he thought about losing her.

"Thank you." He kept his eyes ahead. "Anyway, I went home to Colorado for a while but I didn't fit in and so when Brayden told me about this place…" He shrugged. "I've been here ever since." He rarely talked about Erin, but after everything they'd gone through together, he trusted Summer. Still, it left him feeling a little vulnerable talking about someone he'd once loved so much and lost.

The stretch of landscape up ahead was becoming more elevated. The Jeep climbed over rock after rock while Axel gripped the wheel and prayed they wouldn't tip over.

"We should be getting closer to where Brayden stores the snowcat, although it's hard to tell for certain. I've only been here a few times with him."

Summer leaned forward. "Is this his property?"

"Yes. He owns this area at the base of the mountain all the way up to his house and down to the left side."

"I see something up ahead." Summer pointed.

Axel squinted through the driving snow and saw it, too. "That's the shed for the snowcat."

Almost there. He could leave the Jeep parked inside and head up in the snowcat.

As they neared the shed, something seemed out of place. He stopped and shut off the lights.

"What's wrong?"

"The door is open... Brayden would never have left it like that."

Her rounded eyes met his. "Maybe he's inside."

That would be the logical assumption and yet nothing about what they'd gone through so far made sense.

"Wait for me here," he said. "Lock the doors and don't let anyone in."

"Axel, maybe we should turn back..."

He glanced behind them. Nothing. "We can't keep fighting the elements like this. We need help." He was concerned about Abram and Lainey and their family. Were they safe? The traffickers had proven ruthless in their pursuit of Summer. They wouldn't think twice about forcing innocent people to talk.

Axel looked her way and did his best not to show his concern. "I'm sure the wind blew the shed door open. But let me make sure."

Her troubled eyes held his for a long moment before she slowly nodded.

Axel slipped the handgun into his pocket and got out. He forced out a breath and eased toward the shed. As soon as he rounded it and looked through the opening his heart sank. The snowcat was missing. Had Brayden taken it into Elk Ridge after all?

He stepped inside and looked around. Normally, if Brayden worked a shift during bad weather such as this, he'd take the long way. It didn't make sense, but they had a bigger problem. He wasn't so sure the Jeep would make it up the mountain in these conditions.

Brayden did have a radio that was part of emergency services and if they could reach the cabin, Axel could use it to call in what was happening. It was their only choice.

He stepped out into the night and glanced back at the open door. Still, why would Brayden leave the door open? It was unlike him to do so.

With questions rattling round in his head, Axel returned to Summer and got in.

"The snowcat is gone," he told her and saw her fear return. He gave the only answer that made sense. "Brayden must have taken it into town." He explained about the radio. "If we can reach Brayden's place in the Jeep, we can call the sheriff."

Her attention was riveted on the looming mountain ahead.

"If I'm remembering correctly, there's a spot to the left that isn't quite so steep. We'll try that."

But finding it in these conditions wouldn't be easy. He'd only seen it a couple of times.

He buckled his seat belt, and they started forward. Axel flipped on the lights. Creeping up to the mountain base, he once more leaned forward and concentrated on what he could see in front of them.

"I think I see it." He slowed to give himself time to observe the area carefully. There were no landmarks visible now, but it looked like the right spot.

Axel eased toward the path. The first rocks of the mountain were difficult and had him wondering if he'd made a mistake.

The terrain jostled the Jeep as he crept over it. Summer braced herself as best as possible and watched the scene unfolding in front of them.

"Are you okay?"

She forced out a yes she clearly didn't feel.

Even with the snow chains, the mountain was more than the Jeep wanted. Several times, the vehicle slid backward when they encountered more ice than snow.

Summer bit back a scream as they slid sideways and slammed against a boulder.

Axel exhaled a shaky breath. "Sorry about that." He glanced down at the boulder that was blocking his door from opening.

"Are we stuck?" Her fearful eyes searched his.

"I'm not sure." He eased on the gas. The Jeep struggled to gain traction. After sliding backward, the rock scraped along the side of the hood. Axel eased onto the brakes until the vehicle came to a sideways stop when it connected with another boulder.

"Third times a charm," he said lightly to ease her mind.

After a moment, she laughed. "That was scary."

"Yeah." He hesitated before trying again. The chains finally caught and they inched up the mountain and out of the icy spot.

He could still see the shed. The direction of the tracks for the snowcat troubled him. Brayden never used the vehicle anywhere except to clear a path for himself up the mountain.

"Something's wrong, isn't it?" Summer had picked up on his worries.

He blew out a breath. "It's not like Brayden to use the snowcat to go to town. For one, the tracks can't go on the paved road without tearing it up."

Her brow creased. "Do you think Ray's men took it?"

It made more sense. If they'd stumbled upon the snowcat and knew its purpose, they could use it to travel in the storm.

"Let's keep going," he answered. "The sooner we get to Brayden's place and the radio, the better."

Summer settled back against her seat while

Axel tried to let go of his misgivings. The tracks weren't leading up to Brayden's place. But it would be okay. It had to be okay.

# Chapter Eight

The slow climb up the mountain was nerve-wracking. For every few feet they climbed, the Jeep would hit another patch of ice and slide backward.

Out of the corner of her eye, Summer spotted a silhouette. "There's someone else here."

He jerked to where she pointed. "That looks like Brayden's snowmobile." It was still about a good hour away from daybreak and difficult to see. Summer couldn't believe the things she and Axel had gone through since he found her the previous afternoon. Her attention was glued on the vehicle moving their way at a fast pace.

Axel frowned and moved the Jeep behind another boulder and parked. "If it's Brayden, he may have heard the noise earlier despite the weather"

She started to get out, but he stopped her. "I need you to wait here. I'll be right back." He looked over his shoulder at Camo. "You stay with Summer, boy."

He looked to the snowmobile light and frowned. "That's an odd direction for Brayden to be coming from."

Axel tucked his handgun into his pocket and got out while a prayer for his safety raced through Summer's thoughts.

He eased to the next boulder and took cover but not before the snowmobile spotted him. Instead of his friend waving, the man on the snowmobile opened fire.

Summer screamed and ducked low. More shots followed. Axel was shooting at the snowmobile.

The exchange ended only to be followed by a crashing sound. Then there were no more shots.

Summer rose and tried to see what was going on. The snowmobile appeared to be on its side. She got out along with Camo. Both moved to where Axel now stood at full height.

"That's definitely not Brayden," he told her. "Wait here."

He eased toward the unconscious man with Camo standing guard near Summer. The snowmobile had struck a boulder hard enough to crush the front of the vehicle.

Axel checked for a pulse.

Camo growled and turned. Before Summer had the chance to see what had the dog spooked, Axel yelled, "Watch out!" and ran toward her.

She swung in time to see two men in a standoff with Camo. A larger vehicle with tracks stood just off to their left. The missing snowcat.

Axel raced past her as Camo engaged one man.

"Get him off me!" the embattled man yelled.

The second was caught between helping his partner and zeroing in on the threat Axel posed. He whipped his weapon around and prepared to shoot.

"Get down, Summer," Axel yelled, and she dropped to the snowy ground.

Gunshots pierced through the night, whizzing past her head.

The sound of a scuffle could be heard. Axel was battling the man who had shot him while Camo continued to fight the second person.

Summer had to do something. She jumped to her feet and ran toward the struggle.

Axel and the man were locked in hand-to-hand combat. The two fought for control of the weapon in the shooter's hand.

She found Axel's gun on the ground where he'd lost it. Though Summer had never fired a weapon before, she'd watched Ray many times when he'd hold one on her or one of the other women. When she had a clear shot at Axel's attacker, she put her finger on the trigger and aimed. She fired. The noise ricocheted around the countryside.

She opened her eyes and saw Axel's shock before her bullet struck the unidentified man in the forehead. He didn't have time to scream. He died instantly.

Before she could react to the knowledge she'd taken a life, another shot was fired. She whirled toward the second man, who was trying to kill Camo.

The dog had the man's arm in his mouth and wasn't letting go.

"Drop the weapon," Axel yelled with the deceased man's gun in hand.

Summer got a good look at the man's face and recognized him immediately. DT. One of Ray's inner circle.

The man shifted his weapon from Axel to Summer. Axel didn't hesitate. One shot and the guy was dead.

Reaction set in quickly. Summer dropped the weapon as if it burned. She'd killed a man.

Axel saw and reached her side. "No, don't go there, Summer. Those men were going to kill us. You did what you had to do."

She pulled in several breaths before slowly nodding. Having to be put in a situation where you had to take another life was awful, but Axel was right—there was no other choice.

Axel looked back at the dead men. "Let's get out of here. We'll take the snowcat. It should be safer." They started for the snowcat that was still running. Camo loped in front of them, unharmed. "I'll grab our supplies and then remove the key and battery from the Jeep. If more of the ring heads this way, I don't want them using the vehicle to come after us."

She started toward him. "Let me help you."

He shook his head and held the passenger door open for her and Camo. "Stay here where it's warm."

Once they were safely inside, he disappeared into the swirling storm.

Summer kept her eyes glued to the direction he'd gone. An eerie sense of being watched had her jerking toward the place where the men lay.

The weather made it next to impossible to see anything. Nothing moved.

*Just the residual effects of what we've gone through so far.*

She struggled to keep from screaming when Axel appeared on her side carrying a battery and some of their supplies. "Got them," he said, then stopped when he noticed her expression. "Are you okay?"

She clasped her hands together and searched for calm before nodding. "But can we get out of here before someone else shows up."

He smiled gently. "Copy that." Axel stashed the supplies and battery behind their seats before getting in on the driver's side. He studied the instrument panel for a minute. "I've driven this thing before with Brayden, but it's been a while."

With his attention on the dash, Summer studied his profile and was grateful to this handsome man who had saved her.

Growing up, when she and Hannah would attend youth singing, they'd talk about the young men in the group and which ones they thought were attractive. After Ray, well, she'd seen men as monsters.

But she didn't believe Axel was like those

men. She'd witnessed his friendship with Abram and Lainey—the way he and his friends looked out for each other. And she'd seen his kindness toward her. The vehicle lurched forward, and they were on their way. Just traveling a few feet made it easy to see the difference in stability from the Jeep.

"Does your friend keep his snowmobile in the shed?" She'd seen inside the building. It didn't appear large enough to fit this snowcat as well as a snowmobile.

"Not that I recall." Axel's frown deepened. "But that was definitely Brayden's snowmobile." He glanced her way and forced a smile. "I'm sure it's like you said and he left the snowmobile down here."

But she could tell he didn't really believe that.

"Let's just get to Brayden's place and get help," Axel told her.

His attention went straight ahead as the snowcat eased along the snowy mountainside as if it weren't anything.

"How much farther?" she asked while absently stroking Camo's fur. Everything about this nightmare had stretched her nerves to the breaking point.

"Maybe another mile. It's hard to judge when you're going uphill."

Summer settled into her seat and tried to relax. They were almost there. Brayden had a way to reach the sheriff despite the storm. It was going to be okay.

For the first time, she let herself think about the future. Summer glanced down at her stomach. The baby. Her child was everything to her. She'd find a place for them.

"It'll be dawn soon. Although with this weather, it won't make it much easier to see. Are you hungry?" he asked, his strong, sure voice penetrating her doubts.

She turned her head. "I'm okay for now."

"Once we reach Brayden's I'll make you something to eat." Something shifted in his eyes. "I'm sorry you've had to go through all of this."

The sincerity in his voice made her believe him. Axel wasn't like Ray or the others she'd known.

"It was my mistake. I left the life I loved because someone told me he cared about me. I brought shame on my family." She shook her head. "That's why I can't ever go back. I've hurt them so much." She turned away when the tears were close.

"You made a mistake," came his soft voice. "You were young and you trusted a man who lied to you—who used you. Don't blame yourself."

She wanted to believe him...

"What Ray did to you was horrible, inexcusable," he added. "But it wasn't your fault."

She slowly faced him. "Thank you, Axel." She knew his words weren't some magic fix-it-all. And she'd have years ahead of her to find a way to lay to rest what she'd gone through, but hearing someone else say it meant everything.

Ray had berated her. Told her she was worthless. That no one else would ever want her. Her self-esteem was empty. But when she looked into Axel's eyes, she didn't see any of those things. Only a man who believed in her worth. He'd proven himself trustworthy over and over again since they'd met by risking his life for her. Axel made her want to be the person he saw in her.

She was so beautiful. The thought hit him out of left field. Erin had occupied his thoughts for so long. Nothing else had found room in his heart or in his mind. Until now. But he couldn't deny that since he'd met Summer, she'd occupied all his thoughts. Hearing her story broke his heart. Knowing that she blamed herself made him want to tear apart her tormenter and everyone connected to him. How could any human being do such terrible things to another?

As the snowcat jostled over the precarious terrain he thought again about Brayden's snowmobile. Though his friend had two, it didn't make sense that Brayden would leave one in the shed. Brayden would never leave the machine out in the elements, especially if he knew there was a storm coming, and as a sheriff's deputy, he'd be aware of what was in the forecast.

If the second snowmobile wasn't at Brayden's place, then it was possible Ray's crew had been to the house. The thought was unsettling.

He shared his concerns with Summer.

Her grip on the door handle tightened. "Do you think we'll be walking into a trap?"

"We can't dismiss the possibility. I'm thinking they went to Brayden's earlier, perhaps in the Snowcat and searched it. I told you there is a way to reach it from one of the county roads but it's a long route and so far, all we've seen them driving is cars."

"Unless they walked in?"

"Perhaps, but it would be a long way." He struggled to untangle answers that were illusive due to lack of sleep and the frantic pace they'd been forced to endure.

"When we get closer to Brayden's place. I'll hike up to the house and check it out."

"I'm going with you."

"That's not a good idea. They could be there waiting."

She shook her head. "I'm going. Axel, this is all about me. You're in this mess because you helped me. I'm going."

He admired her courage, but he was worried about her and the baby. "All right," he said at last.

Camo seemed to realize they were discussing something important because his full attention was on the conversation.

"You can come with us, too, Camo." Axel assured the canine. "We'll need your skills to let us know if there's trouble."

The dog settled down with his head close to Summer's hand.

"He's really taken to you." He hesitated before adding, "I meant what I said earlier, Summer. I have plenty of room in the cabin. You have a place to stay as long as you want. You and the baby."

She appeared overwhelmed. "You don't even know me. How can you offer me a place to stay and—"

"Because I see who you are even though you don't. I see you and I trust you... I care about you."

He hadn't thought he would say that again to a woman.

She smiled into his eyes. "You are a special person, Axel. Thank you for helping me."

"Anytime." Their gazes held for a long moment. Feelings he thought were no longer part of his being formed a lump in his throat that wouldn't go away no matter how many times he tried to swallow them.

Erin's pretty face appeared in his mind's eye. He'd told her he had something important to tell her. She'd been eager to get together...

His mouth thinned.

How could he think of another woman when Erin had given so much?

He dropped his hand. If Summer thought it odd, she didn't say so. She placed her hand on

Camo and faced forward watching as he continued to plow the snowcat through the snow.

At times, Axel wasn't sure what was the hardest. Not being able to tell Erin how much she meant to him or declaring his love only to lose her.

"How long have you known Brayden?"

Summer's question pulled him back from the heartache. "Going on eight years now. We served together for five. I've been out of the service for three."

"It must be hard to adjust to civilian life." Summer was watching him. Her gaze flicked over his taut jaw. The way his hands tightened on the snowcat's wheel as he tried to find a way to explain the nightmare of adjusting to life beyond war.

"It was." Axel barely recognized his voice. "I watched many of my friends die over there…" And he'd taken lives. More than he could remember except in his dreams.

"I'm so sorry," she whispered sincerely. This woman who had gone through so much had compassion for him.

"I don't usually talk about it because it's hard. Maybe one day, I'll sit down and unload my heart." He tried to make light, but her empathy didn't go away.

"Maybe one day I will as well."

He dragged in several breaths and slowly nodded. Both he and Summer were survivors. They had scars that wouldn't go away easily.

"Maybe we can help each other heal," he whispered and watched as she shivered but didn't look away.

"I'd like that. I don't think I can do it on my own."

He didn't think he could either, but he wanted to try and get better…for her.

For the first time in a long time, his smile felt genuine.

He focused ahead and realized he had hope again yet he was facing a dangerous situation. So much was at stake. Summer's life and her baby's were on the line.

Glimpses of something unexpected grabbed his attention and he stopped the snowcat.

"What's wrong?" Summer asked, her attention going in the same direction as his. "Are those lights?"

"They are." Axel didn't like it. "If Brayden's home, he'd be sleeping. If he's at work, there's no way he'd leave the lights on."

"You think it's Ray?" She studied the landscape, and he struggled to give her an answer.

"Possibly. I think this is as far as we should go in the snowcat." He turned to her. "It will be difficult walking from here but if Ray's people are inside, advancing on foot will give us the element of surprise."

He held out the weapon he'd taken from one of their attackers and she immediately shook her head. "Just as a precaution in case."

She reluctantly accepted the gun from him.

Axel searched her face before opening the door. He got out, and Camo followed immediately. Axel rounded the machine and held out his hand to help her down.

She stood beside him, and he could feel her trembling.

"It's going to be okay," he said softly.

She looked up at him with huge eyes that tugged at his heart.

He pointed through the storm. "This way."

Axel stayed close to her side. She was also eight months pregnant after all and he was worried about the baby, too.

He caught glimpses of the lights from Brayden's house, and his breath came in short gasps. The adrenaline rush he'd felt many times during battle had his senses heightened.

Axel glanced down at his dog. Camo appeared to have fallen back on his military training. No more loping around exploring different things. His full attention was on the ground. The dog's keen senses had hit on a trail. The only question was who it belonged to.

They reached the first stand of pine trees that grew around the cabin. Brayden had chosen a place among the trees to build his home down the mountainside from where he'd grown up.

The place was powered by both solar and a generator. Axel had learned a lot about construction from his friend, who'd learned it from his father.

He eased closer to the edge of the small, wooded area that Brayden had left deliberately to block the wind. The house was lit up as if every light in the place was on.

"I don't like it," he said to himself before turning to Summer. "Let's check the garage." He pointed to the left at the detached structure Brayden had built.

With Summer close, all three headed for the garage. If Brayden was indeed home, then his vehicle would be parked inside. If not, it could mean two things: Brayden had left, or Ray's men had stolen the vehicle and the second snowmobile that Brayden owned like they had the previous one.

He reached the side of the garage where there was a small side door. Brayden never left it locked. Axel opened the door and went inside. He didn't have to flip on the overhead light to see Brayden's Blazer there.

He bent over with relief. "He's home. He must be getting ready to go to work."

He stepped outside and closed the door. "Let's get out of the weather."

They reached Brayden's front porch. The curtains were closed. Brayden rarely kept them that way.

He turned to Summer. "Wait here with Camo."

She nodded, picking up on his anxiety. Axel pointed to the side of the house where they'd be out of sight, and Summer moved to the cover.

Once he was certain they were safe, he eased along the porch to the front entrance. There was no way to see inside, and he had no idea what he would be walking into. If he walked in and found Brayden, it would be a huge relief.

His friend told him he usually locked the

doors at night. Axel tried the door. It twisted freely in his hand. Immediately, Axel's hackles were up, and he had the handgun ready as he carefully stepped inside.

That no one shot at him was a welcome relief. "Brayden, are you here?"

Silence was the only answer. Axel stepped farther into the living room and took in what was before him. A dying fire in the woodstove. And a kitchen that showed no signs of Brayden preparing breakfast. Though Axel didn't know Brayden's work schedule, Brayden was generally up before dawn to start his day. And daybreak had begun to lighten the horizon despite the storm.

"Brayden, are you still asleep?" Axel eased toward the bedroom. The door stood open. The bed was empty but had been slept in recently. He went over and felt the mattress. Cold. Where was Brayden?

He knocked on the bathroom door thinking perhaps his friend had gotten sick. When there was no response, he entered the space. Empty as well. A search of the rest of the house proved something was wrong.

He hurried outside and brought Summer and Camo in.

Summer looked around the house, clearly realizing the owner was absent. "Where's your friend?"

"He's not here." Axel was worried and trying not to show it. "I didn't check to see if the second snowmobile was in the garage. I'll be right back." He stepped outside and tried to get his thoughts together. Perhaps Brayden had had to leave in a hurry and hadn't bothered turning off lights. What Axel knew for certain was that Brayden had been asleep at one time but had gotten up. But what would give him cause to take the snowmobile over the Blazer that was equipped with snow chains and more than capable of covering the rough terrain that led to the county road?

The answer was he wouldn't have, unless he'd gone down the way Axel and Summer had come.

None of it made sense. Axel covered the rest of the way to the garage and opened the side door once more. As soon as he flipped the lights on, the dreadful truth slapped him in the face. The snowmobile was there.

They'd taken Brayden.

# Chapter Nine

Summer paced the living room. She was worried about Axel.

Camo seemed to be mirroring her steps. She stopped and looked down at the dog. "He'll be okay, boy." She hugged Camo's neck. The dog stared up at her with troubled eyes. "Don't worry. Axel's got this."

As soon as the words were out, the sound of footsteps on the wooden porch had her jerking toward the door. She let Camo go and pulled the gun out of her pocket.

The door flew open, and her heart exploded in her chest. When Axel appeared, her relief was physical. He closed the door and bolted the lock.

"Is the snowmobile still in the garage?" She scanned his taut expression.

"Yes, but there's something else. The SUV's been tampered with and so has the snowmobile."

"They've been here." Her eyes held his. "What about your friend?"

The grim expression on his face assured her Axel was concerned. "He's missing." Axel's attention shifted from her to something beyond her right shoulder.

She turned as he hurried toward a desk that was set up on the opposite side from the woodstove. She followed him over.

He picked up a microphone that was detached from a machine.

"It's broken." He turned distraught eyes her way. "The police radio is broken."

There was no doubt in Summer's mind that Ray had ordered this. The only question was why? "I don't understand why Ray would come after your friend. He has nothing to do with me."

Axel was still holding the broken mic. "I'm guessing they came here looking for us and managed to catch Brayden sleeping. They took him by surprise before he had the chance to defend himself."

"But he's not here. They didn't…kill him."

Axel flinched at her words. "Maybe they figured he'd be able to help them in some way." He stared at the mic. "They're gone for now.

If I can get the radio working again, I can call for help." He ran a hand through his hair. "Do you have any idea where they might have taken him? What about the house you escaped from? Can you find it again?"

Her stomach clenched. The thought of going back there made her sick but if it saved Brayden's life then she'd do it. "I think so. It's isolated. If Ray's men thought Brayden could help them locate us in some way, they might take him there to…" She couldn't say the word torture. Ray and his goons had perfected that art to force people to talk. She remembered the time some of the girls had run away. Ray captured one and had tormented her until she'd given up the location of the rest. And then she'd disappeared. The other girls never came back. Summer had no doubt Ray had killed all of them.

"Brayden's strong." Axel examined the radio. "They really did a number on this."

"What can I do to help?" She'd asked because she had to do something.

Axel turned to her with a gentle look. "Just rest. I know you're exhausted." He went over to the woodstove and added some logs and kindling to it. Soon the kindling caught, and the fire began to penetrate the cold. He pulled up the sofa close to the fire. "I'll see if I can make us something to eat and take another look at the radio." Summer used the restroom and then returned to the living room. She stretched out and tried to shut down her mind enough to sleep but it was impossible.

She heard Axel moving around in the kitchen.

"Can't sleep?" he asked coming back in. He handed her a bowl filled with stew.

She stifled a yawn. "No, I can't. Too much on my mind."

"I get that. I checked the radio. It's a bust. I think they may have taken some part of it to keep anyone who found it from getting it to work and calling for help." He sat beside her. "In other words, us."

A disturbing thought occurred er. "Unless they weren't thinking of us but Brayden."

Axel's frown deepened. "I'm not following…"

"Maybe they came here thinking they'd gotten your address wrong, and that you lived here. They broke in, but Brayden managed to escape. They could be looking for him."

Axel shot from his seat. "If he's out there on foot, he's in danger." He paced the room while holding his injured shoulder. "I don't even know where to start looking for him. In this blizzard, he won't last long."

"We don't know for certain that's what happened," she reminded him. "Is there any place close where Brayden might go for help?"

"My place," he said and pulled a face. "Abram and the Amish community are closer but there are no phones."

"What should we do?" Summer had no idea where to go from here.

He turned toward the radio. "I'm praying Brayden was able to make it out of the house without being caught. Right now, we need the sheriff involved in this dangerous situation because we can only keep running for so long before we're found."

Summer couldn't hold back her frightened reaction.

He came back over and sat down beside her. "I'm guessing based on what they did to the radio, there's no way I can fix the Blazer or the snowmobile." He huffed out a breath. "There's only one thing I can think to do. Go back for the snowcat."

She had a feeling this was what he'd say but still the thought of hiking back to the machine wasn't a welcome one.

"I think the sooner we get going the better." Axel pulled out the sat phone and gave it a try. His frustration was clear. "It's not going through."

She slowly lumbered to her feet. The concern on his face for her made her feel special. Summer hadn't felt that way in a long time.

Axel rose beside her. Only inches separated them. "I'm sorry I have to take you with me, but I would be too worried leaving you here by yourself, even with Camo."

She didn't feel worthy of his concern. All the terrible things she'd been forced to do played through her head, assuring her she was dirty and no one would ever love her.

"I'll be okay." Her voice was barely a whisper, his attention on her face.

"You deserve someone to love you and treat you and your baby right."

She swallowed but the lump in her throat wouldn't go away. "I want to believe you."

He tucked her hair behind her ear in an unexpected gesture that had her sucking in a breath. Yet, for once she wasn't repelled by Axel's gentle touch.

"It will get better. There are people who can help. I can help. I want to."

She believed him. "I trust you, Axel. I don't trust anyone else."

"Thank you." He seemed moved by her admission. "Then let me help you through this. I won't leave your side."

She could get through just about anything as long as he was there.

"Right now, we have to get out of here. Those men are still on our tail and could be anywhere. They're good at disabling things. If we lose the snowcat..."

He didn't need to finish. They'd be on foot and subject to Ray's men as well as the weather. "I'm ready. I can make it," she said even though she wasn't so sure.

He looked at her with awe before going over to the door with Camo at his heels. Axel cracked it and looked out. Even if the threat was out there somewhere waiting, it would be impossible to see or hear them.

"Stay close to me," he told her, and she willingly agreed.

Summer slipped out beside him and closed the door. Fear-fueled adrenaline swept through her body replacing the exhaustion. She stayed so close to Axel that whenever he stopped, she bumped into him.

He eased toward the edge of the porch and then off it. Camo was right at his side.

Together, they started toward the woods once more. Every step scared the daylights out of her. Summer was relieved when they reached the trees, because it allowed some amount of coverage.

"Let's take a break," Axel suggested. "The cold makes it hard to catch your breath."

She was too busy sucking in air to answer. Eventually, her heart rate slowed and she could breathe normally.

"Ready?" he asked after they'd rested for a few minutes.

Summer wasn't anywhere close to being ready to start walking again but she had to be strong for Axel. He couldn't fight this battle alone. "Yes, I'm ready."

He searched her face before they began moving again. Fighting the wind made it seem as if they weren't making any progress at all. Each step was a battle. The howl of the wind through the trees overrode every other sound. Their pursuers could be right on top of them, and they'd never know it.

Although the skies had lightened now with

dawn, the storm and the woods made it still difficult to see anything.

After stumbling several times, Axel looped his arm through hers to keep her steady. Even Camo seemed to be struggling.

"Let's stop for a second and catch our breath again," Axel said when he noticed Summer struggling even though they hadn't been moving long.

She huddled close to him, using a group of aspen trees for some protection from the biting wind.

"It's getting harder to see where we're going," Axel said close to her ear. "Our earlier tracks are covered up by fresh snow." He pointed straight ahead. "I think this is the way."

After they'd rested for a while longer, they started walking again. Through the snow, something caught Summer's attention. She stopped. "What is that?"

Axel focused on what she was seeing. "That's a light. It could be Brayden."

The light disappeared with the swirl of the storm. "Where'd it go?" She waited but it didn't return.

"Let's keep heading that way. If it's Brayden, he could be turned around in the storm as well."

Once they reached the place where the glow had been, they saw that the ground was cluttered with footprints. More than one set.

"That's not Brayden—or if it is, he's not alone." Axel frowned as he studied the prints. "I'm more worried about Ray's people. Let's see if we can get back on track for the snowcat. We need to extract ourselves from this situation and the only way to do that is to get to the snowcat."

She agreed. As much as she didn't want to think about Brayden being out here with dangerous men, every second they were out in the open she felt exposed.

"Which way?" She'd long since lost the direction of the vehicle.

"To tell you the truth, I'm not a hundred percent sure, but I think it's this way." He pointed to their left.

Once more, they started walking. At the edge of the tree coverage a downhill trek waited.

The boots she wore had some traction on the bottoms, but the ice beneath the snow had her slipping and sliding. If it weren't for Axel's grip on her arm, she would have gone down.

"This is dangerous, let's stop." Axel's breathing was labored like hers. "How are you holding up?" he asked when he noticed her clutching her stomach.

Summer was too exhausted to answer. Cramps continued to shoot across her midsection from the endless walking. She couldn't imagine the stress this was putting on the baby.

"Let's rest for a bit." He dusted off a fallen tree for her to sit. Through the limited visible space, every angle looked the same.

"I don't see any other way down," Axel told her after a few moments' rest. "But thankfully we don't have far to go. Are you okay with continuing?"

She wasn't but they didn't have a choice. "I'm okay."

Axel kept his arm through hers as they slowly headed down the mountain. Summer didn't remember the snowcat being this far away. Had they missed it in the storm? "Where is it?"

"I don't see it. It's possible that in the storm we've been going the wrong direction." He glanced around them.

The thought was terrifying. What if they couldn't find it or their way back?

Camo trotted away and was quickly swallowed up in the whiteout.

"He may be on to something." They quickly

followed when he barked. An object soon appeared through the snow. It was the snowcat. The dog stood next to it sniffing the tracks.

Axel laughed. "Thank you, Camo." The dog looked up as they approached. "Let's get out of here." Axel opened the door and helped Summer inside. Camo leaped up into the cab, no doubt happy to be out of the weather.

Axel got in and started the machine once more. He didn't waste time heading back up the direction they'd come at a slow and steady pace.

"Who do you think was behind the light we saw?" she asked.

Axel looked her way. "There's no doubt it was one of the people searching for us. They probably found the snowmobile and the three dead men and figured we were behind it."

She wondered about those who had been at Brayden's home. Where had they gone and what had they done with Brayden?

The snowcat continued climbing. "It shouldn't be much farther until we top the mountain," Axel told her. "From there it should be fairly smooth going. We need to reach the sheriff's office."

Those were welcomed words and yet Summer couldn't let herself relax. Ray was coming after her with everything he had. Did he know about the evidence she'd stashed away? If he did, she didn't believe it would matter how much money the baby might fetch—he'd kill Summer to silence her and probably not before he tortured her to find out where she'd hidden the thumb drive.

Something moved in the storm off to her left. She squinted through the windshield, but it was gone. Had she imagined it? Was she seeing bad guys everywhere?

She drew in a breath.

"Everything okay?" Axel asked.

"I'm not sure. I thought I saw something to my right."

Axel glanced past Summer. "Wait, I see something, too." The words barely cleared his lips when gunfire exploded around them. The all-out weapon's attack had him swerving away as shots whizzed off the snowcat. If they lost the machine, they'd be on foot and there was no way of knowing how many people were out there.

They headed away from the shooters. "There's no place you can get that's safe. The cab is all glass," Summer shouted.

And the speed they were capable of going

wasn't fast enough to outrun the men. The shots continued to rain all around them.

"I count two shooters," Axel told her while searching to her right where the men continued firing on them. "Can you drive this thing?" he asked unexpectedly.

The only thing she'd ever driven was a buggy back on the farm. Ray had drivers who moved the girls from place to place.

"It's simple. Here's the gas and the brake. Take the wheel and head away from the shooting. I'm going to try something."

As much as she didn't want him to put his life in more danger, a standoff might be their only option.

Axel opened the door and waited for Summer to take the controls.

He jumped out and slipped toward the back of the machine. She shut the door and kept driving, remembering what he'd told her.

A round of shots coming from behind had her jerking that way. Gun barrel flashes coming from Axel's direction were followed by a distant scream. He'd hit one.

The firing continued. Summer ducked when several of the shots pinged off the glass. Camo growled and leaped into the seat she'd vacated. "No. Camo. Down, boy."

The dog did as she asked.

She glanced back and saw Axel using the cover of the snowcat to protect him from the gunfire that continued. A heartbeat later, another scream confirmed the second shooter was down.

Was that all there was?

Axel appeared beside her and knocked on the glass. She jumped in alarm, but found the brake pedal and pressed down as he opened the door and climbed in. She was glad to give him back the controls.

"I think that was all of them for now." He closed the door and hit the gas pedal. The snowcat started up again.

"Where'd they come from?" She knew Ray had lots of men keeping his organization running. He'd bragged about how he had a virtual army protecting him.

"They're probably the same ones who were at Brayden's place. There could be more."

She had no doubt.

The machine topped the mountain and moved onto level ground. At least that was something.

Getting through the woods with the machine

was difficult. The trees grew close together. There was barely room to walk in some places.

Axel maneuvered the vehicle to the right. "Brayden cleared a path especially for the snow-cat. We need to find it for easier traveling."

As they moved along, Summer couldn't get what had happened back there out of her head. These men seemed to know the layout of the land well. Something Ray told her once flashed through her mind and she grabbed Axel's arm without thinking.

"What is it?" His attention went to the darkness at her side.

"Ray told me he still has family here that he visits... He'd know the area."

She shivered at the thought.

"Did he ever say where he lived?"

She tried to remember anything useful and couldn't. "No, only that he'd lived here before, oh, and I think he mentioned having a brother."

"Does the brother still live here? I'm wondering if he's using his brother for intel as to what's happening in the area. Where the police are working. Things about the previous case that still aren't settled."

"I don't know." She wouldn't put anything

past Ray, including using his own flesh and blood to get what he wanted.

As she glanced out at the darkness pressing in, Summer could almost feel the danger lurking just beyond the safety of the cab...waiting to pounce.

Axel could barely see anything in front of them. Would they be able to find the road leading into town? Normally, the snowcat wouldn't be traveling under these severe conditions. Brayden used it when it was daylight and not in the middle of a blizzard.

In the middle of a storm, it was impossible to see danger until they were right on top of it. If it hadn't been for those men using flashlights and Summer just happening to glance in that direction, they both could be dead.

"Can you think of anything else Ray might have mentioned in the past that could help us?" He knew it was a long shot, but he needed to know.

She leaned back in her seat. "He said a lot of things. Ray loved to hear about himself. He used to brag about how far he'd come from his simple upbringing. He'd make fun of his family as if they were beneath him."

Axel's mouth thinned. "How did he end up in Ohio if he's from around here?"

"When we first met, he told me he was working for a business in town. Of course, that was a lie. I overheard him telling some of his cronies once that he had worked his way up to run the organization. He'd become successful with his bosses in the past by knowing just the right type of girls to pick."

The man's brutality was revolting. "When this is over, I'm going to make it my personal mission to bring him down," he said with enough anger, it had her turning toward him.

She slowly smiled. "Thank you, but I don't want you going down that dark path. I don't want anything bad to happen to you."

The look in her eyes took his breath away. He studied her pretty face for a second longer before staring straight ahead. There was no denying he cared about Summer—how could he not. She'd suffered so much at Ray's hands and yet she was still fighting. He swallowed several times but the lump in his throat wouldn't go away. She put him to shame. Though his faith had grown strong, he'd held on to the anger he felt over losing Erin all these years. He'd blamed God. Himself. The enemy for her death. He'd let it isolate him from most forms of human contact. Brayden was the only close friend he had, and Axel believed it was because they shared what it was like to have seen combat. It was hard to explain that to a civilian.

Summer had her hands clasped over her baby as if protecting it from the dangers outside. Camo was curled up at her feet as if he'd known her forever. She must have felt him watching her, because she turned. Just for a moment, their eyes held. Things he wished he could understand there gave him hope. If their future together was only brief and he was to be there for her and her baby for a short time, it would be enough.

He looked away and pulled out the sat phone once more. Not that he had much hope, but he didn't want to think he'd left anything on the table without trying everything he could to save them.

The sudden static on the line gave him hope. He dialed for help. It rang once and then dropped.

"Almost," he said with frustration. "I'll keep trying." Maybe it was just the location.

Through the darkness, the landscape in front of them became confusing. The trees were getting shorter. Before he put two and two together, he realized they'd reached the edge of cliff on the way down.

"Hold on." He just had time to get out before the snowcat flew off the side of a steep downhill fall.

Summer screamed and closed her eyes.

Axel gripped the wheel tight and braced for a hard hit. He reached for Camo who was hunkered at Summer's feet. The machine struck the ground hard and plowed along for several hundred feet, taking out trees along with it.

Another scream from Summer followed. They were headed for a sheer drop-off.

Lord, please don't let us die here. The prayer tumbled through his head as he fought with everything he had to keep the machine upright.

The brakes seemed not to be in effect as the speed picked up. One of the tracks on the snowcat snapped free, jerking the machine sideways.

"Axel, watch out!" Summer warned.

"I can't control it." He gritted his teeth and stomped on the brakes until he could smell them overheating.

"If we go over it's going to be bad," Axel told her. So many things he wanted to say didn't feel right in the moment.

The snowcat shuddered along as it brought down trees. He stood up and stomped even harder. Axel fearfully watched the trees coming up quickly. Several were huge pine trees. He could no longer steer the machine but if they could hit one of the trees, it might stop their momentum. A large tree appeared in front of them.

"Oh no, oh no, oh no." The words slipped from his lips as he watched the nightmare approaching. He barely got the words out before the snowcat slammed against it at full speed. The sound of metal crunching—glass breaking—was like nothing he'd heard before.

"Cover your eyes with your arm," he managed and closed his eyes to keep shards of glass from damaging them. The impact of the crash seemed to keep going forever. Axel smacked his head on the side of the shattered window and felt the world around him go black.

Axel had no idea how long he'd been out, but he awoke to pain. Everywhere. Coming from his temple. His shoulder. His face stung as if needles were attacking it.

A low moan from close by had his eyes shooting open. Had it come from him or…at his feet,

Camo looked up at him. The dog appeared unscathed. "You okay, boy?"

Camo acknowledged his concern with a lick. The dog hadn't been strapped in. Axel couldn't imagine what he'd gone through.

Axel turned his head toward Summer, and another sharp pain followed the movement. He struggled to focus. Her head was against the headrest and turned slightly toward him. She wasn't moving.

"Summer!" He swiftly unbuckled himself and shook her. "Summer, are you hurt?" The baby!

She had a dark smudge in the center of her forehead. No doubt where she'd smacked it against something.

He tried to use his right hand to examine the injury, but the pain was too much. His shoulder had slipped out of joint upon impact.

"Summer, wake up." He shook her again and she moaned, her eyes slowly opening.

She stared at him confused for the longest time. "What happened?"

"We crashed. Can you move? Is anything broken?"

She seemed to be in shock. "I'm not sure." She moved her arms and legs. "I think I'm okay." When she finally was able to focus, she gasped. "Axel, your face. You're bleeding. There's glass embedded everywhere."

He lifted his left hand and felt the debris that had struck him. "The window shattered." He searched for Camo who was still in the floorboard at Summer's feet.

He patted the frightened dog. "Good boy."

The snowcat groaned and shifted dangerously close to the edge. The tree was all that was keeping the machine from rolling over the cliff. Axel had no idea if it would hold for long.

"We have to get out of here," he told her. "The tree could give way at any time." He tried his door. It wasn't moving. "We'll have to try and get out through the other side." They switched seats.

The snowcat's headlights were still on. He could see a little bit and the lights from inside the cab would help. Still, one false move.

He shoved at the other door. It was far worse than the driver's side.

"I'll have to crawl out the front." He had a thought and searched through the contents of the glove box. "A flashlight. Thank you, Brayden." Axel clicked it on and shined it around outside. The pine tree was right up against the Snowcat. He focused the light on the ground. The drop-off was just past the tree, which appeared to be half-uprooted.

At eight months pregnant, there was no way Summer could fit through the opening. He'd have to get the door open and fast.

He didn't want to tell Summer how bad their situation was. Axel picked the few remaining shards of glass free and bent over to make it through the opening while being careful not to make contact with his injured shoulder.

Having to use only his left arm made getting free of the snowcat nearly impossible. He dropped down. The jarring of his body hitting the ground raced through his knees up to the injured arm. He bit back a scream.

"Are you okay?" Summer asked, leaning out of the cab.

It took a second for the pain to ease. "I think so." He once again tried the door, but it wouldn't budge. The snowcat was busted beyond use. "I'm going to try and free the driver's door from outside."

With the flashlight aimed at his feet, Axel worked his way carefully around to the other side.

After several tries, the door still wouldn't release. He tried not to show his concern.

"Wait—I remember Brayden telling me he keeps a toolbox in the snowcat." Axel searched through one of the storage compartments and found nothing. "It must be on the other side." As he headed back around, the machine shifted, sliding further against the tree. The tree gave way a little more. Summer screamed. Time was running out.

He hurried to the storage and found a crowbar. He'd have to pry the door open, and he just hoped there was time.

Axel returned to the driver's side and positioned the crowbar against the lip of the door. It was hard to gain enough leverage with one good arm, but he put his entire weight against the bar and the door opened slightly. The snowcat groaned under the movement.

"Hurry, Axel," she called. "I'm not sure how much longer we have."

He gathered his strength and pried again. The door screeched, and the snowcat moved again. Finally the door gave way, and he threw it open.

Camo jumped down beside him, waiting for Summer.

The snowcat slipped further. The tree cracked. "It's giving way! There's no more time." Axel reached up and wrapped his arms around Summer, hauling her from the machine. He fell backward and she landed on top of him.

A loud cracking followed as the tree broke and tumbled down the drop-off. The snow-cat slid off behind it. Several heartbeats later, a thunderous crash resounded from below.

Their only means of escape was now gone.

Slowly he shifted her from on top of him. "Let's get back to Brayden's and treat our injuries." He felt in his pocket and breathed out a sigh. The sat phone was still there.

Axel rose and helped Summer to her feet using his good arm. It took him a second to recall the direction of the cabin.

Once they started walking, Axel noticed Camo had a limp. His friend was hurting.

"Poor Camo," Summer said when she spotted the dog favoring one side.

"Camo, stop." Axel went over to the dog and felt the injured leg. Camo whimpered. "I'm sorry buddy. It's not broken. I'll need to secure it so there's no further damage, though." He peeled off his jacket. Tearing off a strip of cloth to use was next to impossible. "I can't do anything with this dislocated shoulder."

"Here, let me." Summer took the jacket from him and tore off a large piece of the liner.

"You'll have to wrap it tight," he said and hated feeling useless.

She followed his instructions and secured the dog's injured leg while Camo submitted, realizing she was there to help.

Once she'd tied off the cloth, Axel studied her work. "That's a good job. How'd you learn to bandage like that?"

"From living on a farm and taking care of the animals."

He grinned and clumsily slipped his jacket back on. They started walking again. Camo still limped but the brace seemed to help.

He glanced at her. "I'll need your help with getting my shoulder back in its socket."

"Of course. We'll need to get all the glass out of your face before it gets infected."

He nodded. It stung but his shoulder hurt worse. "How are you feeling?" he asked. "You took quite a knock to your head."

Summer felt around the spot that had begun to swell and winced. "It hurts, but it's not too bad."

As they walked, Axel listened for any sign of

more of Ray's men coming but it was impossible to hear anything over the weather.

"Maybe we'll arrive back at Brayden's house and find him there waiting for us." He tossed her a crooked smile, which she returned.

"Wouldn't that be nice."

Axel wasn't holding out much hope. "As soon as I'm patched up, I'll take a stab at fixing the Blazer. We need a way out of here. Heading out on foot in this weather won't be a good idea."

Yet they might not have a choice. They couldn't afford to stay still for long.

Summer stopped. "Look, there are the lights."

Axel focused through the storm in the direction she'd pointed, grateful he'd forgotten to turn off the cabin lights.

As they headed toward the house Axel could feel the effects of everything they'd gone through creeping up on him zapping his strength. They both needed rest. Summer showed clear signs of exhaustion.

They needed to warm up, get something to eat, and to rest—and yet he wasn't sure if they'd have time for any of it.

As they neared, his fear that there might be men inside waiting for them had him wanting to protect Summer. "Stay by the side of the house. Let me go inside and do a quick search."

Once she was out of sight, he opened the door and checked each room, realizing the place was as they'd left it earlier.

Axel went out and brought Summer and Camo inside.

"It's empty. Let's sit for a second." The fire in the woodstove was still burning. He added a few more logs before claiming one of the chairs beside Summer.

"I sure hope we've seen the last of Ray's people for a while. We need time to recoup." He grinned, trying to lighten the moment but failed terribly.

Summer smiled sadly at his efforts. "I'm sorry, Axel."

"Don't be. This is all on Ray." But it did seem as if Ray was taking extreme measures to get Summer back. Was it because of something she knew? He voiced his concerns.

She hesitated for a second. "Ray kept his records all online. He'd have me handle them for him. He had the real names of the girls as well as the ones he'd assigned them. Where he'd taken them from, their ages as well as the names of those in his organization and others that he worked with."

He stilled at the confession. "That could be invaluable to law enforcement."

She nodded. "I thought so. One day when he wasn't looking, I copied all the files onto a thumb drive. I was so afraid he'd catch me, but he didn't. I stuck it into my jeans pocket."

Axel couldn't believe how brave she was. "Do you still have the drive?"

She shook her head. "I was afraid of what Ray would do if he found it. I hid it in the wall of the house before I left."

"You're very courageous, Summer," he said softly.

She shook her head. "I don't feel courageous. Everything scares me."

He searched her face. "It won't always be this way."

Looking at her now, he observed things he hadn't taken notice of before, like how the light caught her blond hair and made it shine. The way her brown eyes seemed to hold flecks of gold in their depths. She had a sprinkle of freckles across her nose. She was beautiful. She needed someone to love her and make her feel that way.

He killed that line of thought immediately. That wasn't him. He didn't have it in him... did he?

Axel cleared his throat. "I'll see if I can find something to treat our wounds." He rose without waiting for her to respond.

In the kitchen he searched cabinets until he found antiseptic and bandages along with tweezers for the glass. He filled a bowl with water and grabbed a couple of towels to clean both their head injuries.

Summer rose as he entered. She looked at him tentatively as if she didn't understand what had just happened between them.

Axel set the supplies on the coffee table. "Do you mind helping me get my shoulder back in place?"

She assured him she didn't. "What do I need to do?"

"First I'm going to lie on the floor on my back." He stretched out on the wood floor and extended his arm, gently bending his elbow so that his palm touched the top of his head.

"Can you support my arm?" he asked through gritted teeth.

She quickly knelt and did as he asked. Axel

drew in a couple of breaths before he rotated his hand behind his head and toward his neck.

He closed his eyes and waited for the pain to lessen before continuing.

"What can I do to help?" Summer asked. Axel opened his eyes. "Exactly what you're doing." He gradually moved the hand down toward the nape of his neck and reached toward the opposite shoulder. He felt a pop as the shoulder slid back in place. Followed by immediate relief.

"Did it work?"

He tested his arm. "It did." Axel rose. "I need something to use as a sling." He searched around until he found one of Brayden's old T-shirts. With Summer's help, they fashioned it into a makeshift sling.

"That feels much better," he said in relief.

"Let me get the glass from your face and treat your head wound."

Axel was happy to take a seat. Setting the shoulder back in place had zapped his small pool of energy.

Summer sat across from him and began gently removing each piece of glass with tweezers. "There are so many." Each piece stung as she pulled it free. A worried frown emerged. She looked him in the eye and a jolt of awareness shot through his frame.

Summer leaned closer as she worked. Her blond hair brushed against his skin as she gently worked the glass free. He could smell her shampoo.

He closed his eyes to keep from showing her his reaction to her nearness and imagined a time when the threat around them was gone. What would happen then? Would she eventually return to her home? Move on and find someone to care for her?

She was a beautiful person who had suffered so much at Ray's hands. She likely needed time to heal before she could love anyone. In his own way, Axel understood that. Would he ever be able to let go of the guilt from his past and love again? Right now, it felt about as impossible as surviving Ray.

# Chapter Ten

Her body ached from the effects of the snow-cat accident. She was exhausted down to her soul and her heart rate hadn't settled to normal yet. Summer wasn't sure how much more she could take, but she was more concerned for the baby's welfare. The child had been restless throughout the night.

*Please, Lord, protect my child.* She couldn't lose her baby.

Summer focused on the final piece of glass lodged in Axel's forehead. "This is the last one." She pulled in a breath and extracted it with unsteady hands.

Axel opened his eyes and looked at her, no doubt seeing her weariness. "Are you okay?"

"I'm fine." She dismissed his concern and held up the tiny piece of glass for him to see.

"Thank you." He started to get up, but she

stopped him. "Not so fast. Let me clean the cuts and your head injury."

He sat back down and clenched his hands while she carefully dabbed a wet cloth over the bloody gash on his head.

"Am I hurting you?" Her brow knitted together. She'd been trying to be careful.

His eyes clouded. "No, you aren't hurting me." The rough edges of his voice had her searching his face.

She lowered the hand holding the cloth. There was something about him that made her wish for things that wouldn't be possible. Her gaze snagged on his lips. A whisper of a sigh that originated from somewhere deep inside, where Elizabeth and all her hopes and dreams still lived, bubbled to the surface. That small part of her wondered what it would feel like to be kissed by Axel.

But she wasn't that woman anymore and too many horrible things stood in the way of her ever being Elizabeth again.

She jerked back. They watched each other through the space separating them. All her uncertainties were there for him to see, and she didn't know what to say.

Camo growled menacingly, breaking the

spell. The dog started for the door. Axel jumped to his feet, standing in front of her. The door flew open, as snow and wind piled in. A man Summer didn't recognize stepped inside, his frantic gaze searching their faces before he fell to the floor unconscious.

"Brayden!" Axel raced to the unconscious man and turned him over. "He's been shot."

Summer shut the door and knelt beside Axel. "How bad is it?" Blood covered Brayden's jacket. She couldn't imagine what was underneath.

Axel opened the jacket and reeled backward in shock. "It's bad." Brayden's shirt was soaked. "He's been shot in the stomach. We need to stop the bleeding."

Summer rose and got a clean towel from the kitchen and handed it to Axel.

He pressed it against the wound. "Can you get some more gauze from the kitchen? There's a roll I can use to bandage the wound after I pack it." He told her where to look, and Summer rushed to the kitchen to the cabinet and found the items.

When she brought them back, Axel had Brayden's sweatshirt pulled up to expose the gash. He removed the cloth. Blood seeped out.

He moved Brayden slightly to see that there was an exit wound.

Summer handed him the gauze and he packed both wounds as much as he could before wrapping it. Though Brayden remained unconscious, he moaned when Axel was forced to turn him over on his side to get the bandage secured.

"I'm sorry, buddy," he said, his expression grave. Once he'd finished, he tugged the sweatshirt back into place.

"That's a serious injury," he told Summer. "The bandage will hopefully keep it from bleeding too much, but he's lost a lot of blood already." He looked over his shoulder. "He's freezing. I'm going to see if I can move him closer to the fire."

Summer moved the chairs out of the way.

Axel carefully wrapped his arm around Brayden's upper torso and lifted him off the floor. Once more his friend groaned in pain. He moved Brayden to the sofa while Summer found a quilt and placed it over him.

Camo came over to sniff Brayden's hand before settling in front of him.

"What do we do now?" Brayden was in serious condition, and they didn't have any way of calling for help.

Axel brought out the sat phone and tried it again. "It's still not connecting." He rubbed his forehead and checked Brayden's pockets. "He doesn't have his cell phone with him— not that it would be any better than the sat phone. There's only one option I can think of. I'm going to see if I can get the Blazer working. Can you keep watch over Brayden?"

She willingly agreed but she was worried about Axel. "What if Ray's people are close? You could be in danger if you go out there alone." Her worst fear was Brayden had been followed.

"I'll sweep the space around the house to check for any sign of them." He started for the door. "Lock up behind me…just in case."

She hated the possibilities left unsaid. At the door, she decided that Axel's searching gaze was something she would remember for the rest of her life. She wished she had the courage to ask what it meant. Did he feel something like her or was it all in her head?

Without a word, Axel stepped out and closed the door behind him. Summer slid both the dead bolt and the chain lock into place before she turned to look at Axel's friend.

Camo made a noise as she approached. He looked up at her with soulful eyes as if he was worried about Brayden, too.

"I don't know what to do for him, Camo." But she did.

Summer slowly sank to her knees and prayed for Brayden. "Please, *Gott*, don't take his life. Please let him live."

Her eyes opened slowly to find Brayden still unconscious, his head positioned at an awkward angle. Summer went to the bedroom and retrieved a pillow before placing it beneath him.

Brayden groaned in pain, his eyes shooting open. "Who are you?" he whispered in a scratchy voice.

"I'm Summer. I came here with your friend Axel."

He looked around the room. "Where is he?"

"Outside. He's trying to get your SUV working so we can leave."

Brayden's frown deepened as he appeared to be trying to remember what happened.

"Someone disabled both the Blazer and your snowmobile," Summer explained.

He closed his eyes briefly. "I remember. They

broke in and came after me, but I managed to get out through the back window. I made it halfway to the county road when they shot me." He stopped and dragged in a couple breaths. "I lost my phone along the way. Wasn't sure I'd make it back. The radio." He struggled to sit up.

Summer rushed to his side. "You mustn't move."

Brayden spotted the radio and fell back against the pillow. "It's busted."

"They wanted to make sure you couldn't call for help," Summer told him.

"It's not safe here." The truth had her stomach in knots. "I did my best to disguise my direction, but I'm pretty sure I left a blood trail. They'll come looking here eventually."

Summer cast a troubled look toward the door. She prayed Axel was able to get the SUV running again before that happened.

"Can I have some water," Brayden croaked. "My throat feels as dry as a desert."

"Of course. I'll get it." Summer went to the kitchen and filled a glass. "Here you go." She held it up to his lips.

Brayden took only a few sips. "Thank you," he murmured, his words slurred.

"You should rest." He didn't respond, but his eyes closed.

Brayden's words played uneasily through her head. *I'm pretty sure I left a blood trail.*

Even in the storm, their pursuers would be able to follow the trail.

She walked to the window and looked out. From the direction of the garage a tiny bit of light shone. "Hurry, Axel."

She checked the locks on the back entrance and returned to Brayden. He appeared to be unconscious again.

As carefully as possible, she checked his wound. So far, there wasn't any fresh blood on the outside of the bandage. That had to be a good sign.

Too anxious to sit still, Summer paced the room. Camo left his post at Brayden's feet and walked with her. She glanced down at the animal who had won her heart almost from the beginning. "Thank you for keeping me company."

Camo seemed to understand.

On her third trip around the room a noise near the front of the house grabbed her attention. A vehicle. Her first thought was Ray's men had found them.

The vehicle stopped. What did she do? She pulled out the weapon Axel had given her. No matter what, she'd do her best to protect Brayden.

Someone knocked.

Summer froze. The gun shook in her hand. The men hunting them wouldn't be polite enough to knock, surely.

"It's me, Summer." Axel. She quickly unlocked the door and opened it. He rushed inside covered in snow.

The Blazer was parked outside behind him. "You got it running."

"I did. Thankfully, the Blazer is old and uses simple means to run. They loosened the distributor cap. I tightened it and the battery cables. It fired right up." He swung toward Brayden. "How's he doing?"

"Resting." She told him what Brayden had said. Axel's hands balled at his side.

"All the more reason to get out of here before they arrive." He went over and studied his friend. "If those men are near the county road, then we can't go that way. We'll have to take a detour."

He gently shook his friend. It took several tries before Brayden awakened.

"Hey, buddy. How are you feeling?"

Brayden cringed. "Like I've been shot."

Axel laughed. "Well, we're going to get out of here and get you some help. The Blazer is running. Can you stand?"

Brayden tried but fell backward.

"That's okay. I've got you." Axel wrapped his arms around the other man and lifted him to his feet. Brayden swayed unsteadily, his full weight slamming into Axel. Axel staggered but managed to hold his friend.

He waited until Brayden appeared steady before they slowly started for the door.

Summer opened the door and struggled to hold onto it when the wind tried to snatch it from her hands. Camo trotted out into the storm, his head darting around as he sniffed the air for danger.

"I'll get some more gauze and bandages for the road." Once the two men were out, Summer grabbed the supplies along with a quilt and pillow for Brayden then shut the door.

"Let's get you in the back seat where you can lie down," Axel told his friend.

Summer placed the pillow inside. She did her best to help lift Brayden into the seat. He screamed in pain when his injured body hit the seat too hard.

"Sorry, buddy." Axel's face revealed his hurt that his friend was suffering.

Summer placed the quilt over Brayden. "He's going to make it," she assured Axel when he seemed frozen in place staring at his injured friend. "But we have to hurry, Axel." She climbed in beside Brayden and put pressure on the wound.

Axel snapped out of his daze and opened the driver's side door. Camo leaped inside.

He put the Blazer in Drive. "It's too risky going the way of the county road but I don't think the Blazer will make it down the same way we came up." He stared out the windshield and she could tell he was fighting fatigue. Though it was now daylight, the storm was creating havoc on visibility. "We'll have to go back through the woods and then down that way. It's not as steep as the path we came up with the snowcat. Still, I hope the Blazer's up to the trek." He put the vehicle in gear and carefully turned it around.

"I hope Abram and Lainey are safe," Axel said. As they started for the trees ahead, he told her they'd be going close to the Amish community once more. "If those men follow, we'll be bringing even more danger close to the community. Unfortunately, we don't have a choice. Brayden needs a doctor's help."

She could tell he was worried. "It will be okay." She touched her stomach. It had to be. She couldn't go back to Ray.

"The good news is it will take us closer to a paved road just past the community."

"That's something." She forced a smile before looking down at Brayden who appeared to be resting. "He's still sleeping."

"Rest is the best thing for him right now." He glanced back at his friend. "I just hope the trip down isn't too harrowing."

The SUV entered the trees at a crawl. Summer hadn't realized it, but she held a tight grip on her seat. The unknown waiting for them was filled with all sorts of dangerous possibilities.

Axel watched behind them. "So far, I don't see any sign of them. Brayden, how are you holding up?" Nothing but silence.

"Can you check on his wound?"

"He's unconscious. I'll check on his injury." Summer lifted Brayden's sweatshirt and her heart sank. "It's soaked through."

"We need to change it." He put the SUV

in Park and got out removing the sling. Camo started to follow but Axel stopped him.

He got in on the other side of Brayden. Working to change the bandage in such a cramped space was a challenge in itself.

Summer handed him the gauze once he'd removed the soiled bandage.

"Keep an eye out for any movement," he told her. "It makes me nervous to be sitting still for too long."

She searched the darkness around them. So far, there was no sign of the bad men, yet she had no doubt they were still out there searching.

Brayden mumbled in his sleep. Summer couldn't make sense of it. "What's he saying?"

"Something about being betrayed." Axel shook his head. "I'm not sure what he's talking about." He finished bandaging and hastily returned to the driver's seat. In a matter of seconds, they were moving again. "I'm really worried about him. He's lost a lot of blood."

Brayden's struggle filled her with guilt. This was her fault. "Ray won't stop until he has me. He doesn't care how many innocent people he hurts in the process."

The storm showed no sign of letting up. Through the swirling snow outside her window something caught her attention, and she leaned closer to the window. "Axel, I see lights again."

His frantic gaze searched through the storm. A glow appeared. "That's close." He whipped the steering wheel in the opposite direction, turning the Blazer away from the lights. "I'm hoping the storm will keep them from seeing us. We can't afford to not use the headlights after what happened with the snowcat."

Once more the lights disappeared. Summer leaned closer, waiting, but they didn't return. "I don't see them anymore." Her frown deepened. "Where did they go?"

Camo jumped up onto the seat beside Axel, a low growl emanating from him.

"What is it, boy?" Axel's attention was on the dog as Camo stared out the passenger window.

Something moved in the snow. Several men became visible. A flashlight beam reached into the backseat where Summer sat. Flashes followed. A heartbeat later, the crack of gunfire confirmed they were under attack.

Axel jerked the wheel to the left and punched the vehicle as fast as he could. "We can't afford to keep going this way for long. The drop where the snowcat went off is just up ahead."

Brayden moaned again. Summer held on tight as the SUV bounded across the rugged countryside.

"Duck," Axel warned. Summer got down low and prayed they'd be able to escape before one of them was shot—or they reached the drop-off that meant certain death.

Another round of gunfire had Axel flinching as the shots fell short of the Blazer. Thankfully, he was able to stay ahead of the men on foot. "You should be safe to sit up. I'm going to start moving away from the cliff now." He carefully changed direction.

Brayden opened his eyes. "I heard gunshots. What's going on?"

"Glad you're back with us." Axel explained the attack. "We're going to head down and skirt around the Amish community."

Axel glanced at Summer in the rearview mirror. This was her story, and he wouldn't tell it without her permission. She slowly nodded and he did his best to explain.

"I can't believe this is happening again." Brayden slowly sat up clutching the quilt. "I'm so sorry you've had to go through such horrible things, Summer."

A simple nod was all Summer seemed capable of giving.

Brayden broke into a fit of coughing that had him grabbing his stomach. His body went limp, and he slumped down on the seat.

"He's passed out again." Summer checked the wound. "Axel, he's really bleeding badly."

"We need a place to get out of sight, but I can't see anything." Axel searched the wintry haze. Beside him, Camo barked a few times. Axel glanced his way. "What is it, boy?"

The dog continued to bark without looking at Axel. He jerked his head forward. "Oh, no. Hold on, Summer." A huge tree appeared from the swirling snow. He couldn't hit it. They couldn't lose their only means of transportation. He had a severely injured man and a pregnant woman. This couldn't happen.

With only a few seconds to spare, he swerved around the tree. Once they were in the clear, Axel breathed out a huge sigh of relief.

"That was far too close. How is he?" Axel stopped the car.

Summer once more checked the wound. "It's bad. Blood has soaked through the bandages already."

"Do you think you can redo them by yourself?" Axel glanced over and cringed at the amount of blood Brayden had lost. He couldn't let his friend die.

"I think so, but we're almost out of gauze and bandages."

His hands tightened on the wheel and sweat beaded on his forehead as he sat forward, getting as close to the windshield as he could just to see anything more than a few feet in front of them.

"How much farther?" Summer asked, her tone worried. "He really needs a doctor."

He tried to think clearly. How far had they traveled? Axel couldn't remember coming this way except maybe once. What if they were going the wrong way? He forced the voices of doubt down. "Several miles, I think." The answer sounded anything but confident. Summer and Brayden were depending on him, and he had no real knowledge of what they'd be facing as they headed down the mountain.

*Lord, please help me. I can't let them down.*

Summer touched his shoulder. He met her eyes in the rearview mirror.

"You've got this."

The strength he saw in her made him believe—he had to. He slowly smiled. "Thank you." Axel covered her hand with his.

After losing Erin, Axel couldn't imagine feeling anything for another woman. He couldn't go through that much pain again. Summer made him see he wasn't the only one suffering. She was fighting for her life and her child's while he'd retreated to his mountain hideout to live in isolation. He didn't want to do that anymore. He wanted to live.

"He's resting a bit more comfortably now." She removed her hand and checked Brayden's pulse. "It's steady. That's something."

She was trying to make him feel better, but Axel had seen enough gunshot injuries during combat to know that the one Brayden sustained was critical. If they couldn't get him medical attention soon... As he continued driving, he searched for any familiar sign, yet all he saw was a storm that was frightening. It swallowed up everything in its path and cloaked any would-be landmarks with white.

He reasoned they were still some ways up the mountain.

One bit of hope he held on to: those men wouldn't be able to communicate with their teammates or Ray. A small advantage. With the storm blasting, he didn't believe the gunfight they'd gone through could be heard by anyone not in the immediate area.

It was going to be okay. *They* were okay. He petted Camo's head. The dog seemed to realize his comfort was needed because he licked Axel's hand.

Laughter bubbled up inside him. "Thanks, boy—I needed that." Camo settled down beside him seemingly unconcerned. If the dog wasn't on edge, maybe it was going to be okay.

"No!" Brayden mumbled several times before his eyes shot open and he tried to sit up. Summer did her best to keep him still.

"Don't try to move. You're still bleeding." Axel did his best to help quiet his friend.

"We have to get to the house," Brayden blurted out.

"You mean your home? Brayden, we left your place a while ago…remember?"

Brayden shook his head and then winced and grabbed his side. "I'm not talking about my place. My old homestead."

Brayden had told him about his family's old place many times. Both of his parents had died within months of each other, and the house had sat vacant for years. When Axel had questioned his friend about his parents' deaths, Brayden said his father had died when his vehicle had gone over the side of the mountain. His mother died a few months later from what was believed to be an undetected heart condition. Axel had always thought it strange they'd died so close together, but he'd heard of cases where one spouse died and the other passed away a short time later supposedly from a broken heart.

"I think he's up to something bad." Brayden slurred his words, his eyes glazed.

"Who?" Axel was totally confused. He took his attention off the stretch of land he could see through the headlights to glance at Brayden.

"He's passed out again." Summer checked Brayden's pulse. "Do you have any idea what he meant?"

Axel shook his head. "No. He could be talking about something he witnessed in battle. Brayden told me he still has nightmares from that time."

"I can't imagine what you both have gone through," Summer said softly.

She was concerned for him. After everything she'd endured, Summer worried about *him*. His heart filled with feelings he didn't know how to deal with. He cared about her. Couldn't bear the thought of Ray winning after all he'd done to her.

"Axel… I'm." She hesitated, and he believed she was going to apologize.

He shook his head. "You've done nothing wrong, Summer. There's nothing to apologize for. You're the victim."

She flinched and he realized he'd said the wrong thing.

"I hate that word." She scraped her hair back from her face. "Even though I am a victim, I don't want to feel like one." She touched her belly. "This little one needs me not to be a victim."

"You've gone through something awful, but it's made you strong—maybe stronger than you ever thought possible."

She didn't look away and his heart responded eagerly to the hope in her eyes.

"I didn't think he would do this. I didn't," Brayden rambled deliriously, and Summer's attention shifted to him. She tucked the blanket around him, which would hopefully help keep him still.

"I haven't seen any sign of Brayden's abandoned house, have you?" she asked.

"No, but even if there was a place, we can't

stop. We've got to get Brayden to the hospital in Elk Ridge."

She nodded and stared out the window. She possessed a beauty that would only grow with time. She had the glow of a pregnant woman, but there was a fighting spirit in her that shone through, too. She would protect her child to the death. And he would protect her because he couldn't lose her. Couldn't lose the woman who had made him feel like a human again.

Going through this ordeal with Summer had reminded him of how good it felt to help someone else. And it had made him realize he'd missed having that special human connection in his life like he'd had before. Sure, he had Brayden and some other friends, but he missed what he and Erin had shared. Missed being attracted to someone. Falling in love.

His and Summer's almost kiss popped into his head. An unexpected tender moment that proved he was still capable of feeling something.

"Axel." The panic in her voice grabbed his attention.

He followed where she pointed. "I don't see anything."

She leaned closer to the window. "I thought I saw a light."

Axel braked and searched through the storm. "There is something. A single light." Was it the Amish community? He didn't believe so. Their homes were lit by lanterns. That light appeared much brighter than what would be put out from a lantern. Had they veered off course and were now heading away from the community? He shared his fears with her. "Not that it matters. If that doesn't belong to a flashlight, then chances are we're somewhere close to a farm."

The relief on her face was intense. "Maybe they'll have a landline."

"It's possible." Though he didn't say as much, he didn't want to dash her hopes. Most people nowadays didn't really have landlines. Still, some of the old timers stubbornly kept them and Axel was certain they'd come in handy when cell service wasn't available.

"Let's head toward the light." It didn't look so far away. Still, with the storm distorting everything, it could be on the other side of the drop-off. He'd have to be careful. One false move could end in their deaths.

Axel eased along at a crawl. After they'd gone some ways, he stopped.

"Do you see something?" she asked.

"No, but I'm worried I won't see the slope

until it's too late." He faced her. "I'm going to get out and walk a little way down."

She studied him, as if looking for something he wasn't telling her.

"I'll be back soon." He got out and closed the door. Axel searched the darkness with a sense of unease slithering down his spine. Where had the shooters from earlier gone? Unless they'd gotten turned around in the storm, he had no doubt they'd keep coming.

He'd taken only a few steps when the confusion of the whiteout set in. Was he heading in the right direction? He turned toward the SUV, the lights barely visible.

Axel drew in a breath and applied reason to the problem. He'd been heading for the mysterious light, so the Blazer would be pointed toward it, which meant the direction he was going should be safe.

Because what had happened so far wouldn't let him relax, Axel retrieved his handgun and checked the clip. Almost empty. He switched out the clip for a full one. As he started walking again, Brayden's strange ramblings niggled at his mind. Was his friend reliving his battle days? Delirium had a way of making even the strongest confused at times. Axel had certainly seen it enough during the war.

He kept going for a while and turned. The headlights were still visible. They would lead him back to Summer and Brayden. He was okay. He peered deep into the winter onslaught. Where had the light gone? It had been there a few minutes earlier.

He panned out farther, but the light was gone. Axel didn't believe Ray's men could've regrouped so quickly after the last attack with no likely form of communication. Was the flashlight coming from one of the Amish farms? Most of the morning chores on the farms would be done by now. It could be someone working…

An uneasy feeling had him swinging toward the Blazer. It seemed miles away as Axel started running for it.

*Crack!* The alarming sound had him ducking low. Gunfire. A shot flew past his right side. Axel raced toward the Blazer's headlights.

Shots continued to fly around him followed by another shocking sight. More lights closing in from the opposite side. They'd almost reached the Blazer. His heart exploded against his chest. As he neared the SUV, he yelled for Summer to get down.

Axel opened fire over the top of the vehicle to force the attackers back.

Grabbing the door handle, he yanked it open. Inside, Camo was on the passenger floorboard.

"Are you hurt?" he asked Summer, who was crouching behind the driver's seat. Without wasting time, Axel jerked the vehicle into Drive and floored the gas.

"I'm okay," she said, clearly shaken. "They came out of nowhere."

His full attention was on keeping the SUV from crashing into a tree as they sped down the mountain while taking heavy gunfire. The back window shattered and Summer screamed. Axel ducked low amidst the rampage. Another round hit the back tire, blowing it immediately. He struggled to keep the vehicle from flipping.

The shooters continued firing relentlessly. Several emerged from the snowy world to Axel's right and destroyed the driver's side window, almost hitting Axel. He swerved and ducked and did his best to keep going.

"Axel!" Summer yelled his name over the noise.

"I'm okay." But they had to get away from the shooters because when the next shot came, none of them would survive.

## Chapter Eleven

Summer covered her ears as bullets continued to bounce off the SUV. Brayden moaned, his panicked eyes homing in on hers.

"Stay down," she told him and gently placed her hand against his shoulder. "You can't sit up. It's too dangerous."

"Where's Axel?"

"I'm right here, buddy. Do as Summer says." Axel explained what was happening.

Brayden's eyes closed. For a minute, Summer thought he'd passed out again. "He's bad. He's just bad," he murmured.

"We're losing them," Axel said over the noise. The shots were no longer hitting their mark.

With the back window gone, cold air and snow blew in, immediately dropping the temperature to below freezing. Summer's breath fogged the air in front of her.

Soon, the firing stopped.

"You should be safe to sit up," Axel said from up front. "We're out of range and they've realized it."

Summer slipped into the seat next to Brayden's feet while the Blazer suddenly sputtered and lurched. "What's going on?"

Axel stared at the gauges. "I think the engine was hit. We're losing oil pressure." The vehicle sputtered again.

"Can we keep going like this?" Summer glanced behind. Though some distance behind, flashlights were coming after them.

"I'm not sure how long. Let's hope we can make it down the mountain and to the Amish community where we can hopefully borrow a buggy and get Brayden to Elk Ridge."

Summer caught his worried expression in the mirror.

The tension in the cab built. More sputtering followed as the engine struggled to keep going.

"We're slowing down," Axel groaned. "This isn't good." The vehicle had noticeably lost speed.

"What do we do?" She leaned forward and looked over his shoulder. The oil light was on.

"I'm going to put it in Neutral. We can coast for a while."

"But not forever." She said what he didn't.

"No, not forever." His attention momentarily reverted to Brayden. "At some point we'll be on foot with an injured man."

Summer's heart sank. She understood what that meant. It would be next to impossible to stay out of sight under those circumstances. And almost impossible to keep going in this storm.

She sat back against the seat and looked at Brayden. So many people had been hurt, all because she'd tried to escape Ray's hold. She fought back tears. "Brayden could die."

"I'm not going to let that happen." Axel's voice was steady. "Brayden's strong. We can't lose hope."

She wanted to believe him. Summer brushed her fingers over her eyes. Crying wasn't going to help anything.

Someone touched her hand. She glanced over and noticed Brayden was awake. He must have seen her tears. She tremulously smiled down at him.

"Where are we?" Brayden croaked, shifting his attention to Axel.

"I'm not sure, but we're in trouble." Axel didn't mince words. "The only thing keeping us going now is the downhill momentum of the vehicle."

Brayden slowly attempted to sit up.

"No, you mustn't." Summer braced her hand against his chest.

"It's okay," Axel told her. "We need his help."

She understood. Without Brayden's assistance, they may not survive. She put her arm around his shoulders and eased him into a sitting position.

Brayden closed his eyes for a second as if trying to regain his strength before looking at their surroundings. "It's hard to tell in these conditions, but I believe we're close to my old farm." He stopped for a couple of breaths. "My dad's old truck is still parked in the garage. It ran the last time I was here."

Hope rose inside her until she got a good look at Axel's face. The probability of that happening was next to impossible.

Still, she needed something to hold on to. Keeping the fear at bay was hard. She could see Ray's smug expression and imagined how pleased he would be when he caught her. The things he'd do to her before he killed her.

"Hey, it's going to be okay," Axel whispered.

"We're not done fighting yet." He watched her in the mirror, seeing all her fears.

She so wanted to believe him.

The vehicle hit a somewhat level space and slowed even more. She glanced out the window at the nightmare storm and dreaded what lay ahead.

The vehicle rolled to a painstakingly slow stop before the engine coughed several times and died.

Axel tried to start the Blazer again, but it was useless. The damage was too great. "Looks like this is it," he murmured. He turned to where Brayden leaned back against the seat. "Can you give me some idea which way we should head?"

Brayden squinted through the snow falling out the side window. "To your left. I'm almost positive about it."

Almost. Would it be good enough to save them? If they got lost in the storm, Ray's people finding them would be the least of their worries.

"Okay, I'll come around and help you out." Axel forced the door open against the wind and jumped down. Camo was right on his heels.

Summer lumbered from the vehicle. The

wind hit her immediately and she almost lost her balance.

"I've got you." Axel materialized close to her. "Hang on to me."

She looped her arm through his. Where she'd once abhorred being touched by anyone, the trust she had in Axel was slowly releasing the power it had over her. *He* wasn't Ray. *He* would never hurt her.

Together, they started around the back of the SUV as fast as the deep snow accumulation would allow.

Once they reached Brayden's side, Axel opened the door. "I'm going to let you go, but I'm right there if you need me."

Summer grabbed hold of the open door as the brutal wind continued to torment her.

Getting the injured man from the back seat took some time. The simple act of getting out of the vehicle left Brayden noticeably struggling for breath. While Axel secured his friend's coat against the weather, Summer caught a glimpse of the bandage. Blood had seeped through the packing and covered the outer dressing. She looked away. Brayden's life was in danger. She couldn't let him die. No matter what, she couldn't let him die because of her.

"We'll take it slow," Axel assured Brayden, who leaned heavily on him. "You're certain it's this way to the house?"

Brayden managed a nod.

With Axel's arm around Brayden's upper chest, they started away from the vehicle. Summer closed the door and stayed close to Axel. Camo quickly took the lead and trotted out in front of them. They'd barely covered any space when Brayden's body went limp.

"He's unconscious again." Axel struggled to hold him up.

"Let me help you." Summer went around to the opposite side of Brayden and positioned her arm just below Axel's.

Walking with an unconscious man between them was difficult enough without the weather playing its part. Cold drilled down through her jacket, past her clothes and chilled her skin after only a brief time of being exposed.

Sweat beaded on her brow. Summer stumbled trying to hold up her share of Brayden's weight.

"Let's take a break." Axel must've sensed her struggle and found a tree to support Brayden.

She didn't have the energy to form a verbal answer. She dragged in a handful of breaths and her body slowly regained strength. Summer watched as Camo inspected the frozen ground around them for scents and eventually gave up.

"It's the weather," Axel said, drawing her attention to him. He nodded toward Camo. "The cold makes it difficult for dogs to pick up scents."

She nodded. "I don't see any lights yet. That's a good thing."

He reached for her hand, and she didn't want to pull free. She wanted to stay here with him—even in the middle of this storm—and let the ugliness that Ray had instilled in her heart heal.

"Yes, it's a good thing." He held her gaze. "Summer…"

She couldn't look away. Summer hung on his every word.

"When this is over, I want to do whatever I can to help you heal." There was something new in his voice. Something like…pity?

Her heart plummeted. He felt sorry for her. She wasn't sure what was worse. That she'd let herself imagine things that weren't there or his pity.

She dropped her gaze to Camo, who had returned to them. "I'll be okay. I just want this over. Once and for all I want to be free of Ray."

He tugged at her hand. "Summer, look at me."

She couldn't. Not with her heart so fragile.

"Oh…no." The drastic change in Axel's tone grabbed her attention right away. The tender moment had passed. He pointed. "Lights. More than one."

Summer swung toward them. Several flashlight beams pierced through the blizzard, which meant they had to be close for them to be able to pick up the lights through the weather.

"We need to get moving if we're going to stay in front of them enough to give us breathing room and hopefully get the vehicle running."

She appreciated him for trying to make her believe that might be possible.

Summer placed her arm around Brayden. With Axel taking on most of the weight, they were mobile again. Each step became a struggle as they moved into the teeth of the wind. She glanced behind. Had the lights gained on them?

"Remember, they're struggling just like we are," Axel said, no doubt to make her feel better. But they had an injured man with them.

Camo sniffed around the ground as if he had hopes of picking up a valuable scent.

Axel suddenly stopped, the instant lack of movement almost pulled her to the ground.

"What is it?" she asked, her attention on his troubled face.

He indicated the ground. "Those are footprints. The snow has partially covered them up. Someone's been this way recently."

"The men behind us maybe?" She glanced over her shoulder again.

"Possibly. If they came this way already, then maybe they won't return if they've cleared the house. Unless they lose their way in the storm."

She and Axel did their best to pick up the pace.

"Do you think Ray knows you have the information from his computer?"

Axel's question jarred her from her weariness. "I'm not sure. I was careful to not draw attention to myself and he never questioned me."

"Still, he knows you have a lot of knowledge about his operation in your head. He's worried enough about what will happen to him if Vitaliy gets wind of his mistake. You know enough to bring down the entire organization and possibly even Vitaliy's part in it. He has to find you."

Axel's words settled uneasily around her. "There's something else."

Summer shuddered as she recounted how

Ray had told her he'd killed some people in the past.

Axel swung his head her way. "You mean more than the girls he alleged to have murdered."

She nodded. "It sounded like it happened before he became involved in all of this... Oh." An unexpected cramp shot through her midsection stopping her in her tracks.

Axel pointed to a nearby tree. "We need to take a break." He slowly lowered Brayden to the ground and leaned him against a tree. "I don't see the lights anymore."

She searched the way they'd come. Nothing but the storm biting at their heels. *Please let them get confused by the storm and not follow us.*

"Like how many people?" Axel asked.

The conversation she'd had with Ray years ago was as clear as the day it happened. "He didn't say. I asked him what he was talking about," she said softly, recalling Ray's reaction to the question. "He seemed genuinely shaken that he'd given too much away, and nothing ever frightened Ray." Axel kept his attention on her face as she told him word for word the conversation. "It happened not too long after I'd been taken. Ray would get in these ugly moods." She recalled the darkness that seemed to permeate every part of Ray when this happened. "He'd go from cruel to terrifying like flipping a switch. Anyway, I'd said something that set him off and he grabbed me by the throat." She touched the spot without realizing it. "I thought he would kill me right then." She forced down the fear that was there when she recalled the talk. "He saw the fear on my face, and he laughed." Summer glanced Axel's way. "He actually laughed as if it were funny. Ray told me I'd better watch what I said, or I'd end up like the others he'd killed. This was before he told me about the girls."

"Why do you think the people he spoke about killing back then were different?"

"He seemed to hint that the murders had happened when he was very young. At the last house I was at before I escaped, I remember Ray kept staring out at the barn. I asked him why, and he said that was where it had happened. He forced me to go inside the barn with him and he'd grin with this maniacal expression on his face. He said they were buried right where they needed to be and then he glanced down at the ground." She'd been so scared.

Axel's hands balled at his sides. "You'll need

to tell this to the sheriff when we get through this. He'll want to retrieve the thumb drive as well. We want to make sure Ray and his crew don't ever walk out of prison again." He glanced at Brayden, who was now awake. "Hey, how are you feeling?" Axel knelt beside his friend.

Brayden sighed. "Like I'm only slowing you down."

"Nonsense. Let me get you to your feet."

"You should leave me," Brayden croaked out. "It will be faster for you two to go ahead without me."

"I'm not leaving you and that's final." Axel lifted Brayden to his feet. The man swayed unsteadily. "We'll get to the house, and you can rest while I work on the truck."

Summer could tell that Brayden didn't believe it. Yet the man answered, "All right, but I can walk on my own for now."

Axel and Summer flanked him on both sides as they started off. Even Camo appeared to be feeling the weight of the weather. Though still out in front, he wasn't full of energy like before because of the injured leg.

Several times, Brayden stumbled, and Axel caught him.

"Let me help you for a while." Axel placed

his arm around his friend. Brayden didn't seem to have the energy to argue.

As they continued downhill, the trees appeared to thin. "What happened to the forest here?" Summer asked. Just a short time earlier they'd been in thick woods.

"They've been cleared away," Axel answered. "We must be getting close to the house."

*Thank You, Gott.*

"Look." Axel pointed to a broken-down fence.

"This is the beginning of the old homestead," Brayden murmured, the exhaustion of the trip showing in his barely audible words. "We're close."

Summer wouldn't let herself think about what an impossibility it would be to get the vehicle running after so many years of disuse. At least they had a place to get out of the weather for a bit and hopefully reach the sheriff.

"Brayden, can you get through the fence on your own?" Axel asked.

Brayden pulled in several shaky breaths. "I think so."

"Good. I'll go before you and help you through." Axel ducked down and slipped between two pieces of smooth wire. Camo slipped under as if it were nothing and trotted through the snow sniffing the air.

Axel lifted the top wire with his hands and put his boot against the bottom wire to give Brayden room to ease through.

As soon as Brayden was through, he stumbled and hit the ground. Axel grabbed for him and helped him up.

"Okay?" He waited for Brayden to respond.

Once Brayden was steady on his feet, he held the wires for Summer. The weight of her pregnancy made it difficult to lower herself enough to get through. The top wire scraped her back as she cleared it. She straightened too quickly and the world around her spun. She closed her eyes and willed the familiar dizziness away.

Axel reached her side quickly. "Are you in pain?" She slowly opened her eyes and looked into his. The concern there warmed her heart. She'd stopped believing in human kindness after what Ray did to her, but Axel stirred up feelings of trust again. Not all men were like Ray. Axel certainly wasn't.

"I'm okay. I stood up too quickly."

He nodded. "Can you keep going?"

"Yes. I'm fine now."

He searched her face, clearly not convinced,

but at this point they had no choice. "Stay close to me and if you need a break let me know. I want to make sure you and the baby are safe."

She kept in step beside him as he helped Brayden along the way. As hard as it was for her, she couldn't imagine how Brayden was struggling. "Do you see the house yet?"

Axel focused ahead. "Nothing. But in this storm, it would be impossible until we were almost right on top of it."

He was trying to make her feel better. She smiled over at him and whispered, "Thank you."

He smiled back. "We're close."

"It's up there," Brayden muttered, his words slurred. "I know it's up there." He lifted his hand and pointed straight ahead.

"You sure?" Axel asked because like her, nothing but darkness and the storm could be seen.

Brayden nodded. "I'm sure."

"That's good enough for me," Axel told his friend. They headed in the direction he indicated.

Soon, shapes appeared through the dense snowfall.

"There's the house." Summer couldn't ever remember seeing such a wonderful sight before.

Axel stopped suddenly.

"What is it?" she asked and wasn't sure she could take too many more bad breaks.

"Those footprints from earlier. I have no doubt Ray's men were down this way at some point. What if they left men behind?"

The thought hadn't occurred to Summer.

He watched the house with a frown. "There's a shed over to the left. I need you and Brayden to wait for me inside. I'll clear the house and garage and come back for you."

As bad as she didn't want him to leave her for a second, she understood the importance of making sure they weren't walking into an attack, and Axel was a former soldier. He'd know how to protect himself.

"Okay," she agreed, grateful for his military background. It had saved their lives.

"You both should be able to get inside the shed and out of the weather," Axel said. "I'll leave Camo to help you keep watch."

The dog's ears perked up at the mention of his name.

They reached the small shed and Axel pried the door open. There was an old riding lawn mower inside that didn't look as if it had run in a while. He helped Brayden over to the lawnmower and eased him down onto the seat. "Rest for a bit."

Brayden didn't respond but held his injured midsection, his breathing labored. Summer glanced around the small space. There were a few tools hanging on the wall. A small workbench that ran along the back wall.

"It's considerably warmer here and it's dry." He was trying to put a good spin on things. "At least that's something."

She would stay positive as well. "Yes, it is." Summer walked with him to the door.

"I'll be back as soon as I can." He touched her face and she didn't back away. How could she? She trusted him. There were so many things in his eyes that she'd give anything to understand. "Stay safe. Protect him." He indicated Brayden.

"I will. Take care of yourself, Axel."

He dropped his hand and slowly nodded. Axel glanced down at the waiting dog. "I'm afraid you have to stay, Camo." The dog's disappointment was clear.

Axel opened the door enough to leave. Their eyes connected briefly before he left, and it felt as if her rock had slipped away.

"It's okay, Camo." Summer stroked the dog's head for comfort. Camo eventually accepted

his fate and went to explore their surroundings while Summer felt her way to Brayden's
side. "How are you feeling?" She could hear
his labored breaths. Having to trek through the
storm had depleted what little strength he had
left.

"I've been better, but I'm hanging in there."

"As soon as we're in the house, we need to
examine your wound. The bandage will need
to be changed."

He still held his stomach. His hand had to
be covered with his own blood. Summer was
so afraid they wouldn't be able to get him the
help he needed in time.

The door to the shed opened. She swung toward it relieved when Axel appeared.

Camo bounded over to him as if it had been
days and not minutes since he'd last seen his
master.

"The place is empty," Axel said. "There's no
sign anyone's been this way in a while" He
came over to the lawnmower, eyeing his friend.
"Let's get you inside."

"I can stand," Brayden told him, and Axel
stepped back and waited while the other man
gripped the steering wheel of the lawnmower

and slowly pushed himself up to a standing position. "Lead the way, brother."

Axel kept close to Brayden as he eased to the door.

"I've got it," Axel told him and held it while Brayden and Summer stepped out into the storm. "It's this way." He pointed straight ahead. Camo ran past them, following Axel's quickly disappearing tracks.

They'd taken only a few steps when the storm swallowed up the shed from sight.

Even though the short reprieve from the frigid temperature had helped, the minimal warmth the shed afforded soon disappeared and cold ate through her jacket and clothes once again. Summer couldn't feel her feet. She staggered and Axel caught her arm.

"We're almost there," he said close to her ear. Those words sounded beautiful and yet reaching the house was only the beginning. They still had to get the vehicle running. Get out of here alive…

*Stop it.*

She did her best to silence the voices of doubt inside that told her she would never escape Ray no matter how much help she had.

"There!" Axel pointed in front of them. The

house appeared through the white. As they neared, she noted there was nothing about its state of decay that was comforting.

Camo bounded toward the structure and up onto the porch while everyone else followed much more slowly. Axel assisted Brayden up the steps while Summer clung heavily to the railing.

Once they reached the door, Axel pushed it open, and they went inside.

The temperature was several degrees warmer, and she noticed that Axel had started a fire in the fireplace.

"Thank you." Summer glanced down at her baby. She was so worried. Would her freedom come at the cost of losing her child?

No! She wouldn't believe that. *Gott* hadn't brought them this far only to lose her child.

"I figured we all could use a little fire to warm up." He pointed to the two chairs in front of the fire. "Sit. Both of you."

Brayden sank down onto one of the dusty chairs and closed his eyes, his breathing still labored.

Summer swung to Axel. "We need to change his bandage before it gets infected."

He nodded. "Let me see if I can find something here."

He disappeared into the kitchen while Summer glanced around the dark room lit only by the fire's glow. She wondered about Brayden's past, his family. Axel had said Brayden's parents died.

"This should work." Axel returned carrying what appeared to be a dish towel. "We'll have to reuse the outer bandage but…"

She understood what he meant. It would have to do.

Summer helped him remove first the outer bandage and then the soiled cloth. The gunshot wound was still bleeding. She could tell from the troubled expression on Axel's face that he was worried.

"It should hold for a while." The bleakness in his eyes when he faced her told a different story. Brayden was fading fast.

"I'm going to check out the truck." Axel straightened. As much as he wished there were food and water to strengthen them, the house hadn't been occupied in years. "When I was in the garage earlier I found a few spare parts. Hopefully, it will be enough to get it running. Can you watch out for Brayden? If he gets worse, come find me." Axel did his best to keep his misgivings from Summer but from the despair on her face he believed she knew how bad things were.

She walked him to the door.

"Do you still have the weapon I gave you earlier?"

"I do." She showed it to him.

"Good. Keep it close. I'll try to hurry. Camo can stay with you. If you hear anything suspicious, get out of sight. If you have to fire, shoot to kill."

She nodded hesitantly. "Be careful, Axel." Her beautiful eyes held his. The depth of caring he saw for him there broke his heart. For the first time in a long time, he had something worth living for and it might all be taken from him.

There were many things he wanted to say but how could he when the worst possible scenario was facing them. Instead, he leaned over and kissed her cheek before slipping from the house.

The door closed quietly behind him. His heart felt as heavy as the exhaustion weighing down his legs.

Axel worked his way to the garage and the

truck that was in bad shape from what he could tell. But it was their last hope, and he couldn't let Summer and Brayden down.

He shut the door against the cold and went over to the truck that looked far older than the twenty years Brayden said had passed since his dad's death.

Opening the driver's door, he noticed the keys hung from the ignition. Not a good sign. That it had been left untouched for years without being stolen meant it probably wasn't running. Axel tried to crank the engine. The battery made a chugging sound but wouldn't turn over. He stopped, not wanting to drain what little life was left in the battery if the main problem lay somewhere else.

He stepped over to the hood and lifted it. It looked as if a community of mice had taken up residence. Who knew what kind of wires had been chewed through.

Using the flashlight, Axel cleaned the nests away and searched the motor. He checked the cables to the battery. One had come loose. After tightening it, he looked around for any other culprits. The radiator still had antifreeze in it, which was shocking. What about fuel?

Axel searched around and found a half-full

gas can and poured it into the vehicle. After trying everything in his expertise, he got in and tried the key once more. This time, the chugging sounded more promising. Axel stopped for a second, his hands shaking. So much was riding on him getting the truck to run.

"Please, God, they're going to kill us and I'm all out of options. Let this thing start."

He pulled in several unsteady breaths and tried again. The engine turned over. The vehicle sputtered several times before running smoothly.

"Thank You." He looked toward the heavens with gratitude.

Axel got out and opened the double doors, preparing to drive to the house, when a disturbing sight amped up the urgency. Flashlights coming from the opposite way he, Brayden and Summer had hiked in. No doubt these were Ray's men.

He hurried back to the truck and drove from the garage without the headlights. Best not to alert their pursuers to their location. He quickly closed the garage doors, hoping if they did come this way after he, Brayden and Summer were gone, all traces of them would have disappeared.

Axel was worried about his friend. The man was fading fast. This was their only hope at getting Brayden the help he needed and escaping the traffickers. They appeared to be coming at them only on foot at this point, but he believed they had to have some type of transportation that would allow them to move the men from the mountaintop.

"Keep us hidden and keep them on foot." Because there was no way they could outrun the enemy should they be waiting near the Amish community with vehicles.

He pushed the negative thoughts aside. They had transportation. At some point he hoped the sat phone would pick up service. They were safe for now.

Pulling the truck up as close to the house as he could, Axel got out, his attention on the lights. They'd covered a whole lot of territory in a short amount of time. He and Summer wouldn't have long to get Brayden out of the house and get away.

He had no idea how much gas the vehicle had. There hadn't been much in the can. Hopefully they'd have enough to reach Elk Ridge.

He knocked on the door. "Summer, it's me,"

he said as quietly as possible. She opened the door with the weapon in her hand.

He explained about the flashlights. "They'll reach the house soon. We should leave now."

The fear on her face doubled.

"There's a blanket in the back bedroom. Can you grab it? I'm not sure if the heater works or not and it will keep you and Brayden comfortable." The single cab truck would be a tight squeeze for them all including Camo, but it ran, and they were close to getting away from this nightmare.

While Summer searched for the blanket, Axel went over to Brayden. "I got the truck running. We can get you to the hospital now." Axel wrapped his arm around Brayden's upper body and helped him to his feet. The stress of being shot and on the run was taking its toll. Brayden was no longer lucid and could barely stand on his own.

"Here it is." Summer returned with the dusty blanket.

"It's because of Daddy," Brayden mumbled.

Axel shot Summer a confused look. "Try not to talk, buddy. We're going to get you to the truck." Axel had no idea what demons haunted

Brayden but right now he was worried for his friend's life.

Without warning, Camo suddenly bounded to his feet and charged for the front door barking loudly. Axel's worst fear became reality. They were too late.

"It's Ray. He's found us." Summer's terror was evident in her tone.

Axel returned Brayden to his seat and hurried to the window. Several sets of headlights were right outside. Where had they come from? More armed men were at the truck. There would be no escaping in it. If they stayed, they'd die. Like it or not, they were back on foot again.

Axel once more assisted Brayden to his feet. "If we can reach the shed… It's our only hope." But then what? Axel had no doubt their hunters would search every building on the place once they didn't find them in the house. But Axel was all out of ideas, and they couldn't stay here.

With Brayden close, he moved to the back entrance and looked out. "I don't see anything." Still, in the storm and at night, Ray's people could be right on top of them without them realizing it.

"Stay close to me," he said to Summer. Walking out onto the back porch took more courage than he imagined. So far, there was no sign anyone was around here.

He stepped from the veranda. Brayden groaned. Summer stayed so close Axel could feel all her fear. Camo's hackles were raised as they trudged toward the shed.

Up ahead he saw its silhouette.

As they got closer, armed men emerged from all around and came after them.

"Hurry, go back to the house!" Axel yelled as the men started shooting. He all but dragged Brayden back to the house and up the steps. Once inside, he slammed the door closed and locked it. Once he had Brayden seated by the fire, Axel shoved the kitchen table against the back door and searched for something heavy to block the front door. He reached for the sofa.

"Let me help you," Summer said.

He shook his head. She was barely hanging on. "I've got it." It took much of his waning strength to shove the sofa against the door, knowing it would only provide a little deterrent to those determined men.

With a prayer racing through his head, Axel tried the sat phone and caught a signal. His legs felt weak with elation. He didn't wait for the dispatcher to finish speaking. "This is Axel

Sterling. We're under attack from armed men near the Amish community at the abandoned farm north of there. We need immediate help." Before the dispatcher could confirm, the call dropped. Axel tried it again, but the signal was lost. Would help come in time?

He rushed to the front of the house. The men were on the porch now. He pushed whatever other furniture he could against the entrance as a barrier that wouldn't hold should they force the door.

Several rounds of fire pelted the house lodging bullets in opposing walls.

"Get down!" Axel yelled to Summer.

She dropped to the floor and covered her head while he dove to shield Brayden.

When the silence returned, Axel tried the phone again. Same results.

*God, please, not like this. Not when I promised to help Summer escape these men.*

"You're surrounded!" someone yelled. "There's no way out. Come out now. Don't make us have to come in after you, Summer."

Summer.

Axel jerked toward her. She had gone as pale as a sheet.

"That's Ray," Summer said in a shocked

voice. "You've got thirty seconds, Summer," her tormentor continued. "Otherwise, I'm coming in after you and you know what I'll do to you and him if you make me come after you."

Summer slowly rose. The defeat on her face was hard to witness. "He's right—he'll kill you." She moved to Axel's side. "He wants me. If I turn myself over to him perhaps Ray will let you and Brayden—"

"That's not going to happen." Axel wasn't about to let her sacrifice herself for him. "I'll die first."

"No." Her face screwed up in pain and she reached up and touched his cheek. "I don't want that. I can't…"

He covered her hand with his and looked into her eyes. "Let me fight for you, Summer. You deserve someone who will fight for you."

A sob escaped.

"I guess we're doing it the hard way," Ray called out.

Something heavy slammed against the door.

"Get out of sight." Axel wrapped her in his embrace and tugged her into one of the bedrooms. "Stay here and get in the closet. I'm going for Brayden."

There was just enough time to haul Brayden into the bedroom and lay him on the bed before the front door gave way followed by the back door.

Axel fired on the advancing men. Camo charged toward one who was almost right on top of Axel.

The perp whirled toward the dog and fired. Camo yelped as the bullet struck his hind leg. The battle-weary soldier didn't give up his mission. He charged the man.

"No, Camo!" Axel couldn't bear the thought of losing his friend. Camo ignored Axel's command. The dog would fight to the death to save Axel.

Axel dove behind the sofa and picked off each person who came into his line of sight, but there were too many. It was a losing battle.

Click, click, click. The sound was one of the most gut-wrenching of all. He was all out of bullets. Falling back on his training, Axel grabbed for the shooter nearest him. Soon, the two were engaged in hand-to-hand combat. It took all his strength to overpower the man and choke him until he lost consciousness.

Axel grabbed the perp's weapon and fired on the two men approaching. Both went down.

Summer's pretty face was all he saw as he fought with everything inside himself to win the battle that was stacked against him from the beginning.

Someone snatched at his arms, imprisoning them behind his back. Another man wrestled the weapon from Axel's hand.

A man he didn't know stopped inches from his face. Axel had no doubt this was Ray. There was something familiar about the man who had caused so much pain.

"Where is she?" The brutality on the man's face spoke of someone who would do anything to get what they wanted.

Axel's stomach clenched when he thought of what this man would do to Summer. "There's no one here but me."

What passed for a smile didn't touch Ray's eyes or wipe the cruelty from his face. "You're protecting her. You know what kind of person she is and you're willing to give your life for her?" The amazement in Ray's voice was clear.

When Axel didn't respond, the trafficker turned to one of his people. "Search the place. She's here."

Ray's attention never left Axel as the armed men began sweeping each room. It didn't take them long to find Summer. She was brought out alone. Where was Brayden?

Axel couldn't take his eyes off her. He tried to break free of his restrainer's hold but couldn't. The terror on her face as she was forced over to where Ray stood made him angry with himself. He'd let her down. He'd promised to protect her, and he'd let her down.

Ray strode over to her and grabbed a handful of her hair.

Summer cried out in pain and shrank as far away as she could get. "Please, no, Ray. The baby. Think about the baby."

A smirk crossed his face as Ray yanked her closer. "I don't want the money I'd get for it as much as I need to eliminate the problem you represent."

"Stop it," Axel yelled. Ray jerked his head back to Axel before motioning to one of his people, who slugged Axel's stomach. The breath flew from his body. The man restraining him was all that held him up.

"You've caused me a lot of problems, Summer," Ray ground out. "This is all your fault. Now I'm going to have to kill him. Are you proud of yourself?" Ray released her and shoved her away.

"Please, Ray, don't," she pleaded. "You don't have to kill him. He's not part of this. It's me you want. Let him be." There were tears falling down her face as she begged for Axel's life.

Ray simply laughed. "Get them both outside." The man restraining Axel forced him from the house. Two men flanked him, all heavily armed. Summer was pulled along by her captor.

*Not like this.* Axel couldn't let it end like this. He couldn't lose her. He...loved her. *Please, God. We need You.*

One thing was clear: Summer had made Axel want to join the world of the living again. He wanted to become a better person. After Erin's death, he never believed love would be possible for him again. Never thought he had anything else to give another woman. But when he looked at Summer, he saw a future with her, and he wanted to have the chance to see if she felt the same way about him. He understood that she'd need time to heal before she could fully love and trust any man again. He'd wait for her as long as she needed because she was worth it.

Summer's frantic gaze locked with his. She silently pleaded with him to do something. Once more, he fought to free himself from their enemies but couldn't. All he had was his words to assure her. "It's going to be okay, Summer." But would it? Would they find a way to escape Ray or die together here in this frozen world.

"Isn't that sweet." Ray came over to stand in front of Axel. "What are you going to do? Fight all of us to save her?" He jerked his head back toward Summer. "You know what she is. She's not worth it."

Anger boiled up inside Axel. "She's worth everything. Everything you took from her."

Ray smirked and motioned to one of his men who put a gun to Axel's head. Ray would make Summer watch him die.

"You want him to live?" Ray asked Summer. "Then you'll tell me where you hid the thumb drive." Her surprise confirmed what Ray had accused her of. "Yes, I know what you did. I kept track of the blank thumb drives in the office. It took me a while to realize one was missing, but when I did, I knew it was you." Ray's eyes gleamed with some dark pleasure at seeing her in pain. "What's it going to be, Summer?"

She shook her head. "I'll never tell you where I hid it and I made sure to get word to the police. They'll have it soon enough."

Just a tiny amount of doubt showed on Ray's face. "You're lying. There's no way you had time to do such a thing."

Summer lifted her chin. "Are you willing to risk everything and anger your boss, Vitaliy? She wasn't happy with you before. I can't imagine what she'll say when she learns how badly you messed up this time."

Ray strode angrily over to her and slapped her hard. Summer's head flew sideways. Axel fought against his restraints but couldn't break their hold.

"You're lying." Ray kept his hand raised and inches from her face. Summer never flinched away. It broke Axel to imagine the things she'd gone through at this man's hands that were far greater than a slap to the face.

Something caught Axel's attention near the front of the house. In the open doorway, Brayden leaned against the frame.

No. Stay hidden, he mouthed, trying to warn his friend.

Brayden didn't listen. He stumbled from the doorway. Axel expected him to be shot immediately. He looked a lot like Brayden.

"What are you doing here?" Ray dropped his hand and crossed the snowy landscape to the porch where Brayden was now barely hanging on. Ray saw the amount of blood Brayden had lost. "What happened?"

"Jimmy, I figured you were behind this somehow!" Brayden exclaimed. "I recognized some of your old friends from back in the day shooting at me. I knew you had to be up to something bad on the mountain near my place, but I still can't believe you'd do something this awful."

Jimmy. Axel recognized the name immediately because Brayden had spoken of the cousin who was like a brother to him. The one his family had taken in when Jimmy was just a child. Jimmy—Ray was Brayden's family.

## Chapter Twelve

Brayden was related to Ray? Summer saw the resemblance between the two now. She'd heard Ray talk about his straitlaced brother who tried to get him to change, but she'd never put it together that Brayden was that brother. Ray's people had shot his own brother.

"I knew you were up to something bad," Brayden rasped while gripping the porch rail, his weak body swaying.

Ray appeared contrite for half a second.

"Dad was right about you," Brayden muttered with disgust on his face. "There's something terribly wrong inside you, Jimmy. Mom was just too blind to see until you killed her and Dad."

Summer was mesmerized by the exchange between the two cousinss. Something dreadful had happened to this family. Was it what had caused Ray to become this monster?

"They got what they deserved!" Ray yelled angrily before regaining his composure. "Look, I'm sorry you got yourself involved in this, Brayden. You were always good to me, but I guess I knew having a deputy for a 'brother' was going to get in my way." Ray smirked at his cousin before he started for Summer. "We need to get this over with and clear out in case someone around called the cops." He glanced over his shoulder. "Like my brother."

"You don't have to do this, Ray." Summer clutched her belly as a sharp pain had her doubling over. Her baby. She couldn't let him kill her baby. She pulled in several breaths before saying, "Just leave. We won't tell anyone."

Ray stepped inches away from her. "You think I don't know as soon as I'm gone that you and your friends here will give the evidence you stole from me to the cops." He grabbed her arm painfully. "I destroyed everything else. All the computers, everything that ties me to… Where'd you put it."

She lifted her face to his and stared him down. Ray grabbed her arm so tight, his fingers dug into it. "Where is it?"

"Leave her alone. She doesn't have your

stuff," Axel yelled, drawing Ray's attention to him.

"You care for her." Ray seemed surprised. His attention returned to Summer. "And you have feelings for him. This is the last chance to tell the truth before he dies."

"No. Please, Ray, no," Summer pleaded.

Ray's glee was clear in the smile that spread across his face.

The man holding the gun on Axel suddenly jerked toward his right. Summer caught a glimpse of an injured Camo flying toward Ray. Camo grabbed hold of Ray's leg. Ray screamed as the dog's canines buried deep.

"Get him off me!" Ray raged while slapping at the dog.

Axel grabbed for the distracted man's weapon, and Summer ran to help him as the man fought to keep possession of the gun.

"Get down, Summer!" Axel yelled, finally gaining full control of the handgun. He aimed the weapon on the man, who raised his hands in surrender.

Summer hit the frozen ground and covered her head as Ray's men fired on Axel, who returned shots. He scooped Summer up and ducked behind the truck.

"Stay here," he instructed. "I'm going to get Brayden."

Summer peeked through the window of the truck in time to see Ray finally managed to shove the injured dog off him and whirl toward Axel ready to shoot. Before he could fire a single shot, the woods around them lit up with headlights.

Dozens of vehicles moved in led by a snowplow. The driver of the plow let the rest of the vehicles pass by. As they drew close, the sheriff's department emblem was emblazoned on the side of several. An ambulance was there as well. Joy rose in her chest. They were saved. Axel's call had gone through after all. She hadn't been sure. More than half an hour had passed since he'd placed the call and she'd begun to lose hope.

Axel grabbed the fading Brayden and hauled him over to the truck.

Soon, the sheriff's department was engaged in battle with the attackers. Axel edged toward the back of the truck and assisted.

Summer caught movement to her left and whirled toward it. Ray loomed beside her. He grabbed her arm and hauled her up beside him with the gun to her head. "You're coming with me. I want that thumb drive." He yanked her along with him to the closest vehicle.

She tried to scream but Ray clamped his hand over her mouth. "Oh, no you don't. You're going to show me where you hid that evidence."

Her frantic eyes searched for Axel. In the chaos around them, would he notice she was in danger?

Ray reached the vehicle and opened the door. He shoved her inside. Before he could get in after her, Axel materialized beside him and shoved his weapon against Ray's temple.

"It's over, Ray. Give up."

Ray tried to get the handgun into position to shoot Summer, but Axel pressed his weapon harder against the man's temple. "I wouldn't do that if I were you."

Throwing daggers Summer's way, Ray eventually dropped the weapon and raised his hands. Axel grabbed the gun and tucked it in his pocket. "Are you hurt?" he asked her.

Summer shook her head. "No, I'm okay." She leaned back against the seat, her hands shaking at how close to death she'd come once more. She noticed that Ray's uninjured men were now surrendering.

Ray saw that he was defeated and yet he wasn't going quietly. He continued to rage at Summer and assure her he'd make her pay for betraying him.

A sheriff's deputy came over. "I've got him." He took control of Ray. After searching him and finding yet another weapon, the deputy handcuffed him and led him away.

"Let's get you out of here." Axel held out his hand. Summer clasped it and let him help her from the vehicle. She wrapped her arms around his waist and held him close.

"Is it really over?" she asked, her voice shaking. After so long, was she finally free of Ray?

"It is," he said softly against her ear. "It really is."

"Brayden." She remembered how seriously injured he was. "He needs help."

Axel clasped her hand and together they hurried over to where Brayden was receiving medical assistance.

"How is he?" Axel asked the EMT examining his friend's wound.

"He's lost a lot of blood," the paramedic replied. "We need to get him to the hospital right away."

Axel nodded and stepped back as Brayden was taken to one of the waiting ambulances.

Another EMT came over to Summer. "Ma'am, you should let me examine you. You've obviously been through quite an ordeal. How far along are you? Are you experiencing any pain?"

"Yes, some earlier, but I'm okay right now." Summer couldn't imagine how awful she looked. "I think I'm around eight months."

The EMT gave her a curious look and she did her best to explain what she was certain of.

"I promise I'm going to take good care of you," the paramedic assured her. She held on to Axel's hand while the EMT did the examination. "You're in remarkably good health all things considered. Still, we need to get you to the hospital to run some further tests."

"He's right, Summer," Axel told her.

"I'm not leaving without you." And she wouldn't. Then Summer noticed something disturbing. "Camo." The dog heard his name and limped over. At first, Summer thought it was the injury he'd sustained with the snowcat accident until she saw blood above the old injury.

"I'm so sorry, boy." Axel knelt beside his injured friend.

"Here, let me take a look." A second EMT brought his bag over and carefully treated Camo's leg while Axel told him about the previous injury. "Looks like the bullet went straight through. I don't see any serious damage from the earlier accident. I'll bandage it up, but I would suggest you take him to your vet as soon as possible."

"I will, thank you," Axel assured him.

Sheriff Wyatt McCallister and two of his deputies came over and introduced themselves.

"Are you the one who called this in?" he asked Axel.

Axel told him yes. "I wasn't sure if your dispatcher got enough from the call to pinpoint our location."

Ray and the rest of his people were being cuffed and loaded into the waiting cruisers.

"Thank you for saving my deputy." The sheriff shook his head. "This will take a lot of sorting out." His attention went to Summer. "How do you fit into all of this, ma'am?"

Axel clasped her hand as she told him her story. Summer didn't realize that she was crying as she spoke until she'd finished.

"I'm so sorry that happened to you, Summer," the sheriff said gently.

Summer felt the weight of the past years lift from her shoulders. "He said he has law enforcement working for him." She waited for the sheriff to deny it. A hard look came and went.

"Unfortunately, it's possible." He explained about what happened previously when an officer and the district attorney had been arrested for assisting a human trafficking ring. "We'll need to get both of your statements soon."

Now that Ray was in custody, Summer was more than happy to assist. "The thumb drive—I almost forgot about it." She explained about stashing it in a secure place at the house where she and Ray and the other members of his crew stayed. "There are other victims being held there, or at least there were, unless Ray moved them. Oh, and there was a woman who visited once. She appeared to be in charge. Her name was Vitaliy."

Sheriff McCallister had listened intently. "Sounds like we'll need to get the feds involved since this appears to be an international ring. We couldn't link the previous arrests to anything international. With the drive and your witness testimony, we can make arrests that will bring down this ring and hopefully get those young women home."

"There's something else." Summer hesitated. What if Ray had just been bragging...or what if it were all true. "Ray claimed he killed some people years ago."

Axel remembered what Brayden had said. "I think Brayden can shed some light on what happened." He told them about Brayden calling Ray by the name of his brother, Jimmy. "Actually, I remember Brayden saying once that Jimmy was his cousin and not his brother. His family took Jimmy in when he had no one else. It sounds like Jimmy killed his own parents as well as Brayden's." Axel's mouth thinned. "That's one disturbed person."

"We'll get Brayden's take on everything as soon as he's cleared by the doctor." The sheriff then focused on Summer. "I'd feel better if you'd go to the hospital to be checked out. After what you've both gone through and considering your lack of medical care, it would be a good idea to get checked out"

Axel turned to her. "He's right. You need to make sure the baby is fine."

"I'd be happy to take you. Give me a few minutes." The sheriff stepped away to speak with his people.

"I can't believe this happened." Summer still

couldn't let go of the fear Ray had instilled in her. How long would it take before she felt safe?

Axel pushed hair from her eyes "It's over, Summer."

As she looked into his handsome face, a sharp pain in her lower abdomen had her clutching her stomach.

"What's wrong?" Axel's worried expression swam before her.

"I think the baby is coming." She doubled over.

"We've got to get you to the hospital. Now." Axel waved the sheriff over. "She's in labor."

"Let's go," McCallister said.

Axel helped her to the sheriff's cruiser and then got in beside her while Sheriff McCallister hit the lights.

Tears swam in her eyes. She was finally going to meet her child and she had nothing to offer— not even a home.

"We'll figure it all out...together," Axel whispered. "You're not alone. You'll never be alone again."

As she looked at the man who had risked everything for her, she saw the future she so desperately prayed for could be hers.

★ ★ ★

"You did good, Mamma," Axel told her when the precious baby girl was placed in her arms. The smile she gave was filled with exhaustion and he couldn't remember anything ever looking so beautiful before.

After everything they'd gone through, to have a new life come from such darkness seemed the perfect conclusion to Ray's reign of terror.

Ten little toes. Ten perfect fingers. A small version of her mother with fine blond hair. The wonder of life made everything they'd gone through to get to this point seem trivial.

"You're sure she's healthy?" Summer asked the nurse again.

"She's perfect," the nurse said with a smile.

Axel sat down beside her and watched the baby in her arms. "Have you thought of a name for her yet?"

Summer didn't hesitate. "I want to name her after my mother. Her name is Abigail." She watched in awe as her daughter looked up at her. "Actually, my mother's name is Abigail Elizabeth. I'm named after her, too."

"Abigail Elizabeth is a pretty name. Your daughter will be named after you and your mother." Axel touched the baby's hand and his heart melted when she latched on to his finger. "Abigail Elizabeth needs to know what a strong woman her mother is. She will be proud of you for what you've overcome."

Summer seemed to fight back tears. "I can finally be Elizabeth again. Summer is dead to me. I told myself that until I truly became free of Ray, I couldn't be the person I was before. Now I can. I'm Elizabeth."

Axel smiled, realizing again that he loved her with all his heart. "Yes, you are."

As she looked into his eyes something shifted in hers. "I'd be dead if it weren't for you, Axel. I owe you everything."

He reached up and brushed away the tears. "You changed my life. If I hadn't met you, I have no doubt I'd still be living in isolation clinging to my grief. I don't want to be that man anymore. You've made me want to be better. You've made…" He hesitated, unable to lay his heart on the line yet. She'd need time to rebuild her life with her child. "You've made me believe in love again, *Elizabeth*, when I thought I'd lost it. I care for you, and I want to be there for you in whatever way that looks like. As a friend and a neighbor, however you want me to be part of your life."

"You gave me hope, too, Axel. I'd forgotten what that felt like." A sob escaped her. "And I care about you, too, but…"

"You need time to heal," he finished for her.

"Yes." Her eyes pleaded with him to understand.

For Axel it was easy. "I'll give you all the time you need. You survived so much. You're a strong woman. You will get through this. What happened won't define you. It will grow you."

With her tears falling he carefully gathered her close and held her while she cried.

When he'd spotted her on that road the day before, Axel couldn't have predicted the journey the two of them would take together. Or the results of that journey, which would prove to be life-altering for both. Thanks to God, everything had worked out. Brayden was going to be okay. He was here at the same hospital as Elizabeth and the baby so Axel could check on his friend, and the sheriff had volunteered to keep Camo until Axel was ready to come home. He felt at peace with the world for the first time in years.

As difficult as it had been, he was grateful for

the struggle he and Elizabeth had gone through because he'd met this amazing woman whom he couldn't wait to get to know better.

# Epilogue

*One year later…*

The familiar countryside near her former Amish home brought fresh tears to her eyes. Elizabeth glanced back at the sleeping baby.

More than a year had passed since she and Axel had been rescued. It made her proud that because of her, dozens of women had been recovered.

And Elizabeth was proud of the progress she'd made through the past year. She'd gotten professional help after what she'd endured and had slowly started to recover from Ray's trauma and rebuild her life with her child.

Watching Abby grow had been a big part of her healing. She'd learned to stand on her own two feet and discovered she was stronger than she imagined.

With the help of Axel, Abram and Lainey,

and her therapist, she no longer blamed herself for what Ray did.

And she and Axel had grown closer. She'd learned what true love really looked like. She'd known she cared for Axel but over this past year, she'd let go of her doubts and accepted that she did deserve to be loved. Axel had shown her how a real man loved, and it was nothing like the hurt Ray put her through. It was gentle and patient. Just like Axel.

She'd slowly grown more confident and reached out to her parents through letters. They were amazingly supportive and anxious to see her.

Now she was ready. Sheriff McCallister had assured her there would be more arrests across the country and internationally thanks to the information on the thumb drive.

Vitaliy proved to be Vitaliy Babanin. A Russian aristocrat who had been on Interpol's radar for some time. Elizabeth had been heavily protected until it was time for her to testify. With her help, they'd busted up an international trafficking ring.

Two police officers from the Polson force in the next county had been taken into custody.

Both appeared eager to talk to save themselves a lengthy prison sentence.

Brayden had also mended over time. Axel had been staying with him to allow Elizabeth and Abby to have his cabin.

Thanks to Brayden, the missing pieces of Jimmy's life were finally known. It was terrifying for Elizabeth to realize the house in the woods where she and the others had stayed was once Jimmy's family home which was over in the next county. At Elizabeth's suggestion, the sheriff had dug up the floor beneath the barn and found Jimmy's dad, who was believed to have left Jimmy behind. He'd never left his property but had been buried beside his wife and younger son whom Jimmy had also killed. Brayden was convinced Jimmy had something to do with his own parents' deaths as well.

The file marked Barn that the sheriff recovered from the thumb drive contained detailed journal entries and photos of the murder of Jimmy's family. The sheriff believed Jimmy kept them as some type of trophy. He was much more disturbed than Elizabeth had even realized.

"Is this it?" Axel asked, drawing her attention away from Ray's deadly past.

She spotted the mailbox next to the drive that led to her parents' home. Everything still looked the same and yet nine years had passed.

Elizabeth had told her parents everything that happened to her. Her mamm wrote back and told her how heartbroken they all were for what she'd suffered. They were excited to meet their granddaughter one day.

After months of exchanging letters, it was finally time to see her family face-to-face.

"This is it." The nervous butterflies returned. How could she face them after everything that happened?

Axel reached for her hand. "They love you. They're excited to see you again, Elizabeth. Remember, they thought they'd lost you forever."

She smiled over at him. Elizabeth wouldn't have gotten through all of this without him. She loved him so much and couldn't wait to marry him one day, but she had to see her parents and brothers first. Had to know they still loved her.

Axel had assured her he'd give her whatever she needed, even if it meant having to say goodbye to her. The thought of losing him hurt physically.

After the terrible things Ray had put her

through, Elizabeth never expected to feel anything again, especially not love.

"You know if you want to stay with your family for a while…"

She didn't let him finish, but she loved him for his selflessness. "I love my family and I loved being Amish, but I can't go back to that life again. It isn't who I am anymore. You and Abby are my future." She prayed the future would include visits with her family, though.

"I love you," he murmured. Every time he said the endearment, her heart became lighter.

"I love you, too."

Axel squeezed her hand before turning onto the driveway.

From her car seat, Abby watched the passing scenery and kicked her feet…just like she had in the womb.

The trees lining the drive were covered in snow. The path curved around the property in snakelike fashion until they reached the clearing near the house.

"Oh." The word slipped from Elizabeth's lips when she got her first glimpse of her former home. "It still looks the same." Only there were signs of aging all around from the peeling paint to the sagging porch.

Axel stopped the truck in front of the home. Elizabeth couldn't take her eyes off it. While she watched, steeped in the past, the front door opened, and her past rose from her memories to become a flesh-and-blood living being.

"*Mamm.*" Her mother still looked the same—maybe a little older—but still the same. And *Daed* was still a good foot taller than his wife. But the biggest change was found in the two young boys she'd left behind. They were no longer boys but young men. At nineteen, Peter would be finished with his *rumspringa*. Eli would be starting his.

Following a bit slower, the family dog, Pepper, came out onto the porch, her dark fur showing white around her face.

Camo had come with them on the trip. When he spotted Pepper, he grew excited.

"Settle down, boy," Axel told the dog.

Tears filled Elizabeth's eyes and she rushed from the vehicle and started for the porch. Behind her, Axel climbed out and got Abby from her car seat. He followed along with Camo, who went up the steps to sniff Pepper.

Elizabeth stopped once she reached the porch and suddenly all the old doubts and fears resurfaced. She'd left them. How could they ever find it in their hearts to forgive her foolishness.

But one look at her *mamm*'s face confirmed she'd been worried for nothing. *Mamm* closed the space between them and gathered Elizabeth into her arms, weeping and laughing at the same time.

"You're home. My little girl is home."

*Daed* and the boys got in on the hugs and all Elizabeth's concerns faded away. She was loved. By these precious people. By her baby. And by the man who had taught her what true love really looked like.

★ ★ ★ ★ ★

# *Romantic* Suspense

## Danger. Passion. Drama.

### Available Next Month

**Targeted With A Colton** Beth Cornelison
**A Spy's Secret** Rachel Astor

**Vanished In Texas** Karen Whiddon
**Christmas Bodyguard** Katherine Garbera

 LOVE INSPIRED

**Trail Of Threats** Jessica R. Patch
**Unravelling Killer Secrets** Shannon Redmon

Larger Print

 LOVE INSPIRED

**Fugitive Search** Dana Mentink
**Witness Escape** Sami A. Abrams

Larger Print

 LOVE INSPIRED

**Sorority Cold Case** Jacquelin Thomas
**Hunted In The Mountains** Addie Ellis

Larger Print

Keep reading for an excerpt of a new title
from the Romantic Suspense series,
LAST MISSION by Lisa Childs

# *Prologue*

*Sixteen months ago...*

The flames consuming Charlie Tillerman's corner tavern lit up the whole town of Northern Lakes, Michigan. The fire cast a sunrise-like glow over Main Street. The arsonist had struck again, setting the bar on fire where it was well-known that the Huron Hotshots, a team of elite firefighters, hung out. That son of a bitch had been coming after them for the past six months.

But some damn firebug wasn't going to beat them. They got out while making sure the other customers got safely out as well. Except for one...

Nobody could find the superintendent of the hotshot team. Not that *everyone* was trying to find him. Someone would be damn happy if Braden Zimmer was never found.

The hotshots were out on the street now, hooking up the hoses, working together to put out the flames before they spread to the other buildings on the block. The noise of the engines was loud, so loud that this particular person didn't immediately hear the shouts. Then they turned and saw hotshot Ethan Sommerly barreling out of the smoke, carrying a small blonde woman over his shoulder. Owen

James, the paramedic on the team, rushed forward to help, pressing an oxygen mask over the woman's face.

"Braden's in the alley!" Ethan yelled.

The woman, the arson investigator, pulled down her mask and shouted, "Get in there! Please, save him!"

She wasn't the only one yelling, though. Another hotshot, Michaela Momber, emerged from the front of the building. She was dragging the bar owner, Charlie Tillerman, out with her. "Clear!" she yelled. "The building is about to collapse!"

Just as she said it, the structure shuddered and imploded on itself, sending out flames and a thick cloud of acrid smoke.

*This was it.*

An eerie silence fell like the building just did. Everybody had to know. There was no way that even the great Braden Zimmer could have survived a building collapsing on him.

But then someone gasped and pointed to the alley between the burning remains of the Filling Station Bar and Grill and the building next to it that had flames licking at its roof and walls. From that narrow space and all that thick smoke, a man emerged. Like Michaela had carried Charlie, Braden was carrying someone, too. The body of Matthew Harrison, that damn kid who'd wanted so badly to be a hotshot, too. He was the arsonist. He had to be the person who'd targeted their team and Braden specifically for not hiring him for the last open position on the Huron Hotshots.

Owen and Ethan and the others rushed forward to help Braden and the kid. While the paramedics treated them, the other hotshots stepped back and cheered and applauded. Tears rolled down soot-streaked faces, tears of relief that their fearless leader was okay.

Everybody was so happy—everyone but one person.

While the others were happy about Braden, they were probably also relieved that the arsonist targeting the Huron Hotshots team of elite firefighters was going to jail. The team should have been safe and might have been if the arsonist was the only one after the team, the only one trying to hurt them.

But there was someone else. And while the arsonist was going to spend a lot of his life behind bars, this person had no intention of ever winding up there and had no intention of ever stopping either.

They weren't going to rest until the Huron Hotshots team was destroyed, even if they destroyed themselves in the process...

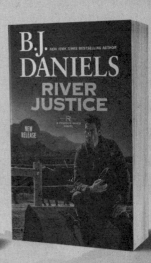

# Subscribe and fall in love with a Mills & Boon series today!

You'll be among the first to read stories delivered to your door monthly and enjoy great savings.

WE SIMPLY LOVE ROMANCE